TWISTOR

TWISTOR

JOHN CRAMER

AVON BOOKS • NEW YORK

AVON BOOKS
A division of
The Hearst Corporation
1350 Avenue of the Americas
New York, New York 10019

First AvoNova Printing: November 1991

AVONOVA TRADEMARK REG. U.S. PAT. OFF. AND IN OTHER COUNTRIES, MARCA REGISTRADA, HECHO EN U.S.A.

Printed in the U.S.A.

RA 10 9 8 7 6 5 4 3 2 1

For Pauline,
who wanted me to,

and David,
who knew I could

ACKNOWLEDGMENTS

Once I complained to David Hartwell that not enough hard science fiction of quality was being published these days. His response was that the fault lay with people like me, who had the scientific background and writing skills to produce good hard SF but were not doing so. That challenge stimulated me to write this novel. David Hartwell, therefore, is the progenitor of *Twistor*. His many suggestions for improvements in style and structure over many months and several drafts have made this a far better book than it might have been in the hands of a less interactive editor.

My wife, Pauline, has also played a key editorial role in this, my first venture into the writing of fiction. Her sense of style and her deftness with point-of-view relationships help me to convert flat scenes into dynamic ones, lifeless characters into interesting ones.

I am also indebted to the patient readers of various preliminary versions of the manuscript who have made useful and sometimes important suggestions: my daughters Kathryn Elizabeth Cramer and Karen Cramer Doyle, and my friends Dr. Ilan Ben Zvi, David and Jan Rowell, Dick Seymour, Judy Gustafson, and particularly Vonda McIntyre, who helped me to avoid many of the pitfalls into which the inexperienced fiction writer can stumble.

This novel is set in the Department of Physics of the University of Washington in Seattle, where I am a faculty member, and it accurately represents the structural layout of the present physics building and campus. David's laboratory is, in fact, my former lab/office in 101 Physics Hall.

However, the physicist characters in the book are not based on any of my colleagues on the physics and astronomy faculties and should bear no resemblance to any particular individuals.

J.G.C.

TWISTOR

PART 1

Problems worthy of attack,
prove their worth
by hitting back.

PIET HEIN
(1905–   )

WEDNESDAY MORNING, OCTOBER 6

The towers and battlements of Physics Hall shone wetly in the morning light filtering through the Seattle drizzle. The structure would have been well suited for shooting arrows and pouring boiling oil down upon some horde of barbarians, were any so foolish as to venture onto the campus of the University of Washington to besiege Physics Hall.

On its north and east sides the 1920s yellow-brown brick structure was embraced by the Suzzalo Library, a gothic pseudo-cathedral of arching marble and stained glass, straining along its angled length to contain its overburden of books as it metamorphosed into Bauhaus glass and concrete at its southeastern terminus. Physics Hall stretched north to south along Rainier Vista, a broad walkway so aligned that when the Seattle weather cooperated it looked out across a large circular pool and fountain past the cityscape of Capitol Hill to a stunning view of Mount Rainier some eighty-five miles to the southeast.

But this particular October morning the sky was overcast, and a light rain dampened the walkway. The arching water plumes of the fountain were absent, leaving only a dark circular pool that reflected the ragged downslope of Capitol Hill, its indistinct edge shading into grayness in the space where giant Rainier belonged. The giant's absence was ignored by the interweaving of bicycles and quick-stepping students on Rainier Vista.

Inside Physics Hall the activities of the morning were beginning to build as the outflow of milling and chattering undergraduates, their eight-thirty classes just ended, diffused from the large upstairs lecture halls to collide with the inflow of nine-thirty replacements. But behind the closed doors on the ground floor, within the long rectangular laboratory rooms, a calmer, more focused atmosphere prevailed. Here, carefully tended by faculty and the most recent generation of graduate students and postdocs, were ongoing long-term experiments that might reveal more about the inner workings of the universe, or at least provide the basis for a Ph. D. thesis or a respectable journal publication.

Behind one glass-paneled door an arcane array of hardware imprisoned a single atom of antimatter, a nucleus made of antiprotons and antineutrons and surrounded by a swarm of positrons. The anti-atom, created at a large accelerator in Geneva, had been carefully imported to Seattle riding in its own electromagnetic trap. It had been held here for over a year, while ever-changing probes extracted secrets of the symmetries between matter and antimatter. In another room a coherent beam of X-rays was meticulously mapping the arrangements of a single layer of atoms clinging to a cold graphite surface, the holographic interference patterns revealing unsuspected regularities and geometrical connections in their configurations. Behind another door a gleaming, rainbowed laser disk spun within its drive. Its data stream, beamed down from an orbiting telescope and captured in plastic, aluminum, and gold, was now with systematic reconstruction yielding an emerging vista, a giant galaxy suspended in the act of a violent explosion that had occurred over a billion years ago. And in another laboratory room just down the corridor, a doorway on another universe was about to open. . . .

David Harrison, in loose sweater, old jeans, and scuffed brown loafers, sat sprawled on the floor beside a rack of electronic equipment. He brushed a shock of dark brown hair from his eyes as he peered into the tangle of wires, ribbon cables, and fiber-optics bundles. Somewhere in this mess two signal leads had been interchanged. All he had to do was find them.

Beside him on the bare concrete floor was a large electrical drawing showing many neat square-cornered lines in a rainbow of colors. It was the latest version of the experiment's control wiring layout, and just minutes earlier it had been traced and labeled by the inhumanly adroit pens of the "coat rack" graphics plotter in the corner. With a small digital multimeter David was beginning the tedium of verifying the correspondence between the beautifully ordered ideal world of electrical wiring represented on the paper and the untidy real world of jumbled multicolored wires, spade lugs, solder joints, and screw connectors in the equipment rack before him. He was confident that he would find the error. But he was also pretty sure that he would not find it soon.

There was a knock at the door. He rose and brushed off the seat of his jeans with his hand, then rubbed hand against jeans. His butt felt cold from sitting on the bare concrete floor. He walked across the cluttered laboratory room to the brown varnished door, noting the tall shadow on the frosted pane. He could hear the shrill sounds of high-pitched child-voices. It was Paul and the children. He felt a rush of pleasure and smiled broadly as he pulled the door open.

"David!" they said in unison as the door came open. David noticed how their voices echoed from the bare concrete floor, the white plaster walls, and the high ceiling of the room. Jeffrey Ernst, age six, and Melissa Ernst, who had just had her ninth birthday, charged across the threshold and embraced David's knees. He absorbed their small impacts and knelt to hug them.

"Hi, David!" said Paul Ernst. "We've come for the grand tour you promised."

"C'mon in," said David, rising from greeting the children. He took each child by a hand and led them down the long room.

Paul glanced around the cluttered laboratory. "Where's Victoria?" he asked.

"I suppose she's still sleeping," said David. "She wrote an entry in the lab book at three A.M., so she must have gone home after that. We're working shifts. We've really been up to our ears in problems here, but now things are finally coming together." He looked at Paul. "A lot of our progress is due to her. Vickie's very smart, and good with equipment, and she gets things done. I think she's the best experimentalist graduate student in the department."

His friend nodded. "The CalTech undergrads we get as graduate students are usually pretty good, and Victoria is better than most. She took my advanced quantum mechanics class last year," he continued, "and all three quarters she got one of the highest grades in the class. She beat out some of our hotshot theory grad students. As I recall, she had one of the better scores on the qualifying exam, too."

"Well," said David, "this mess will soon be collecting her thesis data. She and I have invented a neat trick for manipulating the drive field. Vickie calls it a 'twistor' field because of the way it twists and contorts the electric and magnetic fields. She's taking George Williams's quantum gravitation class now, and she says the time structure we impose on the field is an electromagnetic analog of one of the twistor operators in Roger Penrose's hyperdimensional calculus."

Paul nodded noncommittally.

David noticed that Jeff, perhaps bored with the adult conversation, was beginning to fidget. He smiled at the boy, gesturing toward the shining array of equipment that occupied most of the central part of the room. "This," he said, "is our new experiment. We had to work some to cram it all into this little seven-by-fourteen-meter lab room. Some parts were scrounged from an older setup of Professor Saxon's, some were bought from commercial suppliers, and some were made in our machine and electronics shops. We spent a long time deciding exactly what we wanted, and we designed a lot of it ourselves. Now all the parts are here, it's all put together, and all we have to do is make it work." He thought of the wiring error yet to be found and looked across at the wiring diagram spread on the floor.

Jeff crowded between David and Melissa. "David, does this stuff ever make sparks and blow up, like the things the scientists on TV use?" he asked.

"That's a good question, Jeff," said David. "Our stuff doesn't do anything so spectacular when it breaks. Maybe it would be easier to fix if it did. The hardest part of doing this kind of physics experiment is making sure that each part of the experiment is working the way it should and that all the parts are working at the same time. About half the equipment you see here isn't for actually *doing* the measurements; it's for checking to make sure that the other half of the equipment is working."

Looking for something to amuse the children, David led them to the far end of the room near the windows. Here an old wooden desk had been converted through some feat of amateur carpentry into a control console. In its center were a small computer and a color monitor flanked by two short electronics racks.

"This is where we sit to run the experiment," he told them. "This computer sends and receives messages from the equipment and puts them in a form that we dumb humans can understand. It has a part that does very fast calculations and another part that draws pictures for us on this monitor to let us know what's happening in the calculations or the experiment. We make things happen by moving this 'mouse' around and clicking its button." David moused up the main desktop, selected the speech synthesizer utility, and fed it a text file. A stylized human face appeared on the screen, and with realistic lip movements and facial expressions it recited a bit of text which was a short commercial for the computer.

"And that," said David, turning to point to the stainless-steel sphere in the center of the apparatus, "is the most important part of the equipment. Inside is the sample holder where we put the material we're studying: a perfect single crystal, a special arrangement of atoms that we want to learn about. We pump all the air out of the sphere so there's a vacuum inside, like in space. Then we make it very cold.

"The lowest temperature possible is called absolute zero. We cool our crystal sample down to almost that temperature. When they're cold enough, we can learn about how atoms behave in crystals. Then we make special waves in them."

"I have a crystal at home," said Melissa. "It's very pretty. Can we see your crystals, David?"

David nodded, opened a metal cabinet, and took two plastic boxes from a clear plastic drawer. "Here are some natural iron sulfide crystals that we've been using." He handed shiny black cubes to Jeff and Melissa. "You can keep 'em if you want."

"Are you sure you aren't going to need those?" asked Paul.

David shook his head. "They're nice crystals, and we went to some trouble to get good ones," he said, "but they turned out to be worthless for the calibrations we had in mind."

Paul nodded. Melissa seemed very pleased as she held the dark crystal cube near the desk lamp, examining it closely.

"What's that thing?" asked Jeff, wrinkling his nose and pointing to a wheeled cart supporting a brown tank with a green rubber hose and copper nozzle.

"That's a tank of helium gas, Jeff. We use it to check our equipment," said David. "Helium is the second smallest atom of all, lighter than everything except hydrogen. We use it to find leaks in our equipment, because it can find even the tiniest hole in a steel or aluminum container and squeak through it into our leak detector. We squirt helium around on the outside, and if it finds its way to the inside we know we have a leak. And helium also has another use, too."

From a bottom shelf of a cabinet David produced two red rubber balloons and some string. He held each balloon to the nozzle, filled it with helium, tied off its neck, and attached a string. The red balloons bobbed on the strings as he gave them to Jeff and Melissa. "Sir and madam, I present you with the second lightest element in the known universe!" he said dramatically. Then he winked at Paul.

"Is Allan around?" Paul asked.

David shook his head. "He's off to D.C. for some big National Science Board meeting at the NSF. He's amazing. He really has the connections. He persuaded a guy at Argonne to send us some huge single crystals of fluoridated layered perovskites. You should see the X-ray diffraction patterns. They're the most beautiful perovskite crystals I've ever seen. Just what we'll need after we get this kludge working." Allan Saxon was the senior professor for whom David worked as a postdoc.

"Allan knows everybody," Paul agreed. "He has a reputation in the department for keeping tight control, making sure everyone under him is working flat out. Does he give you enough elbow room, David?''

''He was a bit hard to deal with when we were having equipment problems,'' said David. ''Nothing I couldn't handle. But he brightens right up when he smells progress. Just now he's very friendly and helpful. He's busy writing proposals and editing that AIP journal, so he leaves Vickie and me to do most of the lab work.''

Paul nodded. ''Kids, I'm afraid we have to go now,'' he said. ''David has work to do, and we've interrupted him long enough.'' Jeff protested, but David assured him that they could come back again for another visit soon. Grasping their balloon strings with one hand and holding their crystals carefully in the other, they filed out the door.

''See you later!'' David called after them.

''See you tonight, David,'' said Paul. ''And thanks.''

'' 'Bye, David!'' said Jeff and Melissa together as they walked down the hallway, balloons bobbing.

David turned back to the problem at hand. Too bad, he thought as he arranged himself on the floor again, that doing physics experiments isn't all flash and dash and helium balloons. The dogwork always has to be done first, and sometimes after it's done there isn't any good stuff anyway. Carefully he resumed the checking of each of the several hundred connections, gradually eliminating possibilities and progressively closing in on the obscure wiring mistake. He looked at his watch. Vickie ought to be here after lunch, he thought.

Victoria Gordon, her red hair overflowing her yellow helmet and streaming in her wake, eased her ten-speed down the long gentle slope of Densmore Avenue North, squeezing a brake handle occasionally to kill excess speed. She'd worked quite late last night, completing most of the wiring for their new experiment. This morning she'd slept in until nearly noon to make up some of the missed sleep of the previous week. Her head still felt muddy, but it was clearing in the crisp air.

The view of Lake Union with its backdrop of downtown high-rises spread below her at the end of the street, opening

ever wider as she coasted downhill. The morning drizzle
had burned off. The transcendentally wonderful smell of
baking bread grew as she approached the Oro-Wheat Bakery
on Pacific Avenue North. She sometimes bought their day-
old bread in the little bakery shop, but the smell of the bread
baking was the best part, a treat she savored every morning.

A gap in the traffic on Pacific allowed her to head east
to join the Burke-Gilman Trail. It paralleled Pacific above
the lakefront north of Lake Union and the Ship Canal. When
gaps in the massive blackberry vines along the trail per-
mitted, there were marvelous views of the city, the water-
way, and its boat traffic. She enjoyed riding on the pleasant
and relatively automobile-free link between her co-op house
in the Wallingford district and her laboratory at the university. The breeze off the lake now smelled fresh and clean,
with the barest hint of fish and diesel oil from the boatyards
down the slope. She contoured around a slower cyclist,
deftly threading through the walkers and joggers taking their
lunch-break exercise.

She glanced downhill to the right. It was cool, but that
didn't seem to have deterred the wind surfers who dotted
Lake Union near Gasworks Park. Victoria considered their
dedication to an essentially empty activity and smiled to
herself. It was nice to have something better to do with your
life.

She passed under the I-5 bridge, so high above her that
the hum of her own wheels was louder than the freeway
noise. The massive bridge pillars near the trail were rather
like giant redwoods, but done in concrete gray. Now the
sequence of marinas, run-down boatyards, and the occasional posh lakefront restaurant was giving way to the outer
fringes of the university's sprawl: converted older buildings,
landscaped parking lots, new buildings under construction,
plots of grass, and rhododendron beds.

Victoria's mind began to slip into work mode as she
neared the campus, reviewing what was on the menu for
today. First on the list was the redesign of the radio-
frequency control interface. Those nifty phase-control chips
were going to allow a whole range of new tricks with the

RF control system, if she could just find a way to shoehorn them into the crowded control card.

She pictured the card layout. Those analog-to-digital converter chips took lots of space on the present card, and that new LSI chip from National might just be substituted for the whole mess of them, if only it was fast enough. She'd have to check that with Sam.

The upper stands of Husky Stadium in edgewise perspective loomed ahead like the twin jaws of a monumental bear trap. Fuzzy thinking is a trap, too. She tried to bring the design problem into sharper focus as she turned off the trail at Rainier Vista and pedaled harder. She liked to use this last upslope beside the lush green lawns of the campus leading to Physics Hall to add some final stress to her leg muscles.

A new card layout clicked into place in her mind's eye. It wasn't even going to be very difficult, she thought, grinning. David would be delighted.

Allan Saxon reached down and massaged his rump. It was getting numb, he decided. Arthur Lockworth, Presidential Science Advisor, had been droning on and on for most of an hour. He was informing the NSF's National Science Board, of which Saxon was a member, of all the wonderful things that the administration had done for science in the past year and was planning for the coming year. He painted the bright canvas with broad strokes, skipping over the damage done by political pork-barreling, the opportunities missed through shortsighted budgeting, the initiatives lost because Lockworth's masters had no real understanding of science.

Lockworth's resonant voice shifted timbre, a clue that he was at last reaching his conclusion. Saxon breathed a sigh of relief and glanced around the room. The board members, their chairs oriented to face Lockworth at the podium, sat around a long oak table. Behind them was a ring of seats occupied by National Science Foundation people, a few news reporters, and some observers from the scientific societies and organizations.

This had been a miserable meeting. The big-science contingent of the board had grabbed the initiative and never relinquished it. All the plums distributed here had dropped into other pockets. Funding for the NSF's Science/Industrial Initiatives, Saxon's pet project, had been neglected. The board's enthusiasm had focused on new funds for the National Gravity-Wave Telescope Project and the Neutrino Earth-Scan Initiative. Well, there would be other meetings, Saxon thought. His time would come.

Lockworth finally droned to a stop. There was determined applause when he finished. Lockworth looked up inquiringly, and Saxon put up his hand. "Yes, Allan?" Lockworth said.

"Arthur," said Saxon, "we're all impressed by the breadth and vision of the administration's long-range plans for science . . ." He paused while Lockworth absorbed the compliment and smiled. ". . . but there is one area that this administration persists in neglecting." The smile faded. "I refer," Saxon continued, "to the NSF's longstanding program for promoting the infusion of the fruits of basic science research into the industrial sector. The Science/Industrial Initiatives program has been at a flat funding level for the past three years, without even adjustments for inflation—"

"Allan," Lockworth cut him off, "the administration has a vigorous program aimed at the preservation of the competitive edge of our nation's industries. We have worked with Congress to implement a generous investment tax credit program for promoting more private-sector funding of scientific research . . ."

"That's fine for Bell Labs and IBM, Arthur," Saxon broke in, "but it does nothing for the small entrepreneur who's trying to start a business based on high-technology innovation. He'll be taking a loss for the first few years of operation. Those tax credits are worthless to him. The small innovator is the wellspring of our technology-based economy, yet your administration is stifling this important activity by neglecting the Science/Industrial Initiatives." Saxon looked up at Lockworth, now standing beside the podium and leaning on it with one hand. The squeaky wheel gets the grease, he thought, and this is a better place to squeak than most.

"I would agree with you, Allan, if I believed that the S/I Initiatives were the best vehicle for matching our excellent university research base into the technological development stream. But I and my staff at the OSTP have made a detailed study of the effectiveness of that S/I program, which the previous administration pushed rather hard. We've determined that in the balance it just wasn't cost effective. That's why we're de-emphasizing it. There has to be a better way. I would, of course, be interested in alternative approaches. . . ."

Saxon nodded. That was a foot in the door, at least. Lockworth fielded several questions from others, but Saxon ignored them and gathered his papers in preparation for the cab ride to National for his flight to San Francisco.

"Professor Saxon?"

Saxon glanced up. A man stood looking down at him. He wore a rumpled tweed sport coat, a stained yellow necktie, baggy brown slacks, and scuffed loafers. He needed a haircut. He might have been a faculty member, except that this wasn't a university.

"I'm Gil Wegmann from *Newsweek*," the man said. "I wonder if you'd tell me what was behind your dialogue with Lockworth just now. Would you say that the administration was screwing over the tech-innovation entrepreneur?"

"I wouldn't want to say that," Saxon answered carefully. "They're phasing out an NSF program that I consider to have been highly successful. I think they're making a big mistake."

"Are you an entrepreneur, sir?" Wegmann asked.

Saxon looked uncomfortable. "Well, in a way . . ."

"In what way, Professor? Do you have a business on the side?"

Saxon cleared his throat. "I'm part owner of a small venture-capital company that specializes in exploiting certain aspects of condensed matter physics that may have applications in, for example, the computer industry."

"Did you have one of those grants you were talking about when you started the company, Professor?"

"Well, uh, yes, we did have a small S/I grant, but most

of our startup was funded by the private investment of venture capital.''

"Don't you think you have a conflict of interest, Professor, sitting here on the National Science Board and pushing federal programs that would directly benefit your company?''

Saxon stood up. He could feel his scalp prickling in the back, a sign that his blood pressure was rising. He took a deep breath. "No indeed, Mr. Wayland. My company is already started, and is unlikely to get any further federal research support, particularly under the present administration. I bring to the board an experience in both basic research and private enterprise, and that is very valuable in our deliberations, as I'm sure the chairman will tell you. I resent your implication, Mr. Wayland—''

"Wegmann, sir. I think I understand, Professor Saxon. Thank you for your comments.'' He turned and moved to corner another board member before he could escape.

I hope none of that gets into *Newsweek*, Saxon thought. We don't need that kind of publicity just now.

David sat at the control console. The snarl of wires had been folded back into its recesses. During his lunch break, after the elusive wiring fault had been discovered and fixed, David had stopped by his apartment to change from the jeans and loafers of the morning to a white shirt, creased slacks, and polished black shoes. A dark tweed jacket hung from the window handle, and through the panes behind it campus buildings were visible in the gathering darkness.

Across the room Vickie sat at the little design computer, manipulating a pattern of red, green, and blue circuit traces on a circuit board layout. She moved a mouse over a large digitizer pad, circuit structures popping into existence and reforming themselves as she coaxed the design slowly toward an optimum.

"Jesus H. Christ!" said David, peering more closely at the vacuum gauge. "Vickie, watch this! When I take the RF up by a megahertz, the vacuum gauge goes *down*! It just clicked down to the 10^{-9} scale and then popped back up. Look, it reproduces! There it goes again!" He moused the cursor to a spot on the control screen labeled OSCILLATOR [INCREMENT], clicked, and then leaned back in the swivel chair, trying to watch the row of orange digits labeled FREQUENCY (MHZ) and the meter labeled VACUUM (TORR) at the same time, although they were at opposite sides of the console.

Vickie rose from the design computer and walked over to the control console. Despite the loose jeans, rumpled sweatshirt, and unbrushed red hair, David noted, she seemed remarkably attractive this evening. He felt distracted, and recalled Allan's warning comments about involvements with the female physics graduate students.

"Really, David!" said Vickie, pointing at the apparatus that they had meticulously designed, constructed, and assembled over the past few months. "I told you this kludge had ground loop problems—" Walking up behind him, she peered intently over his shoulder at the console vacuum meter, then reached out and tapped it sharply near the bottom. "—but you had to start running the full-blown experiment before we'd done the final component debug. The vacuum can't be that good. Considering all that Apiezon bear-crap you pasted over the leaks, we're lucky it isn't hissing at us."

The object of her derision was the beach-ball-size stainless-steel sphere in the center of the room, girdled by sculpted coppery coils and spiked with vacuum feedthroughs and a large blue-and-silver ion pump. A plume of condensed water vapor and a rim of frost marked its nitrogen exhaust vent. Silvery dewars stood at one side to supply liquid nitrogen and helium for the cryogenics inside.

Yesterday David had used the department's only functioning helium leak-checker to discover tiny air-to-vacuum leaks in several of the welded joints. These he had peened shut with a small hammer and then for good measure temporarily sealed them with dark brown leak-sealant putty. The sharp chemical smell of a spray-on vacuum sealant still hung over the equipment. These were stopgap measures until the machine shop foreman could spare some welder time to fix the leaks properly.

The sphere stood on aluminum I-beam legs attached to

an elevated concrete slab in the center of the room. Framing the apparatus in three dimensions was the outline of a cube made of thin wooden sticks. Along the surfaces of the sticks were taped many turns of chestnut-brown enameled wire. These formed Helmholtz coils that nulled out the Earth's magnetic field in the central region of the apparatus.

David leaned back and looked beyond the control computer, studying the red-and-black coaxial cables and gray ribbon leads that snaked across the floor from the console's underside to the components of the experiment. "Guilty as charged, ma'am," he said, looking up at her. "Guess I've been pushing too hard. I wanted us to get some good data today before I had to bug out for dinner. I'm having my weekly Wednesday night dinner with the Ernsts." He gestured at a brown sack in the corner, the red top of a wine bottle projecting above its edge. "I'm bringing that bottle of Chateau La Tour '82 tonight. It cost me too much so I wanted to have something to celebrate."

"But instead," she said, "it looks as if Vickie Fix-It has some work to do while you're gone. We've gotta find this bug before we can make any more progress." Her eyes unfocused. "Hmmm. Maybe if I hooked a 'scope to the vacuum meter drive circuit I might zero in on the problem . . ."

David nodded. "Sam Weston was down in the electronics shop about half an hour ago. I think he's working late on something tonight. Perhaps you could persuade him to help."

"There's an idea," said Victoria. "Sam's super at debugging electronics. If I can just keep the topic of conversation away from sex and survivalism, he should be a big help."

"Just kick in his kneecaps if he gets out of line," said David. Although he'd never seen any evidence of it, Vickie had a reputation among the graduate students as a martial arts expert.

She smiled. "You're coming back tonight?" she asked.

"Yeah," said David, "I should be back by about midnight. As we both know too well, 'Physics is what physicists do late at night.' At least it's when *I* seem to get the most done. If you can fix this RF glitch, maybe I can accomplish something on the owl shift. I should be good 'til about three A.M. Allan's still in D.C. smooth-talking the NSF, so I have the honor of teaching his Physics 122 class again tomorrow morning at eight-thirty. Guess I can't stay up too late; I haven't made any notes for the lecture yet.'' He grinned.

"I was under the impression that you real physicists didn't need lecture notes," said Vickie, grinning back. "They did give you a Ph.D. in physics at Illinois, didn't they? Doesn't that mean you know everything in the 122 textbook, at least?"

"Oh sure," said David, "only the students get kinda upset when I start using partial differential equations and Riemann tensors to demonstrate that water runs downhill. It's real work to get it on the right level. But there are compensations. It's just amazing how much you learn when you want to explain what you already know to somebody else. . . ." He shook his head, musing. "Particularly to the articulate, socially adjusted algebra-illiterates that are admitted to our institutions of higher learning these days. This morning I had to spend ten minutes to get across the idea that when you divide by a number smaller than one, the result gets *bigger*. I guess they couldn't do that one on their fingers and toes."

She laughed, a rich contralto.

"Anyhow, Vickie, I gotta go," he said, reaching for the wrapped wine bottle. "If the food's overdone because I'm late, I may not be invited back. If you can bring some modicum of order to this chaos by the time I get back, it will be sincerely appreciated."

"OK," said Vickie, "but you go easy on that Chateau La Tour. I can't have you staggering back and falling into my apparatus. I need a Ph.D. too, you know."

As David turned down the long hill toward the university's east gatehouse, Lake Washington appeared on his right. The water shimmered with the reflected lights of the lakefront houses of nearby Laurelhurst and the longer reflections from posh Hunt's Point across the lake. A row of stationary red taillights punctuated the long low silhouette

of the Evergreen Point Bridge, indicating to David that there
was another jam-up there, on that well-known "car-
strangled spanner." It was nice that Paul lived on this side
of the lake.

David thought about Vickie. She was a remarkable young
woman. He'd never before worked with anyone so capable,
so smart, and at the same time so nice to have around. The
traffic light at Twenty-fifth Avenue Northeast turned green,
and he accelerated.

He was going to have to watch himself. Romance at the
workplace is generally a bad idea. Particularly the physics
workplace. He could think of a few cases where scientific
coworkers had become romantically involved. Almost never
had it ended well. If the relationship broke up, it became
difficult working together afterwards. And if it lasted it was
even worse. The conflicting demands of two careers, of
retaining scientific objectivity in criticizing each other's
work and ideas, and the eventual problem of finding jobs
together usually seemed to destroy such pairings within a
year or so.

He curved left at the Laurelhurst intersection and headed
north along Sand Point Way. But she was beautiful and
enormously talented, very intelligent, and remarkably good
with equipment, a natural with the hardware. He couldn't
think of anyone else quite like her. And there were a few
examples of successful physicist couples. . . . David rolled
down the window and breathed in the cool night air off the
lake as he slowed for the pedestrian crossing at Children's
Orthopedic. Watch it there, guy, he thought, and shook his
head as if to clear it.

He continued north along Sand Point Way, a broad street
with a tree-studded esplanade, and thought about Sarah and
their final quarrel. Was he too self-centered for a lasting
relationship? He'd always considered himself to be a nice
person. Thoughtful, considerate, even tempered . . . but it
seemed that when he became at all involved with a woman,
everything eventually exploded in a barrage of accusations
about his character flaws. After it happens for the third time,
you begin to wonder. . . . He continued down Sand Point

past the Federal Records Center and the entrance to Magnuson Park.

He recognized the brown-and-gold sign for the Seventy-O-One condos coming up on the left, his signpost for the place to turn. Downshifting, he clicked the turn indicator and drove uphill into View Ridge, passing large houses with manicured lawns.

Paul's house stood at a sloping corner near the top of the tall ridge overlooking Lake Washington. It was of traditional northwest design: brown wood tones with stone accents, cedar shake roof with a wide stone chimney, a broad, raised deck, and window walls of Thermopane glass facing on the sweeping view of the lake and the Cascades. The day, begun in overcast, had turned cool and clear with the arrival of darkness. The waxing October moon was not yet up, but a sprinkling of stars to the east was already penetrating the urban sky-glow. David parked by the line of rose bushes in front.

Paul Ernst was slipping a CD of Bach cantatas into the player just as the doorbell chimed. He heard Melissa and Jeffrey already racing across the slate entryway to the front door, squealing with excitement! He rounded the corner just in time to greet David as Melissa was closing the door. "David! Welcome!" he said. He accepted the proffered Bordeaux-shaped bottle and held it up for examination. "Wow! 'Appellation Pauillac Contrôlée, Chateau La Tour, 1982!' She was a good year, *oui*?" he asked. "What, may I ask, is the occasion for this superior product of the vintners' art?"

Melissa and Jeff swarmed over David as he shrugged off his topcoat. Jeff took the coat and carried it to his father for hanging in the closet. Both children suggested coyly that they might like piggyback rides to the living room.

"Mmmm! I smell something absolutely wonderful!" said David, raising his voice and projecting in the direction of the kitchen. Then he turned to Paul. "Yeah, '82 is near the top of the Bordeaux scale," he said. "There hasn't been a better year there in the past decade, though the '93s are looking good so far." He dumped Jeff on the long L-shaped sofa and went back for Melissa. "I bought it on impulse last week when I thought that tonight we'd be celebrating the final debugging of the new experiment. But, as it turns out, that celebration would be just a bit premature. . . ." He dumped Melissa on the sofa near Jeff and sat down between them, putting one arm around each, giving them a squeeze and heaving an exaggerated sigh of contentment. The children snuggled against him, and Melissa rumpled his hair. Paul detected a note of forced good humor in David tonight in place of his natural good spirits. Perhaps he needs a bit of cheering up, he thought.

"You mean that chrome-plated mound of fancy hardware we saw this afternoon still isn't working?" he asked in mock surprise. "Why don't you guys design equipment that works? By the way, David, the children were very impressed with your lab. On the way home Jeff asked why I wasn't allowed to have neat stuff like yours."

David laughed. "What did you tell them?"

"I tried to explain," said Paul, "that a theoretical physicist works mainly with paper, pencil, and brainpower, that I didn't need elaborate equipment. I'm not sure they bought my story. I told them about all the thousands of kilobucks that the misguided funding agencies take from our important theoretical work to lavish on your ill-conceived experiments. But they decided that the crystals and the balloons provided sufficient justification for continued support of experimental physics." Paul offered David a bowl of nuts. He looked closely at David, watching to make sure his teasing hadn't irritated his friend.

"Aw, come on, Paul," countered David, joining the familiar game. He was clearly more cheerful and relaxed now. "What would you theorists find to spend real money on, should someone be foolish enough to give you some? How many pencils and note pads do they have to buy you guys before you're happy, anyhow? Why, when you guys do latch on to some money you promptly embarrass the rest of the physics community by gathering at phony institutes and conferences held at beach resorts and ski lodges to fritter away dollars that might be better used for experiments to demonstrate the holes in your partially baked theoretical ideas." Paul had spent a month at the Aspen Institute for Theoretical Physics for the past several summers, and David frequently reminded him of this.

David leaned back and smiled, as though awaiting Paul's counterpunch, but at that point Elizabeth Ernst emerged from the dining room, wiping her hands on a towel. "I hope you two aren't arguing about funding again," she said. "My God! The only thing more boring than listening to a radio interview with an athlete is listening to scientists talk about funding. And did I understand that you ham-handed experimentalists are out to put my poor husband out of business?"

"What's fun-ding?" asked Jeff, wrinkling his nose.

David turned to Jeff and said, "Funding is money that governments and foundations give scientists like your dad and me every year so that we can have fun for the rest of the year. That's why it's called FUN-ding, Jeff!" He winked, then turned to Elizabeth and said, "There is one thing that's more boring than either of those: have you ever heard an interview with the lawyer of an athlete?"

She grimaced.

"Anyhow, Elizabeth, you needn't worry about us experimentalists causing any problems for your husband. He's found himself a nice ecological niche that's well insulated from the harsh environment of the real world. His theories can probably survive indefinitely, unblemished by embarrassing confrontations with experimental reality."

"Is that a virtue?" asked Elizabeth, raising her expressive eyebrows and looking at her husband. "I thought physics theories were supposed to be testable."

"What David's saying in his colorful but bombastic way," said Paul, "is that in my field of theoretical physics our pursuit of the underpinnings of nature has led us further and further away from anything that can be directly tested by doing experiments. The size scale is too small; the energy needed is too big. In the area of theoretical physics I'm looking at now, all the experimental work was over and done with before the Big Bang had expanded to the size of a pinhead. God has closed down the experimental laboratory until the next time around, if there is one."

Elizabeth looked from David to Paul. "This is all news to me," she said. "I thought you guys had a hot line to the innermost secrets of the universe."

"We do," said Paul, "in a way. The lack of tests is a real problem, but what can we do except keep looking for ways to keep the theory honest. This work is what I do best . . . and the field is one of the most exciting in all of physics. We're predicting wonderful and outrageous things. We study model universes with spaces of ten or even twenty-six dimensions, all but four of them rolled up like submicroscopic snails. We use geometries made of tiny looping strings where points would be in ordinary Euclidian space. We've found unlikely symmetries that can explain all the forces of nature. We predict exotic particles with strange properties and enormous masses. We're doing many, many lovely things . . . but none of it seems to be relevant to here-and-now reality, because we can't make testable predictions. It may all be just mathematics. Sometimes I wonder if we're the successors of the old scholastics, doing the modern equivalent of calculating how many angels can dance on the head of a pin."

"Can angels dance on a pin?" giggled Melissa, her interest kindled. Elizabeth grinned, shook her head, and disappeared in the direction of the kitchen.

"Sure they can, Melissa, if the pin is big enough and the angels are small enough!" said David, and winked.

A tinkle of glassware could be heard in the distance. "Dinner is served," announced Elizabeth with a fake English accent.

"Now there's a higher reality we can get our teeth into," said Paul, leading the way to the dining room.

2

WEDNESDAY EVENING, OCTOBER 6

The electronics shop was located deep in the basement of Physics Hall along with the machine shop, the glass shop, the helium liquefier, and the other technical services for the experimental activities of the Department of Physics. Victoria was pleased to see that a light still burned behind the shop's frosted glass door panel. She opened it with her master key and entered. The room was lined with cluttered workbenches, now mostly unattended.

At one bench a broad-shouldered figure was at work. Sam Weston, seated on a high stool, was peering closely at a spotlit rectangle of green translucent circuit board, his straight black hair hanging down over his forehead. One side of the board was dotted with rectangular black integrated circuit chips and cylindrical resistors and capacitors bearing brightly colored stripes. But Sam seemed more interested in the other side of the board, which was covered only with silvery printed circuit traces.

"Problems, Sam?" Victoria asked.

"Oh, hi, Vickie," said Sam, raising his head. "Yeah, this module is from the FermiLab setup of the high energy guys. Their FastBus rig doesn't work, and they need it, like, yesterday. The ICs all check OK, so I think it must have a broken trace or maybe an open capacitor."

"What does the diagnostic computer say?" Vickie asked.

"Diagnostic computer? Surely you jest! You'd need a data base of nominal parameters for that. These folks don't document anything, let alone enter the nominal circuit specs in the computer. So I get to check the damned thing by hand, like back in the Dark Ages. I don't even have a circuit

diagram. And I don't get overtime for working nights, just
comp time. My kids are beginning to have trouble remembering what Daddy looks like."

"Poor Sam!" said Vickie. "I've got sharp little eyes. Let
me look." She gently took the circuit board from Sam and
held it so the spotlight illuminated it from behind, light
showing through the translucent Fiberglass. After a few
minutes of peering and poking, she said, "Hmmm. What's
this little line on the trace here, Sam?" Taking a felt-tipped
pen from the workbench, she drew a black circle on the
green-and-silver surface.

"Lemme see that!" said Sam, gently taking the board
and simultaneously reaching for his digital ohmmeter. With
a delicacy which belied his large blunt hands he carefully
touched the red and black probes of the meter to points on
either side of the almost imperceptible line within the black
circle. The meter's silvery LCD readout read OFF SCALE.
Then he moved one probe until it just touched the hairline
crack. The readout jumped through a cascade of digits and
settled on 0.007 OHMS. "Vickie, you're an absolute marvel!" Sam exclaimed. As Vickie watched, he took a slightly
smoking soldering iron from a bracket on the bench and
touched it to the offending region, dabbing with the end of
a silvery coil of solder.

As the solder flux melted, a smell of hot resin filled the
air, conjuring in Victoria's memory a vivid world of piñon
campfires, and mountain hikes in the Sierra, and Mark. No,
she said sharply to herself, that was over a year ago; it's
finished. She wrenched her attention back to the here and
now.

Sam had clipped aluminum shielding to both sides of the
board and was slipping it into a module slot in a nearby
rack labeled FASTBUS. As he flipped the power switch up,
red, green, and yellow LED indicators began to dance behind tiny holes in the multimodule panel. He pushed a button
labeled DIAGNOSTICS and the pace of the dance increased,
then stopped as the legend CHECK OK appeared on a tiny
liquid-crystal screen on one of the wider modules. "It's
fixed!" he said. "By God, that lousy trace was the trouble!
Vickie, I owe ya one."

"And, as it happens, Sam," said Victoria, giving him her most winning smile, "I'm here to collect!"

David drained the last ruby drop from his wineglass, dabbed his lips with the white cloth napkin, and smiled contentedly. The food had been excellent. He and Elizabeth shared an interest in gourmet cooking, and she had done particularly well this evening.

Paul looked from David to his wife and said, "Elizabeth, you've outdone yourself this time. If the Moral Majority ever finds out about the hedonistic pleasures of doing physics and closes down basic research as a licentious and immoral activity, we can always open a restaurant. You can be the cook, I'll be the maitre d', and David can be the wine steward. We'll clean up, I tell you!"

"Yes, cleaning up is an excellent idea," Elizabeth said, smiling. "You four can start your training as busboys right now. Grab some of those dishes, and let's take them to the kitchen."

"What about our story!" cried Jeff, looking concerned as he picked up his plate.

Melissa chimed in sternly with, "Yes, Mother! David has to tell us our story before bedtime." In the past ten months, as David's once-a-week dinner with the Ernsts had grown into a habit and a tradition, the event of the evening for the children had become a story from David before bedtime.

David had met the Ernsts when he was newly arrived from Los Alamos. He had gone on a hike in the Cascades with some other people from the physics department, including Elizabeth and Paul. They had all enjoyed the hike, and as they were driving back to Seattle, Elizabeth had invited David to come home with them for dinner. After the dinner that evening David had, on impulse, told the Ernst children a little Ozark folk tale about the Hobyas to help in persuading them to go off to bed. From then on David had been pegged as the Ernst family storyteller.

As a child, David had been fascinated by folklore and mythology and had been encouraged in this by his mother, a successful novelist. He was surprised now by how well he remembered the old fairy tales and how smoothly he was able to tell them for the Ernst children. He found that he enjoyed the opportunity to use this otherwise dormant talent. And there was another unexpected aspect of the arrangement. David usually felt uncomfortable around children. Never before had he had young children as his very good friends who were enormously delighted to see him whenever he appeared. This was a new experience, and he found that he rather liked it.

Elizabeth seated herself in the big chair and picked up the textbook on cognitive psychology that she had been working her way through, finding the place where she had stopped. After Jeffrey had started the first grade, she had found a part-time job doing psychological counseling. She'd earned an M.S. in psychology while Paul was in graduate school, but she needed to brush up on some of the basics.

Across the room David was sitting on the sofa between the children, and Paul had seated himself at the far end of the sofa and was looking at some physics preprints. "All right, kids," David said, "this is a very old story, but I'm going to tell it my own way, not the old way. OK?" The children nodded solemnly. "Once upon a time," he began, "in a faraway kingdom, there lived a young boy named Ton."

Jeff giggled. "Ton? That's a funny name!"

"It was a very common name where Ton lived," David replied seriously. "Now listen quietly if you want to hear the story." He mugged a comic scowl at Jeff.

"Ton's mother and father loved him dearly, and he was very happy. His father had a prosperous business in their village, and his family owned three books."

Jeff and Melissa looked at the book-lined living-room walls and giggled, apparently finding the notion of owning only three books a comical idea.

"A bright clever boy, Ton learned very fast. His mother taught him how to read and write. Ton's father was a master armorer who made weapons and armor from steel. He taught Ton many things: how to make steel from red iron ore and coal, soften steel in the forge and shape it, rivet and weld pieces together, make weapons and armor, harden steel, and sharpen the edges of a new blade. As Ton grew and learned, he was able to be of more help to his father.

"One day when Ton was riding his pony along the seaside, leading a pack horse with a load of coal for his father's forge, he was captured by a band of corsairs."

"David, what're cor-sairs?" asked Jeffrey, cocking his head.

"Corsairs were free-lance pirates, usually from northern Africa, who specialized in capturing people and selling them as slaves," said David. "Very bad guys!" He glanced at his audience, then continued: "Struggling with his captors, Ton tried to escape. He bit one corsair on the arm and drew blood. He was beaten until he thought he would die. He was taken to a ship and thrown into a dark hold, where he was chained with other miserable prisoners. He was sick for days from the beating. The smell of the dirty prisoners was awful. The only food was rotten, with maggots squirming in it. The eternal rocking of the ship made him so seasick that he wanted to die."

Classic format, observed Elizabeth, unable to concentrate on the textbook in her lap. It's a variant of the "Jack and the Beanstalk" myth, right out of Bettelheim. A young boy with a peculiar education is thrust into a different world and confronted with seemingly insoluble problems.

"After what seemed years but was only a few days, Ton was taken ashore in a strange, dry land. The corsairs put him in a cart with other captives and took them all to a great slave market in the center of a noisy, foul-smelling city. Ton was made to stand naked on a round stone block before ugly bearded men wearing strange robes and shouting in a language he could not understand. He was sold as a slave to the highest bidder.

"As it happened, Ton was bought by an evil magician."

"David, are magicians always evil?" asked Jeff, round eyed. Melissa was looking annoyed.

David laughed. "Not always," he said. "In the older times a magician was a person who tried to control nature without trying to understand it. Sometimes they resorted to things they knew were evil because they were desperate to find the control they sought. Magicians would kill animals as sacrifices and chant spells, trying to make something happen or to make something change.

"After the scientific method was invented, people began to realize that it was actually possible to understand nature. Magic, which involved little real understanding, lost out. Now magicians are only entertainers who create the illusion of magic by using trickery. Today scientists like your father and I have accomplished some of what the old magicians attempted. We've gained some control over the forces of nature by first understanding them."

Jeff looked seriously from David to his father to make sure a joke wasn't being had at his expense. Then, satisfied, he smiled.

"The magician," David continued, "whose name was Zorax, took Ton to a hut deep in the forest to be his servant. Shortly after they arrived, the magician gave Ton a bitter potion to drink and made him stare at a candle flame until he fell asleep, while Zorax chanted words that had something to do with a 'rope spell.' When Ton awoke, he could remember little of what had happened, only the image of Zorax's compelling eyes.

"Ton soon learned his duties in Zorax's household: carrying water, washing loathsome pots coated with the odorous gummy residue of potions, disposing of the horribly mutilated remains of small animals killed in Zorax's experiments, cleaning the hut without disturbing the books, packets, bottles, boxes, jars, cages, and apparatus scattered everywhere, and gathering wood from the forest.

"Frightened villagers left food for Zorax every day at the same spot, seeking to appease the powerful and dangerous magician. So Ton did not have to gather food, but only to carry it the short distance to their hut."

This Zorax seems to have his own ways of obtaining "funding" for his experiments, thought Elizabeth.

"Ton was allowed to roam in the forest, but soon he learned that after he had gone a certain distance from the magician's hut he was unable to go any farther and so he couldn't run away. The 'rope spell' that the magician had cast on him prevented his escape more surely than if a rope had actually been tied around his neck."

That must be rather like being Allan Saxon's postdoc, thought Elizabeth, looking at David appraisingly.

"One day," David continued, "when Ton was in the forest gathering wood, he saw something large looming among the tall trees. Pushing through the brush, he came upon a clearing. In its center was a high tower surrounded by tumbled stones. The ruined tower, which might once have been part of a castle or fortress, stood alone. There seemed to be no way to enter or to climb it: no doors, no ladders, no footholds. Ton shouted, asking if anyone was there.

"There was an answering call, the voice of a girl. The stone tower was high and the walls were thick, so they had to shout back and forth for a long time before Ton was able to understand her story. The girl's name was something like Elle, she was the daughter of a king, and she was being held prisoner by an old magician. Zorax? Ton wondered, but she didn't seem to recognize the name."

The unattainable girl, thought Elizabeth. Interesting.

"Abruptly, Ton noticed that the light was failing and that it was quite late. He called goodbye to Elle, promised to return, and quickly left. To avoid a beating from Zorax, Ton had to run all the way back to the hut with his heavy burden of wood. The magician gave him a piercing look when he entered the hut out of breath and stumble-footed, but the old man said nothing."

David stopped and looked at each child apparently checking on their interest. Elizabeth looked across the room. Both children were clearly enjoying the story, looking at David with rapt attention. Paul seemed to be listening, too.

"The very next day," David continued, "Zorax told Ton that the time had come for him to earn his slave-price. There was a great task that Ton must perform, and if he did it correctly and well he would be freed from his slave-bond. Ton was suspicious of the magician's unusual generosity, but he said nothing. Zorax told him to pack some food and drink in a large basket. They left the hut walking in a direction that Ton had never explored. After a time Ton was suddenly brought up short. The rope spell prevented his further movement. The magician turned, looking annoyed, and uttered a single unpronounceable word. It was as if the invisible rope had been cut. No force now held Ton back, and he was free to follow the magician.

"They continued to walk until in the early afternoon near the base of a mountain slope they came to the tumbled ruins of what must have once been a large town. They followed an overgrown trail down to a place at the lowest part of the mountain wall, where Zorax indicated that they would halt and take their refreshment from the food and drink that Ton carried.

"After they had eaten, Zorax ordered Ton to clear the brush from a large rectangular rock slab at the base of a cliff. When this was done, the magician took some wax from a bag that he carried and roughly pressed it into Ton's ears, until Ton could hear nothing more than the rush of his own blood and the beating of his own heart. Zorax took some papers and packets from his bag. His lips moved so that he must be saying long and complicated words, but Ton could hear nothing because of the wax."

Must be classified information, Elizabeth thought, remembering David's comical stories about the extremes of Los Alamos security measures.

"After a while, the magician stopped," David went on, "held his arms out over the flat rock, and looked expectantly down at it. Nothing happened. Then for another long while Zorax chanted words and gestured more vigorously, then waited. Again nothing happened. Finally, looking very troubled and nervous, Zorax dug some dirt away from one edge of the flat rock, undid one of his bundles, and placed its contents in the small dug-out depression. He opened a gray flask and poured a clear liquid into the depression. Then he backed away, his lips moving furiously as he said more words, and this time his efforts were answered by a bright flash, accompanied by much dust and smoke and a shaking of the ground. And the great rock moved. It lifted, shifting sideways and revealing a dark round opening in the ground."

David may claim that magic and science are different, Elizabeth thought, but that sounds just like experimental physics to me.

"As the smoke cleared, Zorax removed the wax from Ton's ears. He dropped a rock into the hole. After it had fallen for about a second, they heard it hit something solid. Zorax nodded and gave Ton his instructions.

" 'Climb down this rope until you reach the floor below. Then you must light this candle. In the chamber below you will find a long tunnel which leads back into the mountain. You must follow that tunnel past three side passages, two on the right and one on the left. When you have passed the last of the three passages, you must continue straight ahead until you come to a door. It will be locked, but you should be able to get it open, for it is very old. Beyond the door you will find a chamber. In the chamber are three objects: a roll of fabric like a rug, a leather bag, and a weapon. These you will bring back to me without examining them.

" 'There will be many other things that you will see in the passages. There will appear to be rich treasures, jeweled weapons, golden coins. These are only traps and illusions, and you must leave them completely alone! If you do not, you will probably be instantly killed, and in any case will never be able to return above ground again. When you have brought me the three valueless mementos that I have described, mere souvenirs which I desire only for sentimental reasons, I will set you free. Do you understand this, boy?'

"Ton nodded. Zorax lifted the rope, which he tied around Ton's slender waist. Then Ton wriggled through the tight hole, which had a burnt sulfurous smell from the recent explosion, and he was lowered to the cool damp surface below. Zorax then threw a burning stick into the hole, and Ton used it to light the candle. Ton untied the rope, and holding the candle high he looked around . . ."

David glanced up at Elizabeth. The signal for bedtime, she thought. She closed the book with a snap, rose, and said, "I'm afraid, children, that that's all the story for tonight. It's time for bed now."

"Darn!" said Jeffrey, wrinkling his nose.

"Aw, Mom!" said Melissa, "You always stop the story at the most interesting part."

3

WEDNESDAY NIGHT, OCTOBER 6

Trailing red and black multimeter leads, Sam Weston grunted and eased his body from under the experiment control console. Victoria looked up from the oscilloscope on the cart before her and raised an eyebrow.

"Vickie, my love, if there's any coupling between the RF and the vacuum readout I sure can't find it. As far as I can tell, your little radio frequencies go just where they're supposed to and don't do any broadcasting. The vacuum-gauge electronics are all packaged in a nice copper-shielded box, and the leads from the gauge tube even pass through RF-traps on the way in. The gauge itself is all DC. I couldn't force RF into that circuit with a crowbar. There may be a spook in your hardware, but it ain't from RF getting into the vacuum readout."

"Yeah, Sam," said Vickie, pulling back a strand of coppery red hair, "I was coming to the same conclusion. I picked up the campus FM station on my 'scope, but I don't see our frequencies on any of the lines. Something else must be wrong."

"So," said Sam, standing up, "I'm afraid that's all I can do for you tonight, sweetie. It's gettin' late, and if my wife ever found out I was consorting all evenin' with a beautiful redhead, I'd be in for some real trouble." He dropped several of his tools into a camouflage-patterned olive drab tool box with the number "3" stenciled on each end.

"Hey, Sam," said Vickie, "why is that toolbox with the funny paint job 'number three,' and why do you have all those odd-looking tools and meters in there? They don't look like anything from the electronics shop."

"They're special, honey," he answered. "After the bomb falls, there ain't gonna be any nice wall sockets where you can plug in your little soldering irons and drills and oscilloscopes. This is my number-three toolbox. Number one's at home, and number two's in my Jeep. Everything in these boxes is self-powered, and there's a little solar-cell recharger unit, too. It's all done with batteries, little gas cartridges, stuff like that. After the Big One, mine'll be the only stuff that works.

"You know, Vickie, you ought to give a thought to what you'll do when the time comes. It's coming, you know, and it's not that far off. We've got our place up in the Cascades all ready. You'd be welcome to join our group."

"We've talked about this before, Sam," said Vickie, slightly amused, "and you're not going to convince me that it makes any sense to worry about such things. I want to get my Ph.D., not dig myself a hidey hole. In the Middle Ages a good part of Europe was convinced that the world was going to end in the year 1000. They fully expected the Second Coming and Armageddon, and they did some pretty odd and unbelievable things to prepare themselves. They must have been quite disappointed when the millennium came and nothing happened.

"You'd better watch out, Sam," she continued. She liked to tease him, but she was careful not to hurt his feelings. "This survivalist stuff can have a bad effect on your character. After you've made all these preparations, done all that work, and spent all that money, aren't you just a tiny bit disappointed every time the international situation gets a little better or tensions drop a notch? Don't you worry that you won't be able to get the benefits of all your investment?"

He looked at her for a moment, then sighed. "Vickie, honey, I guess the ants couldn't convince that grasshopper that winter was comin', either. Anyhow, I got to get home. You think about what I said, though, OK?"

"OK, Sam," she answered, "and thanks for all your help. We didn't find any RF pickup, but we're that much farther along in knowing we have to look somewhere else. David's going to be disappointed, though, when he gets back from dinner. Anyway, thanks! Now I owe *you* one."

"Naw, we're even, Vickie," said Sam. "G'night!"

Victoria turned back to the control console as the door shut. She moused up the supervisor program on the control computer and clicked the data file containing the settings that David had been using. Then she set the oscillator to manual and slowly turned the black knob to change the frequency while she watched the vacuum gauge. As she tuned, the gauge abruptly dropped to the 10^{-9} scale. The spurious vacuum improvement again: the problem was still there. "Shit!" she said to no one in particular.

She had an idea. Maybe this frequency wasn't unique. She slowly swept the drive frequency from one end of the oscillator range to another, watching the meter. Only at the one value that David had found did the vacuum meter drop. She changed the oscillator range switch and tried again. As she tuned, the meter took an abrupt drop. She backed over the frequency several times to check that it was really there, then noted its value in the logbook.

Reaching for the black knob, she continued the search. At another frequency the meter dipped again. She blinked. Curiouser and curiouser, she said to herself as she recorded the third new frequency in the logbook.

Returning from the children's rooms, Elizabeth smiled at David. "That was a nice story, David. You haven't lost your touch. Where'd you get this one? I don't think I've encountered it before."

"It's funny, Elizabeth," David replied, "I don't actually remember. When I was a kid I was absolutely fascinated with mythology and folklore. On my tenth birthday my mother bought me good facsimile reproductions of all twelve of Andrew Lang's *Fairy Books* that were originally published in England around the turn of the century. You know, *The Blue Fairy Book, The Green Fairy Book, The Crimson, The Lilac*, and all the others. They had beautiful pictures and wonderful stories, and I practically memorized them. I think maybe that's where I read this story. It sounds a bit like 'Aladdin' from the *Arabian Nights* or Hans Christian Andersen's 'Tinderbox,' but it's different from both of them.

Tonight it just popped into my head. I'm not sure I was remembering all the details; I may have improvised a bit."

"It was a seamless, polished delivery," said Elizabeth, still considering the psychological implications of the story. She thought it was good for David to tell stories to the children, and she enjoyed listening for clues to his inner conflicts. "You know, David, you're very good with children. Which reminds me, how are you and Sarah doing? I don't believe I've heard you mention her lately."

"Sarah and I are *finito*, as of a couple of weeks ago," said David. "I think it's the Curse of the Harrisons at work again."

"The Curse of the Harrisons?" Elizabeth frowned. "That sounds like a bad gothic romance. What is it?"

"It's an infirmity which has afflicted most of the male members of my family for generations," said David. "We have a weakness for intelligent women. But we're not very tolerant, I'm afraid. Quirks, hang-ups, and neuroses drive us right up the wall. I'm still looking for a lady who's smart *and* well adjusted. But our society does terrible things to the psyches of adolescent females who betray the stigmata of intelligence. Nothing against Sarah. She's a fine person. I was just hoping she was different.

"So the bottom line, Elizabeth, is that Sarah and I have decided to go our separate ways. She had become increasingly jealous of the long hours that I put in at the lab. It got so we argued all the time when we were together. I suppose it's just as well. During this present rather precarious phase of my career it's better that I don't devote too much time to the pursuit of females, intelligent or otherwise. It can be a full-time job."

Elizabeth deliberately gave him a pained look. Poor David, she thought, I hope you grow out of it. "Cheer up," she said, "you only have to find one, you know. Your afflicted ancestors seem to have managed it."

Just then, Paul, who had gone to the basement to "stoke the computer," returned. He and David walked to the kitchen for the after-dinner cleanup.

I wonder what his mother was like, Elizabeth thought as she settled back into her chair.

* * *

David was standing at the sink, rinsing the dinner dishes and handing them to Paul to place in the dishwasher. While Paul was doing some rearranging, David looked out the kitchen window, considering the shimmering reflections of the lights from Kirkland across the lake. The residences of Bellevue made densely packed points of light that shaded to a continuous galaxylike glow on the more distant hillsides of Somerset and Newport Hills. Farther south the traffic on the Evergreen Point Bridge seemed to be moving now. He handed Paul another dish.

"So you're having problems with your hardware," Paul said. "Anything serious?"

"Well, you never know how serious an experimental problem is 'til after you understand it," said David, "and by then it's usually not a problem any more. This one's particularly insidious because it makes our diagnostic instruments tell us lies. Vickie and I are just putting the finishing touches to the new perovskite holospin-echo rig."

"I'll bet Allan's excited," Paul said mildly.

"Well, Allan's out of town right now," David answered. He considered just what he wanted to say to Paul about Allan Saxon. "That's OK, though. Even when he's around his forte isn't debugging hardware. His talents lie in other directions. He has some pretty good ideas for where to push, he gets the NSF contracts that pay the bills and our salaries, he gets the shop time, and he gets us the very best samples to play with. Right now he's pretty involved with his national committees and his business ventures." *And it's damn hard to get his attention*, David added silently to himself. "But anyhow, we're setting up to look for holospin wave excitations in some of the more exotic warm superconductors. We're going to have the best setup in the world, if it ever works."

Paul nodded.

"But so far we haven't even been able to get to square one," David continued. "That'll be when we put a sample in the chamber. We're still on square zero, working on the 'null' part of the experiment to make sure that we don't get false signals from the equipment when nothing's inside. But at the moment we do get unexpected results without a sample." He described what had happened that evening at the laboratory. "It's weird!" he concluded. "Vickie thinks it's an RF power leak."

As he was speaking, Elizabeth came in from the living room and opened the refrigerator. "RF power?" she said. "That sounds like a political movement. 'Power to the Rs, not to mention the Fs!' You guys certainly have your own language."

"It only seems that way," said David, handing Paul another plate. " 'RF' just means 'radio frequency' or high-frequency electricity. We're using something like TV transmitter to pipe electromagnetic energy into our experiment. We're driving the system with high-frequency radio waves."

"What happens during the commercials?" asked Elizabeth with an impetuous grin.

"We have a special circuit that cuts out the commercials, the game shows, and the wrestling matches," David said, laughing. "We prefer to use soap operas and new-wave music. It's much smoother."

"Paul told me that you've been working with warm superconductors," said Elizabeth. "I remember hearing about them five or six years ago when they were making the covers of *Time* and *Newsweek*. What ever happened to them?"

"Oh, they're still around," said David, "but the floating trains and the superfast computers described in the magazines are taking a bit longer than was advertised. Warm superconductors were special in the first place because they have a special crystal structure called a layered perovskite. It's a flat crystal plane like a checkerboard with copper atoms in the centers of the squares. The copper atoms in the red squares have spin up and those in the black squares have spin down."

"Wait, David, let me get this straight," said Elizabeth, holding up a hand. "As I recall, atoms have a permanent 'spin' rotation about their axes that also gives them a magnetic field like a little compass needle attached to each atom. If the needle points up or down, then the atom has spin up or spin down. Right?"

"Right," said David. "The atoms of copper resemble

little spinning tops, and can point either way."

Elizabeth nodded, measuring coffee beans into the grinder.

"OK. About two years ago it was discovered," David continued, speaking more loudly over the noise of the grinder, "partly by our own dear Professor Allan Saxon and his students, that in these checkerboard crystals of some of the warm superconductors there's a new and previously unsuspected kind of ordering. Waves called holospin waves move through these crystals by changes in the spin directions, rather like the waves you see when the wind blows over a field of wheat. You know, like 'amber waves of grain.' But these waves are special because instead of being like a regular wave pattern, they're more like a hologram." He handed Paul some silverware.

"That isn't much help, David," said Paul. "The workings of holograms are not widely understood. I'm not sure that I understand how they work in every detail. There are some tricky phase aspects of the wave interferences—"

"Never mind the details," David interrupted. "The only thing you need to know about them is that if you break off a small piece from a big hologram, it still shows the same picture as the whole thing but with less resolution. That's because the holographic ordering, the encoding of the picture, is spread out over the whole thing rather than localized in any one place on the hologram.

"And it's the same with the waves that we make in our superconductor samples. It's called 'holospin order,' and the wave disturbances that move in funny ways through the crystals are called 'holospin waves.'" He paused to run the plastic scrubber over the inside of a pot.

"Allan Saxon told me that those are the hottest thing in condensed matter physics just now," said Paul. "He said that a holospin transmission cable made from one pair of warm superconductor strips could carry simultaneously an almost unlimited number of messages of very high bandwidth. It will revolutionize communications, he said, and there are lots of other applications, too. Should I believe him?" He shook some detergent into the dishwasher, closed its door, and turned it on.

They dried their hands and adjourned to the living room. Paul stirred up the fire he had started in the stone fireplace. David stared into the fire, musing. "Sure you should . . . at least in this case. The application potential is real enough," he said. "I turned down a tenure-track faculty job at a pretty good university to come here for a second postdoc so I could work with Saxon and get in on the ground floor of this. And we're beginning the second generation of experiments. These will be the ones where we learn to fully understand the phenomenon: how it works, and what it's good for."

"But you're having problems?" said Elizabeth.

"Yeah," said David. "Our equipment is lying to us. Vickie thinks some funny resonance in the vacuum-readout electronics is the culprit. That would explain all the facts, but it doesn't feel right to me. I've used almost the same hardware in a dozen other experiments, and I never saw anything like this. It's true that we're making some pretty strange electromagnetic fields. The field vectors are rotating, precessing, and jumping according to an intricate program that we set up. But there's no reason that that should produce what we're seeing.

"Anyhow, Vickie is now checking things out while I'm over here wining and dining. I promised I'd be back about midnight to take over. I'll work a few more hours tonight and try to flush some bugs out of the system. As a psychologist, you should understand this, Elizabeth. If you interact closely enough with a complicated system, it'll eventually tell you what its problems are. And somehow it works best in the wee hours."

"You guys have your own pagan religion," said Paul, shaking his head. "Instead of sacrificing sheep, you sacrifice sleep. Do you suppose there's any chance at all that you're seeing a real effect, not just an instrument glitch?"

"Look," said David, "we're talking about a volume of empty space about the size of a baseball acting as a vacuum pump and absorbing lots of energy at the same time. There's no physics I know about that could account for that."

"I know some physics that could, if the energy density were, say, 10^{32} electron-volts per cubic centimeter," said Paul. He smiled ruefully. "Some of the oddball superstring theories I've been playing with lately would seem to say that you can make space itself do tricks if you fill it with the right amount of energy. Trouble is, that 'right amount' hasn't been around since the Big Bang.''

"We ain't making any Big Bangs in my lab, buddy!'' said David. Then he paused and smiled. ''You might say we're close, though . . . the power's only off by thirty orders of magnitude.'' He winked at Paul. ''That's closer than some of your predictions, I believe.'' They both laughed.

Elizabeth disappeared in the direction of the kitchen and soon returned with a tray of steaming coffee cups. ''David,'' she said, ''if you're going back to work tonight, you'll certainly need some of this.''

"I'm afraid it's going to take more than coffee to get the job done tonight, Elizabeth,'' said David, taking a cup and saucer from the tray. ''You have anything that makes you smarter instead of just more wide awake?''

"Wish we did!'' said Paul. ''I could use some of that myself.''

4

THURSDAY MIDNIGHT, OCTOBER 7

David pulled into the Fifteenth Avenue Northeast entrance to the central parking garage. At this time of night there was no guard in the glass-walled booth as he drove past it to the short ramp up to the A level. He selected an empty spot near the southeast corner, parked and locked his car, and climbed the garage stairs to the exit at the corner of the Administration Building. Across Rainier Vista he could see lights in the windows of their lab in Physics Hall. Vickie's still at it, he concluded, smiling to himself. As he walked down the broad granite stairs and headed across an open space, the bell in the campanile to the north slowly tolled twelve. Midnight, he thought. He was still feeling pretty sharp. Maybe he could get something done tonight.

He unlocked the outer door with his building key and let himself in, then walked along the dimly lit hallway to his laboratory. It was an unusually quiet night, he observed. None of the usual night owls seemed to be working in the other labs tonight.

Victoria looked up from the console as he let himself in. David noticed that she looked unusually tired. "Maybe I should have called you at the Ernsts and told you to save yourself a trip," she said. She told him what she had been doing. "And I found two new frequencies where the same thing happens. The vacuum improves, and the RF power shows a load increase," she said. "It's spooky!"

"I didn't want to say anything that might have dampened your enthusiasm," said David, "but your vacuum gauge resonance theory smelled wrong to me then. Driving over, I was wondering whether we could be making a cyclotron resonance with free electrons in the sample volume. Maybe stray electrons get up some speed, collide with gas molecules in the vacuum, ionize them, and the fields sweep them out. That would explain both the power loss and the improved vacuum."

Vickie frowned and shook her head. "If that works," she said, teasing, "you'd better patent it quick. It makes a far better vacuum pump than this one we bought for several thousand dollars."

"Yeah." David sighed, nodding agreement. "That point had occurred to me also. I guess it's a lousy theory. I'm grasping at straws, Vickie. Maybe if I play with this miserable beast for a while I'll get some better ideas. Anyhow, you look as if you could use some rest. We can't have you expiring from exhaustion before we even get you a Ph. D. You have to wait 'til you're a postdoc for that."

Victoria looked at David, frowning. "Don't worry about me; worry about yourself," she said. "I know your disgusting work habits very well, David Harrison. You're quite capable of forgetting the time and working all night. Remember that you have a class to teach tomorrow. You can't afford to hang around here for more than an hour or so, no matter how interested you get in our hardware problems. I'm going to set this timer, see. When it buzzes, you have to go home. OK? Promise?"

"Vickie, if I'd wanted to work with a mother hen, I'd have gone into zoology," said David, slightly annoyed. "I'm well aware that I can't work much longer. That damned eight-thirty lecture is only about eight hours away now.

"But speaking of mother hens, how are you doing with Flash?" asked David, seeking to change the subject. Vickie's sixteen-year-old brother was now living in her rooming house. He had come to Seattle at Vickie's widower father's request after a brush with the law in southern California. Last month Sarah and David had gone with Vickie to SeaTac Airport when young William Gordon arrived. He was a tall scrawny kid with acne and Vickie's red hair. They'd had a nice dinner at David's apartment that evening, and David had tried to interest him in physics. But William, or "Flash," as he had insisted on being called, seemed more interested in David's new portable Macintosh III computer and his collection of science fiction hardbacks. He had told David that if they ever let him out of high school he was going to get a fast degree in computer science and make lots of money.

Victoria shrugged on her jacket and backpack. She frowned and said, "William is doing OK, I guess. He just started as a senior at Roosevelt High School, and he got into the classes he wanted. His teachers say he's turning in assignments on time and doing well in class. And the Seattle police, unlike the L.A.P.D., don't pay him a visit every time some hacker cracks a bank machine."

"So he's reformed?" David asked.

"I've got my fingers crossed," she answered. "William claims to have learned his lesson, and he gives the appearance of being a serious student. I haven't the time to watch him continuously, of course, any more than Dad could in Santa Monica."

He nodded, waiting.

"David," she said, "I don't think William has completely given up hacking."

"Why?" he asked.

"Because last night when I got home I noticed that my modem was still warm," she said. "He may have just been dialing into bulletin boards, but he might be trying to crack commercial systems again. I'm worried."

She looked at her watch, frowned, waved at David, and left. For a minute David looked unseeing at the closed door, musing over how cold and empty the room suddenly felt with Vickie not in it.

Then he turned his thoughts back to the present problem, the glitch in their experiment. He seated himself at the experiment console and moused up the control program. Scanning several of the new parameter files that Vickie had generated, he selected one and tried it. He didn't have to look at the vacuum gauge to know that the problem was still there. He could hear the reed relay click as the automatic mechanism changed vacuum scales. He began to experiment. He tried changing the field in the superconducting magnet; he tried altering the rotation rate of the field preces-

sion system; he tried playing with the relative phases of the
electric-mode and magnetic-mode driving fields. Nothing
helped.

He'd been working for about an hour when he noticed
one peculiarity. Watching a field pickup with an oscilloscope, he saw with surprise that the field was not making
a single "twist" as it was programmed to do. Instead it
was "tumbling," repeating the rotation cycle over and over
again. He'd found a bug! Backtracking the symptom, he
discovered that it originated not in the electronics but in the
programming. A few days earlier he'd made a small "improvement" in the control program. Apparently this change
had brought with it an unwanted side effect: instead of
making a single twistor rotation pass, the field rotation was
cycling again and again.

Relieved that he had at last found a fixable problem,
David corrected and recompiled the program, then activated
the field cycle. The result was a disappointment. While the
vacuum excursion was now much reduced, it was still there.
And the strange loss of RF power was now bigger than
before. The program bug had not created the problem, it
had only aggravated some other glitch that was still present.
It just didn't make any sense.

David, feeling frustrated, got up from the console and
walked around the room, topping off the liquid nitrogen and
liquid helium reservoirs inside the apparatus and tightening
a brace to reduce vibrations from the mechanical first-stage
vacuum pump. As his hands worked automatically, he had
an idea: if you can't twiddle parameters to make things
better, why not see what it takes to make them worse? The
rotating field volume of the system was carefully adjusted
to be well inside the boundaries of the sample holder and
the magnetic guide field. But suppose the problem was
coming from some stray field getting where it didn't belong.
By readjusting a few currents he could make the field volume
bigger—much bigger, in fact. There was plenty of drive
power for that. They had been quite conservative in esti-
mating the power needed, and as a result the driver units
were considerably overdesigned. If he could make the prob-

lem worse, then perhaps its source would become more apparent.

He returned to the control console and moused up the program that he and Vickie had developed to design and model the unusual coil configuration of the apparatus. He set the nonlinear least-squares search feature of the program to find settings that duplicated the same twistor field shape but with a diameter that was, say, eight times larger.

The computer settled into its search procedure. It took a while. It usually needed about twenty minutes for its central processor to search out optimum parameters in the complex parameter space of possibilities. While the search code wandered about in its arcane way, mapping the parameter space and seeking a minimum in the chi-squared goodness-of-fit value, the system's powerful display processor had nothing to do. So, for the user's amusement, Vickie had arranged the program to produce a perspective view of the chi-squared space being searched, a spectacularly colored graphical representation showing a mathematical terrain of tall mountains, rolling foothills, and broad deep valleys. The colors of the surfaces were selected using an algorithm that, on a blue-washed background, mapped mathematical mountains with white tops, brown central regions, and green bases.

As the lengthy search proceeded and the contours of the terrain were filled in, David settled back to wait for the result. He realized that the emerging scene with its snowy mountain summits, brown slopes, and green valleys looked very much like the Cascades he had explored the previous summer. He remembered his first climb. The winter snows of the central Cascade Range near Seattle had melted enough for safe mountaineering, and Paul had invited him along on "an easy Class Three climb." He remembered it well. . . .

The four of them had been climbing Kaleetan, a minor two-thousand-meter peak in the Central Cascades. Paul had been in the lead; David was second, in the novice position; followed by Rudi Baumann and George Williams, both quantum-gravity theorists.

The monotony of the uphill plodding had lulled David into daydreaming. He was just fitting his boot into the next

step that Paul had provided when he heard a shout. Back
along the white slope marked with dark footsteps he saw
George, last on the rope and heaviest of the party, momentarily frozen in the act of losing his footing as a snow step
crumbled away. As David watched, George flailed, pivoted,
and toppled into a downward slide, head first on his side.
He twisted, pivoting on an elbow as he planted the short
wide blade of his ice axe in the snow to halt his fall. That,
it seemed, was a mistake; George was falling too fast for
that maneuver. The broad blade bit out a shower of snow,
and the ice axe jerked and was wrenched from George's
grip, his acceleration continuing unchecked. A clearly enun-
ciated ''Shit!'' echoed resoundingly from the nearby rock
walls.

David felt his heart speed up from an involuntary adrenaline spurt. He watched as George's red-clad figure moved
leisurely down the slope, trailing the dark rope, moving
toward the jagged rockfall below, twisting as he maneuvered
into a stomach-down, head-up position. George was trying
without much effect to slow his fall by digging toes and
elbows into the snow. The rope straightened, stretched, and
stiffened, shedding snow and moisture as it became a vibrating line. George was slowed momentarily as the impact
hit Rudi, now kneeling in the snow, the narrow spike of his
ice axe planted about halfway up the blade.

But David could see a problem developing. The climbing
rope, which should have absorbed the shock at Rudi's waist,
well centered on his braced position, somehow become
draped over his shoulder instead. The impact levered him
up and backward, and now he was sliding down the snow
slope head down on his back, his axe blade pointing use-
lessly toward the sky.

I'm next, thought David. We're like dominoes. Those
two falling now are both heavier than I am. George must
mass about one-hundred-twenty kilos, and Rudi perhaps
ninety. When that quarter ton of meat hits the end of the
rope, I'll never be able to stop them. They'll drag me off
too, and then there will be three of us falling. We'll pull
Paul off, and that will make four. We're going to end in a
pile of broken bodies on those sharp rocks down there. In

a day or so maybe someone will find what's left of us. We're going to die right here, right now. And this was only supposed to be a Class Three climb!

Somehow the thoughts racing through his head seemed to calm David, as if someone else was about to die as he observed remotely. With control and precision he kicked deep toeholds in the snow and then nudged out depressions for his knees. He made sure that the rope was positioned correctly, then chopped the long thin blade of the ice axe into the grainy snow, his right hand gripping its top at the cross of the tee while his left held the handle so that it passed under his right arm, adjusting the stance until it felt right. It all seemed to be taking quite a long time.

The impact, when it came, was not the sudden crushing blow that David had anticipated. The climbing rope was surprisingly flexible, like a rubber band. He could feel it stretch as the force built and the rope cut deeper into his waist. He was slowing them! He had the brief illusion that his braced position would hold, that the two would stop. But then the rough snow crumbled beneath his left foot and he too was falling, the rubber-band effect now accelerating him to join his comrades in their tumble to the rocks.

He was sliding on his stomach, feet down. His axe blade was cutting through the crusted snow like a knife, a plume of frosty fragments streaming out behind him as he slid. In his right hand the ice axe pulled with a force that was close to the limit of his strength. But he found that by levering back to reduce the axe blade's bite in the snow he could bring the force down a bit. He slid on, cursing and working to dig in his toes.

This must be using up a lot of the available gravitational energy, a detached corner of his mind murmured. Energy-in is energy-out is force times distance: $E = mgh = \int F \cdot dl$. A big force over a long distance might just do the trick. Hell, maybe I can stop them! With new optimism he gritted his teeth and dug in the blade deeper, until he was straining with all his strength against an enormous force. He couldn't do this for long. Was it his imagination, or were they slowing down? He became more certain that they were slowing, that the drag on his arms and the pull of the rope on his waist were diminishing. *Maybe*, he thought, *may-be* ... Then, quite unexpectedly, he stopped.

David looked back up the steep slope at his track. He had traveled about forty meters down the incline, his trail through the snow delineated by grooves from his boots and the jewel-edged black line cut by his axe blade. He looked up to where Paul was set and ready, face down in the snow, feet, knees, and ice axe braced for the impact that now would not come. There was still a little slack in the rope.

David exhaled a laugh, jerked twice on the rope as a signal, and stood up shakily. Downslope, Rudi was still lying on his back, head downhill, his ice axe blade still pointing at the zenith. Farther down, George was getting slowly to his feet and cursing fluently in several languages as he combed snow and ice from his bushy beard.

The blood still singing in his ears, David inhaled deeply, brushed himself off, and looked around at the snowcapped peaks and the green valleys far below. It's wonderful to be alive, he thought. It wouldn't do to die just now, when things have been going so well at the lab. He grinned.

The computer made a beeping noise, signaling that it had found a steep descent trajectory. David shook himself. The view of the Cascades on the display screen shifted back to a representation of a mathematical surface.

The calculation was nearing completion. The program had found a deep minimum groove in the chi-squared surface and was sliding along a channel that headed downhill at an increasingly steep angle. Like a slide down a snow field, David thought. The search code raced along this "creek bed" until it emptied into a broad green valley with a deep blue depression at one end. It targeted on the depression, dived into it, and settled, rocking back and forth at its very bottom. Then it registered success by playing a few bars from "The Ride of the Valkyries," a feature that Vickie in a moment of CalTechie exuberance had added. David smiled.

He moused the packet of final fit parameters that the search code had generated into the control program and configured it for a count-down-to-run of five seconds. He moused the cursor to the (ACTIVATE) control on the computer screen and clicked. The settings were fed to the driving circuits, and there was a brief wait while the static fields and power levels stabilized. Then the computer's synthesized "voice" produced by the control program counted in the usual way: *"Five! . . . Four! . . . Three! . . . Two! . . . One!"* and finally, *"Activating!"*

David was looking directly at the large stainless-steel sphere when it disappeared, accompanied by a loud hollow *pop!* Immediately wires and small metal parts cascaded to the floor and the auto-fill circuits of the helium and nitrogen supplies cut in, the severed feed lines spouting clear streams of the cryogenic liquids and gouts of steam as water vapor condensed from the chilled air. Cut water lines added to the mess. A glass vacuum gauge, now unsupported but still attached to its black cable, swung diagonally, colliding with the floor in a crash of shattering glass punctuated by blue-green flashes from its shorted electrodes. Its power supply gave a loud click as it responded to the overload condition.

"Jesus H. Christ!" said David Harrison, staring at the empty space where, just one second earlier, the culmination of ten months of hard work and a net expenditure of $47,362 from Allan Saxon's National Science Foundation grant had rested.

PART 2

Properly, there is no other knowledge than that
which is got by working; the rest is yet all
a hypothesis of knowledge, a thing to be argued
in schools, a thing floating in the clouds, in
endless logic vortices,'til we try and fix it.

THOMAS CARLYLE
(1795–1881)

5

THURSDAY MORNING, OCTOBER 7

A bleary-eyed David Harrison looked out at the upward-sloping sea of student faces, then put the last transparency of his lecture on the overhead projector and hammered on the final concept concerning capacitance and energy storage. Some of the students were watching attentively, some flipping notebook pages, some yawning or reading newspapers at the back of the two-hundred-seat lecture hall. He had been teaching Allan's Physics 122 class all week, and he noticed that he was developing something of a fan club. The three attractive young ladies in the second row were sending him messages of dewy interest and anticipation. Good, that means they're awake, he thought.

He glanced at the large wall clock at the rear of the sloping theaterlike classroom. The time was 9:09 A.M., still eleven more minutes before the bell. Time for the demo, he thought, and walked behind the slablike lecture demonstration table. He pulled the heavy glass Leyden jar capacitor onto the aluminum sheet next to the department's antique Wimshurst machine.

The Wimshurst machine was a large electrostatic charging device straight out of the nineteenth century, a thing of tinfoil and turning glass plates and tinsel brushes and balls and cranks and round leather sewing-machine belts. As he turned the crank, the twin glass plates rotated in opposite directions, and between the silvery ball electrodes the apparatus produced a fat blue spark. The spark was accompanied by a curiously satisfying *Fwap!*, and a sharp ozone smell. A dozen bored faces turned to see what was going on. The "fans" clapped with delight and smiled.

"Now," said David, "we're going to have a little demonstration that may teach us something about capacitance and energy storage. This big object is called a Leyden jar capacitor, and it's just like the one described in your book. It has cup-shaped metal conductors on the inside and outside, kept apart by the jar-shaped glass insulator. The insulator is quite thick, and it can hold many thousands of volts without electrical breakdown. Now I'm going to put a big electrical charge on it . . ." He paused, leering at the class and beetling his eyebrows. ". . . with this Wimshurst machine, which I have borrowed from Dr. Frankenstein's laboratory deep in the Physics Hall basement," he added, using his best Karloff imitation. That got a laugh.

"We're going to try and learn something about stored energy," he continued, resuming his normal voice. He stopped cranking and picked up a long insulated rod supporting a C-shaped conductor that ended in two shiny balls. He held the C across the terminals of the Leyden jar. *Fwap!!* went the spark as he shorted the capacitor. "See," he said, "I can store lots of energy in this capacitor because it holds a large voltage and has a big plate area. Now watch this one." He turned the crank again and heard a satisfying sizzling noise as the Wimshurst machine again charged the device. "This time, inspired by the work of Dr. Frankenstein, we are going to dissect our patient," said David, mugging a demented grin. The fans giggled.

As he turned to get the other insulated rod, he spotted Vickie standing just outside the exit door of the lecture hall, watching. Uh-oh, he thought to himself. For the first time in recent memory, he was not pleased to see her. Using the pair of insulated rods, he disconnected the large juglike capacitor from the machine, pushed it down the table to a second grounded plate, and grasped its metallic outer sheath by a projecting handle. "This is a special kind of Leyden jar capacitor. It comes apart," he said as he grasped an insulated handle on the inner conductor and pulled. The inner electrode, a blunt cylindrical piece of metal that fitted snugly into the interior of the jarlike glass insulator, pulled out easily.

Then he grasped the top edge of the glass, pulled it away

from the outer conductor, and set the glass vessel on the table. There was a slight sizzling noise and a heightened smell of ozone. Then he picked up the inner conductor by its handle and touched it to the outer conductor. The class, now well conditioned, was expecting another big spark. The tiny *pop* that occurred instead was an anticlimax. There were a few nervous laughs.

"OK," said David, "we've disarmed the beast by touching the inner conductor to the outer conductor. It's dead. Now let's put it back together." He picked up the glass insulator in both hands and slid it into the cup-shaped outer electrode. Then he picked up the inner electrode from the grounded sheet by its insulated handle and slipped it into the glass cavity.

"Now," said David, "how many of you think the electric charge is gone and the capacitor is discharged?" Most of the class raised their hands. "Does anyone think it's still charged?" No response. "Well then, since it's all discharged, would anyone like to volunteer to touch the inner and outer conductors at the same time?" He mugged the demented grin again and beckoned. The fans giggled, the class shifted nervously, and there were a few nudges and uneasy laughs. No one volunteered.

"I congratulate you on not having the courage of your convictions," said David. He touched the C-ring across the electrodes, and there was a startling *Fwap!* as a large blue spark jumped across the connection. The class buzzed with excitement. "D'you see that?" asked David. "It was still loaded with electrical energy! Now the question is . . ."

The serious students, sensing a possible item for the next test, opened their notebooks and began to write.

". . . where was all of that electrical energy hiding when I touched the metal parts together? Now I'm not going to tell you the answer. I want you to think about this and talk about it among yourselves until Monday . . . Professor Saxon will be back, and he'll explain it to you then." The fan club looked disappointed.

"And don't forget that you have a problem set due on Monday also. Any questions? No? OK! Class dismissed!"

As if triggered by his last words, the class-break bell sounded.

As David turned away from the lecture table, perhaps a dozen students from the first few rows charged up to the front table to get a closer look at the demonstration and to ask questions. These were the curious and interested ones, the ones who made it worth teaching the class. A student, one of the fans, asked if he would be teaching other classes next quarter, or if he would be teaching this one again soon. He said no, and she looked disappointed.

He excused himself as soon as he could manage it. He felt good. Despite his spotty preparation, the lecture had gone quite well, and the demonstration had knocked their socks off. Then he saw Vickie waiting at the exit door and looking rather irritated, and his mood fell.

He collected his transparencies and notebook at the over-head projector, then threaded his way to the exit door half-way up the rows of seats. Vickie was standing there, green eyes blazing.

"David, what happened last night?" she said, her voice unusually shrill.

"Uh, let's wait 'til we get to the lab to talk," said David, leading her down the hallway.

"I read the logbook and played back the data files. None of it makes any sense at all. What happened, David? Where's the cryostat? Where are the coils and the sensors?" Victoria's voice rose. "Where's my thesis experiment, dammit!"

David closed the door of the lab, put his lecture notes on a corner of the workbench, and slumped onto a wooden chair. Vickie still looked upset, but the walk from the lecture room to the laboratory had calmed her somewhat. She was still standing, however. "David," she said, tapping a foot on the concrete floor, "what the hell is going on?"

"I wish I knew, Vickie." He inhaled deeply and paused to organize his thoughts. "Sit down, and I'll tell what happened. Maybe you can tell me what's going on."

She sat in the other chair and glared at him.

David carefully described what he had done after she had

left the previous night. "While I was looking straight at it," he said finally, "the whole bloody chamber just disappeared! There was a sort of *pop* sound, and then there was nothing there."

She blinked but said nothing.

"I guess I was in shock for a while after that. I remember shutting off the water, the power, and the cryogenic fillers, and then I spent a long time just writing down everything I could think of in the logbook, trying to arrive at some rational explanation. But I was just going over the same ground again and again, and it was getting late. Finally I decided that the best thing to do was to go home, so I went. I made myself a stiff drink and went to bed. It's strange," he added lamely, "I slept like a baby. When I woke up this morning I barely had time to scribble out a few transparencies and get to the lecture." He paused, waiting for Vickie to say something, but she sat silently staring at him. David felt a compulsion to continue talking, to fill the silence with words.

"Vickie, the goddamned thing just disappeared! I know that sounds crazy, but that's what happened. The chamber we spent the last six months designing and building is gone, and I don't know where it went or how to get it back."

He felt rather desperate for a moment. Why didn't she say something? But then something triggered an old memory, and he felt himself growing more calm and thoughtful. "You know," he began, "once when I was a kid we found a huge light bulb in a garbage bin near the football stadium. I guess it was for the stadium lights. Anyhow, I threw a rock and hit it, and it broke with a loud funny *pop* and smashed all to pieces. The *pop* was an implosion, the air rushing in to fill the vacuum that had been in the bulb. Last night when the chamber disappeared, the *pop* sound it made was exactly like that. I think the damned chamber imploded!"

"God, David, that's weird!" said Victoria, frowning. Then she added, "How could a hunk of stainless steel implode without leaving a trace?" Without waiting for an answer, she blurted, "Have you *told* anyone yet?"

"What am I supposed to tell them? That our chamber

imploded and disappeared? I might as well say a billy goat broke into the lab and ate our equipment." He walked over to the concrete slab still holding the four upthrust chamber supports, their brackets truncated. He kicked at a scrap of metal lying on the floor. Then he stopped, bent down, and picked it up. It was a stainless-steel flange that had been welded to the chamber. He examined its inner surface, then touched its edge very carefully with his finger.

"David, what about Allan? You've got to call and tell him what happened. And wow, he's going to be mad! I can hear him now. It's his NSF grant, and his laboratory, and his equipment, and his professional reputation. David, he's going to take this as a personal insult. It would be best to tell him by phone. That would give him a chance to cool off a bit while we're out of shotgun range."

"Yes, that should be done soon," David agreed, but his thoughts were elsewhere. "Hmmm, this is interesting. Come here and look at this, Vickie!" He held out the piece of metal. He had noticed that the surface where it had been attached to the chamber was strangely shiny, like a polished mirror. She took it in her hand and examined it. She touched the edge carefully. "It's so smooth and the edges are so sharp! It would be hard to get a finish this smooth even with the precision surface grinder in the main shop." She bent down and examined some of the other pieces of metal, ceramic, glass, and plastic that littered the floor. "They're all the same way, David. How could that be?"

David picked up one of the larger metal pieces, the stub of a brace, and examined his reflection in its shiny inner surface. He walked to the window where the late morning sunlight was slanting through the glass. Holding the shiny surface so that it reflected the sunlight, he brought the sun's image to a brilliant spot on the palm of his other hand. "It focuses!" he said, quickly removing his hand from the hot spot. He walked across the room to the workbench, picked up a meter stick, and returned to the window. With the mirrorlike surface he cast a bright image of the sun on the wall under the windowsill and used the stick to measure the distance from the reflecting surface to the wall.

''What are you up to, David?'' asked Victoria, walking to the window to stand beside him.

''If you look carefully,'' he answered, ''you can see that all of these shiny surfaces are slightly concave, like fragments of a shaving mirror. I was using the sun's image to measure the focal length of this big one. It's just about forty-six centimeters. That means, if I remember my freshman physics right, that the radius of curvature of the reflecting surface is twice that, or ninety-two centimeters.'' He walked quickly to the control console and moved the mouse through a rapid series of operations. ''Yes, I thought I remembered that number from last night. Vickie, the curvature of these surfaces matches the size of the field I set up just before the chamber disappeared. My field solution was for a sphere with a radius of ninety-two centimeters!'' He sat at the console, his chin in his hands, and was quiet for a long time, not moving, his thoughts far away.

Vickie was checking more of the pieces. ''They all focus the sun at the same distance,'' she said. ''They all have the same radius of curvature.''

''Hey,'' said David, suddenly looking up, ''what ever happened to that first set of field coils we made, the ones that had to be done over because they had those big ugly sextupole and octopole field components?''

''I gave them to Sam,'' said Vickie. ''He said that maybe he could use them for the electron spin resonance setup in the senior lab.''

David smiled. ''Well, maybe we're not dead yet. Look, Vickie, we've lost our chamber, our cryostat, our sample holder, our superconducting solenoid, all of the stuff we spent so much time building. But it occurs to me that we still have all the power supplies, the driving electronics, and the control computer. And whatever gobbled up our hardware, the boundary was outside the volume where the vacuum and the cryogenics were, so those things probably didn't matter. Maybe we don't need all that stuff to do it again. So let's just reproduce the external field conditions and see what happens.

''You know, the unique thing about this experiment is that tricky spherical rotation of the twistor field that we devel-

oped. Nobody's ever made a field do anything like that
before. Vickie, maybe we've found a real effect. If you
think about our problems of last evening, perhaps those
funny vacuum gauge 'resonances' were just a smaller version of whatever took out the chamber. Perhaps we were
just making gas molecules disappear instead of stainless-
steel chambers. Let's go get those coils back from Sam and
see if we can reproduce the effect.''

"Wait a minute, David,'' said Vickie sternly. ''Just wait,
now! Think! Do you realize how crazy that sounds?''

David paused for a moment, then grinned. ''As some
famous physics pioneer must have said at one time or another,'' he said, holding two fingers against his upper lip
like a mustache and pointing upward with the index finger
of his other hand, ''Der nutty problems machst für das crazy
explanations!''

Vickie giggled, shaking her head and rolling her eyes
upward in mock despair.

"And this explanation, Vickie,'' he continued, ''is just
about crazy enough to be right. Cross your fingers. Maybe
we can get you a Ph. D. out of this mess yet!'' He walked
quickly to the door, motioning her to follow.

As they walked down the corridor toward the stairs,
Vickie said, ''David, aren't you forgetting Allan and the
disappearance of his expensive equipment? You've got to
call him.''

David slowed and gave her a pained look. ''Problem is,
I don't know where Allan is, so I can't just pick up the
phone and dial. I'll have to ask Susan, his secretary, to track
him down. Then I get to tell him that the sky is falling.''
He sighed. ''I do not look forward to that conversation,''
he said.

6

THURSDAY MIDMORNING, OCTOBER 7

The Megalith Tower loomed over Market Street, a featureless prism of black glass that contrasted bleakly with the whites and beiges of the other buildings of downtown San Francisco. From its thirty-third floor, the gray blanket of fog over the Pacific Ocean, somehow held back at the Golden Gate Bridge, looked like a shag carpet about to be unrolled over the bay.

Allan Saxon tapped his fingers on the chrome armrest of the black leather designer chair and felt himself becoming increasingly upset. Yesterday in D.C. the National Science Board meeting had not gone at all well. His fellow board members were even more self-serving, stubborn, and pigheaded than usual, and his pet projects consistently received the short end of the funding stick. Then he had drunk too much first-class booze on the much-delayed flight from Dulles to San Francisco and hadn't slept at all well after he reached the St. Francis.

And it had now been well over half an hour since he had arrived at the Megalith Tower and seated himself in the elegant reception area of Martin Pierce's outer office. Under slightly different circumstances he might have found advantage in the wait, an opportunity to arrange some afterhours recreation with Martin's stunning blond receptionist. But after yesterday's reverses he was in a petulant mood and didn't feel he had the patience for such games. Dammit, who did Martin think he was to keep him waiting so long? Perhaps he should invent another appointment and leave! But no, he couldn't afford to put additional distance between himself and Martin. There were problems enough already.

The ivory telephone made a bland musical sound. The receptionist answered it and listened for a moment, then turned smoothly toward him. "You have a long-distance call, Professor Saxon," she said with a smile that she probably also used in swimsuit competitions. "You can use the second office on the right if you'd like more privacy."

"That's very kind of you, Darlene," he said, hoping he remembered her name correctly. "I don't have any secrets, but perhaps I'd be less of a nuisance if I took it in that office."

"Oh, you're nev-ver a nuisance, Professor Saxon," she said, awarding him The Smile again as he turned and retreated down the hall.

He seated himself at the polished walnut desk and pushed the flashing button on the telephone. "Hello! This is Allan Saxon," he said.

"Allan, I'm glad Susan was able to track you down," said a voice which he was able to identify as that of David Harrison, his postdoc at the university.

"Hello, David," he said. "What's up? What can I do for you?" What's so important that he'd call me here, he wondered.

"Well, I doubt if there's much you can do from there," said David, "but I wanted to give you the bad news without delay. There's been a major breakdown in our experiment. Some of the equipment was damaged and will have to be replaced."

The words were like a blow to the pit of Saxon's stomach. "Which equipment, David? What the hell happened?" His voice rose a bit in pitch. He stood, ready to take action.

"Well, the vacuum chamber, the superconducting solenoid, the sample holder, the cryopump heads, and the field coils are all unusable. There was some kind of implosion that took them out. We're going to have to replace them completely."

"My God! An implosion? Was anybody hurt? What about you and Vickie?" Saxon's mind spun, trying to grasp, to visualize what had happened. Were there injuries? Were there to be insurance claims, accident reports, paperwork, lawyers?

"We're just fine," came David's voice, "except that we're still a bit stunned. Losing all that work and hardware, I mean." That sounds a bit lame, Saxon thought.

"What exactly happened? Can anything be salvaged? What caused it?" Saxon recalled the optimism he'd expressed just yesterday to his NSF contract monitor and considered the obstacles, without new results to show, that he would face in obtaining more funding for the project.

"I'm afraid that the hardware near the chamber is a total loss. We aren't sure what happened. We were doing preliminary tests. I was just about to start the coil calibrations late last night when there was an implosion. We're still trying to reconstruct the sequence of events, so I can't tell you much yet. The only thing we're sure of is that we're going to have to start over, almost from scratch. Maybe half the hardware is still OK . . . the power supplies, regulators, and control circuits.The control computer is fine, too. But all that machine-shop work that you pulled strings to get done in a hurry will have to be done over, no question."

There was the odor here of a cock-and-bull story, Saxon thought. "David, I don't understand. What imploded? How could it destroy that big hunk of stainless steel? It sounds crazy!"

"It is crazy, Allan! That's what I'm trying to tell you. It's completely insane. We don't know what imploded. All we know is that all the hardware in the center of the rig is gone."

He was covering something up; Saxon was sure of it. Had he done something stupid that he was hiding? The bloody incompetent! "Gone! What do you mean, 'gone'! Vacuum chambers and cryopumps don't vanish into thin air! There must at least be some pieces you can analyze to figure out what happened."

"There are no pieces, Allan. Everything within about a meter of chamber center is gone. Vanished."

There was silence for a moment. Theft! He must have stolen the equipment. The bastard! An eruption followed. "Goddammit, Harrison, when I get back I'm going to kick your ass into orbit! This story of yours is the most ridiculous fabrication that it has ever been my misfortune to hear. You expect me to believe that fifty thousand dollars' worth of hardware just vanished into thin air! I'll find out where you're hiding it, or who you've sold it to! You'll go to jail! I'll have you blacklisted! You'll never be able to get a job even sweeping out a physics building. You're not going to rob my laboratory and get away with it!'' Saxon could feel the back of his scalp tingling, the usual sign that his blood pressure had risen too high.

"Allan, please calm down," said David in a soothing voice. "Nobody is trying to rob you of anything. Nobody is trying to put anything over on you. We have a problem, and we need your help. We're doing some checks now, to try to get some more information. You can look things over when you get back and decide for yourself. I wanted to bring you up to date now, so you can be thinking about it. We don't understand what happened. I thought perhaps you might have some ideas."

"I have a very good idea what happened," said Allan, then paused, and cleared his throat. There was nothing to be done from here, he realized. Better not to burn any bridges. "But I will certainly examine all the evidence when I return, and I expect all the evidence to be there. Don't throw anything away or change anything. I'll come to my own conclusions and determine what course of action to take." He paused a moment. What would others in the department think? Better to keep the lid on. "And be careful to whom you talk. Don't mention this to anyone! I, at least, have a reputation to consider." He took a deep breath. "I'll be flying back tomorrow afternoon. I'll see you and Vickie in my office at seven tomorrow evening and hear your report. And it had better be damned good, Harrison. Goddamned good! Now goodbye!"

He slammed the receiver into the cradle and took several deep breaths. He shouldn't lose control like that, he thought. It gave jackasses like Harrison the opportunity to assume the voice of calmness and rationality, leaving him on the defensive. He must try to stay calm. He'd need perfect control for his meeting with Martin Pierce. That young asshole! he raged silently to himself.

He got up from the desk, breathed deeply again, and

walked back down the hall to the reception area. Darlene was talking quietly into the microphone of a small comm set when he returned. He inhaled the scent of her perfume, full of musk and implications. She looked up to give him The Smile again as he sat down. "I was just talking to Mr. Pierce. He's real-ly sorry to keep you waiting so long, and he says that he'll only be a few minutes more. Can I get you some coffee, Professor Saxon?"

"Yes, coffee would be nice, Darlene," he said, thinking that what he actually needed was a stiff drink. But he quite admired the view as she walked down the hall to the coffee maker, and he began to wonder how much progress he could make in the next few minutes.

It was fully twenty minutes later when Martin Pierce, thirty-ish, tall with a charcoal gray three-piece business suit, silk tie, and neat British officer's mustache, finally emerged from the inner office and welcomed Allan warmly. Too warmly, considering the situation, Saxon thought as Pierce guided him into the large, well-appointed corner suite with its sweeping view of the San Francisco waterfront and Marin County beyond. "Please, be seated here, Allan." He waved to a designer chair of rosewood and black leather. "Excuse me for just a second. I'll have to rearrange some appointments so we will have enough time to work on our problem."

Saxon grimaced as he sat down in the low comfortable chair, then smiled. As Pierce walked away, Saxon considered that perhaps it wasn't so bad that the bastard had kept him waiting. Now he had some moral advantage, with Pierce a bit on the defensive. Ignoring the view, he silently marshaled his arguments.

Pierce strode to Darlene's desk in the outer office, glancing back to make sure that Saxon was out of earshot. "That call of his probably was important," he said in a low voice. "At least it's worth following up. Thanks for setting him up, listening in, and then bringing the recording to my attention. You deserve another efficiency bonus. Now here's what I want you to do while I have him in the office. First, type a transcript of the call into a computer file. Combine that transcript with our dossier file on Saxon, then make a

copy with all references to Megalith removed so that it might
have come from anyone. Put the final version in my file
area on the computer system. Second, have Communications set me up with a secure net-path using at least five
untraceable nodes. I'll need to contact the spooks we deal
with in Seattle with no possibility of a traceback. Our in-
vestigators there can dig up some more information on Dr.
Saxon and his little friends and what they're on to.

"Finally, when the old lecher comes out of my office,
see if you can get him to invite you out this evening without
being too obvious about it. If you can manage it, get him
well lubricated and see what you can get him to tell about
what he's been doing. I want to know all about his so-called
business enterprises and also his work at the university,
particularly this new experiment that was discussed in the
phone call. You know the routine. And enter your report
into his dossier file tomorrow morning."

"Sure," said Darlene, winking at Pierce and giving him
The Smile. "The old fart thinks he's God's gift to women.
It oughta be easy."

Pierce leaned down, patted her bottom, and strode back
to his office. Seating himself behind his uncluttered oiled-
rosewood desk, he looked across at Saxon. Saxon was
dressed as usual, a bit more dapper than the garden-variety
academic with his neat blazer and coordinated slacks, Italian
loafers, and one of the oversize silk bow ties that he affected.
He needs a haircut, Pierce thought, noting the bushy hair,
and he looks a bit down in the mouth this morning.

"Well, Allan, we have a problem," Pierce began. "Let
me start with a review of the facts." He glanced down at a
note pad, the only item on his broad rosewood desk. "My
company has provided you with an interest-free loan of
$273,000 and moreover has leased to you at nominal cost
about $400,000 worth of electronics equipment of the high-
est quality. In return for our generosity we hold twenty
percent of the stock in your corporation and the option for
an exclusive license on the holospin wave memory technique that you have patented and that you and your colleagues had contracted to make into a commercially
marketable ultrahigh-density picosecond cycle storage de-

vice for us. That development effort has now collapsed. It appears that neither your stock nor your patents are worth a nickel.''

Saxon started to object, but Pierce raised a hand. He did not want Saxon interrupting his carefully prepared presentation. "When the development of this memory device began to go sour," he continued, "you agreed to do a bit of extra work for us, disassembling certain pieces of electronic equipment for analysis, determining their operating characteristics, and reassembling them so that they were exactly the same as before. I stress the word 'exactly.'

''Last month we delivered to your laboratory a new military command computer which one of our associates had been able to 'obtain' for us for a brief period of time. You and your former graduate students, your present business associates, were to disassemble the computer and determine the function of certain proprietary components used in the device. You were then to reassemble it so that it was in exactly its original condition. You supposedly carried out your task and returned it to us. But after our associate had returned it to the place from which it had been borrowed, someone discovered that it was not functional because one circuit board was missing from inside the device.''

Saxon looked uncomfortable.

''Our associate is now under suspicion,'' Pierce continued, ''and has been suspended from his former position. An investigation is being conducted. Things may get worse, but the present situation is bad enough: a valuable contact of ours been eliminated from further participation in our enterprises. He may go to prison and will almost certainly be of no further value to us.

''Your little business enterprise has failed us twice, first by failing to deliver the commercial device you had promised and now by bungling a simple operation which any marginally competent technician should have been able to accomplish. Standard business practice would dictate that we should call in our interest-free loan and our leased equipment at once. I would be interested in your thoughts as to why Megalith should wish to provide your company with any further favors or to continue our association.''

"Look, dammit," said Saxon, "when I reluctantly agreed to help a bit with some of your 'industrial product evaluation' work, I never agreed to do anything illegal. If you bribed someone to steal that unit, that's your problem, not mine. We did learn what you wanted to know about that tricky little computer unit and delivered our report. Moreover, that missing circuit board was found under a circuit diagram only about an hour after your courier had left, and I immediately tried every means I knew to contact you. But you didn't return my calls until the next day, when it was too late."

Pierce frowned. He must get this back on track, he thought. "The fact remains, Allan, that you and your colleagues screwed up," Pierce's voice rose in pitch and amplitude and his face lost its bland expression for a moment, then resumed its tranquility as he continued, "what was basically a simple and routine job. Your carelessness has damaged one of our more important projects, perhaps beyond repair. I have no interest in your recriminations and accusations. My company holds most of the cards in this game. And you should consider that your professional reputation will not be enhanced if it becomes known that you have been engaged in illegal industrial espionage on a secret military device. I would be interested in hearing your thoughts on how this problem can be resolved." He looked across at Saxon, who was agitated, struggling for control.

"OK," said Saxon, inhaling deeply and passing a hand through his graying hair, "as you've said, you hold the cards. Steve was the one who actually left the circuit board out when he reassembled the device. I've already disciplined him with measures that are as severe as is feasible. If I were to do more, he'd probably quit. He was always careful as a graduate student. I still don't understand how he could have done such a dumb thing.

"In any case, you know the financial situation of my company well enough to know that we're in no position to pay damages for our mistake. And considering the nature of the problem, I don't think our liability insurance would be of any help. But we can try to take this into account in future transactions. And I can absolutely guarantee you that there will be no further problems of this kind. I think that it's in Megalith's interest to continue the present arrangement. I'm afraid that's the best that I can do."

Pierce gave Saxon a penetrating glance. "And what about the holospin technology? Have there been any recent developments that might lead to possible applications?" he asked softly. *Let's see what the bastard will say*, he thought.

Saxon looked straight at Pierce. "Absolutely none, Martin. We're continuing to work on the holospin memory device, and we may eventually find a way around its fundamental problems. In my laboratory at the university we're continuing our basic research work. We have some new apparatus that's about to come on line, and we expect to be learning some interesting things in the next few months. I've just learned that our new project has had a setback, but when it works it should provide powerful new insights into the basic holospin wave phenomenon. If and when there is any new information at all, you'll be the first to hear, of course."

"Of course," said Pierce. *He's a smooth liar*, he thought. *He knows he's sitting on something important, and he doesn't even blink.* "I've talked this matter over with our president, Allan. I went to bat for you. And I believe that I have convinced him that a continued association with your firm would be of value to Megalith. However, there will be a price. We will require a one-half interest in the patent rights on your present and any future holospin wave devices, as well as a forty-nine-percent share in your company's stock. Neither is of any current market value, but things do change and we could eventually profit from one or both of these items."

Saxon shook his head and sighed. "You bastards are always after that last drop of blood, aren't you? But . . . OK, I'm not in any position to argue. I'll need an agreement of continued support under the new arrangement for a minimum of three years. If that is acceptable, then we have an agreement." He stood up and looked across the desk.

Pierce paused, looked at Saxon for a moment, and stroked his chin. Then he rose and shook the offered hand. "Our lawyers will be in contact with you next week, to work out the details.'' He walked around the big desk and accompanied Saxon to the door. Darlene shot them The Smile as they walked from the inner office. Pierce excused himself and walked quickly down the long hall, then glanced back over his shoulder. Darlene was smiling and standing to greet Saxon.

All that could be seen of Vickie when David entered the laboratory was a pair of worn sneakers projecting from under the control console. ''Your dinner awaits you, madame,'' he said, holding up the warm Kidd Valley bag containing a large hamburger and fries.

They had been working all day and most of the evening to construct the field mockup of the vanished equipment. Where yesterday there had been gleaming aluminum, crystalline glass, and satin-finish stainless steel, now there was wrinkled duct tape, rough wood, twisted wire, red C-clamps, and oddly positioned lab jacks. But the extra set of coils that David and Vickie had retrieved from Sam now occupied approximately the same position as their predecessors. The epoxy-coated outer coils were held in position by wooden braces, and the bare copper inner coils were clamped against the outer ones with Styrofoam spacers and twisted loops of wire. David surveyed their work. It certainly wasn't beautiful or elegant, but it was almost finished.

''Just a minute,'' came a muffled voice from under the console. ''Whose brilliant idea was it, anyway, to attach the main terminal strip to the most inaccessible part of the console? Mine, I guess.'' There was a pause and a grunt. ''There! It's done.'' Vickie crawled out from under the equipment console and brushed the more obvious dirt from her blue machinist's lab coat, several sizes too big for her. She moved some copper-red hair from the immediate vicinity of her nose and sat down at the table where David had placed the bag. ''Mmm! That collection of cholesterol, fatty meat byproducts, and toxic preservatives smells absolutely wonderful! Thanks. And where's my change?''

''Here you are,'' said David, handing her a few coins. ''So where are we?''

"Juff ah mi-ut!" said Vickie from behind a mouthful of hamburger.

David walked slowly around the equipment, checking connections. Several times he paused and used the small digital multimeter to verify the integrity of a contact or the quality of the electrical insulation. He used a steel tape to check several distances, and once gave the knob of a laboratory jack a few turns to improve a position. Finally he was satisfied with the alignment and returned to the table. Vickie was just putting the remnants of her hurried meal into the trash can. "Thanks, David. That sure beats the peanut butter and crackers I had for lunch," she said.

He smiled at her. She ought to eat better. "So what's left to do?" he asked.

"Up to you," said Victoria. "Depends on whether we're going to calibrate these coils properly or just assume they're close enough to the old ones for the purposes of this hare-brained test of yours."

"There's no way they could be exactly the same, with all that hardware missing," said David, gesturing in the direction of the equipment. "Let's just give it a try and see what happens this way. Chances are, it won't do much in this condition. But if it doesn't, we can calibrate the coils, find a way to simulate the impedance loads that the missing stuff contributed, and try again. We'll do it by successive approximations, one step at a time. So first of all let's give it the smoke test." He walked to the console and started switching on power supplies and control units. After that was done he turned and systematically examined the coils, then the power supplies, sniffing for the telltale odor of burning insulation or fried transistors, touching the critical load points, shunts, and heat sinks for signs of overheating. Satisfied, he went back to the console chair and sat down.

He moused open the control folder and looked over the dozen or so data files, each with its icon representing a page filled with tiny numbers. "Let's start with the small-volume field, the one you were using when I got back from dinner last night," he said. He carefully adjusted the oscillator to the frequency recorded as yesterday's "resonance" setting. He clicked the appropriate data file and moused the control program into the manual operation configuration. A simulated control panel of dial indicators and push buttons had appeared on the screen of the control computer, and he clicked on the button labeled (ACTIVATE) . There was a pause. Then from across the room came a soft *pop*, as from a light bulb breaking.

"What was that sound?" asked Vickie, standing up.

"Beats me," said David. "Go over by the coils and watch. I'll do it again." Again he clicked (ACTIVATE) and again there was a soft popping sound.

"David, it's coming from the center of the field!"

They tried the test several times more, always with the same result. Both of them were too caught up in their thoughts to say much. Finally Vickie said, "Stop for a minute; I want to try something." She went over to the workbench and picked up a piece of heavy, white-jacketed electrician's wire. She bent a hook on one end and draped this over an upper coil, so that the wire hung approximately through the center of the field. "Now! Try that," she said. "I want to see what happens when a solid object is in the field."

David nodded and activated the field sequence. Again there was the popping sound, and the lower portion of the wire fell to the floor, leaving the hooked wire, now much shorter, dangling from the upper coil. "Jesus!" said David.

Vickie retrieved the wire stubs and examined their ends. "Smooth and shiny, just like those pieces from the chamber," she said. She held them out to David, then returned to the workbench for two more pieces of heavy wire. These she balanced on the side coils so that they formed a white horizontal *X* across the central region of the field coils. "OK . . . again," she said.

David activated the sequence. The now-familiar *pop* echoed through the room, and an instant later four stubby wire ends fell to the floor. He laughed, with just an edge of hysteria in his voice. "Holy shit! Vickie, do you realize what we've discovered?"

"What?" said Vickie, looking over at him.

"What we've got here," he announced with a crooked grin, "what we've discovered," almost breaking up com-

pletely, "is a unique and com-plete-ly new and un-prece-
dented way . . ." he could hardly talk now for laughing,
". . . of cutting wire!"

On the large bed of his suite at the St. Francis, Allan
Saxon lay on his stomach. "Al-lan," Darlene said, as she
massaged his bare back, "how do you manage to be such
a fa-mous pro-fes-sor and still run an important business at
the same time?"

Saxon rolled over and looked up at her, savoring the view.
I wonder what she's up to, he thought. His finger traced the
crinkled aureole around her erect nipple. He was getting his
third wind, he decided. "It isn't too difficult," he said.
"The basic research work that we do at the university leads
to applications that feed into my business. And the techniques that we develop at my business lab are often useful
for our basic research at the university." At least, that was
how it was supposed to work, he thought. "Does Martin
ever say anything about our work?" he asked. Might as
well see what he could find out.

"Mr. Pierce never discusses things with me like this,
Allan. I love to watch you talk," she added. "Your eyebrows
are so expressive. What are you doing now at the university?
You seemed so excited when you came back from your
telephone call this morning."

Saxon explained to her in some detail about their holospin
wave experiments, and her gaze never left his face. She
was a remarkable girl, he decided. Talented in many ways,
and interested in physics, too.

7

FRIDAY MORNING, OCTOBER 8

Martin Pierce turned from Darlene's neatly typed report, which had been waiting on his desk when he arrived at his office this morning. She was good, he thought. In more ways than one. He lifted an oiled rosewood panel, unfolding the built-in computer terminal that opened from his desktop. He adjusted the angle of the high-resolution color display plate, switched on the terminal unit and logged in, then called up the special program that the Megalith Communications Group had prepared for him. It was time for another bit of spook work.

Industrial espionage was a primary tool of Martin Pierce's operation at Megalith. The company survived by spotting new technologies and sewing up patent rights and exclusive license agreements before their value became apparent to the bigger, slower-moving corporations competing for the same turf. But there were severe dangers to the corporation if one were caught with a hand in the cookie jar. Therefore, the intelligence operatives who were used to provide the essential inflow of information about developing technologies were never corporation employees; they were kept at a discreet distance from the corporation proper. Deniability is as essential in business as in politics.

Modern computer communications made possible almost complete isolation, protection, and damage limitation for both parties in the operation. The operatives in Seattle had no inkling of the identity of their employer, only that from time to time requests from one Broadsword for certain information or actions appeared in their computer systems. After the operation was completed, reports were posted in

Broadsword's private encrypted area on the same computer system's disk storage area. The deposit of funds of an appropriate sum in a numbered Swiss account always followed shortly thereafter. It was a sanitary and satisfying arrangement for all concerned.

Pierce entered his private encryption key and the program shifted to graphics mode, displaying a full-color map of the North American continent, adding each of the links leading from San Francisco to Seattle to the display as they were established. The route was remarkably indirect, crossing the continent four times. But that, after all, was the idea. Finally the last link in the chain was forged and the map disappeared, to be replaced by the message **User Name:**. Pierce typed BROADSWORD, and the computer responded with **Password:**. Pierce typed EXCALIBUR. The computer then responded with **Second Password:**, and Pierce typed ARTHUR.

**Welcome to the PSRS HyperVAX 98000 running under VMS 8.7.
This is the Puget Sound Reference Service.
Library reference services and literature searches are our specialties.**

came the response. This was followed by a **$** prompt. Pierce responded by typing RUN UPLOAD, then completed a set of responses which caused the newly prepared **SAXON.TXT** file on Pierce's system to be transferred to the **[BROADSWORD]** disk area of the Puget Sound Reference Service computer system. A pie chart appeared on Pierce's terminal screen, the ''slice'' corresponding to that fraction of the file which had been encrypted with an encryption key known to PSRS, transferred, and checked for accuracy. The slice grew larger and larger until it was the whole ''pie.'' Then the display disappeared, to be replaced by:

New file [BROADSWORD] SAXON.TXT successfully created.

Pierce then entered the message describing his needs:

$MAIL
MAIL > SEND/ENCRYPT
PASSWORD: EXCALIBUR
To: MANDRAKE
Subject: SAXON SURVEILLANCE
Text:
Establish soonest Class III surveillance on the residence and workplace of Professor Allan D. Saxon. Reference encrypted file [BROADSWORD] SAXON.TXT for details including authorization of related activities. Use encryption key DOG. Special attention to experiment in progress at Saxon's laboratory at University. Full operative reports and transcripts of all recordings to be posted in the [BROADSWORD] account within 12 hours of collection. Original recordings to be sent Federal Express to F&G Enterprises, 1436 Avenue of Americas, Suite 356, New York, NY 10047 within 24 hours of collection. Operation authorized for 14 days, renewable.

Pierce logged off the system and disconnected, folded the terminal back into his immaculate desk, and smiled. There was something deeply rewarding about a job well done.

The balding man of middle age sat down at his scratched metal desk beside the line of ill-matched file cabinets. A sign with the legend PRESIDENT, PUGET SOUND REFERENCE SERVICE, SEATTLE, WASHINGTON stood at a corner of the desk. The old VT-220 terminal on the littered desk of the president of PSRS made a "beep" sound as he logged into his computer system. The message **You have 1 new Mail message.** appeared on the terminal screen. He called up the **MAIL** utility and read the new message. It was from "Broadsword," one of his anonymous clients. He decrypted and read the file **[BROADSWORD] SAXON.TXT,** then retrieved a battered pad from his pocket and made a few notes from the screen. He was glad to have the business. Broadsword was a good customer who paid promptly, and the cash flow had been a bit sluggish lately.

This particular operation was going to require some backup operators, at least one a muscle type. He knew that his usual experienced help was presently tied up on another assignment, so it was going to be necessary to line up some new recruits. He picked up the phone and began to dial. Maybe he could get a lead from some of his former CIA contacts: the Company usually took care of its own, even after their people had dropped out for a more sedentary lifestyle.

Several phone calls later he made a connection. He settled for three operators he'd never used before who had only so-so recommendations. It was certainly getting difficult to find good help these days.

When Paul Ernst arrived at his office in Physics Hall at 10:03 A.M., David and Vickie were already standing at his door. They both looked rather bedraggled. He wondered what was behind David's call earlier this morning to request a meeting.

"I hope I didn't cause any problems, asking you to show up so early," said David with a note of broad sarcasm. "I know you theorists don't come to work before noon."

Paul shrugged. "Actually, I've been at work since seven by dial-up to San Diego," he said, letting them into his office and waving them to the chairs opposite his desk. "The Cray-4 at the UCSD Supercomputer Center is now crunching on a twelve-hour symbolic integro-differential equation reduction for me. By the time I finish dinner tonight it should have the answer for me. But you said you needed some theoretical advice. What's up, David?"

David took a deep breath. "Do you remember the other night when I was telling you about the problems we'd been having with our experiment? You said that you had a theory that could explain space acting as a vacuum pump and doing other weird tricks, if the conditions were right. Well, weird tricks we now have in great abundance," said David. "Our twistor field is making things disappear!"

Paul blinked. I'm not getting this, he thought. "Do you mean that it makes objects harder to see?" he asked. "Maybe it's some distortion in the glass—"

"Paul, there isn't any glass, or any stainless-steel vacuum chamber or cryopumps either. They've disappeared."

Paul recalled the massive equipment setup that David had shown him and the children a few days earlier. Disappeared, he thought, that's crazy.

"We've been having weird effects at certain frequencies with our spherical rotating field," David hurried on. "When I came back here after the dinner at your house night before last, I decided to do a test by increasing the field volume. I made it almost two meters in diameter, big enough so the boundary was outside the coils and chamber and pumps. And when I activated it, everything within the boundary just disappeared. The braces at the edges of the field volume were cut off clean, smoother than a good machinist could make them. And the cut surfaces are concave, with a curvature that matches the field radius."

"Whoa! Wait a minute," said Paul, trying to make some sense out of what David was saying. "First, what's this 'spherical rotating field' business? There can't be a spherical field! That would violate several of Maxwell's favorite equations."

"OK," said David, "imagine a globe of the Earth, but now the lines of longitude are lines of magnetic flux and the lines of latitude are lines of electric flux, with the magnetic lines looping back on themselves inside the globe at the poles. To a rough approximation, that's our spherical field. But the whole thing is spinning, like on an axis through the north and south poles of the globe. That couples the magnetic field to the electric field. But instead of oscillating and reversing the field directions, we've got it rigged so that the whole axis of rotation shifts by ninety degrees. Vickie and I designed some coils that set that up. We call it a 'twistor' field. There are some games that we can play with holospin waves in solids after we put a cryogenically cooled sample in this twistor field. But we haven't progressed that far because our equipment keeps disappearing."

Paul shifted uneasily in his chair, looking for a moment out the window and then turning back to David and Victoria. There was a long pause before he finally spoke. "OK, I think I understand more or less what you're doing with the fields. Now tell me precisely what you observed." This is a pretty good story, Paul thought, considering the possibility that David and Vickie were playing a joke on him. "And tell it slowly," he added.

David carefully described what had happened in the previous thirty-six hours. Paul rubbed his chin. He was beginning to get the drift of the story. They wanted him to believe that a considerable volume of matter had disappeared from their laboratory because it was in a particular electromagnetic field. David was his good friend, but this was ridiculous. Electromagnetic fields do not make things disappear.

"Of course," David continued, "we didn't believe that any such thing was possible. So yesterday we dug out some of our old reject coils and made a mockup of what had been there before. No vacuum hardware or cryogenics, but about the same twistor field. And, goddammit, Paul, the same thing happened! Vickie and I have been up all night making things disappear. We even made the wires inside a light bulb vanish without breaking the glass envelope." He held out a large clear industrial-size light bulb to Paul for inspection.

Paul looked into it and shook his head. Inside there was no filament, only two short wire stubs projecting from the glass holder. He looked appraisingly at David. A trick? Any competent glassblower could produce such "evidence."

David turned to Victoria. "Tell him, Vickie! He thinks I'm crazy."

"Not crazy," said Paul carefully, "but you have been working rather too hard lately." David has a strange sense of humor sometimes, he mused. Maybe he's punchy from overwork and is trying to play weird jokes on his friends.

Victoria's face reddened slightly and her green eyes flashed. "Sure we've been working hard, Professor Ernst!" she said. "But what David described is exactly what happened. I was there too for most of it, and we both saw the same things. It's a perfectly reproducible effect. Any material within the twistor field disappears at the time of the field rotation."

Vickie's a sensible person, Paul thought. How could she have become involved in this prank or whatever it is? What's going on?

"But we're wasting time, Professor Ernst. Look, you
don't have to take our word for it. We have a working model!
Come on down to the lab. We can make things disappear!
We can even make your skepticism disappear." She smiled.
"Provided, of course, you're willing to put it in the twistor
field."

Paul sighed. He could see no reasonable alternative to
going to the lab with his wacko friend and his confederate.
He might as well be a good sport and let them complete
whatever it was they were about. But it had better be
good. . . .

Twenty minutes later, Paul was convinced. He had put
sticks and wires and even a steel bar into the small region
in the center of the coils, and each time the central part of
the test object had vanished with a *pop*. David had even
allowed him to do the whole operation himself, while David
and Vickie had stood with backs turned and arms folded
against the far wall of the room. Paul had heard of sleight-
of-hand experts deceiving supposedly sophisticated scientists, but there was no possibility of deception here. He
simply had to believe that he was observing a real effect.
He felt a rising sense of excitement. A real effect!

"Did you tell Allan about this?" Paul asked. He was
wondering how far the news of this miracle might have
spread already.

"I talked to him yesterday," said David, "but I only told
him about the chamber disappearing. We hadn't reproduced
the effect with the spare coils yet."

Paul nodded. He was very pleased to be the first, aside
from David and Vickie, to know about what he had already
begun to think of as the "twistor effect." "After all of this,"
he said, gesturing at their apparatus, "I need a stiff drink.
How about some machine-shop coffee." He smiled at their
grimaces. "We can get our caffeine fix first, then go to my
office and discuss what this means."

David closed the lab, and they went downstairs to the
department's large machine shop. The machinists main-
tained a large coffee percolator there and, according to ru-
mor, also used the dark brown liquid for the loosening of

rusted bolts and nuts. They all filled their mugs from the percolator and then took the elevator to Paul's third-floor office.

"Thanks for giving me the first look at your wonderful discovery," said Paul. "It's very exciting to be on top of an unexpected experimental result like this. We must work to understand it better. Much better. Perhaps that's where I might come in . . ." He struggled to speak calmly despite the excitement he felt. It's incredible, he thought. I hardly know where to start, there are so many questions in need of answers. He paused and grinned at them. "You know, it's wonderful to have a theoretical problem with a working experiment to provide answers! I'd forgotten what it was like."

"Yeah, and it would be wonderful to have some way of explaining our weird results," said David. 'A more impor-. tant question for me just now, however, is when I'm going to get some sleep. Vickie and I stayed up all night making things disappear. We've been going for about twenty-eight hours straight. It has been very exciting, but now the adrenaline is wearing off." He shook himself. "What questions did you have in mind, Paul?"

Paul walked to the blackboard on the wall opposite the windows. "Let's make a list." He picked up a piece of chalk, becoming increasingly excited. "We'll start with these," he said, and rapidly wrote: (1) How much energy is used in producing the effect? (2) Does the amount of energy depend on whether or not an object is in the field? (3) When you change the field size, does the energy load change? (4) If you reverse the field rotation quickly enough, can you make the object come back? (5) If you put a radioactive source in the field, does the radiation vanish when the source disappears?

"I could think of a couple of hundred more questions," he said, "and so could you if you weren't so tired. But these will do for a start. Get me the answers to some of these, and maybe I'll be able to help you with a theory."

Victoria produced a small note pad from her purse and quickly copied the questions. David stared at the blackboard, rubbing his unshaven chin. He seemed to be having trouble keeping his eyes open and yawned.

"I think I'd be too excited to sleep," Paul said, rubbing his hands together. "This is going to be fun, by God. This is a whole new phenomenon, and we've got it all to ourselves to play with." He remembered then that he was leaving out Allan Saxon. "Whatever this turns out to be," he continued, "it's not an effect that anyone had even suspected before. It's a crack in the seamless structure of our understanding. It's enormously important, and we've got to treat it accordingly. Now go home, both of you, and get some sleep if you can. You've earned it."

"OK, Paul," said David. "At the moment I don't need much persuasion. But I can't sleep long. Vickie and I have to be back here this evening. Allan's returning, and he wants 'a full report' on what's happened to his equipment. I hope we can convince him as easily as we convinced you that we're neither lunatics nor thieves." David headed for the door, stifling another yawn, and Vickie followed.

Paul looked after them. That will be an interesting meeting, he thought.

Later that morning a balding middle-aged man in thick horn-rimmed glasses, a worn tweed coat, gray sweater, baggy slacks, and new Adidas running shoes appeared at the reception desk of the campus architect's office. "I'm Professor Johnson from the physics department," he explained to the secretary. "I'm stuck with being the chairman of the departmental space committee. I've got to find offices for three new faculty members. I need to look at the drawings for the Physics Building. Maybe there's a concealed broom closet or elevator shaft we've missed."

She looked up at him. She was very busy, and she wondered how she could get rid of him with a minimum of disruption.

"We've got to put them somewhere," he added, then regarded her with a lopsided grin.

She stood and led him to the microfilm cabinet, where she showed him how to use the index and the film reader. She left him making notes and sketches and went back to the large stack of correspondence that her boss had dumped on her this morning.

He left after another twenty minutes, complaining that he was going to be late for his class. She shook her head. Another basket-case faculty member, she decided.

Just before noon Sam Weston knocked at the door of David and Vickie's laboratory. When no one answered, he tried the door and found it unlocked. Entering the room, he immediately spotted the electric drill that Vickie had borrowed yesterday. As he bent to disconnect it from the electrical outlet, he jostled the equipment frame. Sam watched as a brown object about the size of a tennis ball that had been resting hidden in the hollow of a projecting bracket rolled out from under the apparatus, off the platform, and across the floor to bump to a stop against his shoe. He picked it up and examined it.

It was a perfect wooden sphere a couple of inches in diameter. Its surface was glassy smooth, with a beautiful reddish wood grain. Curiously, it smelled like new-cut wood, perhaps cedar, and it felt damp. Sam shook his head. How did Vickie and David have time to do artsy-craftsy stuff like this and still work so hard on their experiment? He put the sphere carefully down on the control console, picked up his drill, and let himself out.

The reddish wood gleamed in the bright sunlight that streamed through the window.

8

FRIDAY AFTERNOON, OCTOBER 8

In the early afternoon of the same day a man of about thirty with a mop of hair, pressed gray trousers, a neat blue blazer, necktie, and polished black shoes entered the Physics Building. He was carrying a black attaché case bearing the white, blue, and green logo of U.S. West Communications. He made his way directly to the basement and found an unnumbered door in a back wall. He produced a ring of keys, but there was some delay in opening the door. After about a minute, however, it swung open, revealing the telephone wiring for the Physics Building. He produced three small gray plastic cases embossed with the Western Electric logo and, using the adhesive backings of the units, carefully attached each in turn to the bare upper part of the inner panel. He studied them, making sure that they appeared to be part of the standard equipment. After consulting a computer printout he connected a few wires and closed and locked the door. That part was easy, he thought.

He made his way upstairs to the main hallway and walked along it, consulting his notebook, until he found the laboratory room he was seeking. He knocked, but there was no answer. He tried the door and found it unlocked. Entering, he looked around at the bewildering array of wiring and hardware. He crossed the room to a desk with a black telephone. He placed his case on the desktop and opened it. Ignoring the telephone, he removed a pair of small objects in clear plastic boxes. In one of them he inserted a tiny disk battery, snapped the back closed, peeled off an adhesive strip, and attached it to the undersurface of the desk. Then he crossed to the blackboard and, after the same procedure, attached the other to the underside of the chalk rail. He removed a small box with a meter from his case, pulled out a short antenna, and twisted a knob on the box while watching the dial. Satisfied, he put the box back in the case.

Retreating to a corner of the room, he aimed a small camera at the assembled equipment. He repeated this action from the other three corners of the room. Then, after a brief examination of the contents of the desk drawers, he closed his case and left. Consulting a computer printout, he headed for the office of Allan D. Saxon, Professor of Physics. It was then 3:47 P.M., Pacific Daylight Time.

Allan Saxon wheeled his BMW along Fifteenth Avenue Northeast, following the boundary of the main campus until he came to the entrance to the underground parking garage. He drove past the parking guard, who nodded to acknowledge his annual parking permit and C-1 sticker, and pulled into a parking slot in the southeast corner of the nearly deserted A-level parking area. His slim gold wristwatch told him that it was now 6:45 P.M.

He felt awful. He had awakened about noon in the St. Francis with a horrible, although deserved, hangover. He was regretting his haste in setting up this appointment. But no, he had to find out what this jackass Harrison had been up to before things went any further. Imploding hardware indeed!

He let himself into Physics Hall with his building key and went directly to the mail room. He sorted through the large pile of letters and manila envelopes in his box. The bad news was that there were two papers from the *Physical Review* and one proposal from the National Science Foundation, all in need of immediate review. The good news was a generous check from General Avionics for the consulting he'd done last month. He felt a little better as he walked down the hall to his office in the south wing.

At 7:03 by his wall clock there was a knock at his door. Saxon opened it to find Victoria Gordon standing outside, wearing her usual jeans and sweater and looking a little sleepy. As he invited her in, he spotted Harrison turning the corner at the far end of the corridor, stifling a yawn as he

approached. He waited at the door while Harrison entered
and slumped into one of the wooden chairs opposite Saxon's
desk. Victoria sat very erect in the other chair, her hands
folded in her lap. Saxon walked to his desk, sat down, and
glared at Harrison. "Now! What in Hell's name has been
going on around here?" he said.

"Well, Allan," Harrison began, "it's like this . . ."

As Harrison activated the twistor field, there was the
characteristic *pop* and the ends of the one-inch steel rein-
forcing bar dropped to the laboratory floor with a loud clank.
"Good lord!" said Allan Saxon. He had been persuaded
by Victoria and Harrison to come to the laboratory, and
Harrison had repeated the now-familiar procedure for him.
But to increase the dramatic effect, David had used a piece
of heavy steel re-bar that he had "borrowed" from a nearby
campus construction project. Victoria picked up the steel
ends and handed them to Saxon. He examined them, touched
the smooth surfaces, and gave a low whistle. It's true, he
thought, by God, it's true.

Victoria looked at Saxon and David hunched in front of
the control computer. The change in Saxon was hard for her
to believe. He looked and acted twenty years younger. His
eyes sparkled, and he talked faster, as if he were impatient
to get to the next word. When he's like this, she thought,
he's almost a likable person. She walked up to the other
side of the console and asked, "OK, gentlemen, are we
ready to try reversing the effect?"

David looked up at her. "Yes, let's go for it. I've twiddled
the control program's instruction list so that when it finishes
the usual sequence of twistor field operations it will pause
it for a few milliseconds and then do the same sequence in
reverse."

"Physical phenomena are usually reversible," Saxon
commented. "The twistor operation makes objects disappear, but do they reappear if we reverse the sequence?"

"Let's find out," she said. Saxon seemed to think the
reversal test was his idea. She could barely restrain herself
from telling him that Paul Ernst had suggested it first.

"Did you get some more of that heavy wire we were using?" asked David. "I've got the field set for a ten-centimeter-diameter sphere, so we'll need at least that much."

"Sure, I brought up several big rolls from the storeroom," said Vickie, walking to the cabinet. "But this time let's make it easy on ourselves and just hang the whole roll over the coils. We can pull down what we need for each test." She extracted a large white roll of electrician's wire from the cabinet and in a few minutes had securely suspended it above the coils, one end unrolled so that it hung down to pass through the central region of the coils. Saxon walked over to inspect the arrangement. He bent the wire so that it was hanging closer to vertical and stepped back.

"OK, let's try it," said Saxon. He had taken charge. David nodded and moused the computer into the activation cycle. There was the usual *pop*, but slightly muted this time, and two pieces of wire fell to the floor. One was the usual end piece. But the other was the wire section which had passed through the central region of the coils. It was cut smoothly at both ends.

"Holy shit!" said David. "We got it back!"

"Yes," said Saxon, "it would appear that the reversing trick works."

Vickie picked up the longer of the two pieces of wire. "I thought you said the field diameter was ten centimeters," she said. She held the wire against a piece of green paper lying on the console. "This piece is only eight-point-three centimeters long. I don't think we got all of the wire back."

"Better check the parameters, Harrison," said Saxon. "Maybe there was a mistake in the settings."

"Sure," said David. He moused up the editor program and opened the data file that had specified the operation. "Nope, the parameters are fine," he said, "but let's see what happens when we jiggle one of them." He changed a number in the file and closed it. "I had the time delay between the two twists set for about fifty milliseconds, plus a few for the twistor operation itself. I just reset the delay for one hundred milliseconds. How about some more wire, Vickie?''

"OK, but wait a minute." Using a plastic ruler and a black marking pen, she made a succession of equally spaced lines on the flat white plastic-surface of the wire, then numbered the lines with tiny numerals. "There," she said, "now we can tell where the missing wire came from." She pulled out enough wire from the roll so that a length of wire containing the new markings hung vertically through the center of the field coils. "Ready," she said, retreating a few feet.

The same muted *pop* echoed through the room, and the wire pieces again fell to the floor. Vickie quickly retrieved them and examined the marks. "Aha!" she said. She held the longer piece of wire against the stub still dangling from the roll. "The missing piece came from the bottom of the wire within the coils. The top edge matches the piece on the roll." She paused and compared the wire with her plastic ruler. "And now more than half of the ten cm is missing. There's only about four centimeters left." She noticed that Saxon seemed lost in thought.

David walked to the blackboard and drew an elongated L. "If we delay by fifty milliseconds we lose one-point-seven centimeters." He marked equal divisions on the vertical and horizontal axes and then drew a small cross above the horizontal axis. "If we delay by one hundred milliseconds, we lose six centimeters."

"It's five-point-seven centimeters, actually," said Vickie, consulting the ruler.

David nodded and drew another small cross on the blackboard, higher above the horizontal axis. "Now let's assume that if the time delay were zero, we wouldn't lose anything." He drew a third small cross at the elbow of the L, then drew a rising curve through the three points. "A parabola, maybe," he said.

"Maybe the wire is falling," said Saxon. "Let's see, if it falls five-point-seven centimeters in one hundred milliseconds, that's an acceleration of . . ." He punched numbers rapidly into the slim gold watch-calculator on his wrist.

". . . eleven-point-six meters per second squared. Not quite 'g,' but close."

"Wait a minute!" said David. "Those time delays we're using are the ones I'm giving to the computer program. But there's also the delay caused by the field changes themselves. That should be . . ." He consulted a notebook. ". . . about nine milliseconds."

Saxon poked at his wrist calculator again. "I'll be damned! That gives an acceleration of nine-point-eight meters per second squared! That's Earth-normal acceleration due to gravity. The wire is *falling* out of the field. How much we lose depends on how much had dropped below the bottom edge of the field sphere."

David nodded. "Wherever our wire's going, it's still in the Earth's gravity field."

Earth-normal gravity, thought Vickie. It's gone, yet it isn't.

Saxon suddenly yawned and looked at his watch. "God! It's almost midnight!" he said. "You young folks can stay up 'til all hours if you want. But I've had a very long day, and I've simply got to get to bed. I was worn out before I even arrived here." He smiled, then grimaced. "And dammit, I haven't even had dinner yet! Shall we continue our investigations here at, say, one P.M. tomorrow?"

David nodded in agreement.

Vickie looked at Saxon. It must be tough to be so weary that you to need to quit just when things are getting interesting, she thought.

"In any case," Saxon continued, "I believe that we've got our hands on a very important discovery. Truly important. But I must caution you to be careful. Don't say a word about this to anyone yet. And I mean anyone!" He turned and strode to the door, letting himself out into the hallway.

David followed Saxon outside. "Just a minute, Allan," he said, leaning against the lab door. "It may be a bit early to discuss, but I think that we'd better write up a report on what we've got for *Physical Review Letters*. This effect is going to create a whole new field of physics, and it should be published as soon as possible. I also think we should find some theoretical help very soon."

"I disagree," said Saxon firmly.

David recognized Allan's expression as the familiar one of stubbornness.

"We must do all of the definitive initial exploratory work before we publish or reveal anything to anyone," Saxon continued. "We've plenty of time. No one is likely to stumble upon this effect by accident." He gestured back at the lab. "This field configuration is too unorthodox."

David frowned and looked as if he were about to argue.

"Look, David," said Saxon, "I've a very good friend who once made an important experimental discovery. A week after he made it, he went to an American Physical Society meeting and happened to mention it to some 'friends' over dinner. Before he knew it, several groups were working on his effect and publishing more papers on it than he was. And after a few years a theorist received the Nobel prize for developing the theory describing the effect. But no prize was ever given for the prior experimental discovery because the experimental contributions had been distributed over too many groups. Le's just keep very very quiet about this, at least for the moment. OK?" He looked penetratingly at David.

David was feeling a bit stubborn himself. "OK," he said carefully, "for the moment we won't tell anyone who doesn't already know. But while we're working to learn more, I'm going to start preparing a draft of a *Physical Review Letters* paper describing the basic twistor effect. We can discuss its submission in a week or so. Allan, we simply can't sit on this thing forever; it's too damned important."

Saxon frowned, then nodded. "Very well," he said, "but be extremely careful with any copies of the draft paper."

"I will," said David. Saxon turned and strode down the hallway toward his office at the other end of the building.

David reentered the lab and smiled at Vickie. "He doesn't want to publish," he said to her, shaking his head. Absently he picked up a small polished sphere of reddish wood that lay on the control console. He gently hefted it, his thoughts far away.

In a van parked on Fifteenth Avenue Northeast across from the campus a balding man wearing headphones nodded as he switched the input signal from the first to the second digital disk audio recorder strapped to the side shelf. He removed the disk from the first machine and placed it in an envelope. On the outer envelope he wrote, *Voice, University Physics Lab, Friday, 10/08, 19:00-24:00*. Things are going very well, he thought.

Vickie lifted her bicycle up the worn gray steps onto the porch of the old house on Densmore Avenue North and put it in a place out of sight from the street, chaining it to the peeling white bannister. She quietly opened the weather-stained front door and entered, then closed it and tiptoed across the hardwood floor, avoiding the squeaky spot. She felt in the darkness for mail on the hall table, but there was none. Then without turning on the light she walked through the kitchen to the basement stairway.

She moved quietly. It was now after one A.M., and she didn't want to disturb any of her housemates. The old house was subdivided into bedrooms rented to miscellaneous students who shared the bathrooms, kitchen, and living-room areas. Vickie didn't know her housemates very well. Their majors were in uninteresting areas like business or communications or phys ed or civil engineering, and their personal habits tended toward the untidy, but they were quiet and didn't hassle her.

As she glided silently down the stairs she could see that a light was on in her basement bedroom. She looked inside. "William, what are you doing with my Macintosh?" she said to her red-haired younger brother, who was sitting before the screen of her vintage computer, his hand poised over the keyboard. "You're using my modem. You're hacking again, aren't you?"

William (The Flash) Gordon, sixteen-year-old convicted hacker, looked up from the screen a bit bleary eyed, the light reflecting from his thick gold-framed glasses. She noticed that his acne was getting worse.

"Hacking?" he said disdainfully. "Hardly! I'm just using your account on the Physics HyperVAX. A friend of mine who consults for Microsoft and Boeing wanted the new high-speed frequency-domain transform routine that somebody in Physics is supposed to be using. I just found a copy in Sam Weston's area. It's written in FORTRAN instead of a civilized computer language, and it's hardly structured at all, but it is the program my friend wanted. There's no accounting for taste-o."

Victoria felt slightly relieved. At least this wasn't likely to lead to another brush with the law. "How did you know my password? Anyway, I never said you could use my account."

"Aw, Sis," said Flash, "it's easy to see that you always type your first name when you log in. That's not very secure, you know. You really should choose a less obvious password."

"I certainly shall!" said Victoria. "Did you ask before you copied Sam's program? You can't just go around lifting people's software, you know."

"Well, he didn't protect his area, so I figured that he wouldn't mind. If you like, though, I can send him a MAIL message from you saying that you made a copy-o."

"I copied it! You mean *you* copied it," said Vickie, her eyes flashing.

"Well, sure, if you really want everybody to know that I've been using the Physics VAX," said Flash with a suspiciously bland expression. "I thought you wanted me to kinda keep a low profile."

She walked up behind him and peered more closely at the screen as she said, "Well, I guess Sam won't mind. I'll tell him on Monday. What's this letter you're reading? Saxon? Is that Professor Saxon?"

William looked a bit uncomfortable. "See, your thesis supervisor, Professor Saxon, had this subdirectory in his area that was triple protected. It was the most tightly locked-up subdirectory on the whole system. That made me curious to see what he had in there that was so secret, so I gave it the old peek-o."

"William!" shouted Vickie, then put a hand over her mouth as she realized that several of their housemates were sleeping in the bedrooms just above. "You promised me when I allowed you to come here from Santa Monica that you'd cut out all of this hacker stuff. And now I find you poking around in the private files of my thesis supervisor. This is simply awful!" Then she looked again over his shoulder at the screen and said more quietly, "What'd you find?"

"Well," began Flash, "most of his stuff uses some weird-o encryption system, so I can't read it just yet, but from the items in clear text he's running a business on the side."

"Sure, everybody knows that," said Vickie.

"There's a lot of junk about patents and licenses," said Flash, consulting a printout. "Sis, what's a 'holospin-wave memory device'?"

"I don't know," said Vickie, frowning. "My thesis project involves holospin waves, but I never heard of holospin-wave memory. That is odd, isn't it."

"Yeah," said Flash. "Anyhow, your professor must've screwed the pooch-o. There's a long letter in there to a guy named Pierce at the Megalith Corporation about how your prof's company couldn't make this whatchamacallit memory gizmo work after all. And there's another letter about some kinda goof-o that a guy named Steve made."

"That's probably Steve Kosinski," said Vickie. "He was Professor Saxon's grad student until a couple of years ago. He got his Ph.D. and took a job as vice president of Allan's company, I heard."

"Anyhow, it doesn't look like your prof's doing too well in the harsh world of business. He was asking them for more time on some loan. Lemme show you." Flash reached for the keyboard, but Vickie caught his hand.

"Time to quit now, Inspector," she said. "It's very late. Tomorrow I'm going to change my password, and you may *not* use my VAX account any more! Is that clear?"

"Sure, Sis. Nooo problem," said Flash, smiling to show that there were no hard feelings.

"It's now after one in the morning, and I need to get some sleep. Log off and get out of here," said Victoria, sitting down on the bed and removing her sneakers.

Flash nodded and quickly typed a few lines, switched off the modem, and then shut down the old Macintosh. He slipped a diskette into his shirt pocket and stood up. "G'night, Sis!" he said, closing the door.

Victoria could hear him moving around in his room next door as she undressed. She must write to Dad soon, she decided.

SATURDAY MORNING, OCTOBER 9

Paul Ernst was reclining on the long sofa in his living room, reading the *Seattle Times* and glancing occasionally out the east-facing window wall at the Saturday morning activity down on the lake near Magnuson Park. The Hobie-Cat enthusiasts were having a regatta. When the door chimes sounded, he looked at his watch, wondering who could be at the door at this time of the morning. It was just after ten. He put the paper on the coffee table and walked to the front door. Looking through the peephole, he could see that David stood on the doorstep. A bit early for a visit, he thought. He opened the front door wide and smiled.

"Hi, Paul," said David. "Hope I'm not intruding. I need to talk to you."

"Nonsense! You couldn't possibly intrude," said Paul. Then he turned in the direction of the kitchen, from which the sounds and smells of frying bacon were emanating. "Honey! It's David! Set another place for breakfast!"

The children immediately ran into the entryway. "Hi, David!" said Jeff, still in pajamas. Melissa, looking rather sleepy, took his coat and, stretching to reach the pole, hung it in the hall closet.

"Come on in and have a seat," said Paul, gesturing in the direction of the sofa and the view of Lake Washington backed by Mount Rainier. David sank into the sofa and the children immediately took up their stations on either side of him. He gave them each a hug.

"So how did it go with Allan Saxon?" asked Paul, noticing that David looked a bit subdued.

"That's what I need to talk to you about," said David.

"We did our magic disappearing-wire act for Allan last
evening, and we were able to convince him that we have a
real effect. He's very excited now, and he's dropped the
matter of the missing equipment, at least for the moment."

"David, can you do a magic act?" asked Melissa enthusiastically.

"I guess I can now, Melissa," said David with a rueful
smile. "I make things disappear. I'll be sure to invite you
to my next performance."

"I wanna come to th' p'formance too!" said Jeff.

David nodded. "Anyhow, Paul, Allan insists that we
should keep the whole thing a deep secret. Not a word to
anyone. He had some story about a friend of his who talked
too freely and missed a Nobel prize. I didn't mention that
we'd already told you about the twistor effect."

"Why not?" asked Paul. "I would have thought that the
best way of dealing with Allan's secretive nature would be
to tell him that people already know about your results."
Damn Saxon and his paranoid secrecy, he thought.

"Yeah, maybe so," replied David unhappily. "Trouble
is, Allan has a very short fuse, and Vickie and I had just
gotten him calmed down. Besides, when I called him in
San Francisco on Wednesday, he did tell me explicitly to
keep quiet about our problems with the experiment. Also I
didn't want to get you involved in some confrontation with
Allan. He's a powerful man in the department, and he'd
make a bad enemy. I thought we'd let things cool off for a
few days while I convince him that we need theoretical
help. I think I can get him to ask you for help, if I keep at
it. He just wants to make sure we don't get scooped by
another group."

Paul looked at David closely. He isn't very good at being
devious, he thought. "Well," he said, "I think it would
have been far better to avoid all this secrecy. But handle it
your way. I'll respect your wishes. At least for the moment."
And please don't screw it up any further, he thought.

"Look, Paul, I don't like secrecy any better than you
do," said David. "Remember, I worked at Los Alamos for
two years. I was in one of the 'window dressing' basic
research groups where essentially nothing was classified,

but I saw the effects of secrecy at first hand. When you're not sure if you can talk about something, you don't talk. And so you aren't able to share ideas, to be stimulated by the other guy's ideas or by the problems he has in understanding yours. And you sort of get into the habit of keeping quiet about what you're doing, even when it isn't classified. The result is that research goes very slowly, if at all, and often stagnates. Los Alamos made me a firm believer in open research, free discussion, and publication in the open literature. That's why I left LANL to come here. I have no interest in doing research that way."

"I completely agree with you on that," said Paul. Then he remembered the list of questions he'd written on the blackboard yesterday. "Were you and Vickie able to make any progress on our questions about the twistor effect? What about the energy dependence?"

"Boy, have we got some good stuff for you," said David, brightening. "We worked on it 'til late last night. Vickie put in some shunts with ADCs to monitor the current flow better, and I set the control computer to integrate the net power usage as a part of the transition procedure. It shows that for a particular transition frequency, the net energy required for a twistor transition goes as the cube of the diameter of the field sphere. So the energy per unit volume is holding constant."

Paul nodded. Just as it should be, he thought.

"But there are several frequencies that produce the popping noise," said David, "and each of them needs a different amount of energy for the same size of field sphere. There's something interesting going on here. I put a summary of all the frequencies, energies, and field sizes in a data file and mailed it to you on the Physics HyperVAX. See what you can make of it.

"And, Paul, do you remember yesterday when we found that one frequency that produced a kind of clunk noise?"

"Sure," Paul nodded, "but then we couldn't make it happen again."

"Right!" continued David. "That frequency shows a definite power drain. And we also found another frequency that draws power but doesn't make the pop sound."

"Curious," said Paul. "If the pop is caused by an implosion when the air disappears, what does the absence of the pop mean? That the air doesn't disappear?" His mind chased after a random thought that it couldn't quite grasp. . . .

"Paul! Children! Come to breakfast! You too, David!" called Elizabeth from the dining room.

"David," Melissa said sweetly. Elizabeth looked over at her daughter, wondering what she was up to. "Could you tell us more of the Ton story, since you're here, and we're here, and everything?"

David put down his coffee cup and looked at his watch. "I guess so," he said, "if it's OK with your parents . . ." He looked at Elizabeth and she nodded.

"Good!" said Jeff, and pulled his chair closer to the table.

"Well," David began, "you'll remember that Ton had just been lowered into a dark underground passage at the base of a mountain." The children shook their heads in agreement.

"At first Ton could see nothing. His eyes had not yet made the adjustment from the bright daylight above. But slowly, as his eyes adjusted to the gloom, he was able to see that he stood in a long passage walled with stone. Ahead, in the direction that Zorax had indicated, it did lead back into the heart of the mountain. But in the opposite direction it ended nearby in a jumble of cut stone blocks and dirt.

"Ton followed the tunnel until he came to a side passage on the right. Deep within the opening he was able to make out many large bags spilling silvery coins and bars on the rough stone floor. A vertical slab of stone, like the blade of a guillotine, was propped up with a single rotting wooden beam. Remembering what he had been told, he continued on along the main tunnel until he came to a passage on the left. It contained baskets and bags of golden objects, cups and bowls, arm rings and crowns, bars and coins. Ton noticed one coin near his foot. He touched it with his toe and noticed that it felt cool and substantial, not at all like an illusion. But again he remembered his instructions, and turned and continued along the passage."

Ton sounds rather like David actually, thought Elizabeth. He doesn't trust theories, he tries things for himself. And he's goal oriented, not too interested in money. A good story for children, a good role model character.

"After a while, Ton came to the third passage," David continued, "which was on the right. This one contained bags of jewels and bejeweled objects. Near the doorway was a beautiful little jeweled dagger. Ton, armorer-apprentice that he was, could see that the workmanship was exquisite. He thought of how delighted his father would be with such a gift and reached out for it. But remembering the magician's warning, he hurried on along the main tunnel.

"He walked for quite a while. Just as he was beginning to worry whether his candle would last, the passage ended at a massive barred door with strange runes carved upon it. The door must once have been a formidable obstacle, for it was made of thick oak and bound with heavy wrought iron, but many decades of dry rot and decay had done their work. Ton gave the door one stout push with his foot, and it collapsed backward.

"He walked beyond the door and looked around. Before him was a catafalque upon which rested a skeleton clothed in once-rich garments that had long ago moldered to rotten rags."

"What's a catafalque, David?" Melissa asked. Jeff looked annoyed at her interruption.

"It's a special stand for holding up the coffins and dead bodies of important people," David said, then took a sip of coffee.

"Oh," said Melissa.

"Behind the skeleton," David continued, "a broad curved shelf had been cut in the native stone where the passage ended. Ton walked around the catafalque to the shelf and examined its contents. There was a roll of woven material tied with a cord, a bag the size of a small melon, and a corroded swordlike weapon with a thin shaft ending in a sharp point. These must be the things that the magician had described. Ton carefully took the three items and turned to leave. As he was passing the catafalque again, he noticed that clasped in the bony fingers of the skeletal hand was a small book handsomely bound in a light-colored leather. Hesitating, with trembling fingers Ton took the book from the grasp of the corpse. Lifting it for closer examination, he caught the leathery odor of its binding and heard the sound of its crisp pages. Suddenly he had the vivid memory of his mother teaching him to read. Without considering what he was doing, he clutched the book and hurried with his burdens past the skeleton and back up the tunnel.''

I see, thought Elizabeth; he isn't tempted by money, but he can't resist the possibility of new knowledge.

"He slowed as he passed each side passage, and the glint of precious metal and jewels pulled at him. But he kept straight on the path. Finally, just as his candle was guttering out, he came to the point below the hole where he had entered this underground world. The area below the hole, which had previously seemed dim and gloomy, now was illuminated with sunlight so bright that it hurt his eyes.

" 'Zorax! I'm back, sir!' called Ton.

" 'Excellent!' crowed the magician. 'Did you find all of the mementos that I described?'

" 'I did, sir!' called Ton.''

Elizabeth could see the children squirm with relief at the successful completion of the dangerous task. Just wait, she thought, David's going to end with his usual cliffhanger.

"The magician lowered the rope. Tied to it was the basket which Ton had carried. 'Put all of the objects in the basket, and I will pull them up,' said the magician. 'And I will, of course, pull you up afterwards,' he added, his voice taking on a faintly sinister tone.

"Ton considered his situation. 'If you don't mind, sir,' said Ton, 'I would like to be pulled up at the same time. I'll tie the rope around my body and hold the basket with the objects in it.'

"The magician spluttered and became very angry. He said terrible things to Ton, threatening him with awful consequences. In strident tones he commanded that Ton place the three objects, which he now called 'treasures' and 'amulets,' into the basket at once.

" 'You mustn't think that I don't trust you, sir,' Ton told him with careful respect. 'It's only that my father taught me always to bargain carefully, even with one so great as yourself, and I could not go against my father's teachings. I hope that you understand, sir.'

"Zorax became more and more agitated and shouted fouler and fouler curses in a voice that became louder and louder, but Ton remained steadfast, for he was now very suspicious. As the magician's rage increased, he began to kick big rocks and large sticks into the hole. Then there was silence, then a loud explosion. The explosion was followed by a great shaking of the ground itself, and there came from behind Ton in the tunnel the sounds of cave-in and collapse. And following the explosion and its aftermath there came a wind and a great crash like a blow, and the little hole above him suddenly winked out, leaving Ton in utter and absolute darkness . . ."

David looked from one child to the other. "I think that will do for now," he said. "But we'll continue next Wednesday. OK?"

Jeff and Melissa seemed far away as they nodded.

Over a second cup of coffee, Paul asked, "What about the reversibility of the effect? Did you have a chance to try that?"

"Oops!" said David. "I almost forgot to tell you the most interesting part. Yes, we did try reversing the twistor operation. And it is reversible. We can twist and then un-twist, and when we do, we get the wire back. Or at least part of it."

"Only part of it?" said Paul, frowning.

"Yeah," David continued, "we only get part of the wire back. Part of it falls out of the transition region. So if there's a time delay between the twist and the un-twist, part of the wire drops below the field sphere and doesn't come back. Vickie proved that it's pulled downward, and Allan calculated that the acceleration is essentially nine-point-eight meters per second squared. Wherever the wire goes, it's still in the Earth's gravity field. Isn't that weird!"

"Weird?" said Paul. "No, it's exactly what should be

happening if my suspicions are correct. Look, David, since the mid-eighties theorists have been developing 'superstring' theories that explain all of the particles and forces in the universe in terms of 'superstrings.' Instead of masspoints, particles are described as tiny extended loops in a space that has the normal three space dimensions and one time dimension, plus six or more extra dimensions that are all curled up or 'compactified' into little loops. The development of this theory went very fast at first, and there was a lot of excitement. We thought maybe 'The Theory of Everything' was at hand. But in the last few years theoretical progress has bogged down because there's simply no contact with experiments, no tests to be done to show us where we part company with reality. It was beginning to look as if all the experimental work in this area was over and done with in the first femtosecond of the Big Bang.''

''Yes, I believe you've mentioned that before,'' David said.

Paul realized that he'd probably slipped into lecture mode. ''OK,'' he said, ''but here's the new part. I've found a superstring variant that looks very interesting, except that it has a sort of ungainly appendage. It predicts the existence of extra 'shadow matter' particles in addition to the normal ones, particles that share the same space-time and the same gravity with normal matter but are completely noninteracting in all other ways. The two kinds, shadow and normal, completely ignore each other except through gravity. There would be two distinct types of light also, with each kind of light interacting only with its own kind of matter.''

''Is that why you call it 'shadow matter,' '' asked David, ''because only its gravitational shadow could be detected? Invisible matter and even invisible light . . . sounds like H. G. Wells or something. And you think it has something to do with our recent results?''

''Maybe,'' said Paul. ''Since yesterday I've been playing with the idea that your twistor apparatus, in rotating the electromagnetic field as it does, somehow precesses all the particles in a certain volume of space, using one of the extra dimensions as a rotation axis, so that normal particles become shadow particles. If that were to happen, the Earth's gravity would still be there, so an object converted to shadow matter should still fall. It's as if the particles are still physically present, but they have been made invisible and noninteracting. Or maybe it's better to consider that the matter inside the sphere has been moved to a universe next door—call it a 'shadow universe'—where it still feels the pull of Earth's gravity but nothing else.''

"That's wonderful!'' said David. "It really fits with what we've been seeing.''

"Anything else in the way of new results?'' asked Paul.

"As a matter of fact, yes,'' said David. "I once read a Paul Davies book that made a big deal of the delicate balance of the physical constants in our universe that's required for the existence of living things. So Vickie and I decided to see if a living thing could survive a brief exposure to the other side of the twistor transition. Vickie has a friend who's a psychology graduate student, and she lent us a white rat. His name is Neil Tailstrong, the extradimensional astro-rat.''

Paul laughed. Melissa looked interested.

"We put Neil into a sealed jar and dropped him through the twistor transition,'' David continued. "The astro-rat office of mission control is happy to report that both Neil and the launch vehicle came through the transition with no apparent problems.''

"Do you still have him? Could we see him?'' asked Melissa.

"He's not at my lab anymore,'' David said. "Neil's returned to his normal place of residence in the psych department's rat lab, where he's being checked periodically to make sure he stays healthy. If he survived his trip to your shadow universe, it can't be immediately hostile to life.''

Paul smiled. "That's indirect evidence that the forces between shadow particles are the same as for normal particles,'' he said. "That's very nice to know, David.''

Elizabeth looked up from her reading to glance from one of them to the other but didn't say anything.

"The other news item,'' David continued, "is that I didn't have the equipment to try your test with the radioactive source, but I did make a small permanent magnet disappear. Since gravity still affects materials after the twist, I was wondering if we could use some kind of magnetic suspension to keep things from falling out of the field during a transition. But it didn't work. I had a Hall probe mounted just outside the field sphere, but near enough to register the magnet's field. As soon as the transition hit, the reading from the Hall probe dropped to zero and stayed there. Magnetic fields don't get through.''

"Great! It's wonderful to make predictions that work,'' said Paul with a feeling of rising excitement. "Now I'll make another prediction. I'll bet you can't make an electrically charged object completely disappear. When you try, most of it will go. But you'll leave behind enough electrons or positively charged ions to make what disappears electrically neutral.''

"Yes,'' said David, standing up excitedly and walking over to the window, "I think maybe I can test that. I could borrow some of the hardware from the Physics 122 lecture demonstration I did last week. The old Wimshurst machine might work nicely.''

"And watch the energy required,'' said Paul. "There may be a small extra energy loss in separating off the charges because of induced fields.''

David looked at his watch. "Guess I have to be moving along. Vickie and I are meeting Allan at the lab at twelve thirty, and I have to do my laundry first.'' He turned to Elizabeth, who sat reading a novel at the other end of the table. "Ever notice, Elizabeth, how the guys in works of literature never have to worry about doing their laundry?''

She looked up at him. "Probably the writers have better taste than to mention it,'' she said, and smiled.

He grinned back. "Thanks very much for the breakfast, Elizabeth,'' he said. "I feel like a new man.'' He tickled Jeff, got up, and headed for the door.

Elizabeth smiled after him, then turned back to her book.

Paul sat for a long time, thinking about what David had said. Then several ideas began to take form. He stood and walked toward the stairs. As he moved toward his basement computer link, the symbols of an algebraic manipulation task for the UCSD Cray-4 began to assemble themselves in his head.

* * *

Martin Pierce had been in his office in the Megalith Tower for most of Saturday morning, working on a report for the president. He looked up as a beeping sound came from the built-in computer terminal in his broad rosewood desk. Ah, he thought, that's to remind me to check on the progress of the agents in Seattle. He levered the flat display screen into position and logged on, then established a secure link to the PSRS system. The connection was established and the message **User Name:** appeared on the screen. Pierce provided the two passwords, and the usual PSRS header message followed:

**Welcome to the PSRS HyperVAX 98000
running under VMS 8.7.
This is the Puget Sound Reference Service.
Library reference services and literature
searches are our specialties.**

Pierce made a directory listing of his **[BROADSWORD]** area and found that there was a new file there called **S931008.TXT**. He downloaded the file to his own computer and logged off the PSRS system. Then he decrypted the new file with the prearranged ''DOG'' decryption key. The file was a transcript provided by Mandrake of the recordings collected yesterday over the time period from seven P.M. until midnight from the voice and telephone surveillance of Saxon's laboratory and office.

Pierce read the transcript twice carefully, made a few notes, then deleted the decrypted version of the file. It was corporate policy that sensitive material could be left on the system disk in encrypted form only, never as clear text. He was pleased that his plan was proceeding well. His instincts had been correct: some important discovery had recently been made in Saxon's University of Washington laboratory. That much, at least, was clear. And Saxon's little speech to the others about the importance of secrecy was particularly interesting. Secrecy from whom?

He reached for the telephone. He would call Saxon in

Seattle to make a friendly inquiry as to how things were working out with the laboratory "setbacks" Saxon had mentioned on Thursday. Saxon's reply would be very telling. Pierce smiled.

10

SATURDAY AFTERNOON, OCTOBER 9

Allan Saxon cursed fluently as he threaded his BMW through the football traffic on Montlake Boulevard. When he had suggested that they meet at the lab at twelve-thirty, he'd forgotten that the Huskies would be meeting their latest victim at the stadium at the same time. He was already running late, even without this traffic crush.

He'd been delayed by a curious telephone call from Martin Pierce, who had called from San Francisco to ask about the "reverses" he'd mentioned on Thursday in connection with the new experimental equipment. The nosy bastard. Saxon smiled as he thought how he had deceived Pierce by describing a mysterious implosion that had destroyed some of the equipment. He had given not even a hint of the twistor effect. If this hand is played right, he thought, I can cut all ties with Pierce and his sleazy crowd, secure all the application patent rights for the effect, and perhaps collect a Nobel prize as a bonus.

Finally Saxon reached the east gatehouse of the campus. He drove around the paying customers, pointing to the annual permit sticker on his windshield when the guard looked up. He followed the curving road around the campus past the Faculty Center and the Engineering Library to the turnoff for the rear of Physics Hall. When he reached the small parking area behind the building he was relieved to see that one lone spot had not yet been expropriated by the football crowd. It was marked with a wheelchair symbol and a DISABILITY PERMIT ONLY sign. But it wouldn't be checked on Saturday, he decided. He pulled in.

Entering the laboratory, he found David Harrison and

Victoria Gordon already there. Harrison was sitting at the computer console, and Victoria was energetically cranking the antique Wimshurst machine that Allan recognized from twenty years of E&M lecture demonstrations. A round brass doorknob was suspended from a transparent cord, perhaps monofilament fishing line, at the center of the apparatus, and a fine wire connected it to the whirling glass and metal contraption. A curved piece of aluminum sheet was clamped in position near the doorknob, and a piece of coaxial cable led from the aluminum and its stand to an oscilloscope nearby, which in turn was connected to the control console by a flat gray ribbon lead.

"Now!" said Harrison, and Victoria touched a C-shaped conductor across the electrodes of the machine, producing a fat blue spark and a loud *crack*. "OK," said Harrison, "I've got the calibration. Let's do the real thing." Already at it, thought Saxon, seating himself in the wooden chair as he tried to understand what they were doing.

Victoria cranked again, and the glass disks spun. Finally she said, "That ought to do it, David." He nodded and did something behind the console. The characteristic *pop* of the twistor transition echoed through the room and the doorknob disappeared. Victoria rose and ran to the console. Saxon followed her.

"Wow! It's true!" said Harrison, pointing to a pair of jagged curves on the monitor screen.

"What's true?" said Saxon. "What are you people up to?"

"We're investigating electric field effects," said Victoria enthusiastically. "The question is, if we put an electrically charged object through the twistor transition, what happens to the electric field outside the transition region? If the E-field just stopped at the boundary, that would violate Gauss's law, wouldn't it?"

Saxon nodded uncertainly, grappling to visualize the problem. "Sure," he said finally, "electric field lines have to stop and start on charges, so you can't simply chop them off."

"Right!" said Harrison. "So the question is, what does happen? I bought a doorknob and some fishing line on my way in and snarfed the Wimshurst machine from the lecture demonstration setup room. We charged the doorknob negative, and then twisted it. We compare that with discharging the doorknob with a spark.''

He gestured at the screen. "Our nifty new subnanosecond digital oscilloscope saved both traces and then dumped them to the computer, and here they are. The spark kills the field fast, on the lower curve. But when the doorknob disappears, the trace falls much more slowly. That's just what you'd expect if all the extra electrons were left behind, probably attached to air molecules on the surface of the field boundary. They'd have to travel through air at a slow diffusion rate to get to grounded conductors and kill the field. So the electric field stays around much longer. Only electrically neutral objects can make the transition. With a charged object, you leave the charges behind.''

"That's a very nice result, Harrison," said Saxon. "You two are doing very well. How can I help? I came in to provide some ideas, but you don't have any shortage of them at the moment." Saxon was feeling a bit unnecessary. He didn't know what to suggest next. Then, too, there was the stack of papers and proposals on his desk awaiting review. "Maybe I should leave you to finish what you're doing and check back later."

"Sure, Allan," said Harrison, taking the hint, "if you have other things you need to do . . .''

"Well, as a matter of fact, I have some reviewing to do, if you're sure you can spare me," said Saxon. He noticed Victoria frowning slightly. She walked over to the oscilloscope cart and watched the screen closely, then twisted a knob.

"No problem," said Harrison. "But Allan, if you've got a minute, there is something else we need to talk about. I've been thinking over our discussion last night about secrecy. I just can't do it that way. We need help in understanding what's going on here. This is too important to keep sitting on it. We've got to go public, and we must do it very soon. If we don't, we're cutting ourselves off from the ideas and stimulation of the department and the whole physics community."

Saxon frowned, dismayed at the direction of the conversation. To his left Victoria was still peering at the oscilloscope.

"Science can't progress that way," Harrison continued. "For your one example of a guy who was done out of his recognition there are lots of examples of people who published quickly with no bad consequences. And there are examples of people who sat on a discovery until someone else discovered it and walked away with the credit. I left Los Alamos to come here because I don't like secrecy in physics research. I don't tolerate it any better here than there."

Saxon felt himself growing upset and struggled to regain his composure. His doctor had warned him again about his blood pressure. He had felt this issue had already been settled, and he resented having to deal with it again. "Look, Harrison," he began with superficial calm, "there's more to this than just adding to your publication list or even becoming the next Nobel laureate. My instincts tell me that the twistor effect is going to have commercial applications that are unimaginable. Extremely valuable applications, David. To give you just one example, do you have any idea how many hundreds of millions of dollars are now being spent by the Department of Energy just to develop methods of disposing of nuclear waste? And here we're sitting on a device that can make anything—anything including nuclear waste—disappear!"

Harrison looked as if he wanted to object, but Saxon continued. "Harrison, when something like this goes into the open literature the patent rights virtually evaporate. It becomes part of the public domain." That's not quite accurate, Saxon thought, but I won't confuse him with details. "We must proceed very carefully. We must protect our own interests. The stakes are too high to get hung up on petty questions like whether secrecy is nice or isn't nice. This isn't philosophy, David, it's real life. This is the chance of a lifetime, and we must be careful to gain the maximum advantage from this opportunity."

Saxon suddenly noticed that Harrison's face and neck were developing a reddish tinge. I don't need to get into a shouting match with this jackass, he thought. Better keep him working while he's making good progress. "Wait!" he said. "Don't argue with me now, Harrison. Think it over. Think about what you could do with the wealth and opportunity that this discovery of ours can provide. You're young, and you have your whole career in front of you. I'll be in my office, if you need me. And we'll talk more about this later, after you've had a chance to think."

David looked bleakly at the closing door. How can you argue with a greedy asshole like Saxon, he wondered, and shook his head.

"David, say something," said Vickie from across the room.

"You mean about Saxon?" asked David, mystified.

"Say anything, talk, make noise," said Vickie. "Sing a song, maybe."

"Hmm, a song. How about this one? *My name is Moses; they call me Moe; Hello, hello, hel-lo, hel-lo!*" he sang in a loud carnival-barker singsong, walking over to the oscilloscope. "*I told the Pha-raoh; we had ta go; Hello, hello, hel-lo, hel-lo!*" He noticed that the high-frequency trace on the oscilloscope changed its structure in time to his syllables. "I should've brought my guitar," he said more softly. "What the hell is that?"

"It's the E-field pickup plate," said Vickie in a quiet voice. "It's acting as an antenna, picking up something. It has a high-frequency component that modulates in frequency in synchronism with your voice. Or mine!" she added. She walked over to the field coils and unclamped the pickup plate and its wire lead, then returned to the oscilloscope cart, holding the pickup at arm's length. "Testing!" she said. "It's still there, David. Sing more!"

While Victoria prowled the room, rolling the 'scope cart and waving the pickup, David continued: "*My name is Daniel; this is my den; Hello, hello, hel-lo, hel-lo!*" Vickie halted near the control console, then dropped to her knees. "*You pussy lovers; can step right in; Hello, hello, hel-lo, hel-lo!*"

"David, come here!" said Vickie. He crouched beside

her and she pointed to a thickish oval plastic plate, about the size of two thumbnails, attached to the undersurface of the desk. Looking closely, he noticed that it was printed with the logo of a well-known office furniture manufacturer. He watched the oscilloscope screen as he tapped the little nameplate. The rough sine wave on the screen snarled, then stabilized. Reaching into his pocket, he fished out his small red three-blade Swiss army knife. He opened the knife blade and pried the object loose, and it dropped into his hand. Vickie walked to the workbench and returned with a sheet of heavy aluminum foil. She carefully wrapped the object in the foil and looked at the oscilloscope screen. The green trace on the screen had gone flat. She carefully opened the foil wrapping for a moment. The trace jumped, then flattened again.

"David, I think this thing is a bug. Somebody is bugging our lab and has been listening to everything we've been saying! This damned thing was broadcasting our voices on some FM band!"

"I always wanted to be a media performer," said David. "Hope the folks out there in radio land like bawdy songs."

As he spoke, the trace on the oscilloscope screen began to climb, shifting with his voice. Victoria frowned and waved the pickup again. "Sing some more, David," she said quietly.

David took up the refrain again: "*My name is Jesus; the Son of God. Hello, hello, hel-lo, hel-lo!*" Vickie turned and moved toward the blackboard. "*I've come from hea-ven; to save your bod. Hello, hello, hel-lo, hel-lo!*" Kneeling, she examined the underside of the chalk tray, then beckoned David. He joined her and spotted a second oval plastic "label," this time bearing the logo of a manufacturer of educational equipment. He pried it loose and handed it to her to be encased in aluminum foil like its twin. The oscilloscope trace went flat again.

It remained flat for the next ten minutes while David and Vickie took turns singing, counting, reciting limericks, doing anything to make sounds that might be registered.

*   *   *

Allan Saxon sat at his desk staring, not seeing the sheaf of typewritten pages before him. He just wasn't in the mood to review the papers, he thought, not with the twistor effect on his mind. Reaching a decision, he picked up the telephone and called the unlisted home number of Dr. Steven Kosinski, the vice president and general manager of his company.

Steve answered and immediately complained about being taken away from the television set just when the Huskies were about to score. Saxon ignored his objections and began to lay out their new plan of action. Their company was going to start a major new development project, an important application of a new electromagnetic phenomenon called the twistor effect. Steve was to start making preparations first thing on Monday. Saxon would arrange to have the basic apparatus delivered late Wednesday afternoon. By that time Saxon wanted Steve to have a technical team assembled and ready to go to work on it on a three-shift, twenty-four-hour basis.

Suddenly, Saxon had a premonition of things going wrong. Steve had a morale problem from the circuit card incident, Saxon thought, and lately he'd just been going through the motions of company management. If he screwed up this project . . .

"Steve, this is going to be big, very big, for both of us," Saxon told him. "We'll have the inside track on an important new technology."

Steve grunted agreement.

"You and I are going to have to work our tails off in the next few weeks," Saxon continued. "But you're soon going to be wealthy, Steve. Very wealthy. Think you can handle that?"

Steve said he thought he could. Saxon detected more enthusiasm in the response.

As he was about to terminate the call, he had another thought. "By the way, Steve," he said, "if that son of a bitch Martin Pierce or anyone else from Megalith calls you, you don't know anything at all about any of this. Understood?"

"Understood," said Steve.

Saxon put down the telephone and sat for a long while, thinking.

Sam Weston looked up from the disemboweled computer on his workbench when David and Vickie entered the electronics shop. Vickie extended a pair of aluminum-wrapped packets. "Whatcha got there, Vickie?" he said. "I'm too old to sniff cocaine. I'm already too confused as it is."

"Nothing like that, Sam," said Vickie. "David and I think that we've been bugged!"

"So what? I've been bugged every day since I took this job," said Sam with a crooked grin. "Oh, you mean 'bugged,' like spy stuff! Hmmm. Lemme see those." He took one of the packets and unwrapped the foil. He examined the logo, then turned it over and peeled the double-face foam adhesive away from the back with a small knife. Underneath was a ring crack near the edge that encircled the back of the object. Sam inserted the tip of a jeweler's screwdriver at a point where the ring widened. He lowered the handle of the screwdriver and there was a sharp click. Carefully he lifted off the back plate, revealing a circular blue object centered on the oval, a microcircuit along one end and a silvery disk on the other. Taking a sharp-pointed pair of tweezers from the workbench, Sam removed the disk. "It's a watch battery," he said, putting it on the bench. He took the other packet and repeated the procedure. Then he turned to Vickie and David. "Yep, you were bugged. Where'd you find these?"

Vickie described the sequence of events in the laboratory.

"Clever!" said Sam. "Even if you happened to spot 'em, you'd figure they were put there by the manufacturer. And the sequence thing. They must have been set up so that the one on the desk did the broadcasting while the one on the blackboard remained dormant at low power until it stopped receiving a signal from the other one. Then it went into action itself. That way if one fails, the backup takes over. And if they both fail in rapid succession, it tips off whoever planted them that their scam is blown and that they'd better head for the bushes.

"Gee, Vickie honey, you sure bring me interesting toys.

Now I'm gonna have to dissect these babies to find out how they work." He patted one of the disemboweled listening devices. "With folks this clever, I'll bet there are some tricks I can learn from 'em."

Victoria and David carried their coffee cups to an isolated table in a corner of the basement eating area of the Husky Union Building. It was a large orange-carpeted room with white tables and fabric-covered hemispherical light fixtures suspended from the ceiling. This afternoon it was almost deserted. What customers there were had gone across the corridor, where a TV set was carrying the football game still in progress across campus.

As they seated themselves, Victoria looked around furtively. Maybe the HUB is bugged too, she thought. David leaned down to examine the underside of their table but reported finding only abandoned chewing gum on that surface.

Sitting upright, he looked across the table at her. "Allan must have done it, the bastard," he said.

"Why would he?" said Vickie, frowning. It didn't make any sense. "He doesn't need to bug his own lab. If he wanted a recording of what was being said, he'd simply set up a tape machine and tell us it was for documentation or something. No, I think it was my brother." William was quite capable of this kind of thing, she thought.

"The Flash? Why him?" asked David. "He wouldn't have the money to buy goodies like the ones we found. And look, I tried to get him interested in physics, but no luck. I even invited him to come over and help us after school. If he wanted to know what we were doing, he'd just come to the lab and hang around."

"Maybe you're right," said Vickie, feeling a bit relieved. "But who does that leave?"

"I don't know," said David. "The FBI, the CIA, the KGB, the Boy Scouts, the Radio Amateurs' League, the League of Women Voters..." He paused and licked his lips. "We don't know much about what Allan is into with his business ventures, do we? Maybe it has something to do with that."

"I happen to know something about Allan's enterprises," said Victoria, thinking what she could say without implicating William, "but I can't tell you how I found out. Allan's in deep debt to an outfit called the Megalith Corporation, and his business is tottering on the brink of bankruptcy."

"Oh," David said, and looked thoughtful. "Maybe I see why he's so interested in turning a profit on the twistor effect. Well, it's clear we need to tell Allan about the bugs. If he planted them he'll wonder why we didn't tell him, and if he didn't plant them then they're something he needs to know about. I'll let him decide if the cops should be brought in." David took a sip of coffee, then looked across at Vickie thoughtfully. She found his gaze vaguely disturbing.

"Tell you what," he said finally. "You and I have been working some long hours lately. I think it's time for a break. After we go back to the lab I'll have to tell Allan about the bugging, and you can return the borrowed hardware. Then we close down the lab for the rest of the day. You go home and get ready, and I'll take you out to dinner. I know a great seafood place at Shilshole over on the Sound. We can watch the sunset over the Olympics and talk more about this. OK?" He looked at her inquiringly.

Victoria regarded David quizzically for a moment before she replied. He'd never invited her out alone before. She found, on considering it, that she rather liked this development. "All right, David," she said at last.

"Great!" he said. "It'll be easier to get a table if we get there early. This time of year the sun sets at about six-thirty. I'll pick you up around a quarter to six, OK?"

She nodded.

Later, as they walked from the HUB into the autumn sunshine, Victoria felt more relaxed. But as they strolled back toward Physics Hall she found herself scanning the shrubbery furtively for lurking spies and hidden surveillance devices.

Allan Saxon looked up from the proposal that was spread out on the desk before him. "Come in," he called through the door. It was Harrison. He had a funny little meter in his hand. "Hello, Harrison," he said. "What's the latest discovery?"

"This," said Harrison, slapping a small object on the table top.

Saxon adjusted his reading glasses and peered at it. Then he picked it up and turned it over in his hand. It was a thin plastic oval with a manufacturer's label on one side and a recess on the other showing microelectronics within. "What the Hell is it?" he asked, replacing the device on the desk top and looking up.

Harrison didn't answer. He was kneeling on the floor and moving the meter, which Saxon now recognized as the field-strength meter from the electronics shop, as if it were a Geiger counter. Finally he put the meter down and took a small red-handled knife from his pocket. He pried something from the underside of Saxon's desk and attacked the back of the object with his knife point, popping off a thin plate and extracting a small battery. He put the object and battery on Saxon's desk. It was identical to the other one.

"What in Hell . . ." Saxon began, but Harrison signaled him to silence with a wave and a finger on the lips. He moved slowly around the room, stalking an invisible prey, and soon repeated his actions, this time removing a similar object from the undersurface of a low shelf of the built-in bookcase. He deposited the new object before Saxon on the desk with the others and walked once more around the room, watching the meter. Finally satisfied, he sank into the straight-backed chair. "Bugs," he said.

"What do you mean, 'bugs'?" Saxon asked, although the significance of the little objects was already becoming apparent to him.

"The lab and your office," said Harrison, "have been the recent objects of electronic surveillance. These things on your desk are bugs, clever state-of-the-art electronic listening devices that broadcast everything said in both rooms on high-frequency FM. By a lucky accident our new ultra-high-frequency oscilloscope picked up the signals, and Vickie found them. We thought perhaps there might be some in here too, and indeed there are. Allan, somebody is so interested in what we're doing that they've bugged the lab and your office. Do you have any idea what the Hell's going on?''

Saxon felt suddenly sick, as if he'd been punched in the stomach. He looked down at the devices. His mind whirled. Pierce would do this, that filthy son of a bitch, he thought. He turned to Harrison, looking him straight in the eyes. ''I know nothing of this, Harrison, nothing at all. You're sure they're bugs?''

''We could see on the 'scope that they were broadcasting our voices, and a few minutes ago Sam Weston cut one of them open and found a tiny microphone inside. We're as sure as we can be without catching the guy who planted them. I'd be careful about what you say on the telephone, too. Sam says telephone surveillance and voice surveillance usually go together. Allan, could this have anything to do with your business ventures?''

Saxon spread his hands. ''I would not have thought anything connected with my business was worth spying on. Our new work here is the only thing that makes any sense. But I haven't mentioned it to a soul.'' He looked sharply at Harrison. ''Have you?''

Harrison ignored the question. ''Look, Allan, this bugging incident demonstrates the futility of trying to keep our twistor discovery secret. These little things aren't cheap.'' He gestured at the bugs. ''Sam says they probably cost a thousand dollars each. Somebody with enough money to buy sophisticated, expensive equipment is out there on the other end of those bugs. They've heard everything we've said for the past few days, and they surely know what we've got. If there ever was a reason for keeping our work under wraps, that reason no longer exists. We've got to get our discovery out in the open, where it belongs.''

Saxon glared at Harrison, searching for a way to refute his argument. ''What are you driving at?'' he said finally.

''I've been writing papers,'' said Harrison. ''I'm almost finished with one describing the experiment and one about the equipment. I'd like to finish them off, with your help if possible, and send them off for publication as soon as we can. Once that is done, there won't be any point in bugging anyone.''

Later, when Allan Saxon calmed down, he remembered losing his temper at that point. He couldn't quite remember all that he had said to Harrison, but the gist of it was that they needed tighter, not looser, security. The only way to achieve it was to move the whole experiment to the company laboratories in Bellevue so that it could be better protected. Harrison had objected and he'd ordered him out of his office. You just can't get good, loyal, respectful postdocs any more, he thought.

On Fifteenth Avenue Northeast at the western edge of the main campus a nondescript commercial van was parked. The balding man eased into the driver's seat, started the engine, and drove unhurriedly away from the university in the direction of the I-5 freeway.

He shook his head as he drove, wondering what could have gone wrong. Something must have alerted the subjects in the physics laboratory to the fact that their room had been bugged. They must have found both of them, too. The devices had gone dead within five minutes of each other. About half an hour later he had heard someone come into the professor's office, and the units there had gone dead, too.

But dammit, these people were supposed to be amateurs! It required the latest and most sophisticated detection equipment to find bugs like these. It just didn't make sense.

Well, at least the telephone taps were still in operation. Those didn't broadcast. One simply dialed into them and "milked" them once a day. He'd need advice now from Broadsword on how to proceed. Broadsword was not going to be pleased.

11

SATURDAY EVENING, OCTOBER 9

David backed carefully out of his parking slot in front of his apartment on Fuhrman Avenue, drove west past the Red Robin, and turned north onto Eastlake. Half a block ahead, red lights began to flash on the University Bridge. Damn, David thought, somehow that bridge always decided to go up when he was in a hurry. But checking his watch, he saw that he had enough time.

The north end of Seattle is separated from the rest of the city by the Lake Washington Ship Canal, a man-made channel that cuts from Puget Sound on the west to Lake Washington on the east. The break is stitched back together by seven bridges. Two of these are high fixed spans, but the other five, the old University Bridge among them, are low to the water and must be opened whenever a sailboat toots its horn.

David drummed his fingers on the steering wheel, watching as the lights flashed, the red-and-white-striped barriers unfolded like Japanese paper cranes, and the steel lattice bridge spans levered upward, slackening the electric trolley wires they supported. He turned on the car stereo and pushed the selector button for KING-FM, a classical music station that he liked. The music soothed away his minor feelings of annoyance. He watched as the mast tip of a lone sailboat passed at a leisurely pace across his field of view. Then the bridge lowered and reassembled itself, the lights stopped flashing, and the barriers retracted. He was feeling pretty good after his shower, he decided, and he looked forward to the evening ahead. His feeling of paranoia after the bugging incident had passed. It was probably Allan's problem, he thought as he accelerated over the bridge to Eleventh Northeast, not his or Vickie's.

He turned west onto Northeast Forty-fifth Street and headed away from the university in the direction of the Wallingford district. After a while he began to look for a street sign indicating Densmore Avenue North. He found it just beyond Wallingford Avenue, but then had to circle around a playfield that interrupted the street before he reached Vickie's house.

From a previous visit he knew that the bell didn't work and that Vickie's housemates often didn't answer a knock at the front door, so he simply let himself in. Vickie's brother William, a textbook in his lap, was sitting on the faded orange living-room sofa facing the dim flatscreen wall TV, an MTV rock band gyrating in the background. He waved as David entered.

"Hi, Flash! Is Vickie ready?" David asked. He wondered if she'd had that kind of acne as a teenager. Probably not; her complexion was quite good.

"She said to tell you that she'd be a few minutes more. Have a seat, David."

"OK," said David, sitting gingerly on the sofa to avoid a protruding spring. "How are things at Roosevelt High? You get into that science fiction class you wanted?" David had discovered last month that he and Flash shared an interest in science fiction. It had been the single contact point from which he'd been able to reach Vickie's younger brother. He remembered that Flash had been trying to get into an honors English class called "Science Fiction and Universal Philosophy" or some such.

Flash nodded without enthusiasm. "Yeah, but it's a mite weird-o. First we had to read some New Age crap about Hinduism. Then Mr. Rebarth made us read *The Martian Chronicles*. I hated it even the first time I read it, which this wasn't. It's terminally artsy-fartsy dumb-o."

David nodded in sympathy. He'd never had much appreciation for Bradbury's free-form approach to scientific facts.

"After that we did a unit on Buddhism, and that was paired with *Starship Troopers*. That old Heinlein thing might be OK, if you'd never been shown the glaring holes in it by reading *The Forever War*.''

David blinked. He'd enjoyed *Starship Troopers* when he read it years ago. He coveted some of those early Heinleins for his collection of SF hardcovers, but after the author died in '88 the prices for his first editions had become astronomical.

''Now we're doing *Neuromancer*,'' Flash continued, ''which Mr. Rebarth says signaled a new direction in the late eighties toward hi-tech cyberpunk. Yuck-o! Punk-tech is more like it. Jeese, this Gibson individual must never have heard about bandwidth or transmission-speed limits. He thinks that once you plug the wires into your damp little head, you can download the whole universe in zero time-o. He oughta try downloading a coupla megabytes over a 4800-baud line sometime, if he's got a few spare hours. But Mr. Rebarth thinks cyberpunk is just wonderful because it makes you think about the disenchantment of the postmodern era, and it's so technologically realistic. Jeese-o!''

''I hope you're not letting him get away with anything,'' David inserted noncommittally.

''When it gets really deep-o, I mostly just hang quiet,'' said Flash. ''After class I just mosey up to Mr. Rebarth and get him to tell me what he wants me to tell him in the writing assignments. Then I just give it back to him verbate-o. He says he just loves my work because it contains so many good ideas, and it's so well thought out, so I get me a good grade-o. Teachers just love fresh new ideas, as long as they've seen 'em before. Isn't that the way it's always been in high school?'' He looked owlishly at David.

David paused for a moment, then nodded. ''I guess it has,'' he said finally. Well, that kills this topic, he thought. Wonder what we can talk about next.

At that moment, however, he was saved from further discursive struggles by the appearance of a transfigured Vickie. She was wearing a scoop-neck creation of white knit that looked both expensive and fashionable. She was very beautiful, he realized, and he felt suddenly disoriented, tongue-tied and awkward for the first time in recent memory. Then Vickie smiled her familiar smile and his perception

shifted, his self-possession returned. He told her how wonderful she looked. She whispered some admonishment to
Flash, and they walked together to David's car.

David glanced back at the house. Flash was standing on
the porch watching their departure, a bemused expression
on his face.

Ray's Boat House was on Shilshole Bay, just north of
the channel to the Chittenden Locks that isolated the fluc-
tuating tides and salt water of Puget Sound from the un-
varying level of fresh water in Salmon Bay, Lake Union,
and Lake Washington. The view from their table—of the
sound backed by the snow-dusted Olympic Range—was
breathtaking this evening as the sun lowered to meet the
jagged horizon. This evening the view was spiced by the
varied boat traffic traveling to and from the locks.

David liked Ray's. It was probably the best seafood restaurant in Seattle, though old-timers always claimed it had
possessed more character before it had burned to the water
and been rebuilt a few years earlier. He'd been lucky tonight;
with only two hours' notice he had been able to reserve his
favorite southwest corner table. David considered his sudden impulse to bring Vickie here. This was an upscale,
pricey restaurant. Was he trying to impress her? Was he
matching Vickie against Sarah, who didn't like the place?
Sarah preferred the Windjammer further down, with its view
of the yacht moorages.

He looked across the table at Victoria. He still couldn't
quite believe the transformation. She was ravishing in that
white dress. He took a deep breath. They had already ordered and were working on their salads, and the waiter now
brought the bottle of the Hugel Gewürztraminer that David
had selected. David sniffed and then sipped. "Good nose,
good balance," he pronounced. "This place had very good
whites," he said to Vickie, "and this Alsatian is one of
their best. It's light and flowery, and it tricks you into
thinking that it's going to be sweet until your taste buds
sort out its balance and finish."

"Couldn't prove it by me," said Vickie. She studied the
sunset through the pale amber liquid, sniffed, sipped it

gently, and nodded. "It does smell a bit like flowers, though. I got that part, even though I come from a family of beer drinkers. Hmmm, Chateau La Tour and now Gewürztraminer. How does one learn to be a wine snob, David? Looks like fun." Her compressed smile showed that she was teasing him.

"Just schtick with me, kid," he said, Bogartesque, and winked. His wine expertise wasn't impressing Vickie as it had Sarah, he thought. "My boss at Los Alamos," he went on, "was a devout enologist or, as you might put it, a first-class wine snob. He discovered that I have a very discriminating palate, and he helped me to educate it. If you want the unclothed truth, there isn't a whole lot else to do in Los Alamos. My taste buds are now well calibrated. You should see me in action at a blind tasting. My great-grandfather was supposedly a wine merchant and importer, so perhaps it's genetic.

"And it has proved to be a valuable skill since I came here. On Wednesdays I'm teaching the Ernsts about good wines, and they're keeping me well fed." Might be fun to introduce Vickie to wine snobdom too, he thought.

"Paul is nice," said Vickie, watching a passing boat. "I like him very much. We're fortunate that he's willing to work with us on understanding our experiment. And he's so enthusiastic."

"Yeah," said David, "Paul's been a good friend ever since I came to the department, but up to now it's been strictly outdoorsy or social things. I had no idea that I'd ever be working on something that connects with his brand of way-out particle theory. It had somehow never occurred to me that those guys were actually interested in experimental work. But it's clear that Paul is. You know, he thinks I goofed by not telling Allan that he knows about our results."

"He doesn't have to work with Allan," Vickie said. "We'd just gotten him calmed down when the subject of secrecy came up. He'd have blown up all over again. And that reminds me, David, what was his reaction to the bugging business?"

David sighed. He didn't want to spoil their evening together with the subject of Allan Saxon and his temper tantrums, but this was something she needed to know. He described to Vickie his encounter with Saxon that afternoon. "He said he's going to move our experiment to his company lab in Bellevue so that it'll be 'better protected.'" David stopped abruptly, trying to control his anger.

Vickie looked upset. "That's awful, David. Can he do that?"

"I told him that I wasn't going to help in doing anything of the kind. I said I was employed by the university, not by his company. I said I'd quit before I'd allow our experiment to be moved. It was about then that he ordered me out of his office. But I think maybe he'll come around when he's cooled down and has a chance to think about it." David considered that. He wished he were more certain that Allan could be convinced.

"David! Would you actually quit?" Vickie's voice sounded higher in pitch.

"Damn right I would," said David. "I hadn't told you or Allan yet, Vickie, but a few weeks ago I got a good job offer from Cal-Berkeley for a tenure-track assistant professor position, starting in September of next year. We're still negotiating over details like salary, start-up money, and teaching load. I haven't accepted yet, but it's one of the best departments in the country. I think I could easily arrange to go there earlier than September." David noticed that Vickie was growing visibly more upset. He paused, searching for what to say next.

"I'd feel like a louse, though, leaving when your thesis project is only half done," he hurried on, "and with you getting little or no help from Allan."

"I couldn't stand in the way of an opportunity like that, David," she said, frowning.

"But what Allan wants to do is simply unacceptable," he continued. "I'm seriously thinking of leaving this place. Look, Vickie, if it comes to that, why don't you come with me to Berkeley?"

"David?" said Vickie, wide eyed. "What are you suggesting?"

David stopped short, considering how that had sounded.

He himself was more than a little confused by what he had just said, by what he really wanted. "My intentions are honorable, ma'am," he mugged, trying to regain his balance. "Or mostly honorable," he added with a crooked grin. "I'll bet I can get you graduate status there so you can finish your thesis doing a proper investigation of the twistor effect. It's our discovery, and Allan's trying to run away with it. But Allan doesn't understand half of our tricks with the field coils. He couldn't reproduce the work without us, not if he had to start from scratch." The thought of going to Berkeley and leaving Vickie here suddenly wasn't acceptable.

She shook her head. "David, look, I've invested over three years in graduate school here. I've made good grades in the courses, I passed the qualifying exam on the first try, and in another year, or maybe two, I should have my Ph.D. I can't just pick up and leave. I'd have to start all over again." Her lower lip trembled.

"OK, I know it's complicated," said David. "But it's not impossible. On Monday I'll find out what is possible. Maybe it's not as hard to switch schools as you think. There are waivers and special permissions and things. But here's the worst part. I'm not sure that you can finish your thesis here if Allan hauls our equipment away. Just before he threw me out of his office, I asked him what would happen to your thesis project if he did decide to move the equipment. He said something about maybe finding you a new project. I'm afraid that he's not going to let valuable hardware be used for a mere thesis. Not if there's big money to be made with it. Look, there has to be a way—"

"Shit!" said Vickie, taking a gulp of her wine.

The formally clad waiter, arriving with their poached salmon with hollandaise sauce and wild rice, looked rather offended.

David felt better after the excellent meal. He sipped the last of his Gewürztraminer and looked speculatively at Vickie as he considered the shape of the evening. He'd turned on the old Harrison charm and she was more relaxed now, in the glow of the fading sunset silhouetting the Olympics. Perhaps a stroll on the beach, a nightcap at his apartment, and who knows . . . Their eyes met. "It's still warm enough for a walk on the beach down at Golden Gardens," he said. "Would you like that?"

She considered him for a moment over her wineglass. "David," she said at last, "I'd love that, but I have a problem. I mean, another problem besides Allan. My brother is up to something, and I have to watch him very closely. The judge in California told him to stay strictly away from computers. But last night I caught him using my account on the Physics HyperVAX, and doing . . . dangerous things. When we were leaving tonight, I had the distinct feeling that he wanted me out of the house because he's up to something again. I have to go home to check on him soon . . . I'm afraid I'm not very good company when I'm worrying about William."

David covered his disappointment. "Sure, Vickie," he said, cocking his head to one side. "It would be good for me to turn in early for a change anyhow. We've been working pretty hard lately. Another time when we're not so tired, OK?"

"Deal!" said Vickie with a faint smile. She turned to study the dying sunset.

David looked across at his passenger as they headed east from Shilshole on Northwest Market Street through the Ballard business district, wondering just what had gone wrong. He felt depressed. She'd been nice about it, but he'd definitely been rejected, he decided. Judged and found wanting. He supposed that he'd been "self-centered," as Sarah would have put it, in trying the romantic route with Vickie when she was concerned about her brother, her thesis, and her whole future. His mind churned in agitation as he drove under the Aurora bridge and into the Wallingford district. This would not do.

When they reached the old house on Densmore, he asked if he might come in for a while to talk. She looked at him for a long moment and then said, "Sure."

Vickie showed him into the long narrow living room. Two of her male housemates were seated on the orange sofa

near the front window gazing at the fading flatscreen TV
that hung on the wall. Vickie led David the length of the
room to an over-the-hill overstuffed chair, one of a pair
facing away from the window, well away from the TV.

"I'll be right back," she said. "I need to see what William is up to."

The housemates, an overweight fellow with a blond crew-
cut and a smaller man with wiry black hair and a ringing
voice, were watching a cablecast of a pro football game.
There were cheers as their favored team took possession of
the ball. A beer commercial followed.

In about five minutes Vickie returned. She sat down in
the empty chair, poking some of the herniated cotton back
in place. "He actually was writing a paper for his English
class. I'm relieved." She glanced at David. He was feeling
uncomfortable.

"I feel the need to clear the air a bit," he said, looking
across at her. "I have a sense of things heading in the wrong
direction. What I wanted to say is that I like you. A lot. I
want to see more of you. A lot more." He looked at her,
almost as if waiting for a blow. From across the room there
were moans from the TV watchers as a pass went incom-
plete. "Shit!" said the wiry-haired man.

She considered him. "OK," she said, "refreshing hon-
esty. I like that. You're a wonderful person, David. I like
you too. I feel a sort of 'gradient,' you know, a sense of
rising intensity.

"But we have a good working relationship right now. A
very good one. Unique and rare. We're getting things done,
and it's very exciting. Sometimes I can't quite believe it,
it's so exciting. It's why I went into physics in the first
place. I can't do anything that would endanger that."

"Go, man!" the big blond shouted from across the room,
as a back broke through the line for good yardage. Victoria
looked momentarily annoyed.

"What would happen to all of that," she continued, "if
we were to get involved and then it didn't work out? We
would have destroyed something very valuable."

David looked at her directly. "Yes, I know that argument," he said. "I've thought about that a lot over the past

week. What you just said is what I've told myself perhaps a hundred times. I guess I've decided that you're worth the risk.'' He grinned at her. ''I think that we can build on the rapport we've already established. I want to try. And if things should not happen to work out, though I can't visualize that, well, I'm not a vindictive person. I've never had problems being friends with former lovers . . .'' Before he completed the sentence he realized that he had said the wrong thing.

Vickie winced. ''I have,'' she said in a small voice, and was far away for a moment. Then she looked at him and smiled, but her eyes looked damp at the corners. ''OK,'' she said. ''I've never planned anything this rationally before, but why not? We do have a huge amount of data to collect, starting early tomorrow morning. So let's wait to go out again, until maybe the middle of next week when things ease off a bit. Perhaps our problems with Allan will be resolved by then, too . . .''

''And we can try to get to know each other,'' David finished.

''Yes, I'd like that,'' she said. Her smile must have had several kilowatts of power behind it.

''OK!'' said David, feeling that somehow he had risen through a dense cloud into the sunlight. From across the room there was a roar of appreciation as the favored team scored. ''Yeah! Touchdown!'' yelled the blond, and the smaller man stood and clapped.

Vickie walked David to the door.

Alone at his apartment later, he felt her lingering kiss on his lips for a very long time.

12

SUNDAY MORNING, OCTOBER 10

Vickie awoke feeling wonderful. She lay for a while in the bed, savoring the vague feeling of heightened well-being. David, she thought. Am I falling in love with David? Her skin tingled, as if the blood were rushing through her body at a greater speed then usual, vibrating as it went.

She rose, put on her robe, and padded down the hall to the bathroom. The long shower didn't wash the feeling away. If anything, it made it more intense. As she dried off with the rough towel, her skin seemed to sing. Thoughtful, she collected her toothbrush, toothpaste, hairbrush and a few other items in a small plastic zip-bag.

Back in her room, she slipped the zip-bag and a few articles of clothing into her backpack. Might as well be prepared, she thought.

David hadn't slept at all well. He had gone to bed early and awakened after about an hour, thinking of Vickie. The rest of the night he had alternated between restless dozing and thinking of the previous evening and how he might have managed it better. Finally toward morning he had drifted off, only to be awakened by the cruel rasp of the alarm.

Now he stared at his face in the mirror as he shaved. He looked awful, he thought. He was hung up. Hooked. And she didn't want to see him outside the lab until the middle of next week. That was infinitely far away. This was only Sunday.

But everybody has to eat, even Vickie. He checked the freezer. There was a stack of prepounded and -floured scallops of veal, each wrapped separately. They had cost him some considerable trouble to locate at the Pike Place market and to prepare properly. Scaloppine Marsala. And perhaps a light burgundy, the Beaujolais nouveau maybe. No, rather one of those excellent Spanish Rioja reds. The Marqués de Riscal's product was still well represented in his closet "cellar." There was frozen broccoli in the freezer and a jar of Romanian artichoke hearts in the pantry. Not bad.

"Be prepared," he'd learned in the Boy Scouts. Well, he was.

When Victoria arrived at the laboratory at 7:58 A.M., the first thing she did was to start checking the room. With the high-frequency scope at maximum sensitivity she'd been able to pick up a few FM stations and some SCR spikes from the electrical power lines, but no bugs. David, arriving with a thermos of coffee and a huge Danish pastry, had helped with the bug search. He'd suggested that it was his singing that had driven them away.

Over the coffee and Danish they had both been rather quiet. Vickie had been thinking of the previous evening and was feeling awkward with David. She had sensed that he was also off balance, and she had been careful to keep things on a professional level. David had followed her lead, and soon they had slipped into the familiar work routine.

David had decided that the radioactivity checks were next. He'd driven to the nuclear physics laboratory on the other side of the campus. There he had borrowed a disreputable-looking scintillation counter rig for gamma ray detection and used their radon source-maker to "cook" an aluminum foil test source, transferring a few microcuries of radioactive thorium 226 to a hot spot in its center. Vickie had gone to the undergraduate modern physics laboratory on the fourth floor of Physics Hall and borrowed a thin-window ion chamber.

Now they were set up to detect both gamma rays and charged particles. They could test for the persistence of radiation after a twistor transition. The shiny source was hanging from a thread in the center of the twistor apparatus and the counters were clamped in place just outside the field sphere.

David moved the mouse to the (ACTIVATE) ACTIVATE region of the control computer screen and clicked. He had activated the synthesized voice from the control program, and now it began to count down. *"Five! . . . Four! . . . Three! . . . Two! . . . One! . . . Activating!"* it said. There was a *pop* sound. At a leisurely pace, the needle of the scintillation counter's rate-meter coasted downward to zero. On the computer screen a histogram display of counts recorded per unit of time showed a more abrupt transition to a flat-line trace.

Victoria studied the trace on the digital oscilloscope connected to the ion chamber. "The beta counts from the source stop at transition time," she observed. "Paul was right."

"I get the same from the gamma rays," said David. "I guess it's like Allan said. If nothing else, we've got a way to dispose of nuclear waste. Our hardware may become the flush toilet of the twenty-first century." He frowned. "But first we'll need to find out what's on the other end of the sewer pipe."

"Yes," said Vickie, "I wonder how it looks on the other side of the transition. I wish I could stick my head through without losing it. Hey, that's another use for this thing: a no-mess guillotine! No unsightly heads to dispose of after the event."

"Great," said David without enthusiasm. "Hmmm, maybe we could drop my thirty-five-millimeter camera through the transition and rig it to click while it's on the other side."

"I've a better idea," Victoria said. "Chuck Swenson, a grad student in astronomy, was showing me one of the new cameras they've been using at Kitt Peak and Mauna Loa. It uses a CCD, a charge-coupled device, to digitally record image sweeps that are programmed into the optics. The data is burned into a little high-density read-only memory cartridge. You can set the optical sweeps for extremely high resolutions and even record color-wavelength information if you don't mind using more ROM space. It's made for telescopes, but it also comes with its own lens if you want to use it that way. You can even do sound and movies, if you want to devote the ROM space to that." She typed a word into the computer terminal and pointed to the screen. "Yeah, he's logged into the Hyper-VAX right now. Let's go up and see if we can borrow it."

At nine on Sunday morning, Martin Pierce, still wearing Chinese silk pajamas, used the IBM PC/System 4 computer in his elegant bedroom to do a secured indirect link to the Puget Sound Reference Service computer. He found several files waiting for him in the [**BROADSWORD**] area. He downloaded the encrypted files, broke the link, and decrypted them with the PC. The first file was routine, a list of the library books and journals accessed by Saxon and his group at the university's library within the past two months. The second file was a message informing him that all four of the voice pickup bugs placed in the university physics building had been discovered, that the phone taps remained in place, and that PSRS intended to continue the surveillance operation with the remaining equipment and without replacing the bugs unless directed otherwise. The message concluded by requesting instructions on how to proceed further. Pierce frowned, then read the transcripts of the recordings. As he read, color rose in his cheeks.

A picture of the events in Saxon's university lab was emerging. The twistor effect, a whole new phenomenon . . . and it was made with essentially tabletop apparatus. The thing must be worth millions, even billions. This bastard Saxon was keeping it all to himself. That in itself was an indication of its value. Well, he wouldn't get away with it. Since Saxon wasn't allowing anything to be written down, the apparatus itself held the key. And now he was going to have it moved. . . .

Pierce made a new link with PSRS and typed rapid instructions, then disconnected. He smiled. There was the potential for a very nice gain from this project. And the added spice of properly fixing Saxon for his disloyalty made it even more appealing.

David studied the little CCD camera. It did not look much like a camera to him. "How does it work, Vickie?" he asked. "It doesn't have enough external controls to do all those things Chuck mentioned."

"See that little eight-pin DIN socket in the side?" she asked. "You plug that into a terminal port and download a program that tells the internal processor what to do. There's a C control program that goes with it for doing the setup."

David raised his hands in resignation. "OK, you do the programming; you know C better than I do. I'll rig an orientation device and get some cryostat insulation for a catcher, and we can start the drops. By the way, what's the replacement cost of this little thing, if we should happen to lose it?"

"You don't want to know, David," Vickie said. "A replacement would cost about ten kilobucks, and Chuck said he would also need a posterior transplant."

"He must be a very good friend, to lend you something so valuable," said David, feeling a pang of jealousy.

She looked at him speculatively and smiled. "Not that good," she said.

David worked on the structure of the orientation mechanism, the automatic shutter trip when the twistor field broke electrical continuity, and the soft nest which caught the camera after it fell through on the return transition. Vickie worked on programming for the CCD camera's internal processor. "How do you think I should set the exposure and field of view?" she asked.

David thought for a minute. "Let's make a conservative guess that there isn't going to be much light. If it were my Canon thirty-five millimeter, I'd set it up with fast film, a wide-angle lens set to focus at infinity with a wide-open aperture, and an exposure time of one two-hundredth or less. Can this electronic marvel do anything like that?"

"The CCD cranked up to maximum sensitivity is the equivalent of about ASA twenty-thousand-speed film, if you want to use it that way," Vickie said, causing David to raise his eyebrows. "That kind of speed can cover a lot of sins. Let me think . . . yes, I can configure it just the way you said. The wide-angle lens configuration will get about fifteen percent of a full four-pi solid angle. Is that wide enough?"

"Hmmm, that's an view angle of about forty-five degrees. Sure," said David, "that ought to be fine." He tried to imagine what the little camera was going to tell them. He felt a rising sense of anticipation and squirmed in his chair. He could hardly wait for the result.

"OK, all set then," said Vickie as she typed some final instructions to the HyperVAX, then walked over and disconnected the DIN plug from the camera.

They tried the drop-through procedure first with a plastic bag of bolts and nuts as a dummy load; it worked fine. Then they carefully oriented the camera on a clamped rod and Vickie activated the forward-reverse twistor transition. The small unit plopped satisfactorily into the catcher nest.

Vickie picked up the camera and inserted the DIN plug in the camera socket. The high-resolution image stored in the unit's high-density ROM streamed into the control computer. The computer proceeded the image, repainting it with an electron beam on the graphics display screen. It was black, with a scattering of white spots. They had photographed only darkness, punctuated by occasional dust specks on the optical system, David thought, disappointed. There was no spectacular first view of a shadow universe.

Long experience dealing with the problems and frustrations of experimental physics made him keep the feeling under tight control. He said cheerfully, "OK, let's displace the view angle by about half the field of view. That would be, say twenty degrees, OK?" Vickie nodded and set the unit up for another shot. David repositioned the camera in the suspension and rotated the orientation by twenty degrees clockwise. Vickie activated the transition. The camera dropped into the nest again.

The graphical display showing the second image resembled that of the first, a solid black field with a few dust specks. David nodded. "OK," he said, "can you do a vertical split-screen display with both pictures together on the screen? I'd like to see the right half of the first picture and the left half of the second picture side by side." Vickie worked her magic at the computer console and the twin speckled dark fields appeared. David inhaled abruptly. "Notice anything?" he asked as calmly as he could through the wash of rising excitement. He stood and walked around behind her.

"I see the same pattern on both images, but one pattern is displaced sideways from the other," said Vickie. "David, those can't be dust specks! They have to be outside the camera. They move across the field of view when you change the camera angle."

"I know," said David quietly. "I think they're ... stars." It's too much, he thought, conceptual overload. He sat down in the old wooden chair, put his elbows on the desk and his head in his hands. He sat that way for a long while, hardly moving.

David had oriented the camera so that it was pointing at a particularly dense cluster of "dust specks." Vickie had narrowed the camera's field of view, increased the sensitivity of the CCD, and reset the camera to use its internal diffraction grating as an optical spectrograph. Each "speck" had now become a little stripe punctuated with black dots, the wave-length spectrum of its light. Vickie, an astronomy monograph in her lap, was examining the shot taken in the last drop. "Those black dots have to be absorption lines, David. Look, this one is almost an exact match with the figure in this book. They *are* stars, David! We're sitting inside an enclosed building, and we're photographing stars in the middle of the afternoon!"

David had continued sorting it out in his head as he worked. "We have to find out if any of the stars in these pictures match normal stars in position and also in spectral lines. Paul thinks that when we make something disappear in the twistor field, it isn't actually gone. Instead, it's been converted to what he calls 'shadow matter,' matter that completely ignores normal matter and interacts only with other shadow matter. And it's the same with light: shadow photons only interact with shadow matter. Gravity's the only exception. It's a distortion of space that links all forms of mass-energy: normal, shadow, whatever. This stuff comes from some brand of superstring theory that Paul uses. I've been thinking about how these ideas might apply to what our CCD camera sees.

"Suppose there are large numbers of shadow atoms that among themselves behave exactly like normal atoms. And suppose that a normal-matter star forms. It would make a gravity well that would attract shadow matter also, if any was around. So some stars may be all normal matter, some all shadow matter, and some a mix of both kinds. You might get a half-and-half star made of both kinds of matter and shining with both normal and shadow photons. So there is some chance of a correspondence between the stars in the picture and those in the sky. What we don't know is how much correspondence, except that it isn't one hundred percent."

"How do you know even that, David, when we haven't tried to do any match-ups yet?"

"Because," said David, "for the first shot I pointed the camera so that if our sun were present, it'd be centered in the field of view. It isn't there, so that's at least one star that doesn't have a shadow equivalent in the picture." He was feeling pleased with himself.

She looked at him. "David," she said, her eyes widening, "this is . . . big, isn't it?"

"Yes," he said, the feeling of overload returning. "I've been struggling to comprehend just how big. It's like Galileo looking through his new-made telescope and seeing the moons of Jupiter, a miniature solar system right before his eyes. It's like Newton realizing that the same force that makes the apple fall also holds the moon in its orbit. It's like Einstein at the Swiss patent office coming to the realization that space and time are almost the same thing. Vickie, it's so big I can't get my mind around it. Saying it's going to revolutionize physics and technology doesn't seem sufficient, somehow. We should yell, or dance, or pop champagne corks or something." He felt exhilarated and a bit off balance.

She swallowed and looked at him for a while without saying anything. Then, "We have more checking before celebrations are in order," she said. "What if we're wrong? What if those points aren't stars but something else altogether? Or what if we're somehow just seeing the normal stars of our galaxy in a different way? We need to do a correlation, and I have an idea how to do it. The astronomers have the Yale bright-star catalog on their big disk, a data base that has the coordinates and spectral characteristics of the brightest stars, thousands of them. I can digitize our pictures and then use a fit routine to vary to vary the scale, direction, and orientation of our CCD pictures within reasonable limits and try to do a match-up.'' She paused. "David . . . are we really going to be famous?''

"Of course,'' he said, "our names will be household words. Harrison and Gordon,'' he said giddily. "We'll be like Lee and Yang, or Fitch and Cronin, or Penzias and Wilson, or Crick and Watson—''

"Or Gilbert and Sullivan,'' Vickie contributed.

"Rodgers and Hammerstein,'' he offered.

"Rosenkrantz and Guildenstern,'' she countered.

"Simon and Garfunkel,'' he parried.

"Ozzie and Harriet,'' she rebounded.

"Laurel and Hardy,'' he responded, beginning to break up.

"Or Bonnie and Clyde,'' she concluded, as they both collapsed in gales of laughter.

They had noticed that some of the specks in the CCD picture were fuzzy, and Vickie had set the camera for high resolution in a narrow field of view to photograph a fuzzy speck. Now she was at the color-graphics terminal examining a ROM-dump of the resulting CCD picture. The display showed a rounded central region with two spiral arms. It was clearly a galaxy.

That, David thought, is enough for one day. Too much too fast. He walked over to stand behind Vickie, who was manipulating the false-color palette of the graphics unit to get better contrast for the image. He put his hands on her shoulders and kneaded the taut muscles of her shoulders and neck.

"Mmmmm. That feels good,'' she said. "Too long at the terminal makes my neck hurt.'' He continued to massage her shoulders as she worked. What do you say to someone, he wondered, who's just discovered the first galaxy in another universe?

"Look, Vickie, this has probably been the most wonderful day of my life, and what we've accomplished today I can't even think about without feeling a little drunk or crazy," he said, "but now I think it's quitting time. My mind's getting numb, and I'm afraid I'm going to start making mistakes." And he did not want to make any mistakes in the present enterprise.

"I am getting hungry," she said.

He continued to massage the twin columns of muscle that paralleled her spine. "Well, then," he said gently, "how about some dinner? It's after nine."

She swiveled in the chair and looked up at him appraisingly. "What did you have in mind, David?" she asked. "The sun's already set over at Shilshole."

"Well," he said, "I could fix us some dinner at my place. I've got the makings in the freezer. And maybe you could look over those publication drafts I've been working on." He looked at her inquiringly, holding his breath.

She smiled.

David, sitting at the teakwood desk in his apartment, extracted the diskette from the drive of his little Macintosh III and placed it in the top drawer of the desk, then folded the Mac's flat screen down to cover the keyboard. He looked toward Victoria, her face framed by the mosaic of lights from the University district across the water. "The paper reads a lot better now," he said. "We still need a better way of explaining the field rotation trick, but otherwise it's essentially complete, figures and all."

The dinner had gone well. David had learned to cook a few "specialties" very well, and the scaloppine were among his best. He rose and fetched the gold-wired bottle of the light Rioja from the table and emptied the last into the glasses on the desk. Then he walked with her to the wide glass deck doors and turned, lifting his glass toward the night sky. "To other universes . . . and to us," he said, and drained his glass. She drained hers also and put it on the lamp table.

He gathered her into his arms, and they kissed. Her responsiveness surprised him. It was rather a change from the cool promise of last night's kiss. He held her at arm's length and studied her. "You seem to have come to a decision," he said.

"Yes," she answered. "I've decided that you're worth it too." She grinned mischievously.

He took her hand, and they walked toward the bedroom.

Later, Vickie was stretched out on her stomach, her chin propped in her hands as she studied him. "David . . ." she said.

He looked up at her through half-closed lids. "Yeah?"

"Do you remember that lecture demonstration you were doing last Wednesday?" she asked. "The one where you took apart the Leyden jar, touched all the metal parts together, put it back together, and then made a big spark?" She sniffed the love-sweat where his arm joined his broad chest.

"Yeah?" he answered.

"How does it work?" she asked, tickling the hair on his bare chest with her tongue.

He blinked, shifting mental gears. "It isn't obvious if you haven't worked it out," he said finally. "When you pull the inner conductor out of the glass insulating jar, the electrons have to decide whether to stay on the conductor or on the glass. They give up less energy by staying in the glass cavity, so that's what they do. All of that electrical energy stays in the cavity."

"That's nice," she said, moving toward him.

13

MONDAY MORNING, OCTOBER 11

At ten forty-five, his Monday Physics 122 class out of the way, Allan Saxon walked briskly down the hall to the laboratory. Already this morning he had been able to reach his NSF contract monitor in D.C. and to have a brief talk with Ralph Weinberger, the physics department chairman.

Victoria Gordon and David Harrison were already at work. They were looking at some black pictures hanging by magnets from the blackboard. "What up?" Saxon asked.

"We've been taking pictures of the other side of the twistor transition with a CCD camera!" said Victoria. She looks radiant this morning, he thought. Hard work and long hours must agree with her. But as she began to explain, Saxon felt a rising sense of irritation. Here they go again, he thought. More nonsense, more diversions. Weird astronomy instead of mainstream physics. Stars in the daytime photographed from inside a laboratory.

"I'm not sure I understand your conclusions," he said, examining several of the frames. "They're just white dots on a black background, as far as I can see. Why would you think they're stars? And some of them look elongated and fuzzy. Stars would be points, wouldn't they?"

"Right!" said Harrison. "Look, Allan, here's a times-ten blowup of this fuzzy one here. I just made it. It isn't a star; it's a galaxy! See the spiral arms?"

Saxon scratched his bushy hair. Are they trying to con me, he wondered? Maybe to make me look ridiculous? "Dust specks can have 'spiral arms' too, Harrison," he said, a note of sarcasm unmistakable in his voice. "Just what is it that makes you conclude they're stars instead of

dust or something? Can you identify any known constellations or recognize the positions of well-known stars?"
Saxon struggled to recall what little he knew of astronomy,
which he'd always considered a waste of time and money.

"No constellations or recognizable stars," said Victoria.
"I dumped all the ROM outputs, position, and wavelength
information to the Hyper-VAX and mapped all the image
positions onto a sphere. Here's a Mercator projection of the
brightest ones, about visual magnitude three or less. We've
taken some wavelength data too and generated B-V coef-
ficients. We've tried to match the position and wavelength
data from the stars of each transition we've studied with the
big star-catalog data base on Astronomy's big WORM optical disk. The best correlation gives about a fifteen-percent
overlap between the observed stars and the data base. That's
not very big, but it's far too large to be due to random
chance."

"Neither random nor the same? Sounds to me like a bug
in your programming, Victoria," Saxon muttered. It's just
garbage, he thought. Has to be.

"I'd like to ask one of the observational astronomers to
help with this," said Harrison. "Those guys have lots of
sophisticated techniques for locating and identifying stars."

"Absolutely not," Saxon frowned. "I've already told
you, Harrison, that we can't go around telling everyone
about this just yet." They're trying to use this nonsense as
an excuse for going against my wishes, he thought. The
disloyal bastards. I won't put up with this.

"Allan, I'm sorry, but you can't keep this quiet any
longer. Whoever was on the other end of that listening
device was recording everything we said in here for several
days. And you might as well know that I've told Paul Ernst,
and even demonstrated the effect for him. That happened
on Friday morning, before you'd returned. Guess I should
have told you earlier. Since then he's been working on the
theory of the twistor field for us. He's been making good
progress. But now we need the help of an astronomer, too."

"Damn you, Harrison! You specifically went against my
wishes on this." The fool, he thought. No sense of loyalty.
He can't be trusted. I have to get this equipment out of his

hands as soon as possible, before more information leaks out.

"This discovery is too big to keep secret," said Harrison. "Dammit, Allan, I think the CCD camera is photographing other universes!"

"What the bloody hell does that mean?" said Saxon. "It reminds me of one of those stupid joke-exam questions, 'Define Universe and give three examples.' "

"Look, Allan," said Harrison slowly, "consider special relativity. We're photographing unfamiliar stars and galaxies. Those objects can't be in another part of our universe. If they were, we'd be sending the camera from here to there faster than the speed of light. If you have a way of doing that, you can use it to do paradoxical things like sending messages backwards in time or determining the 'true' reference frame of space. Those things are violations of both relativity and causality."

Crap, thought Saxon. He was growing angry, and noticed that the back of his scalp felt prickly. Blood pressure, he thought, watch the blood pressure. He took a deep breath.

"The more reasonable alternative," Harrison went on, "is that these stars are in another universe . . . a universe parallel to ours, like two sheets of paper in a stack. That doesn't make any paradoxes. Theorists like Paul Ernst have been talking for years about 'shadow universes' as a possible consequence of their theories. My hunch is that the twistor effect has opened a door to these shadow universes."

Saxon snorted in disgust. In departmental faculty meetings he had frequently expressed his low opinion of these untestable fashion-driven fancies of certain particle theorists. It was unthinkable that now his own postdoc was spouting them.

"But first we have to be very sure of that," Harrison continued undaunted, "which is where the astronomers come in. My guess is that our effect will blow the doors off astronomy too. It will allow them to study the stars in several universes instead of just one. And since there apparently isn't any air on the other side of the twistor transition, it'll be like having the Space Telescope in your own laboratory, with no pollution or weather or atmosphere or interference from the sun or moon or the bulk of the Earth. Incidentally, did you notice that Vickie's star maps don't have our sun in them, or even very many bright stars? Our location in the other universes is out in the celestial boondocks.''

Saxon struggled to control his rage and to speak very slowly and precisely. ''I'm sorry that it has come to this, Harrison,'' he said. ''I must remind you that I'm the holder of the grants that purchased this equipment, and in my judgment it's not presently in a secure location. On Saturday I made preliminary arrangements to have it moved to my company laboratory in Bellevue where it will be safe. Just this morning I received permission from our NSF contract monitor and from Chairman Weinberger for the move. It is a fait accompli. This is Monday. On Wednesday at four P.M. the movers will arrive. You can do what you like with the equipment until then, follow any blind alleys you see fit, as long as you have the equipment all packed and ready for them when they arrive. But on Wednesday, it goes. Understand?''

''But the equipment belongs to the university,'' Harrison protested. ''It was given to you to use for basic research. You can't just appropriate it for your private business.''

''The NSF and the physics department think otherwise,'' said Saxon. ''Our government these days encourages the cross-fertilization of university research and commercial applications. My NSF contract, the same contract that pays your salary, has an explicit provision in it for this kind of cooperation. And both the NSF and the chairman have explicitly agreed to moving the equipment. Perhaps you are privy to some legal knowledge that is not known to them?''

Harrison sputtered, then shook his head.

''Now, unless you agree to have the equipment ready to move on Wednesday afternoon,'' Saxon continued, ''I will have to deny you further access to the equipment. Do you agree to have it ready?''

Harrison started to protest, but then nodded.

''And please just stop talking to people about it!'' Saxon stalked out of the room, slamming the door behind him. As he walked down the hall toward his office, he was thinking that he had made a serious mistake in not arranging the move for today. And he should not have told Harrison about the move just yet. He must get better control of his temper. Losing it was bad for his blood pressure.

Saxon had just returned to his office after a leisurely lunch with his colleagues at the Faculty Club when the telephone buzzed. Susan informed him that Dr. Pierce's office was on the line, calling long distance from San Francisco. "Hello, this is Allan Saxon," he said into the receiver.

"Please hold for Dr. Pierce, Professor Saxon," said a voice that he recognized as Darlene's. There was a click. "Allan, how are you?" said Martin Pierce.

"I'm fine, Martin, fine. What can I do for you?" replied Saxon, as warmly as he could manage.

"Well, I believe that we have some further business to transact. I would like you to come here on Wednesday, the thirteenth, to meet with our lawyers and to sign the paper confirming our oral agreement. And I have a new enterprise that I would like to discuss with you."

"I'm sorry, Martin, but I can't make it on Wednesday. I have a class to teach and some hardware problems to deal with then. How about Friday instead?" Things have changed since last Thursday, Saxon thought. I'm not signing any papers.

"Allan, I'm afraid that I must insist on Wednesday," said Pierce slowly in a steely voice. "There are some matters that can not wait."

Saxon's lunch felt suddenly heavy in his stomach. *He knows about the twistor effect*, he thought. *Those were his bugs. Well, let's try confrontation.* "Martin," he said, "we've had some strange occurrences here in Physics Hall recently. Over the weekend one of my graduate students discovered that her experimental laboratory had been bugged with two small listening devices. We later found two similar devices in my own office. They're sophisticated microelectronic devices and must be too expensive to plant without a good reason. You wouldn't happen to know anything about this, would you, Martin?"

Pierce's voice sounded sad. "I'm hurt, Allan, that you

would even ask me a question like that. I thought that we understood each other. I assure you that Megalith is a reputable firm. We do not stoop to actions of the kind you describe, which are not only unethical but also highly illegal. I suggest that you go immediately to the police. They may be able to find those responsible. But I must return to the subject of my call and insist again that you be here next Wednesday morning.''

Saxon thought of the problems that refusing Pierce would bring upon him. It would be easier to go there with his lawyer. The two of them should, if necessary, be able to generate enough confusion to stall any new contractual arrangements. He sighed. ''OK, Martin, I'll persuade one of my colleagues to teach my class on Wednesday. We'll catch an early plane. My lawyer and I will be in your office by ten-thirty. But you must understand that I can only be pushed so far. Our business relations are not improved by your tendency to order me around like your office boy.''

''I do apologize for having to insist on Wednesday, Allan,'' said Pierce. ''We are inconveniencing you terribly, and I'm very sorry to have to do that. But I think that when you hear about our new initiative, you'll find it was well worth the inconvenience.''

After some final discussion of details, Saxon replaced the handset in its cradle. He stared at the wall, thinking of the bugs and what they had picked up while they were in operation. I wonder how much that bastard knows, he thought.

David hung up the telephone and looked across at Vickie. ''I guess it isn't as easy as I thought,'' he said. The confrontation with Allan had made him very angry. He'd called the chairman at Cal-Berkeley immediately to discuss the possibility of his early arrival and to ask about a transfer for Vickie. ''He said I could show up at Berkeley early, if I wanted. No problem, particularly if I was willing to do some fill-in teaching to earn my keep.''

Victoria nodded.

''But having you transfer into their graduate program looks harder,'' David continued. ''The chairman there said it was asking for trouble at many levels. Apparently no university graduate program is willing to admit that their courses and qualifying examinations are equivalent to those of any other university's graduate program. We discussed several ways of doing the transfer, but none of them looks easy. It's doubtful that it could be worked without costing you at least a year or two in your progress toward a degree.''

"Then forget it," said Vickie grimly, shaking her head. "That would be almost like starting graduate school over. I'll just have to make the best of the situation here." Her lower lip protruded a bit; a sign, David guessed, that she was feeling stubborn and angry.

"I agree," David said carefully, "and I don't think that's so bad. The new data, along with the work we had already done, looks more and more like a thesis to me. I've an appointment with Chairman Weinberger at four this afternoon. I'll try to get his help in arguing Allan out of his crazy plans. The worst scenario, however, is that Allan moves the hardware on Wednesday afternoon anyway. That gives us two more days of data collection. I'd give us an excellent chance of accumulating enough data in that time to get you a thesis. And a pretty damn good thesis, at that."

There was a knock at the door, and David walked across to open it. Jim Lee of the astronomy department stood outside. He was a Chinese-American, about forty years old, and had a reputation as the sharpest observational astronomer in the department. David invited him in.

Jim looked from David to Vickie. "I'm not sure what this is about," he began. "You said on the phone that you have some astronomy data you want me to look at?"

David carefully explained the twistor effect and their recent work with it. Lee seemed skeptical. They demonstrated the apparatus. It was soon clear that he was convinced. David was impressed at how rapidly Lee seemed to grasp the new ideas that were being thrown at him. Finally, Vickie showed him the data on star positions and spectra that they had collected with the CCD camera.

It was interesting for David to watch the transformation in Jim Lee, the serious and circumspect professor becoming a child in a candy store as he examined the data files and his excitement grew. He left them after about an hour, laden with printouts and laser disks. As he walked out the door, the soles of Lee's feet seemed to David to be a few millimeters off the floor.

14

David Harrison walked down the long corridor on the third floor of Physics Hall. Along the south side were faculty offices with windows looking out on Mount Rainier. Near the far end of the corridor he came to Paul Ernst's office and knocked.

"Come in," called Paul. David opened the door. "David!" said Paul, motioning him to a chair. "And what have you brought me today in the way of new and mind-boggling results?"

"Just a few more morsels for our captive theorist!" said David cheerfully. "Yesterday I persuaded Jim Lee to look at the data on the stars recorded by the CCD camera. This morning he told me that there are several distinctive spectroscopic binaries that he's sure are like nothing in our neighborhood of the galaxy. The shadow-universe idea is still with us, Paul, and it has its own set of stars."

"Congratulations!" Paul said. "That's impressive progress."

"The other news is that I talked to Ralph Weinberger yesterday about Allan's plan to move our hardware," said David. "He was sympathetic, at least on the surface, but he showed me the part of Saxon's NSF grant stating that cooperation with industry is encouraged, including equipment loans. I don't think it's worth the effort to make a stink at this point. Once decisions like this are made, they become very hard to change. And Allan's too powerful in the department." I don't have the sense of timing or the knowledge or the clout to play an effective game of department political hardball, he thought.

Paul nodded.

"So," David continued, "it looks as if we've only got today and part of tomorrow to work. Vickie stayed up all night taking data, and I'm going on shift after I leave here. Allan has been fairly noncommittal about whether we can continue the work in Bellevue. My guess is that if he and his partners can make the hardware work, Vickie and I will be locked out 'for security reasons.' If not, maybe they'll let us in."

"Surely he wouldn't do that," said Paul. "You two discovered the effect."

"I'm sure he would," said David. "I'm frustrated, Paul. We're making so much progress, and now he's going to pull the plug.

"I haven't had the time to work out many details, but I'm pretty sure that if I have to start over from scratch, even assuming that funds are no problem, it will require months of work just to get back to where we are right now. And my first order of business will have to be moving to a new place where I can do the work. I have that assistant-prof offer from Berkeley that I told you about. I checked. They're willing to have me come early, but there isn't time to arrange for much support."

Paul shook his head. "Allan's being such a bastard about this. At least now that he knows I'm involved, maybe I can talk to him about it. He isn't being reasonable."

"I think there's more to it than just personalities," said David. "Apparently Allan's business is having money troubles. Maybe he sees this as a way of saving the farm."

Paul raised his eyebrows. "Well," he said, "in any case, you're doing the right thing. Collect as much data as you can and don't worry about analyzing it too thoroughly until there's time later. This is pretty rough on you and Vickie, but there's a lot that I can do theoretically if we develop a good data base."

"Yeah, data we have. We're accumulating laser disks full; that's gigabytes of information. Vickie's been stashing backup copies at home, in case Allan should decide to move our data to Bellevue too.''

Paul smiled wryly and shook his head.

''Oh, one other thing,'' David said. ''Vickie discovered something last night that may be of some significance. I told you that we see different star patterns at different twistor transition frequencies. The star patterns from two of the frequencies are perfect mirror images of each other. Any idea what that means?''

Paul paused for a moment. ''Jesus, yes! That's a parity transformation,'' he said, standing up and pacing back and forth. David noticed that his previously serious and somewhat dour expression had changed to one of excitement. ''That's a very important observation, David,'' Paul continued animatedly. ''For the last couple of days I've been using those frequencies that you gave me to try to construct a model describing the twistor effect. Things are coming together. Orthodox superstring theory, starting from the work of Schwartz and Green back in the early eighties, indicated that the universe might have a symmetry called $E_6 \times E_8$, which predicted new particles of shadow matter that only interact gravitationally with normal matter. We've talked about it before.

''There is an unexplained gravity effect, the 'dark matter problem.' Observational evidence says there's more matter in the universe than we can account for,'' Paul concluded.

''Yes, I read a lot about the dark matter speculations when I was in graduate school,'' said David. ''It was quite interesting, but it also looked unapproachable experimentally. Paul, could our results actually be related to dark matter?'' David felt himself catching Paul's excitement. The dark matter problem was important, an unsolved problem of astrophysics and cosmology that had been a nagging worry for a decade or more.

''Perhaps,'' said Paul. ''I've been playing with the idea that your twistor field is converting normal particles into their 'shadow matter' equivalents. I almost gave up right at the start because it didn't work at first. Then I hit on a variant of the orthodox superstring theory in which the normal/shadow matter distinction is treated as a vector—

a spin vector of a certain spin pointing in some hyper-dimensional direction. I call it 'shadow spin.' When I got to vectors of shadow-spin three, it was like finding the Rosetta Stone. Everything clicked into place. Your measured frequencies form a set of energy levels that map perfectly into the shadow-spin three energy states.''

"Zowee! You mean you can predict the frequencies where the transitions come?'' David struggled to grasp the implications of what Paul was saying.

Paul nodded and stepped to the blackboard, writing with chalk as he talked. ''Our normal matter is only one particle state, and there are six others. I found it was confusing to think of that many different states, so I visualize them as seven parallel planes. A particle can lie only in one plane at a time and can interact with other particles in the same plane. Our universe is the middle plane, say, and there are three adjoining 'up' planes and three 'down' planes. Or you can think of these shadow planes as six other shadow universes, all parallel to ours and interacting with ours only through gravity.

''I am, of course, oversimplifying,'' said Paul pedantically.

"Of course,'' David said, with a note of irony, ''but I'll forgive you. Go ahead, Paul, oversimplify some more.'' Six other universes, David thought, struggling to grasp the idea.

"The reason Vickie's observation of a parity effect, the mirror-image star patterns, is important,'' Paul continued, ''is that there are several possible sub-models that work about equally well.'' He sat down again at his desk. ''But only one of them predicts an extra-dimensional rotation that reverses the three spatial directions in the twistor field, effectively 'flopping' everything in the field so as to reverse left and right. Each shadow universe would be connected to ours by two transitions that are mirror images of each other.''

"And that explains the mirror-image pictures?'' David asked.

Paul nodded. ''There's a property of the weak force called parity violation which breaks the symmetry between right-and left-handedness. In the model I'm studying, that symmetry breaking splits the twistor transitions and puts one at a higher frequency than the other. If Vickie found two star maps that are mirror images, that means the two twistor transitions involved must have this broken symmetry. That model, which I wasn't too sure about before, has apparently been verified.'' Paul paused.

There was a smile of great satisfaction on Paul's face, and David remembered what Paul had said just last week about the frustrations of this field, the lack of experimental verification. He's jumped to the pinnacle of his field, David thought. He's the originator of a new, improved superstring model that's just been verified. David felt suddenly elated.

Paul walked to his flatscreen terminal and typed a few commands. The small laser printer beside it hummed for a moment, and Paul extracted a neatly printed sheet of paper. ''Here are the transition frequencies from the S-equals-three model with parity violation. Notice that about half the frequencies here aren't on the list you gave me. You should find out if they're present but were somehow missed. That should keep you busy. And I'll need a data file with the information you've just collected on the star patterns and so forth. OK?'' He looked inquiringly at David.

''No problem,'' said David, taking the paper. He was impatient to get back to the lab to try some of these new settings. ''In an hour or so I'll MAIL you the data file.'' He studied the list of frequencies. ''Hmmm. A lot of these new frequencies are out of our present tuning range. Guess we'll have to modify the hardware a bit to extend the frequency spread. That's easy enough, though.

''Oh, before I forget, Paul, am I still expected for dinner tomorrow night? I should warn you and Elizabeth that after Allan carts off our hardware, I may not be the best of company.''

''Indeed you're expected!'' said Paul. ''Tomorrow is some sort of school holiday, something about a teachers' meeting, so Melissa and Jeff are coming to work with me in the morning. Elizabeth will spend the morning at her new counseling job, then do some shopping at the Pike Place Market. She hasn't confided in me, but I think she's making something special for us.''

"Well, at least I won't have to leave early tomorrow night to get back to the experiment,'' said David morosely. "Bring the kids down to the lab tomorrow, if you want. I'll show them a twistor transition while I still have hardware. Oh, and hey, is it OK if I bring Vickie along tomorrow night?''

Paul raised an eyebrow. "Sure, David,'' he said with a knowing smile. "The Curse of the Harrisons strikes again, eh?''

David sighed, then nodded with a grin. Indeed it had.

At 5:49 P.M., just before closing time, the U-Haul rental agent looked up to see a balding man in a business suit entering the office. "I'm Albert Carter,'' said the customer. "I called you on Monday to reserve a moving van, to be picked up about now.''

"Yes, Mr. Carter. We have it all ready for you, along with the pads and dollies you requested. You wanted the weekly rate, sir?''

"Sure,'' said the customer. "I think we can have it back to you in three or four days, but I'll say a week to allow for problems. Do we get a lower rate if we bring it back early?''

"Yes, sir!'' said the agent. "It's our policy to calculate the final bill using the rate which gives you the best deal. We'd just like to know about when to expect the truck to be returned for our own scheduling. Now I'll need your driver's license and a major credit card.''

The balding man reached into his inside suit pocket and started to withdraw something, then stopped and replaced it. Glancing at the agent, he reached into the side pocket of his trousers, removed a new-looking wallet, and placed a Washington State driver's license and a VISA card on the counter.

A few minutes later he was driving south on Interstate 5. He felt satisfied. Now he had the truck and the uniforms, so everything was ready. Tomorrow morning they'd be ready to put Broadsword's plan into action.

15

WEDNESDAY MORNING, OCTOBER 13

Vickie looked up from the console as David walked into the laboratory at 7:32 Wednesday morning. He was carrying two large white bags from the HUB, each bearing the image of a sled dog on its side. He set one bag aside and opened the other, producing two large glazed doughnuts and two capped Styrofoam cups of coffee.

She was glad to see David. It had been a long night. Her stomach and peripheral vision told her that she had already had too much coffee, but she joined David at the table and picked up one of the doughnuts. She was feeling more optimistic about her prospects for a thesis. Much of the data she needed was safely salted away on laser disks.

"How'd it go?" asked David, then took a bite from his doughnut followed by a swallow of coffee.

"Better than I'd expected," said Vickie. "I got most of the way through the schedule of measurements. There are only a few things left for you to do. I did the modifications to the coils and ran some tests. We can get to the new frequencies OK. But about two A.M. I noticed the number-four driver was overheating. I was able to fix it, though. It's written up in the logbook.

"Oh, and by the way. I borrowed Sam's special number-three toolbox with all the nifty little portable tools in it. It's over by the console now. I left him a note saying where it is. To fix the overheating problem I needed to drill a hole to install a bigger heat sink. Sam has this neat little self-powered drill that just fitted into the available space and saved me about an hour in disassembly time. If you're heading in that direction, take it back to him and say thanks.''

"Sure," said David. He walked over and picked up the logbook. "Yeah, I see that you've done most of the menu. We'll have lots of laser disk-loads of data to analyze after the hardware leaves. All I have left to map are those four oddball resonances that show up on the power meter but don't pop.''

"David," said Victoria, feeling anxious again, "do you honestly think that I can get a thesis out of this mess, with the equipment leaving? What if we discover that something wasn't working, and we need to do it over again?" Saxon was being such a bastard, she thought.

"Look," said David, "any experimental physicist in the world would sacrifice one or more important items of his anatomy to be the discoverer of the effect we've got here. Vickie, it's important! Don't worry about your thesis. Allan can't suppress that, not with Paul and me on your side. Sometimes professors do stick together, but they're pretty careful not to allow graduate students to be mistreated. You'll get your Ph.D., OK. But don't count on its being widely circulated for a while. I'd be willing to bet you that after your thesis goes to the library, Allan will check out all of the copies and lock them up in his office for a long time.''

"How are you coming on those papers we worked over last Sunday?" asked Vickie, getting up from the table. Sunday had been a nice day, she thought.

"That, at least, is going very well," said David. "I incorporated your suggestions, and I found a better way of explaining the twistor field rotation, the part I was having trouble writing. I've got a final draft of the hardware paper on disk, and I'm just about done with the one describing our measurements. But remember, those may never see the light of day as journal publications. At best, they're going to be delayed getting into print. Allan will see to that.

"Vickie, whatever you do, keep out of the conflict, don't take sides in this paper business!" David warned. "It would be better if you didn't tell him you'd helped in writing them, beyond looking over the final result. I'm going to keep the issue of journal publication strictly a matter between Allan and me. What I want to avoid at all costs is getting your thesis held hostage to the suppression of those papers. If you ever hear me tell Allan that I don't give a damn whether you get a Ph.D. or not, that's what I'm up to. We can't allow him to find out that your thesis would be a useful bargaining chip for manipulating me.''

Vickie shook her head. "Politics!" she muttered, putting on her backpack. She turned and surveyed the equipment. "Guess this will be the last time I see this kludge," she said, "if it's actually leaving this afternoon. Goodbye, Kludge! Thanks for the thesis data!'' She walked around it once, trying to commit every contour to memory. She would miss it, she decided, but at least she would still have David.

"Don't forget about tonight," said David. "Remember, I'm picking you up at six-thirty.''

Vickie smiled. "I hadn't forgotten," she said. She brushed his lips with hers as she walked past him to the door.

David sat back from the computer console, once more feeling frustrated. On Monday he'd talked at length to Weinberger about Saxon's plan to move the equipment, but that hadn't changed anything. He'd considered going higher in the university administration, maybe to the Graduate School dean or the provost. But without the support of the chairman, that seemed pointless, and he had decided that for the moment his time was better spent taking data. He could take up that fight again when he had no hardware to worry about.

He consulted the logbook. All the measurements on the list had been completed. He knew he had only about another hour to work before he had to halt the data taking. Sam was coming around at one P.M. to help disassemble things and get the equipment boxed and ready to move.

Now he was following up some new ideas on how to fill his remaining time. He was doing some final calcu-

lations of field settings for a range of field diameters from
as small as a few centimeters to as large as five meters,
about the largest their power supplies could handle. Five
meters was big, he mused. At that diameter the twistor
transition would take out the coils, the supplies, the console—the whole bloody works. He smiled ruefully. Another "accident" would certainly solve the argument about
what to do with the hardware. Now that the pressure to
get data for Vickie was off and he had more time to reflect
on the gross injustice of the present situation, his anger
was rising.

Purposefully, he moused the five-meter settings into the
control program. The control panel appeared on the screen.
He clicked the COUNT DOWN option and moved the cursor
to the control labeled (ACTIVATE) . His hand hesitated on the
mouse switch. No, he told himself, I can't do that. There
would be hell to pay if I did. I'd agreed to do these last
few measurements and have the equipment ready to move
by four this afternoon. Still, it was tempting . . . He took
his hand from the mouse, got up from the console, and took
a deep breath.

I've been working too hard, he thought. He looked at his
watch. It was 10:48 A.M. Coffee time, he thought. He picked
up his cup and moved toward the door.

Allan Saxon and his Seattle lawyer, Dan Marcus, were
escorted by Martin Pierce into a well-appointed conference
room just down the hall from Pierce's office. Saxon was
frustrated. His attempt in the waiting room to interest
Darlene in an evening liaison had met a surprisingly cold
rebuff. He seated himself in one of the leather chairs
around the polished lozenge-shape table. Two people that
Saxon had never seen before were seated at the table.
Pierce performed the introductions. They were from the
Megalith legal staff.

"Well, Allan," Pierce began, "we have a new propo-
sition for you." He put his hand on his copy of the thick
document that Darlene had placed before each of the par-
ticipants. It was a new contract that Megalith was proposing
would replace their old agreement. He proceeded to thread

delicately through the complexities of the massive legal instrument.

Saxon was puzzled. On the surface the terms of this overcomplicated contract were more favorable than he had anticipated, far more generous than those he and Pierce had discussed a week earlier. He looked speculatively at Pierce, droning on and on about the benefits of the new arrangement. What was the devious son of a bitch up to?

Saxon had thought a lot about the bugging incident. Megalith certainly had the resources to set up an operation like that. In all probability Martin Pierce now knew almost as much as he did about the twistor effect. And Pierce wanted it. Saxon smiled and began to leaf through the contract. Now he knew what he was looking for. Somewhere in the bowels of this turgid document were words that would transfer all rights to the twistor effect to the Megalith Corporation. He would find them and nullify their effect.

It was going to be a long day.

Melissa sat looking around her father's office and finding little that interested her. She was becoming bored. It was supposed to be a special day. Her third-grade class had been canceled this morning so the teachers could have a meeting. Daddy had taken her and Jeff to the children's department of the University Bookstore, bought them each a book, and then brought them to his office to help him work. He'd said they would visit David soon, but now he was busy at his computer terminal. She and Jeff had been told to look at their new books. Daddy was very busy with whatever he was doing, and his back was turned.

She nudged Jeff, put a finger to her lips, and pointed to the open door. She whispered in Jeff's ear, "Let's go and see David now!" He nodded, smiling. Quietly they tiptoed outside. Melissa brought her new book to show David the pictures of dinosaurs. They were like the dragons in some of his stories. They walked quietly down the hall to the stairway. On the first floor they found David's lab door. It was unlocked and they opened it. They were going to jump inside and say "Boo!" to surprise him, but he wasn't there.

"His coat is here," said Melissa. "I'll bet he'll be back soon." She put her book on the table by the door. Then she heard David's voice in the hall, talking to someone. "I know!" she said. "Let's hide and jump out and scare him when he comes in!"

"Yeah!" said Jeff. "Let's scare him!"

Melissa led the way to the control console. Together they crouched in the knee space beneath it. It was like a little house.

"This is fun!" said Jeff, and giggled.

David, returning to the laboratory with a full cup of coffee, saw three men in gray coveralls walking to the door of his lab. "Can I help you?" he asked. He noticed that the coveralls had the words WESTERN VAN LINES stenciled in blue on front and back.

The man in the lead, about forty and going bald, consulted a clipboard. "We're looking for a Dr. D. Harrison in room 101."

"I'm Harrison," said David.

"We're here to move some equipment," said the balding man.

David opened the door to the laboratory. "Here's the equipment in question, but the arrangement was to move it late this afternoon, at about four. I'm not done with it yet. You'll have to come back later."

The three men followed David into the laboratory, and he noticed that one of them, a very large fellow with a coarse face and large hands, had closed the door behind him and was locking it. "I'm afraid that's impossible," said the leader. "We have a very tight schedule, and our orders are to move it now."

David frowned and put his cup on the table. "Look, I'm sorry about your orders and your schedule, but I've got a schedule of my own. And I haven't finished. This equipment will not be ready to move until four P.M. You'll just have to come back then. If you have any complaints, I suggest you take them to Professor Saxon, who arranged for this stupid move in the first place." David's rising irritation turned to amazement as he realized that the big man was now pointing a large black gun in his direction. He identified it as one of the new laser-aimed weapons that the police favor, and noticed that the guide beam from the gun was making a small red laser spot on his chest.

"If you wanna leave this lavatory alive, turkey," the big man said, "just hold it right there."

"We have to move this equipment now," the balding man said calmly. "We have our orders. Cooperate with us, and you won't get hurt."

Bugs first and now guns! David's mind was racing. This wasn't about a simple move of the hardware from the UW campus to Bellevue. Saxon wouldn't need to send movers with guns. What the hell was going on here? Who could be behind this? Spies? The CIA? The KGB?

David took a few steps backward. He felt a controlled but rising sense of intense anger and resentment at the injustice of it all. Then it occurred to him that the computer still held the five-meter field settings. "OK!" he said and spread his hands. "Look, if you're that set on moving the stuff a bit early, that's fine. I'll have to get the stuff ready. It will be severely damaged if it isn't shut down properly. I'll have to activate the automatic shutdown procedure. OK?" David pointedly turned his back on them and walked over to the console. He could almost feel the red laser spot on his spine as he walked.

"OK, you can shut it down," said the leader. "But be quick about it!"

"The shutdown is very quick," said David through clenched teeth. "It only takes a few seconds. Look, there are dangerous high voltages here. Please stand back against that wall until everything is safely off." He reached across the console, moused the cursor to the (ACTIVATE) control on the computer screen, and clicked. Then he backed slowly away from the console, moving at a leisurely pace along a path that would take him well outside the field volume and away from the windows. Those might implode from the vacuum produced when the transition hit. The synthesized voice of the control program began the down-count: *"Five! ...Four!..."*

Crouching under the control desk, Melissa heard men's voices in the room. They sounded angry, and Melissa was uncertain about when they should surprise David. When she heard David's computer saying numbers, she decided that the time had come for the surprise. When the computer said *"Three!"* she and Jeff jumped out from under the console yelling "Surprise, David! Surprise!"

David saw the children. The realization of what was about to happen came to him like an electric shock, and his time sense slowed down. As the computer said *"Two!"* he began to move with agonizing slowness across to the console. He knelt slowly to pull the two children to him. He saw them turn to look at him, delight on their faces. They squirmed and giggled. Did he have time to get them out?

"One!" said the control computer.

Melissa squirmed away from him, and David wasted a critical split second in pulling her back again. With the children in his embrace, he turned away from the console. Was it too late? He hesitated for another split second as he estimated the position of the field boundary and considered the consequences of being half in and half out of the field sphere.

"Activating!" said the computer.

The large man was keeping his gun aimed in the general direction of the Harrison turkey when some little kids jumped out from under the messy desk. Reflexively he stepped forward and brought up his laserguided automatic, now extended at arm's length and projecting its target spot on the area of Harrison's heart. He was the muscle, and he had the gun. Nobody was getting away with any tricks on his watch.

"Activating!" said that computer voice. His gun hand suddenly felt numb.

Abruptly, he wasn't looking at the Harrison turkey any more. His arm gave the appearance of pressing deep into a smooth wooden surface. As he pulled it away, he saw

that his hand was missing at the wrist. It looked all smooth
and white and bloody. He could see the bones of his arm
cut off clean and white, and the blood now pulsing from
the severed arteries. He screamed a great animal release
of anger and fear and protest. He'd been in control, goddammit! He'd done it right. He hadn't screwed up. This
couldn't happen!

The balding man stared around the room in disbelief.
There was a strong cedarlike smell in the air. The floor
supports made ominous groaning noises. Where the apparatus had stood an instant ago there was now an enormous
reddish wooden ball that reached almost to the ceiling and
was sunk into the floor. Its sides were smooth, as if polished.
The large man beside him made animal noises, and with
each heartbeat blood spurted from a stump at his wrist where
his hand had been. There were streaks of the bright red
arterial blood down the side of the sphere, and a puddle
was forming on the floor.

The balding man felt growing shock and numbness
spreading across his mind and battled against it, clinging
to clarity. He pressed a blood-soaked handkerchief into
the big man's remaining hand to hold against the wrist
stump. Then he snatched a piece of clear plastic tubing
from a work table by the wall and tied it around the man's
forearm, slowing the flow of blood. He looked at the
quantity of blood on the floor and shook his head in
dismay, then turned to the object that now dominated the
room.

He tapped the wood of the sphere with his fist. It
sounded very solid. Maybe somehow Harrison and the
apparatus were inside. He walked around it, looking for
a way in. Copper tubing on the floor leading up to the
wooden surface was spraying water, and heavy electrical
wires were making blue-green sparks. It didn't look
planned, somehow. His mind racing, he backed to a corner,
removed the small camera from his pocket, and panned
across the scene, snapping four pictures in quick succession.

It's blown, his mind said, *it's blown, it's blown . . .*

"It's blown!" he said aloud. "Execute retreat mode. Let's get outta here!" Shakily he herded his men to the door.

What can I tell Broadsword, he thought as they ran for the truck. Despite his fears, there was no interference outside. The driver waited calmly, the truck engine idling. What kind of shit storm did we blunder into, he wondered. Was this some kind of a setup? With little kids? Guys that disappear? Giant wood balls? Cut-off hands? This is no fucking ordinary job!

PART 3

The knowledge we have acquired
ought not to resemble a
great shop without order and
without inventory; we ought
to know what we possess
and to be able to make it
serve our own needs.

GOTTFRIED WILHELM VON LEIBNITZ
(1646–1716)

16

WEDNESDAY AFTERNOON, OCTOBER 13

It had suddenly become dark and quiet. David felt the delayed adrenaline rush accelerate his heartbeat to a driving thump. The only light was the fading afterglow of the computer monitor screen. The dominant sound was the descending whine of the turbopump spinning down. They were still in the lab, and the power was off! Those new settings must have overloaded the circuits, blown a breaker, and shut down the vacuum system. But this was the middle of the morning, so why was there no light coming through the windows?

The twist! They'd been inside the twistor field when the transition hit. They were on the other side of the twistor transition! The CCD camera had shown only darkness and distant stars on the other side of a transition. They should be breathing vacuum, suffocating in the blackness of empty space. How could they still be alive? Where were they! His mind raced, cycling on emptiness and paradox without a reference point.

David drew three deep breaths, shook himself, and studied what his senses were telling him. He was still crouched near the control desk with his arms around Melissa and Jeffrey, who squirmed closer to him. The cold, hard, concrete slab floor of the laboratory was still beneath him, but he could feel the floor shake slightly, accompanied by small grinding noises. The control console still pressed against his shoulder. There was a strong organic smell like cedar in the air. He could hear his own breathing and that of the children. The darkness was now oppressive and solid, like a wall.

"Are you kids OK?" he asked. His voice rang with a hollow echo that was new.

"What happened?" asked Melissa. "Did those men do something? Why are the lights out?"

"W-we were gonna surprise you, David!" said Jeff.

"I certainly was surprised, Jeff." David was relieved to hear their voices. They were OK. Releasing the children, he said, "I want you two to stay right here until I get us some light. Don't move, now!" He followed the top edge of the desk with his hand and found the middle drawer. Opening it, he found a paper matchbook that he remembered putting there. He struck a match, stood up, and looked around. "Holy shit!" he said.

The light revealed that they were near the center of a brownish dome. It surrounded them on all sides and curved down to meet the concrete floor, which was now a gray circle. The twistor apparatus stood at the approximate center of the circle. David cautiously walked to the nearest wall and felt it. It was smooth, cool, and just a bit sticky, and it smelled strongly of something that was not quite cedar. He could see wood grain in the surface. It was polished wood, like a fine piece of furniture. David turned and looked back, surveying what was left of the laboratory room. He could feel the match burning close to his fingers, but just before he shook it out he noticed a rectangular object next to the desk beside the console. Sam's number-three toolbox! He'd forgotten to return it. He walked through the dark, the remembered view of the room guiding him almost like seeing until his toe touched the box. Bending in the dark, he released the clips and opened it. Inside, his hand encountered a familiar shape. He lifted out the big fluorescent-tube flashlight and switched it on.

The polished curve of the wall mirrored the light, giving the impression of a tiny upside-down human shape some distance away, shining a light in his direction. He propped the light on the console and lifted the toolbox to the flat surface next to the sack lunch he had bought at the HUB this morning. Then he sat on the desk and motioned the children over. They climbed up on the desk beside him, and for a long time they were silent, taking it all in.

"Everything looks different," said Melissa, her voice pitched higher than usual. "What's that funny brown thing?" She pointed at the wooden wall. "Where did it come from? Was there an earthquake? Are we trapped, David?"

David's mind was turning over the problem of why they had breathable air and how long it would last. They might very well be trapped. I have to keep myself and the children calm, he thought, and at least give the impression that nothing is seriously wrong. "No, Melissa, it wasn't an earthquake," he said. "I think we're in no immediate danger. We're in a different place than we were. We're surrounded by wood. I don't know why yet. That's one of the things we'll have to find out. The first thing I need to do is examine that wall around us."

He pointed the flashlight at the wall and walked toward it. Immediately the children stood, about to follow him. He turned back to them. "I want you two to sit here quietly and watch while I get things in order," he said.

"Can't we look too?" Melissa asked.

"It's dark in here," David said, "and it could be dangerous. Just let me check it out first, then you can look too."

Melissa turned to her brother. "Sit down," she told him. "We have to wait for David here."

"I know," said Jeff, sitting down again. Melissa seated herself beside him.

David walked for a distance along the curved wall, holding the flashlight close and studying the wall's shiny surface, occasionally tapping, feeling, or smelling it. It looked like normal wood from a fir tree, a soft wood but very smooth and regular, with occasional color variations. It sounded very solid, very thick. He wondered just how thick it was and what could be outside—if there was an outside. Could a universe be solid wood? Nonsense, he thought, it would go into gravitational collapse.

"Can we look now?" Melissa asked.

"Not yet," said David. He returned to the table and began lifting items out of the toolbox and placing them on the desk. They cast long shadows in the bluish light of the

fluorescent flashlight. "We'll take a quick inventory," he
said. "We need to know how we're set for tools and food."
He put the electronics tools in one pile, the mechanical tools
in a second pile, food items in the third, and miscellaneous
items in the fourth. He was slightly relieved when he found
a small oxyacetylene torch in the toolbox. If the air became
unbreathable, the extra oxygen in its small cylinder would
help for a while. Finishing with the toolbox, he walked to
a shadowed gray cabinet across the room and collected tools
and other objects to add to the piles.

David was thankful that Melissa and Jeff were so well
behaved and cooperative. He wondered how long that would
last. "Well," he said finally, "our food situation isn't too
bad. Vickie and I sometimes do all-night experiment runs
here, so we keep some food in the cabinet. We have powdered milk, instant coffee, tea bags, Tang, sugar, salt, a
full jar of roasted peanuts, some packets of crackers, and
six envelopes of dried soup. Sam had some freeze-dried
stew stashed in his toolbox. And Vickie even left us with
a big jar of peanut butter. This plastic carboy has de-ionized
water in it. The water will taste flat, but we can drink it.
And I hadn't eaten my lunch yet, so we have that too, a
couple of sandwiches and an apple. We have enough to eat
for a while, if we take it easy. You two can help."

"What can we do?" asked Melissa.

"Did you ever go on hikes in the mountains with your
dad?" David asked. This was a far cry from a day hike in
the Cascades, he thought, but it might give them a more
familiar frame of reference.

"Yeah!" said Jeff. "We took a lunch, and we saw a
baby bear once, but Dad wouldn't let us play with it. And
we saw lotsa deers, too, but they ran away."

"Well, this is going to be kinda like that," said David.
"We've got to be sure that we eat something at every meal-
time. But not too much, no more than we absolutely need.
We'll wait for a big meal until we find other sources of
food. OK?" The children nodded, and David added silently
to himself, *if we don't suffocate first and if there are any
other sources of food.*

Jeffrey pointed to the beige telephone on the desk. "We

could phone my mom! Maybe she can help," he said enthusiastically.

David picked up the telephone and held it to Jeff's ear.
"See, Jeff, no dial tone." He pulled on the wire and showed
him the cord, cut off by the twistor transition. "You have
to understand that telephones aren't magic. They're fairly
simple electrical machines. They work by making electrons
jiggle back and forth in wires that go all the way from one
telephone to another. But if the wires are cut, then the
telephone doesn't work, can't work. The lights in here don't
work for the same reason. You have to think of machines
in terms of how they work, not just what they do. OK?"
He smiled.

"OK," said Jeff. He wrinkled his nose and seemed lost
in thought.

David shone the flashlight at the ceiling. He noticed
growth rings in the wood grain near the top of the wooden
"dome" that became more tightly curved near the south
wall, while the curvature of the rings was greater on toward
the north wall. That would be the outside wall, he thought.
He examined the north wall more carefully and noticed that
the ring pattern made a sort of bull's-eye pattern at one point
along the mid-wall bulge. Let's suppose, he thought to
himself, that we are inside a tree. That would explain the
smell and the growth rings. If that's so, then this point is
closest to the outside of the tree. He tapped the wall at the
center of the bull's-eye pattern and listened. It had a hollow
sound here. Returning to the pile of tools on the desk, he
fitted a slim adjustable auger bit in the folding manual drill-
brace from the toolbox. He called Jeff to stand beside him
and hold the flashlight. Melissa stood behind Jeff, watching
intently. David turned the auger slowly. A light brown wood
chip curled out of the hole as he methodically bored into
the center of the bull's-eye.

"What are you doing, David?" Melissa asked finally.

"I think the wall may be thinner here. I'm making a hole
so maybe we can look out."

Melissa looked worried. "What if those men are still out
there?"

"If there's one thing I'm sure of, Melissa," he answered,

"it's that those men are not on the other side of this wall. That's one problem we don't need to worry about." He continued to turn the auger. Suddenly his ears popped. He noticed a hissing noise coming from the newly bored hole. He removed the bit and placed his moistened lips over the hole. He could feel a cold rush of air against their sensitive surfaces. He smeared spittle on his palm and held it over the hole. Momentarily the hissing stopped and a slight bubbling froth formed around the edges of his palm. Air was coming in. He sniffed at it. No odor except the near-cedar smell. Turning to the children, he pointed to the hole. "There's air leaking in now. Wherever we are, there's a higher air pressure outside than in here. I'm pretty sure I can drill all the way through so we can peek outside."

As he bored deeper, the hiss increased sharply, then stopped as David's ears popped again. He continued turning the brace until the auger cut through. He stopped and backed it out, then bent and sighted through the new hole. The smell of new-cut wood was thick in the air as he pressed his cheek against the wall and peered out. Moving his head back and forth across the narrow opening, he could resolve colors, mostly shades of brown and green. There were light brown verticals that could have been tree trunks. Whatever lay beyond the hole, there was certainly more space out there than in here. And more air.

"Can we look too?" asked Jeff.

"Do you see any people?" asked Melissa.

David turned from the hole and felt a rush of giddy relief. He'd been sure they were trapped in an airtight compartment like bees in a jar and would soon die of asphyxiation. He put a hand on the wall to steady himself and smiled at the children.

"You can look if you want," he said, and lifted Jeff to the level of the hole. "I have an idea where we are, now," he said. We have air to breathe, and we can get outside, he thought. We're gonna make it!

Victoria came abruptly back to consciousness, startled. The bedside telephone had awakened her. Its burr had somehow been tangled in a vivid dream that was still evaporating from the surface of her awareness. "Hello?" she said into the receiver, noticing as she spoke the sleep-softened formlessness of her own voice.

"Vickie, this is Sam," came the familiar voice from the earpiece. "I'm sorry to wake you, honey. I know you prob'ly worked all night. But you'd better get right over to your lab. There's been an accident."

"David!" said Vickie. "I mean, is David all right, Sam?" The details of her dream swirled in her head, just out of reach. She and David had been working in the laboratory, and she had been very happy. Then something terrible had happened.

"I don't know where David is, Vickie. There's something here you've gotta see for yourself," said Sam. "If I tried to explain, you'd think I was nuts. How soon can you get here?"

"I'll be there in about twenty minutes," she said. Something had happened to David. She was sure of it, and the thought was a dull ache of dread, an extension of the terrible dream. As she hung up the phone and propelled herself from the bed, she was already plotting a minimum-time strategy of dressing and biking to the lab.

Victoria stood at the door of the laboratory and stared in disbelief. In the space formerly occupied by her thesis experiment was a shiny convex wall of wood. It was a sphere! Ralph Weinberger, the department chairman, motioned her to come inside quickly. He closed and locked the door after she had entered, then asked if she knew anything at all about the wooden object. She shook her head. The room was permeated with an odor vaguely reminiscent of cedar. She walked over and touched the sphere, then walked around it, wide-eyed.

"That thing was here when I came in," said Sam Weston, pointing to the wooden sphere. "There was water squirting all over the place over there, and some cut-off wires were sizzling in it. I cut the power at the breaker box and shut off the valves. Then I called you and got Professor Weinberger. Professor Saxon's out of town today, I guess."

Vickie nodded. "He's in San Francisco," she said, stepping carefully around a puddle on the floor.

"The water's mostly drained away now," Sam continued. "A few minutes ago I went downstairs and looked at what's there. This section of the building doesn't have basement rooms underneath, just a crawl space with a dirt floor and some concrete supports. This big wooden thing comes right through the concrete slab and goes down into the dirt. It's a good thing there isn't a basement room under here or the whole thing would've fallen right through. That big ball must weigh a heck of a lot, dozens of tons maybe."

"Where's David?" asked Victoria, noticing the dark stains on the floor. Was it blood? What weren't they telling her?

"I wish we knew," said Weinberger. "I located his car in the parking garage, but he cannot be found. Tell me when you last saw him."

Vickie described the shift change this morning and the schedule for the day until the time when the movers came. "What do you think happened?" she asked.

"We have no theories," Weinberger answered, "but it doesn't look good, Miss Gordon. I've already called the police, and they'll be here soon. The liquid on the floor appears to be blood."

Victoria looked at it closely. The reddish-brown stuff did look and smell like blood. And there was a disturbing quantity of it in the room. A trail of small spots led to the door. She unlocked the door and followed them outside, down the corridor, and finally to the small loading dock behind the building. The little spots stopped there. She returned to the laboratory.

"What about Allan?" she asked. "Has he been told?"

"Susan has been trying to reach him in San Francisco," said the chairman. "Uh, Miss Gordon, Mr. Weston, I want to caution you both to be extremely careful what you say to the police or to anyone else. We don't want any sensational publicity which might reflect unfavorably on the department. Stick to what you know, please, and do not engage in speculations about what may have happened. This may all be some kind of prank or hoax. We must proceed very carefully. Do you understand?''

"Sure," said Sam, "just the facts."

Victoria looked again at the monumental wooden sphere, then nodded agreement. A knot of despair tightened in the pit of her stomach. David was gone, and she felt a sick certainty that she knew where he was. She looked across the room to the photographs of cold blackness punctuated by glittering alien stars, and she felt a sudden chill.

David braced one shoulder against the curving wood surface and turned harder on the auger, boring the last hole, the one that would complete a large linked ring of similar ones. He had been working for several hours. Now he was hot and sweaty, and his arms were very tired. The new holes formed a shoulder-wide circle centered about the peephole that had provided the first glimpse of their surroundings. Jeff, now seated in a chair, continued to provide light for the operation from the big fluorescent flashlight. As David drilled, the chips falling to the concrete floor had been smooth reddish curls at first, but now they turned brown and uneven as he bored into the outer bark. Finally the auger chewed through into emptiness, and he backed it out.

Turning to the pile of tools on the desk, David put down the brace and bit and selected a hammer. He hit the wooden circle a sound *thwack* and it moved slightly backward. With each successive blow it retreated further. Finally it fell outward, to be replaced by a circle of brilliant outdoor light.

David squinted into the brightness, then jumped back. Something alive out there was looking back at him through the hole! He took a deep breath, fighting for calm against the adrenaline rush the surprise had triggered. He looked out through the hole again.

The confused jumble of colors and shapes framed by the ragged circle finally clicked into register. A beaked head was hanging upside down in the hole, looking in. The head tilted sideways, regarding him with a single eye. Something about that movement suggested a bird. Yes. A large green birdlike creature was peering in at them through the hole. It must be hanging head down from whatever was outside.

Perhaps it had been attracted by the drilling and hammering sounds he had made in breaking out of the tree. Like a chick pecking its way out of an egg.

David extended the drill bit slowly out through the hole. The creature pecked at the drill, made a squawking noise, and was gone. "There are birds in this universe," he said to Jeff, who was standing beside him, "quite big ones."

David studied the scene now visible through the hole. Below, the ground was a peculiar orange-brown color. It was punctuated here and there with shades of green that must be brush and small plants, and he could see a line of bright colors on the ground. Light brown columns, probably the trunks of enormous trees, soared upward out of sight. They were in a forest.

He put a piece of corrugated cardboard over the splintered edges, carefully squeezed his head and shoulders through the hole, and looked around. "We're up in a tree, a very big one," he said. He looked down. The ground was a good ten meters down. A fall from this height could be fatal. They'd have to be very careful. David visualized the sequence of events that had put them where they were. He whistled. If they had materialized only a short distance to the north, they would have been in midair. It would have been quite a fall!

There was a large branch just below the hole he'd made. The green bird was perched far out on the branch, watching him with evident suspicion. Its color matched the foliage of the tree, and from a distance it might have been taken as a clump of leaves on the branch. David looked at it more closely, and blinked. It was not an ordinary bird. It was standing on a pair of taloned feet that gripped the branch, while a second pair of clawed feet projected outward from its breast. It used these occasionally to claw something out of the branch, then peck it into its mouth. The claws looked sharp.

"Come have a look, kids," David called, withdrawing his head. "We've got ourselves a tree house, complete with a four-legged green bird for a watchdog!"

The visibility inside was better now that light streamed in through the hole. Melissa had been sitting across the room; now she ran along the wall toward the spot where David and Jeff were standing. As she ran, her foot kicked against something hard, and she stumbled. She glanced down at the object that had tripped her. Then she screamed. On the floor near her foot was a large human hand. Clasped in the hand was a big blue-black pistol. A brownish smear led down the wall to the hand, and nearby on the floor was a red puddle.

She backed away and pointed at the thing on the floor. David walked over and crouched down. "It's all right, Melissa," he said. "It can't hurt you." Struggling against his own revulsion, he used a single finger to set the gun's safety lock. Then he turned and walked to the lab bench, returning with a large translucent plastic bag. He inverted the bag, put it around his hand, picked up the hand and gun from the floor and reinverted the bag. Finally, through the plastic wall of the bag he pried the gun from the pale thick fingers and removed it.

He placed the plastic bundle on the bench and wiped off the gun with a white tissue. David's father had been a hunting enthusiast, and at age twelve David had been ed-ucated in proper gun handling. He expertly removed the clip from the handle of the weapon, ejected a cartridge from the receiver, and slipped it into the clip. He studied the gun, then held the clip up to the light and counted bullets. "It's a laser-guided flechette pistol, a 'Police Special,'" he said at last. "It points a little red laser beam down the barrel to show where the bullets will hit, to help aim better. It also scares the guy it's pointed at, because he sees the red spot on his chest and knows there'll be a bullet hole just there if the guy with the gun squeezes the trigger just a bit harder. There are twenty little high-velocity explosive bullets in the clip now. Our big one-handed friend has given us a present, a weapon made for intimidation and killing. I hope we won't need it." He placed gun and clip on the workbench beside the plastic-wrapped bundle.

Jeffrey walked over to the bench and examined all three objects closely. Melissa came to stand protectively beside him. David knew that despite Elizabeth's efforts to dis-courage the tendency, Jeff was very interested in guns. But he studied the cut-off hand first. "Yuck!" Jeff said finally, rendering his decision. "That hand is real yucky." Next Jeff studied the gun without touching it. Melissa cautioned him to leave the gun alone.

"Guns are dangerous," David commented. "They mostly hurt their owners and their friends and families. But we may need this gun. I'm very glad that I have it and know how to use it." He placed the gun, its clip, and the plastic-wrapped bundles on the top shelf of the gray cabinet. Later he'd bury the hand in the woods.

"I think we should talk now," David told the children. He coaxed Melissa and Jeff to a spot in the daylight. He pointed to the cabinet and said in a serious voice, "That hand and the gun belonged to one of the men who came into the lab while you were hiding there. They came to steal our equipment. One of them had a gun. He was pointing it at me and threatening to shoot me. When we were moved here, he must have had his hand inside the twistor field. So the field brought his hand along and left the rest of him behind. I guess it cut his hand off. It's bad luck for him that he was hurt, but he shouldn't have been pointing that gun at me."

Jeff nodded his head solemnly, agreeing that justice had been done. Melissa had recovered from her fright and looked interested.

"Now," said David, "I want you both to see where we are, and then we'll talk some more." He moved a box near the new door so that first Melissa and then Jeff could stand high enough to look out the hole and view their new home. It was an amazing change from the university campus.

There was a rich, familiar yet unfamiliar forest smell: green growing things and composted leaves with just a hint of spice. As far as one could see through the woodland dimness, giant trees marched into the distance. They were like no trees David had ever seen. The trunks resembled those of evergreens but were a lighter shade of brown. They had dark green leaves that appeared feathery and club-shaped, more like leaves of a water plant than of evergreen. The ground was covered by an orange-brown carpet of dried leaves, and here and there was the green of low brush.

Looking upward, one saw more green than blue, for an enveloping canopy of feathery leaves blocked all but a few glimpses of sky. Unfamiliar birdcalls sounded from above, and there was also the keening sound of wind in branches.

The children were very quiet. David sat down on the now-illuminated concrete floor and leaned back against the smooth hollow of the wall, and the children joined him. He considered how the children must be feeling about now. They seemed to be watching him for a clue as to how to behave. "Melissa, Jeff," he said finally, "we're in a lot of trouble. We need to think and talk about it.

"First question: Where are we? We're still in my lab, in a way, but at the same time we're very far away from where we were. We're not in Seattle anymore. We're in a place where nobody has ever been before. We're very far from our friends and your family.

"So we'll need to get back. Trouble is, right now I don't know how to get us back. But don't worry about that, I'll find a way." David looked down at the children beside him to see how they were reacting.

"What happened?" Melissa asked. "Why can't we go home?" She looked bewildered.

"That equipment over there is a twistor machine. Vickie and I have been working on it for the last few months. We discovered that it can move things from our world to this one. Those men that came were trying to steal the machine. I had decided to turn it on so they wouldn't be able to steal it. It was set to send itself where they couldn't get it. But we were too close to it when it moved itself, so it moved us here too. Wherever 'here' is."

"This," David gestured toward the ceiling and walls, "is a hole in a very big tree, in the middle of a forest full of other big trees. The wood here," he knocked the curving wall with his knuckles, "is the inner wood of the tree. We have a sort of treehouse to live in. There are animals here; the green bird on the branch tells us that much. But with our treehouse, we should be safe from animals and well protected from the weather.

"We're about thirty feet above the ground. If any of us fell from here, we'd be killed or badly hurt. Our first job is to make a safe way for getting down to the ground. I'm going to put together a sort of rope ladder using that coil of big wire over there. When we're outside we'll have to look around and see what we can find. We don't have much food or the other things that we're going to need, like water and warm clothes. We don't even have a bathroom.''

Jeff giggled, then looked serious, then worried.

"Don't worry, Jeff," said David. "We'll make one."

Melissa asked, "David, how can we be in your lab and far away in a new place at the same time? Shouldn't we be either in one place or the other?"

"Melissa, I can't explain that too well," said David, "because I don't completely understand it myself. But there are other universes, places that are 'parallel' to ours, lying next to each other like the pages of a book. This place is on one page, the place we came from is on another page, and there are still other pages lying very close by. But they're in a direction we can't turn, so we never see them. The twistor machine makes a kind of bubble, and everything inside the bubble is turned in that extra direction and gets swapped from one page to another. Anything inside the bubble on our page is exchanged with whatever was in the same place on the other page. It's like one of those rotating theater stages that pivots, moving one set in front of the audience while it moves another set away. Can you visualize that?"

Melissa frowned and then nodded.

"Just before those men came in, I'd been making some measurements. I had the twistor field set to make a very big bubble, the size of those curving walls you see over there. Those settings were still in the computer when the twistor transition came, so the part of the laboratory that was inside the bubble was rotated here. Most of the lab must be filled with a giant wooden ball right now!"

Jeff laughed at the idea, but then looked around with a worried expression, wrinkled his nose, and asked, "Where are we gonna sleep, David?"

David laughed, "That, at least, is no problem, Jeff. There's a folding cot and two sleeping bags in the cabinet, mine and Vickie's. We keep them here for when we have to watch an experiment all night. You and Melissa can share the cot and Vickie's bag. I'll make myself a mattress out of some of that cryostat insulation over there."

David stood and walked to the hole. "Our first problem is that we've got to make the hole bigger and smoother so we can get out more easily. Then I'll drop some wire down as a climbing rope and climb down. I'll find some small trees or big fallen branches. There's a saw wire in the toolbox, so I can cut them up as rungs for the ladder. Then we can all get up and down easily. We can pull the ladder up at night for safety, like a drawbridge at a castle."

Jeff looked out. "David," he said, "that big green bird's still out there. Maybe you could shoot it with the gun, so we'd have more to eat."

"No!" Melissa objected. "Maybe it's a nice bird; maybe we can feed it."

David looked speculatively at the green bird, still picking at the branch. "No, Jeff," he said, "we're not that desperate for food. Not yet. We don't understand anything about this place, and we can't start by killing things at our doorstep. That bird seems to be eating something on the branch, maybe insects that are attacking the tree. Killing it might indirectly injure the tree. And besides, the gun shoots explosive bullets. It'd blow that bird into little pieces. There wouldn't be enough of it left to make a good bite."

"Oh," Jeff said, "I wouldn't wanna do that!" Melissa smiled.

"We should think of ourselves as explorers, not hunters," David continued. "This is a whole new world where no one has ever been before. We will have to find food and water and firewood as soon as we can, but we have to be very observant and very careful. There may be dangerous animals here. Or snakes. Or stinging insects. Or poisonous plants. We've no idea what we've gotten ourselves into. We shouldn't disturb things until we understand them. We're the pioneers. Since we've discovered this world, we get to explore it. But you must always remember, explorers have to be very careful. OK?"

Melissa and Jeff nodded solemnly. Then Jeff brightened. "David, can we put up a flag, like real explorers? Like those old-time astronaut guys did on the moon?''

"Hey, that's a great idea!" said David, winking at Melissa. "I've got some computer paper and colored pens right here. You can make us a flag, and we can claim the territory! I'll take your picture, Jeff, and when we get back you'll be on television like Neil Armstrong. And Melissa, I want you to go to the cabinet and get out the orange sleeping bag and the aluminum cot. Do you know how to set up a folding cot? Good. Find a nice spot where you two can bed down tonight. OK?" Jeff, a happy smile on his face, immediately set to work gathering materials for the flag, while Melissa rummaged in the cabinet.

David selected a grease pencil from the desk drawer and began to trace a rectangle extending downward from the hole he had made. Their new door wasn't going to be pretty, but it would allow them to climb outside. Then the work of organizing their survival would really begin.

Martin Pierce, seated at his broad desk before the flat screen of his terminal, stared in disbelief at the newly decrypted message from Puget Sound Reference Service. The incompetent fools! The simple scheme for getting the twistor apparatus from Saxon's laboratory with ''movers'' who arrived a bit ahead of schedule had seemed foolproof, a potentially huge gain with a very little downside.

But now the simple operation had been hideously transformed into a scandal involving the disappearance and apparent kidnapping or murder of three people, two of them small children. His agents had left blood everywhere, and a police investigation was in progress. Pierce considered the implications. With children missing and evidence of violence, the FBI would certainly be called in, and nosy reporters would not be far behind. Megalith's isolation from this botched operation must be preserved. If this problem wasn't controlled and cauterized immediately the corporation could be discredited or destroyed, its stocks and bonds made worthless, its corporate officers sent to prison.

Professor Allan D. Saxon was the key. This morning Saxon and his lawyer had done everything they could to generate confusion and delay any signing of agreements. It appeared that Allan Saxon, using some clever ruse that Pierce had not yet penetrated, had managed to thwart Pierce's plans to obtain the twistor apparatus, even while he sat haggling over contract details with the lawyers. He was a tricky, devious son of a bitch.

Saxon must now be hiding the twistor apparatus somewhere, and, as the leader of the research team that had discovered the twistor effect, he knew how to exploit it. And he knew enough to implicate Pierce and Megalith in this mess. If Saxon could be removed from the picture, the whole thing would blow over in a month or so. If Saxon could be made to reveal the present location of the twistor apparatus and provide the details of how it worked, Pierce might yet turn a tidy profit from this operation. But if the bastard told all that he knew to the FBI . . .

Pierce reached for the telephone and dialed Megalith Corporate Security. In a few minutes he was able to determine that Saxon and his lawyer had already boarded a plane to Seattle, out of immediate reach. Pierce was going to have to take charge of this himself.

He consulted his schedule for the rest of the afternoon and tomorrow. Nothing that couldn't be postponed. He gave Darlene the details of how to rearrange his schedule. It was now after four, but if he moved fast . . . He ordered the corporate jet readied and a flight plan filed for a San Francisco-to-Seattle flight to take off at 6:30 P.M. He spent the next twenty minutes preparing, encrypting, and transmitting a set of instructions to PSRS. Then he extracted a prepacked tan leather suitcase from an upper shelf of his closet and headed for the door. It was going to be a long day.

Standing beside Melissa on the mat of oddly shaped orange leaves, David inhaled the strange smells of the forest. He looked up along the massive rounded wall of the tree trunk to his recent handiwork. The crude ladder, two lengths of heavy electrician's wire supporting rough wooden rungs, snaked out of the dark hole ten meters above them and cascaded down the wall of light brown bark to their feet.

The bark had a scale pattern that suggested a colossal brown fish, but the scales projected upward instead of downward. That arrangement perhaps helped to collect rainwater and nutrients during rainstorms. Whatever the purpose of the bark structure, it would make the big trees easier to climb. He frowned. Easier for large animals to climb, too . . .

The large green bird—David was beginning to regard it as the owner of this tree—was now moving along the up-thrust bark of the trunk. It grasped the bark with the talons of its fore and hind feet, and it probed and pecked with its beak into the cupped recesses of the upthrust scales, collecting whatever was there and occasionally tilting its head backward to swallow. David noticed similar green birds on the other trees nearby, but never more than one per tree. *Treebirds*, he thought, local property owners.

He walked to the foot of the ladder and glanced at his watch. It was now four-thirty. The light wouldn't last much longer. He fitted a blank ROM cartridge into the side of the little CCD camera, set it for sequential pictures at tenth-of-a-second intervals, and sighted upward, taking a quick shot of their green treebird at work.

Jeff emerged from the hole, his new-made flag gripped in his teeth, and David started the camera again. Jeff turned to wave triumphantly, causing David to catch his breath, and then began to climb down the ladder. The rapid descent was executed with a carefree skill probably acquired on playground slides and climbers. When he reached the ground, he turned and looked inquiringly at David. David pointed to a small patch of ground that had been cleared of leaves and where the soil was already loosened.

Carefully, Jeff planted the stick in the freshly turned soil of the planet. "I, Jeffrey Ernst, claim this u-ni-verse . . ." he paused to think, ". . . this ter-ri-to-ry in the name of the Uni-ted States of Ame-ri-ca," he recited the words they had composed together. David and Melissa laughed delightedly at the performance. David stopped the camera, and they clapped. Then he took a shot of the computer-paper flag, its crudely formed stars and stripes fluttering and crinkling in the late-afternoon breeze.

He glanced upward. The treebird was regarding them quizzically from its elevated perch.

* * *

They were out of the tree, the flag duly planted. Now David was feeling a growing fatigue. They needed a fireplace and workplace, a center for their activities. That was the first order of business. He pried up another large flat stone. Underneath, white grublike creatures with large brown pincers squirmed and scurried for the cover of leaves. Pink worms, their heads iridescent with bright and changing interference colors, sank into the bare earth. It was a different world, he mused.

As David carried the stone toward the site of what would soon be their new fireplace, he crossed the multicolored line he had spotted from the tree. He stopped and looked down at it. It was an intricate linear pattern made of linked splatters of color, white, red, green, blue, and violet splotches that repeated after a few meters. Now he noticed that the other trees were ringed with similar trains of color, but the patterns were not the same. Curious . . .

He continued to the pile of stones, dropping the one he was carrying beside the others. Sinking down on a mound of orange leaves, he inhaled the rich, mysterious smell of the forest. He must pace himself to avoid complete exhaustion. The light was going fast, and they would need to eat soon. Leaning back, he looked upward, following the soaring column of their tree. It had the familiar tree shape, but that familiarity was an illusion. It was not even close to any tree he'd seen before.

A flying insectlike creature landed on the flat stone and crawled across it. It had the usual six legs and double wings, with a triple-segmented, slightly iridescent blue body. A dangerous-looking triple-pronged trident projected from the rear of its fat, elongated abdomen. The basic insect design was there, yet it did not resemble any Earth insect David could recall. He tentatively extended his hand in its direction, but it flew off.

His gaze moved downward. The dried leaves on the ground, he now noticed, also had an unusual form. Groups of feathery, orange-brown leaflets organized themselves into a shape that was like the club suit of a playing card. The leaf was a fractal, David realized. He could resolve tiny club shapes that formed large club shapes, and those formed still larger club shapes, and so on. Nature was using some genetic subroutine to repeat the same pattern over and over at increasing scale. He smiled, imagining the tiny club shape repeating itself infinitesimally inward, down to minuscule club-shaped molecules. He rubbed one of the leaves between his fingers until it powdered to an orange dust; then he smelled his fingers. The characteristic smell of the forest was there, now greatly magnified. It was a green, resinous, spicy smell. Might taste good in spaghetti sauce, he mused . . .

Again he surveyed his surroundings. If he squinted his eyes, this might almost have been a California forest of giant sequoias. But on closer examination almost every detail was unfamiliar, alien. This is not Earth, he thought, it's a whole new world in another universe. He inhaled deeply, allowing the chill of alienness to penetrate successive layers of his consciousness. He felt so isolated, so alone . . .

Above the dark hole of their "apartment" he could see through the dense upper branches a few wisps of clouds interspersed with blue sky. The great rising trunk gave the illusion of continuing upward to infinity. Yet it was clear that this tree, as enormous as it was, was no larger than most of the others nearby. He stood back and sighted with the CCD camera. He zoomed the lens to maximum focal length, panned up the tree, and then did a slow sweep of the other trees, concluding with a dezoom back to maximum wide angle.

He recalled a family vacation many years ago. His father had taken the family to Redwood National Park in California, and then they'd driven to the giant sequoia groves of Yosemite. Both parks had enormous trees. Some that were thousands of years old. One had been so large that an automobile could drive through it. But the trees in this forest were certainly bigger. Wait 'til Weyerhauser finds out about this place, he thought grimly, recalling hikes in the Cascades on forest trails that wound past the slash-and-burn devastation left in the path of logging operations.

Melissa appeared around the curve of the tree, her arms loaded with dead branches. "There's lots of wood on the ground around here, David," she said. "And I saw some mushrooms, too."

Jeff was just behind her, panting and dragging a huge branch that should have been too big for him to handle. He pulled it up near the pile that Melissa had started. Then he ran over to David. "David!" he breathed. "There was a squirrel on that tree over there! It was a funny greenish color at first, but it sort of flicked its fur and turned brown when it saw me. It ran around the tree, and I couldn't find it any more. David, it had six legs!"

David followed Jeff to the spot, but there was no sign of any squirrel-like animal, only a few treebirds climbing on trunks of the big trees and some smaller birds flying in the high branches of the forest canopy. He squinted upward at the flying birds. There was something odd about the way they flew, but they were too far away to pinpoint the source of the strangeness. Well, forests should have birds and squirrels, he thought, even if they're strange and green and change colors and have too many legs.

17

The fading light through the door-hole was almost gone. David looked at his watch, noting that it was just after 7:40. Sunset came at the same time in this universe, he thought. He peered into the darkness. He thought he could make out vague shapes flitting among the trees. Bats? Or something else? He shrugged and pulled up the ladder, rolling it into a rough cylinder and placing it on the floor near the opening. He covered the door-hole for the night with a large circle of aluminum-covered Fiberglas insulation, secured in place by several horizontal wooden branches tied to the nails driven into the wall.

David felt a sense of satisfaction. The children had been adequately fed, and he'd had enough also. He'd built a cook fire on the forest floor. At first he'd been very careful with the fire, concerned that a larger oxygen fraction in the air or combustibles in the wood might make a fire in this world more dangerous and harder to control. He remembered that some archaeologists had found air bubbles in eighty-million-year-old amber that had a very high oxygen content. But the fire was very Earth-normal, so David had proceeded with dinner. They had dined on their small supply of instant soup, Vickie's peanut butter, and selections from David's sack lunch. He'd set the CCD camera to make stills of them all sitting together at their first dinner.

David had also sampled some "experimental" items: nuts, berries, several mushrooms, and some tuberous roots they'd found growing in the forest near the treehouse. He had made careful notes on where the various items had been found, their appearances, and their flavors. Several items he had rejected after a tiny taste. His small taste samples indicated that one of the nut varieties was quite delicious. A variety of pink berry was very sweet and tasty. One of the mushroom types looked exactly like the morels that grew in the Cascade forest near Seattle. Fried with a dab of peanut butter, it tasted truly wonderful. Nevertheless, he limited his intake to small amounts consumed at fifteen-minute intervals, and he'd refused the children's requests to share in these "snacks." He explained that explorers had to be extremely careful about poisonous plants.

Now they were all in their beds. David had decreed that they must be in bed by sundown. The children had not been happy with the early bedtime. Melissa suggested that they sit down below around the cook fire and sing songs, as her family often did on camping trips. David had rejected this suggestion because of the possibility of dangerous animals. She was unhappy and suggested that a high priority should be given to the making of lamps and candles so they could work in the treehouse in the evenings. He complimented her for having a good idea. Some of Sam's tools did have rechargeable batteries, and there was a small solar recharger in the toolbox, but candles seemed a better solution to the problem of illumination. If there was any way to make the twistor apparatus work, the small power tools were going to be needed for that purpose.

"David, what's today?" Melissa asked from the cot.

He paused. It took a few seconds to realize that it was still the same day that had begun so uneventfully only twelve hours ago. "Today is Wednesday, October thirteenth," he said. David remembered that by now he should have picked up Vickie and taken her to the Ernsts' for dinner.

"Then it's time for our story!" said Melissa triumphantly. "You always tell us a story after dinner on Wednesdays."

"Yeah, David," said Jeff. "You were going to tell us what happened to Ton."

David sighed. It had been a long day, and his mind was numb. But the weekly story was a link with their normal existence. It should help them to make the difficult adjustment to life in this new world.

"OK," he said, gathering his thoughts, "I'm sure you

recall what happened last time. Ton had been kidnapped by corsair pirates and sold as a slave to Zorax, the evil magician. Zorax had sent Ton into some dangerous underground ruins to fetch some things he'd called 'mementoes.' But when Ton had done it and had wanted to be pulled out along with the objects he'd fetched, Zorax became angry and made an explosion that closed the opening. Ton was trapped underground.''

"Yeah!" said Jeff, "What happened after the 'sploshun?''

"After the explosion," said David, "there was much crashing and banging and sounds of cave-in along the passages, and Ton was left in utter darkness. There must have been much dust in the air, because his eyes stung and he coughed a lot. He pressed his face low near one corner of the passage where the air was better, and he waited. It became so quiet that he could hear only his own heartbeat. After a while it became easier to breathe. But there was no light at all. Ton was lost in total darkness. And he was scared, very scared.

"But he remembered that his father had once told him that when you are in a difficult situation, the first thing to do is to take inventory."

"What's enden-tory?" asked Jeff.

Melissa grunted in annoyance.

"Taking inventory," said David, "means making a list of everything you have that you might be able to use. Like we did today when we took everything out of Sam's toolbox and the supply cabinet."

"Oh," said Jeff. Melissa snorted.

"Feeling around in the dark," David continued, "Ton tried to find the things he had brought from the passage. His hand bumped against something smooth. It was the leather bag. He sat in the darkness and undid the thong that held it closed, then opened the top. A faint glow was coming from the bag. He reached inside, and his hand encountered something hard and cool and smooth. As his fingers touched the object, the light from the bag became much brighter. He lifted the object out. It was a crystal sphere, and it glowed brightly with its own internal light. Lifting it to eye level,

Ton could see fuzzy blobs of white and blue and green, but his eyes couldn't quite focus on what was there. As long as the sphere was in contact with his hand, it gave a bright light, but if he put it on the floor and moved his hand away, the light dimmed. Taking the sphere and holding it higher, he looked around. He was still in the passage, which now was littered with rocks and large dressed stones that had fallen from the ceiling. On the floor were the other 'mementoes' for Zorax, the roll of carpet and the corroded old weapon. And there was also the small leather-bound book that he had taken from the skeleton. The basket, with the rope still attached and leading upward, was resting on the floor. Ton pulled on the rope and it came free, its upper end frayed and burnt.

"He rolled up the rope, perhaps five meters of it, and placed it and the rest of the 'mementoes' in the basket. He retraced his steps backward down the passage. It soon became clear what had made the cave-in sounds after the explosion. There were many places where the roof had fallen in, partially blocking the passage. As for the side passages, all of the heavy stone doors had fallen during the cave-ins, completely sealing them. Ton continued down the central corridor, and just beyond the second passage on the right he found that the main passage was completely blocked. The tomb that he had entered was sealed, perhaps forever.

"Ton searched the passage desperately. It was now clear that he was trapped deep underground with no food or water and no way out. He was going to die, soon and unpleasantly. Years from now someone would perhaps find his bones in the tunnel and wonder who he had been and how he had come to be trapped here.

"He lay down on the littered floor and cried in the darkness. It wasn't fair. He had been kidnapped and beaten and enslaved and stripped naked and sold and badly treated and now left to die, and none of it was his fault. He wept bitterly for a long time and at last fell asleep.

"Ton came awake suddenly. Groggy, he reached for the dim sphere, and when the light came to full brightness he could see that nothing had changed. He decided that he felt better, and sitting on the floor of the tunnel, he began to examine his few possessions. The thin corroded weapon had an inscription written along the shaft, but in an unfamiliar script and language. The hilt was functional and unadorned, but showed signs of having once been gilded. Ton, the armorer's apprentice, selected a piece of sandstone from the floor and polished the weapon. The corrosion, probably the remains of a decayed scabbard, came away easily, leaving the rounded shaft bright and shining.

"Next, Ton unrolled the rug. Parts of it were folded over and sewn to the coarse undersurface, but the main part made a rectangle a bit less than a meter wide and about a meter and a half long. Its woven design was intricate and rather beautiful, but the colors had been dulled by time. Ton found a flat level space on the floor and smoothed the rug on it, then seated himself on it. If he was going to die here, he might as well be comfortable.

"Finally, he placed the leather-bound book in his lap and examined it. He found that if he held the sphere against his chest with his chin he could grasp the book with both hands and have sufficient light for reading.

"And so Ton began to read. The pages were handwritten in a thin spidery scrawl, and fortunately were in Ton's native language. But there were many difficult and unfamiliar words. It took him some time to get the drift of the text, but with persistence the general content of the book became fairly clear. This was a book about magic, or, more specifically, about how certain magic objects or talismans were used. Much of the writing was obscure and confusing, but Ton became convinced that Zorax's 'mementoes' were among the talismans discussed in the book. There was much discussion of something called the 'Urorb.' Ton concluded this was probably the very sphere that presently was nestled under his chin. Apparently it could be used not only for making light but also for 'farscrying,' whatever that was. There was something called the 'Surplice' which sounded like the rug he was sitting on, but was apparently intended to be worn like a loose coat and was used for 'farwending.' The description of how to do this was very involved and confusing. And there was the description of a weapon, probably the swordlike object, called the 'Pricklance,' which was used for 'farpiercing.' This also involved the use of the Urorb in some way. That was about as much as Ton was able to comprehend from the writing. The remainder of the book dealt with words, objects, and concepts of which he had no grasp at all. Finally Ton put down the book and released the Urorb, for his neck was getting quite stiff from holding it for so long.

"Lying on his back, he held up the shining sphere and gazed into its depths. The book had said something about fixing a place in the mind for 'farscrying.' He thought of his home, of his mother and father and what they must have gone through when he was kidnapped.

"Suddenly Ton realized that he was looking into his mother's kitchen, and that she was putting bread into the oven. He felt very happy to see her and called out to her. But she showed no sign of hearing him. Her eyes looked red, as if she had recently been crying. He found that he couldn't watch his mother for long without feeling very sad and homesick. So he began to experiment with the Urorb.

"He soon found that by concentrating on any place he knew well, he could produce a view of it. For a while he was fascinated by this, but soon the growing hunger pangs in his stomach brought him back to reality. Farscrying was a powerful trick, but it didn't get him any food or water or any way out of his predicament. He was still trapped."

Hearing deep, regular breathing, David peered through the dimness. Melissa and Jeff were both sound asleep. Too bad, thought David. Just when the story was getting interesting.

He stood, stretched, and walked to the door-hole. He unfastened the branches that held the batting in place and moved it aside. Leaning out through the door-hole, he inhaled the rich night smell of the forest and savored the touch of cool breeze on his cheeks. It was quite dark now, and his dark-adapted eyes could make out patches of stars through gaps in the forest canopy. One star seemed bright. Very bright. Venus? No, it wasn't a planet. It was quite distinctly twinkling. Sirius? Canopus? Perhaps Arcturus? No, it had a soft yellow color, probably G- or K-class.

He tried to recall the brighter stars he'd memorized when,

as a teenager, he'd mapped the Illinois skies with his home-made reflector telescope. He was sure that there was no such star in Earth's northern hemisphere. Interesting. Perhaps some of Sol's neighbors were closer in this universe. The four-plus light-years to Alpha Centauri had always seemed an unreasonably large distance.

The door chimes sounded, and a hollow-eyed Elizabeth Ernst hurried to the door. Her children had been missing for over ten hours. Through the viewer she saw two large men in dark suits. She opened the door.

"Good evening," said the taller of the two, "I'm Agent Bartley of the FBI. This is my associate, Agent Cooper." Both men presented her with wallets containing picture IDs. "We've been assigned to investigate the disappearances," Bartley continued. "We'd like to ask a few questions about your children."

"Come in," said Elizabeth, and introduced herself. She led the agents to the dining room, where a dejected Paul and a worried Victoria Gordon were seated at the dining table. A platter of broiled salmon was in the middle of the table, and on their plates was food that had just been served. Elizabeth performed the introductions and invited the two men to sit down. They did so but declined Elizabeth's offers of food or coffee.

"Agent Bartley and I met this afternoon," Vickie said. "We talked for about an hour." She took a bite of salmon.

Bartley nodded and produced a brightly colored children's book from his briefcase. "Do any of you recognize this book," he asked.

Vickie shook her head. "No," said Elizabeth.

"She hasn't seen it," Paul said. "I only bought it this morning. It's about dinosaurs. Melissa said she wanted to show it to David—" Paul stopped talking abruptly and put his head in his hands.

Elizabeth looked at him with concern. She was worried about Paul. He'd never been able to deal very well with strong emotions. "Where did you find the book?" she asked, turning to Bartley.

"It was on a table near the door in the laboratory room,

ma'am," he said. "The fingerprints on it match the school prints of your daughter."

"What about the blood," Paul asked in a strained voice.

"The red substance found on the floor of the laboratory is definitely human blood," said Bartley. "The lab analysis confirmed that. But we have no matches. We checked Dr. Harrison's blood group and also those of your children. The blood in the laboratory came from someone else."

Paul looked relieved. Elizabeth noticed that he was drumming his fingers on one knee, a sign of tension.

"Now, Professor Ernst," Agent Cooper said, "would you please tell us what happened this morning?"

Paul recounted for them how he had taken the children first to the bookstore, then to his office. "I was working at my terminal and they were sitting reading their books quietly," he said. "Then I looked up, and they were gone."

"I wasn't worried at first." The fingers drummed. "They've been to Physics Hall with me many times before. They know their way around, and it isn't a particularly dangerous place. I thought at first they'd just gone to the restroom or were visiting with one of my colleagues down the hall. But when they didn't return, I became concerned and began to look around. I started on the third floor. Then I got one of the secretaries to check all the women's restrooms. Finally, I thought of David. Since he's a great friend of theirs, it occurred to me that they might have gone to his laboratory. I'd taken them there just last week, and he showed them his experiment and gave them each a balloon—" At the word "balloon" Paul's voice broke, and he was quiet. The finger drumming continued, faster.

"David Harrison is a good friend of the whole family," Elizabeth said, covering the pause. "For the past six months he's been our regular guest for dinner on Wednesday evenings. He brings a good bottle of wine and we have dinner. He and Paul talk physics, and after dinner he tells the children fairy tales." Agent Cooper's face assumed an expression that might have been a smirk, and he wrote something in his notebook.

"What happened when you went to Harrison's lab, sir?" Bartley asked.

Paul cleared his throat, his hand quiet. "Professor Weinberger was there with some campus police officers. Vickie was there too, and she showed me what they had found. The big wooden sphere, and all that blood . . ." He paused for a moment, then continued. "I was very concerned for David, but I didn't connect it with Melissa and Jeff until Sam, uh, Mr. Weston told me that he'd seen the children heading for David's lab a bit earlier. I guess the book clinches it." He shook his head, then stared at the table. The fingers drummed again.

Elizabeth looked directly at Agent Bartley. "What do you think happened to them?" she asked firmly. She wanted the official view. She was not secure with the "twistor field" explanations Paul and Vickie had been telling her.

"There was a trail of blood, ma'am," said Bartley, consulting his notebook. "It led to the loading area behind Physics Hall. We established that a van had been observed parked there with the motor running. We've located the van and traced it. It was rented yesterday by an individual using stolen identification. The van contained bloodstains that match those in the physics laboratory. It was abandoned in a parking area behind the drugstore in the U-Village Shopping Center. A witness at the Goodwill collection station there saw four men in movers' coveralls leave the vehicle and drive away in a car. She did not recall seeing any children with them, but that doesn't prove anything. There may have been others involved who took them before the van was abandoned.

"Our other lead is the listening devices that were found in the laboratory a few days ago. Mr. Weston gave them to us. We've identified them as a commercial product, and we're tracing them back to the supplier. In summary, Mrs. Ernst, we believe Dr. Harrison and your children were kidnapped by the four individuals seen in the physics building."

Paul suddenly looked up, an expression of disbelief on his face. "Kidnapped? That's absurd! What about the sphere? They went through the twistor transition. You can't just leave them there! We've got to get them back, if they're still alive!"

Agent Cooper raised an eyebrow. "We have no information about any 'twisted condition,' Professor Ernst,'' he said. ''What are you referring to, sir?''

Paul looked wildly at the agent, his fingers drumming hard. Elizabeth wondered what he would say next. ''Dr. Harrison and Miss Gordon have been working on a device that makes things . . . it converts . . .'' He stopped abruptly and for the first time looked directly into Agent Cooper's wide blue eyes. Then he looked down at his rhythmically moving hand for a moment. ''Never mind . . .'' he said finally. ''The physics . . . it's complicated. You . . . wouldn't understand.''

Vickie opened her mouth, looked at Cooper, and closed it again.

Agent Bartley looked closely at Paul, then at Victoria, but he didn't say anything. Agent Cooper began to ask a stream of questions centered around David's background, interests, and personal life. Victoria answered most of them.

When the agents finally ran out of questions, Elizabeth felt strangely relieved, as if she had been a suspect held in custody and was about to be released. Bartley gave her his business card, then gave one also to Paul. On the back of each card he'd written a telephone number.

''You already have my card, Miss Gordon,'' he said. ''If any of you receives contacts, ransom demands, or new information, call me at this number immediately.'' Finally the two agents rose and walked to the door.

As Elizabeth showed the agents out, Victoria looked across the table at Paul. He looked in very bad shape. She noticed that his fingers were nervously drumming against his knee. She considered how to get his mind working in more constructive channels. He was staring with rigid intensity at his plate of uneaten salmon. ''Isn't it odd,'' she said, ''that they didn't ask more about the sphere.''

As Elizabeth was seating herself again at the table, Paul gulped down the remainder of his wine. He looked across at Vickie, inhaling deeply. ''No, it's not,'' he said. ''The sphere is a piece of the puzzle that doesn't fit with their preconceived notions, so they're pretending it isn't there or that it isn't relevant. That attitude is hard to penetrate. I couldn't see the point of telling them about the twistor effect," he said. "Even if they believed me, it would only distract them from finding the thugs with the van. And who knows, maybe those people did kidnap David and the children. . . ."

"I doubt it," said Vickie, shaking her head. "That big wood sphere proves that the twistor apparatus is involved in this. It transported itself somewhere, and probably took David and the children with it. Those fake movers must be the ones who bugged our lab. I think they'd been listening and finally came to steal the twistor hardware. I'd guess David set up for a big field and twisted the machine away to keep them from getting it. And I'm very much afraid that he and the children went with it. Otherwise, someone would surely have seen them leave with the movers."

Paul was again staring fixedly at the table and drumming his fingers.

Victoria took a deep breath, trying at the same time to make eye contact with Paul and Elizabeth to project enthusiasm. "OK folks, now for the hopeful news," she began. "We learned some things this afternoon that I think are going to be important. I was late getting here because the results are still coming in.

"You see, I'm a member of a support network at the U of W organized by a group of women graduate students in the sciences. We get together once a month to talk about our work and our problems and our accomplishments, and we help each other when we can. Today I needed help, so I yelled. And I got help. Lots of it."

Paul's fingers stopped. He was looking across the table at her, interested. Elizabeth had also turned to look directly at her.

"A friend of mine in the botany department," Vickie continued, "is doing her Ph.D. on the cell structure of trees. This afternoon she used their scanning electron microscope on a slice of the wood from the big sphere. She says that the microstructure of the wood is qualitatively different from any she's seen before. She had the whole department in looking at it. They're very excited about the 'radical species variant' she's found."

Paul rubbed his chin and nodded.

"I got a chemistry grad-student friend to run a mass spectrograph scan on an ash sample from the wood," said Vickie after she was sure they'd digested the first piece of information. "She discovered that the isotope ratios are all wrong. There's far too much carbon 13 and not enough magnesium 26, for example—"

She was interrupted by the ring of the telephone. Paul jumped, startled. His fingers began to drum again. Elizabeth answered the phone, then called Victoria. She talked quietly for some minutes, making notes on a small pad from her purse. Then she returned to the dining table.

"That was another friend," Vickie said. "She's a grad student in forestry. I convinced her to drop what she was doing to perform an electrophoresis bio-assay of a pulped wood sample for me. She sounded disappointed. She'd heard about the other results and was expecting something spectacular. Instead, she says that the amino acids and proteins in the wood look pretty normal. About the same ratios as normal wood from Douglas fir. There's even a trace of chlorophyll in the sample. The biochemistry, with a few minor differences, looks the same as would be expected for an ordinary fir tree."

"But there were all those other differences," Elizabeth said.

"Yes," Victoria said. "The wood sphere is not from any tree growing on Earth, but nevertheless its basic biochemistry is almost identical."

Vickie noticed that Paul looked more hopeful. He rubbed his chin. "It means that the shadow universe where they went isn't just an empty vacuum," he said. "There's life there, carbon-based life! Advanced plant life at that. Woody trees with green leaves. That kind of tree appeared on our Earth at about the same time as the early mammals, as I recall. The chlorophyll means air with oxygen in it. If that's where David and the children went, they could survive!"

Victoria nodded agreement. "And here's another thing that might interest you," she continued. "I borrowed a ladder from the janitor just before I came here and climbed up on the top of the wood sphere. I wanted to get a look at it from that perspective. From above you can see clear annual growth rings, hundreds of them. The ones with the largest radius of curvature are near the north wall of the lab, and the ones with the smallest are near the south wall. The radius of curvature of the biggest rings is about eight meters. That means the tree they came from must have been at least sixteen meters in diameter. That's bigger than the biggest giant sequoias. When I was looking at the rings, I noticed something else. Near the north wall there's a qualitative change in the wood. Its color becomes lighter, and it's more moist and softer.''

Elizabeth looked thoughtful. "That's how the sapwood looks near the cambium layer," she said. "You know, the living and growing part at the outside surface of the tree that's just under the bark. Perhaps if they are inside a big tree, there's a chance they can get out. David's very resourceful.''

Victoria thought for a moment. "David might just have the tools to do that." She remembered the equipment in Sam's number-three toolbox, which had disappeared along with David and the children.

"Your bio-assay bothers me, Vickie," Paul said. His voice sounded more normal now. "It's altogether too Earth-normal. Could a separate biochemistry that similar to ours actually have evolved in a shadow universe in complete isolation, right down to the same amino acid ratios?''

"That's rather unlikely," said Elizabeth. "It's more probable that there's some kind of connection that allowed the two biosystems to cross-seed each other.''

Paul nodded, but Victoria frowned. "That isn't possible, Paul, is it?" she asked.

"Maybe it is," said Paul. "Yesterday I noticed something very interesting that gives me an idea." He looked from Vickie to Elizabeth. "Have you ever heard of plasmoids or ball lightning?''

"I actually saw ball lightning once," said Elizabeth. "It was years ago. Some friends and I were camping in the Colorado Rockies when lightning struck a tree near us. After the lightning stroke a ball of the blue light ran right down to the bottom of the tree and then very slowly bounced above the ground in big arcs until it went into the lake and disappeared. There was a round burned spot on the ground at each place it had hit, and it made a cloud of steam when it hit the lake. It was spooky.''

"I don't know about ball lightning, but I've read about plasmoids," said Victoria. "A plasmoid is a kind of self-sustaining plasma that generates its own magnetic confinement field, right? A sort of self-contained ball of magneto-hydrodynamic energy.''

"Right," said Paul. "There've been random observations, but no one's ever been able to do a careful study of ball lightning or to produce it in the laboratory. Too much energy needed. The prevailing view is that ball lightning's an extremely energetic plasmoid that's occasionally generated by a lightning stroke, so energetic that it can survive at atmospheric pressure.''

Elizabeth nodded. "Fine, dear, but what does this have to do with our present problem?" she asked.

"Yesterday I happened to notice that the electromagnetic structure of a plasmoid is very similar to that of a twistor field. Plasmoids don't rotate, of course, but otherwise they're almost identical.''

"That's amazing," said Vickie. "Nature discovered the twistor field before we made one.''

Paul nodded. "Now suppose," he continued, "that a lightning ball like the one Elizabeth saw just happened to hit the ground and bounce in just the right way, so that the electromagnetic field was rotated at just the right rate. Then, by a very improbable lucky accident, it might twist everything in the field volume into a shadow universe or from a shadow universe into ours. Probably only tiny organisms like bacteria or moss or mold or fungus spores could survive such a twist, but it would be enough to couple together the evolution of life, at least the early stages, in any parallel shadow systems that contained Earthlike planets.'' He looked at his wife. "Elizabeth, you know a lot more about biosciences and such things than I do. What do you think?''

"Well," Elizabeth said, "I don't know about the physics part of your idea, but I think that if what you described happened only once in a million years that would still be often enough to have a profound effect on the evolution of primitive plants and organisms. There are many well-documented cases in the fossil record of new organisms appearing in a very short period of time and radically changing the ecosystem. It's called 'punctuated equilibrium.' Your scenario might very well lead to roughly parallel evolution in both systems, at least up to the point where the organisms or their seeds and spores got too big or fragile to use the lightning balls as transport vehicles.''

Victoria nodded. She had a feeling of rising excitement. It was beginning to make sense. "And that would explain," she said, "why the biochemistry of the tree wood is so similar but the details of the wood structure are so different. Convergent evolution up to a point, then evolutionary divergence. The shadow universe sounds like an interesting place. Similar but different. David and the children could survive in a place like that if they were careful."

"Paul?" asked Elizabeth, looking perplexed. "How could another planet occupy the same space as the Earth? I mean, wouldn't the gravity be doubled or something?"

"I worried about that when I realized the big wooden sphere in the lab must have come from an Earthlike planet," said Paul. "I think there's a way out. Geophysicists have always had difficulty in explaining how the Earth could be so dense inside. Its center is supposed to have about ten to fifteen times the density of the crust. Even if the interior is mostly iron-nickel under huge pressure, it's still difficult to account for such a big density. It's an old problem that geophysicists have learned to live with and ignore.

"But suppose the interior wasn't iron-nickel but something lighter. Then we could accommodate two or even three Earths superimposed on one another, as long as the others are made of shadow particles that only interact with themselves."

Vickie nodded, considering the new idea.

"So the evidence indicates," said Elizabeth, "that our children and David are probably in a very Earthlike world, with the same gravity as this one and with similar plant life. That makes me feel a lot better. And the children have David to take care of them."

"It also means," said Vickie, "that we need to do a fast rebuild of the twistor equipment and get them back. It took David and me ten months of hard work the first time. But this time it should be much easier; I know which corners to cut and what to leave out. With enough help and enough money I could have another unit ready in perhaps a month. But that's still a long time. . . ."

For the rest of the evening they made plans.

It was a soft, repetitive sound. David came awake from a light sleep and looked around. He held his breath, listening in the darkness that pressed against his straining eyes. The sound came again. One of the children was crying. He slipped from his sleeping bag and slid across the concrete floor in the direction of the cot where they were sleeping.

It was Jeff. He was half asleep, and he was crying softly to himself.

David put his hand on the small head. "What's the matter, Jeff?" he asked. "Are you all right?"

"M-Mommy." The small voice wavered. "I want Mommy."

David stroked his hair. "I know you do," he said. "I know you miss her, especially at night."

Jeff sniffed.

"When you're away from home," David said, "it helps to be with friends instead of all by yourself. I'm your friend, Jeff, and you're here with me. I'll take care of you. We'll take care of each other. If anything scares you, or if there's anything you need, you tell me just like you'd tell your mommy."

Jeff sniffed again. "OK," he said quietly.

David put his arms around Jeff and held him close. Then he settled on the floor next to him, one arm across the sleeping bag. It wasn't very comfortable, but he lay that way for a long time, until Jeff's quiet breathing became very slow and regular. Then David slowly raised himself and looked down at the sleeping child. For a moment his eyes felt moist at the corners, his throat tight. He swallowed and slipped back across the floor to his own sleeping bag.

Much later David awoke again with a start. Where . . . ?

He was disoriented for a moment, then realized he was still in the treehouse. He pushed the button of his watch, flashing its electroluminescent panel. 1:05 A.M. An unfamiliar sound had awakened him. It wasn't Jeff this time. He tried to recall what he'd heard. Then the sound came again, a low, vibrant wail. Carefully he retrieved the pistol and the big four-cell flashlight from their places on the floor beside him and moved silently across the floor to the ragged entrance of their treehouse. He removed the crossed branches, lifted aside the sheet of aluminized Fiberglas insulation that had covered the door-hole, and extended his head slowly into the darkness outside. The rough wood pressed against his lower chest. Nothing was visible in the faint starlight.

Then the sound came again, accompanied by rustling and snuffling noises from a place near the base of the tree. He could make out the sound of deep heavy breathing. There was an animal down there. David pointed the long krypton-bulb flashlight in the direction of the sounds and squeezed the switch button.

Two widely spaced greenish yellow eyes reflected the light. The animal was big—very big. And it was well supplied with curving yellow teeth and sharp dark claws. The large mouth had a long fringe of blood-red beard around its edge. That was all he could see before the creature shuffled bearlike behind the tree, leaving the impression of a mottled brown coat covering a massive humped back. And six legs. There had definitely been six legs. David took a deep breath and replaced the doorway covering. "Great!" he said to himself. "Furry six-legged monsters with big teeth and red beards. That's all we need."

The pistol in his hand looked small, inadequate. The creature had been enormous, and with that array of teeth it must be at least a part-time carnivore. It would take an elephant gun to kill something that size. The creature would hardly notice a bullet from his small-caliber pistol.

How many nocturnal carnivores are out there, David wondered. Do they climb trees and investigate interesting treehouses? He shuddered and lay back on his sleeping pad.

As he placed the weapon on the floor beside him, he recalled the three men who had come to the laboratory the previous morning. He wondered who had sent them and why. Obviously they had some connection with the bugging incident, and they had come to steal the twistor hardware. Saxon's plans for moving the apparatus, if known to these people, might have made a hijacking look easier. All they would have to do was come first with their own moving van, before the real movers arrived. They, whoever they were, must want the twistor apparatus for themselves. And now it was out of their reach. But Vickie wasn't. . . .

David didn't sleep well. The questions in his head kept demanding answers. What was happening now? With himself and the hardware out of reach, the only person who knew all the details of producing the twistor effect was Vickie. A feeling of helpless dread gripped his abdomen. Vickie. She must be in great danger. And he could do nothing even to warn her. His thoughts revolved about Vickie for the rest of a long, sleepless night.

There had to be something he could do.

18

THURSDAY MORNING, OCTOBER 14

Vickie was feeling apprehensive as they approached the office of the department chairman. After their strategy discussion last night, Paul had called Weinberger and asked him to arrange a meeting for this morning, to be attended by the three of them and Allan Saxon. Now Vickie was wondering if the meeting had been such a good idea. She had the sinking feeling that she was well out of her depth at this level of departmental politics.

But as they entered the physics office complex Weinberger greeted them very cordially, almost as if they were old friends he was meeting at the airport. As they entered his large office, he asked Paul in a quiet voice if there had been any word from the police about the children. Paul looked down and shook his head. Along the north wall a long walnut table was placed near the tall windows looking out on the gothic face of the library beyond. Weinberger directed them to seats at the table.

Allan Saxon was already standing behind a chair and leaning against the windows, his back toward the light, his head cocked to one side as if he were listening to a distant voice. He was dressed in his usual attire: dark jacket, color-coordinated slacks, and one of his broad bow ties that rested like a tropical butterfly against his throat. He reached across the table to shake hands with Paul. He smiled warmly at Vickie and raised a hand in a salute, the same gesture he might have used to hail a cab, she thought. He was looking very relaxed, considering all that had happened recently.

They all seated themselves at the table, with Ralph at the head and Paul and Vickie facing Allan. "First," said Weinberger, turning to Paul, "I'd like to make it clear that we are very concerned about the kidnapping of your children, and we understand the strain that you must be under, Paul. You requested this meeting, so I think we'll let you start." Saxon was looking across the table dispassionately, like a line judge at a tennis match.

Paul cleared his throat. "Let me review what's happened recently," he began, "so we'll all be talking from the same basis of information." He was superficially very calm as he described David's demonstration of the twistor effect and his subsequent theoretical work on it. He described the concept of shadow matter and the conversion that the twistor field produced.

Weinberger questioned Paul closely on some of the theoretical aspects of this. He seemed skeptical that Paul's version of superstring theory should be taken as having been verified by experiment. Vickie remembered having heard from some of the theory grad students that Weinberger was a field theorist whose work was somewhat at variance with the superstring approach.

Vickie was impressed with how Paul presented the case. She had seen Paul last night, shaken and unsure, and she understood what control he must be exerting now to hold together like this. Vickie watched the others, Weinberger sitting erect and concerned, Saxon slouched by the window, examining his fingernails.

Paul went on reviewing the incidents of yesterday, describing his last moments with his children. To Vickie his control as he spoke those words seemed icy. "I believe," he concluded, "that for some reason, perhaps to escape the phony movers, David enlarged the twistor field to about a five-meter radius and activated it. He, the children, and most of the apparatus were inside the field sphere at the time of transition. They were twisted to a shadow universe, the one from which the wood sphere came. There's a good possibility that David and my children are still alive. But without food and supplies—"

And air, Vickie thought.

"—they can't last long," Paul continued. "To get them back, we'll have to immediately rebuild the apparatus and reverse the effect as soon as possible. We'll need coordinated effort and support from the department for that. That's what we've come here to request." Paul stopped and looked at Weinberger, who in turn glanced at Allan. Vickie looked too, bracing herself for the explosion.

Allan smiled. "I don't want to question the judgment of my young colleague, particularly when he's under such severe emotional stress from the disappearance of his children. But it seems to me that, as theorists sometimes do, he's chasing up a blind alley. Myself, I've always favored simple explanations. Even Paul admits that his scenario involves theoretical ideas that are not widely accepted. Why do we need all these speculations about 'shadow matter' and new physical effects when we haven't eliminated the far greater likelihood that this was a simple case of kidnapping?" His voice rose dramatically to hammer home the point.

"We know that several men came into this building," Saxon continued, "then left in a van, and that this was coincidental with the disappearance of David and of Paul's children. I've no idea whether David Harrison, or for that matter Miss Gordon, had any previous contact with these men, but it's possible they came to help Harrison remove my equipment to some other place before it could be taken to my corporate laboratory, as I had intended."

Vickie felt rising anger. She glared across the table at Saxon, then at Paul. She noticed that there was color in his cheeks and that his fingers were drumming against his knee.

Saxon paused, smiling. "Of course, I have no evidence of any such thing. For the moment, I'll give both Harrison and Miss Gordon the benefit of the doubt and assume that these events were strictly the actions of strangers. I've no idea what the motives of these terrorists or thieves or whatever they are could be. But I find it likely that they were the ones who planted listening devices in my laboratory and my office. From what they learned by listening in, they must have decided to steal my equipment. They took Harrison along, willingly or unwillingly, because he knew how the equipment worked, and they took the children because they happened to be in the laboratory at the wrong time. I feel that unless the kidnappers decide to ask for a ransom, Paul's children, and perhaps Harrison also, will be released very soon. We have only to remain calm and wait them out.''

Paul's control must have snapped. He made an inarticulate sound and rose from his chair, face red, fists clenched, clearly about to lunge across the table at Saxon. Weinberger clutched Paul's arm, and Saxon held up a conciliatory hand. "I allowed you to talk without interruption, Paul," he said calmly. "I'd appreciate the same courtesy from you." Paul, struggling to regain his composure, took a deep breath and shook himself. Finally, at Weinberger's urging he resumed his seat.

"As for rebuilding the apparatus," Saxon continued, "I intend to do so in my corporate laboratory in Bellevue where the security is better. A university campus simply has too many comings and goings, too many students and visitors and janitors with passkeys, to protect anything that people, for whatever reason, are intent on stealing. We plan to do all the construction for the new apparatus at company expense. There's no need to burden the limited resources of the physics department. And I must point out that Miss Gordon's thesis project is no longer an issue here, since she already has enough data for a thesis. Isn't that so, Vickie?'' He aimed a bland smile in her direction.

Caught off guard, she stammered, "I . . . uh . . . think I may have enough data, but . . . uh . . . I can't really be sure yet.''

Saxon nodded. "Fine. You'll certainly have to analyze what data you already have first. By the time that's done, the new apparatus will be operating at my Bellevue laboratory, and you will be most welcome to come there and take more data if you need it. So I suggest—no, I insist that we allow the police and the FBI to do their jobs and find these criminals. Until they have eliminated the possibility of a kidnapping, I don't see how we can take Professor Ernst's hunches about other universes seriously enough to act on them. And it is clear that no crash program is required to allow Miss Gordon to complete her thesis project. Therefore,'' he said, turning to Weinberger, ''I don't see that any departmental action is required.''

''Wait! Look!'' Vickie exploded, surprising herself with the outburst, ''There's a bloody big wooden sphere in my lab that must weigh twenty tons. It had to come from somewhere. How the Hell do you—''

''Vickie, please!'' the chairman cut her off. ''We must all try to be more rational and less emotional about this. Remember that this is a university campus. Tricks like this are sometimes played. I recall some years ago that the engineering seniors disassembled a Jeep, carried the parts in the middle of the night into the office of the dean of engineering, and reassembled it to stand on the carpet in front of his desk, where he found it the next morning. The university, at considerable expense, hired mechanics to disassemble and remove the vehicle. That was all done very quietly and with no publicity. And the prank was never repeated. That's the way vandalistic pranks like this must be handled. One must have absolutely no publicity, because it only encourages the perpetrators.'' He stopped, giving every appearance of satisfaction that he had laid the problem to rest.

Victoria stared in disbelief. ''But we have mass spectrograph tests—'' she began.

''Please,'' Weinberger interrupted, his voice hardening, ''we've had enough discussion of this prank. Let me worry about dealing with it.''

She looked at Paul and rolled her eyes heavenward. She took several deep breaths. There was no point in arguing further. Still feeling the flush of her cheeks, she turned to Weinberger again. ''There is one other matter that I'd like to bring up, sir,'' she said, trying her best to imitate Paul's tight control. ''I'm very much opposed to the blanket of secrecy that Professor Saxon has chosen to place upon my thesis research. I find it unacceptable. I don't think that I can continue to work in this atmosphere. Therefore, I would like respectfully to request that Professor Ernst be made my thesis advisor. He has already agreed to this—'' She turned to Paul, and he nodded.

''My modified thesis project,'' she continued, ''will consist of the design and construction of the twistor apparatus, which is already done; the analysis of the data from measurements on the phenomenon, which will be done in the near future; and ongoing work with Professor Ernst on the theoretical aspects of the phenomenon." She looked challengingly at Allan, daring him to object.

He smiled at her instead. "Students in our department always have the prerogative of changing advisors whenever they wish, my dear. I certainly value the work that you've done under my direction, but I have no objections at all to the change you suggest, with two minor reservations. First, Paul should immediately assume the responsibility for paying the stipend for your research assistantship out of his Department of Energy contract. And second, I may at times require your services as a consultant when we are rebuilding the experimental apparatus." He looked across the table at Paul.

"The assistantship is no problem," Paul said through clenched teeth. "I'll make the arrangements today. As to the consulting, that's strictly up to Vickie. The department cannot compel her to consult for a private company, even yours, Allan." He smiled grimly back across the table.

Saxon was quiet for a moment. "Of course," he said finally, conceding the point.

Vickie turned to Weinberger. "As a part of my new thesis project, I intend to build a second-generation version of our twistor apparatus. I would like some departmental shop time and some equipment money for this. Can I have it?"

Weinberger paused. "I'm afraid that I will have to agree with Allan on this one, Vickie," he said finally. "The departmental equipment budget is very limited, and there are huge pressures on all of our resources, particularly in the area of technical services. I'm very much in sympathy with your concern for Paul's children and for David, but I simply cannot accept the emotional appeal from a graduate student and a theorist for the allocation of scarce departmental technical resources to rebuild an experiment when its originator and principal investigator, a distinguished senior professor of experimental physics in our department, is opposed. I'm truly sorry."

She looked directly at him, her green eyes flashing. "I take it from your answer, sir, that you have no objection to my construction of a new twistor apparatus provided there is no impact on departmental funds or allocated technical services."

Weinberger blinked. "No, I suppose not," he said mildly.

A few minutes later, after Weinberger had concluded the meeting and shown them cordially out, Paul walked with Vickie to his office. "Those stupid mindless assholes!" she raged as Paul closed the door.

"I guess I'm not surprised at the way it came out," he said dejectedly. "Ralph is not stupid, but he does have to walk a fine line as department chairman. Allan is holding all the cards. One protest from Allan, and Ralph would find himself having to explain to the provost, the dean, or a physics faculty meeting just how and why he'd decided to use departmental resources to rescue people lost in shadow universes. He probably considered that and elected to take the safe way out." He looked at her, hoping that an objective discussion of the meeting would calm her down.

"I do agree," he continued, "that Allan's a pompous asshole. That's well known in the department. But his performance just now wasn't stupid or mindless. He presented a brilliant set of intellectually dishonest and self-serving arguments in defense of his narrow self-interest. He doesn't want the twistor hardware rebuilt in a big departmental crash program. He wants to have the leisure to explore the twistor effect in his Bellevue labs, nailing down applications and patent rights as he goes. He's probably even deluded himself into believing that David and the children will benefit from his approach. Allan's always been good at using his considerable rationality for the purpose of rationalizing." Paul hesitated for a moment. Getting his children back might depend on what he said next.

"Vickie, we must get that apparatus rebuilt. It's the only way we're going to be able to get through to Jeff and Melissa and David. Perhaps we should make a deal with Allan and agree to help rebuild the apparatus his way."

"Wait a minute," said Victoria, her cheeks flushing. "I

know you want your kids back, Paul, but I'm surprised that you'd even suggest such a thing. There isn't any way I'd trust Allan in an arrangement like that. Besides, he wants to do everything in Bellevue under tight security. That isn't consistent with finding David and the children. If we're going to locate them, it has to be done here where they disappeared, not in Bellevue.''

''But what else can we do?'' Paul was feeling increasingly apprehensive as he ran a hand through his short-cropped hair.

''Look, Paul,'' she said, ''I know that I told you last night it would take a full crash program to make a twistor device in maybe a month. And that would be true, if we took the same route as before, the safe route. But we can't afford that route now.

''I did a lot of thinking last night about how to build a second-generation twistor generator. It doesn't have to be that hard or that expensive with the right approach. Much of what we did before with expensive analog systems can be done as well with cheap digital waveform synthesis using microprocessors. And a lot of our time went into perfecting the control program. That's done, and I have the only existing copy of the program.''

''You do?'' Paul said. He looked at her closely, wondering where that left Saxon's efforts to rebuild the equipment.

''It would be nice,'' she went on, ignoring his question, ''to have some of the special circuits that were in the old hardware, but I can make more. I think we can do it ourselves with a few thousand dollars, some circuits from the junk pile, a little borrowing from the stock in the electronics shop, and a few weeks of work. Maybe in less time than that, if I can recruit some help.''

Paul was surprised. ''How is that possible?'' he asked. ''All that hardware . . .'' He recalled David's laboratory tour. Half of the room had been filled with complicated apparatus.

''Remember,'' Vickie said, ''David and I were trying to do something much more difficult when we built up the experiment the first time. We had to spend time and money on systems that didn't work as expected or that, in retrospect, weren't actually needed. The bulk of the cost was for vacuum systems, cryogenics, and superconducting magnets that are not needed for producing the twistor effect. I now know exactly what we want to do, and I've got tons of data from a working twistor field to tell me how to do it better. I think I can design a second-generation twistor machine that will be simple and cheap. We don't need Allan, and I absolutely refuse to work with the bastard.''

"But what about his company in Bellevue?" asked Paul, feeling desperate. "Isn't it likely that Saxon and his people will have a working twistor machine even sooner?" He had to find a way of convincing Vickie to work with Saxon. Surely that would be the fastest way to get the apparatus rebuilt.

Vickie smiled ruefully. "Allan doesn't know it yet, but he's going to have one hell of a time rebuilding the twistor hardware with what he knows," she said. "He never took the trouble to understand the basic principles of the field-rotation trick we used. And it is not obvious, Paul, even if you know what to look for. Now all the twistor programming and hardware are gone away to never-never land and there aren't any other records. After that bugging incident, David and I decided to archive all of our CAD files of shop drawings, circuit diagrams, and board layouts, all of my design calculations, and all of the control programming.

"On Tuesday I put everything one would need to rebuild the twistor apparatus on a single encrypted laser disk. I trashed the hard copies and cleared the files from the hard disks of the HyperVAX and the CAD design computer. For good measure, I got Sam to show me how to do a 'Hard Disk Optimize,' which would make it much harder for even a VAX expert with exclusive use of the system to reconstruct those files from leftover blocks. That one little laser disk is the key to rebuilding the twistor hardware, and it's stored away in a safe place. And only I know the decryption key."

"Vickie, aren't you being rather stubborn?" asked Paul. "Perhaps cooperation would be the best course."

"Paul," she said, shaking her head, "remember Allan's little speech in Weinberger's office, how he clearly enjoyed bending the truth to serve his ends? My grandmother once told me that the best way to coexist with a snake is to keep your distance.'' She smiled grimly.

Paul looked at her appraisingly. ''You're a hard lady,'' he said. ''I think Saxon's in for a surprise.''

Allan Saxon crossed the Evergreen Point floating bridge over Lake Washington at a leisurely pace, matching the speed of his BMW to that of a pretty girl who water-skied the calm water in the lee of the bridge. He waved at her, feeling good. It had been a shock to return to Seattle and learn about the ''incident'' at his laboratory. The quantity of blood on the floor and the great wood sphere presented a puzzle. His new investigations of the twistor effect would have to proceed with caution until that mystery was solved.

He perceived the heavy hand of Martin Pierce in the maneuver with the fake movers. The trick should have worked, but it clearly hadn't. The scenario that Paul had presented this morning was bizarre, but there was a certain logic to it. Harrison must have used the twistor apparatus to move himself and the equipment out of reach. About now Pierce must be feeling very angry and frustrated. Saxon smiled.

The loss of the equipment would set back his plans. But one must land on one's feet. His questioning by the FBI last evening and his confrontation with Paul and Vickie in the chairman's office this morning had both gone remarkably well. Now he must set his business associates to work on the ''rediscovery'' of the twistor effect. Steve and the others were not as sharp as Harrison and Vickie, and it might take them some time. But knowing that the effect existed was a very significant advantage, and with Harrison out of the picture and Vickie without departmental resources for a rebuild, his company had the inside track.

And yes, with any luck Vickie might be induced to contribute her knowledge to the project. She was anxious to rebuild the twistor apparatus. With that fool Harrison out of the way and with her desire to rescue him, Saxon was confident that she could be induced to cooperate. He smiled. Yes, she would cooperate. . . .

* * *

The balding man sat in the back seat of the black car, a
scrambler phone in his hand, as they paced Saxon past the
bridge exit and east along the 520 freeway. "His usual
route," he said into the phone, "is to turn south off 520 at
the 148th Avenue exit and then continue south to Northeast
Sixth Street. Get the 'Road Closed' signs ready. He should
be turning east on Sixth in about five minutes."

"That's a roger, Mandrake," came a voice from the
phone.

He glanced sideways at the other passenger in the broad
back seat of the car. The large man's massive right arm
was bandaged and supported by a tan sling. The hand region
looked unnaturally short and was swathed in white ban-
dages. The man's coarse features were frozen in a grimace
of outrage, his yellow teeth tightly clenched.

The flagman, wearing white coveralls and a yellow hard
hat, waved the red flag back and forth slowly as Allan
Saxon's BMW rounded a curve on the wooded road and
approached him. Construction barriers blocked both lanes
of the road, forcing the car to stop. Saxon lowered the
window. "What's the trouble?" he asked. The man smiled,
nodded, and pointed the shaft of the red flag in Saxon's
direction. From an inconspicuous orifice in the rounded end
of the shaft, a cloud of fine droplets emerged and struck
Saxon full in the face. "Oysters?" he said, a puzzled expression on his face. Then he collapsed across the steering
wheel.

The flagman reached a gloved hand through the open
window, turned off the ignition, and opened the driver-side
door. Saxon tumbled out onto the ground. Just then, a large
black car rolled up and two men got out. Not a word was
spoken as together they lifted Saxon and dumped him un-
ceremoniously in the plastic-lined trunk of the black vehicle.
Folded roadblock signs followed. The two men reentered
the black car, the flagman closed the trunk, and the car
turned around and sped back up the road.

The flagman stripped off his coveralls, revealing a tweed
coat and neatly pressed slacks underneath. He unscrewed

the tiny CIA-issue cylinder of nonlethal nerve gas from its socket in the flag handle, sealed it in a zip-lock plastic bag, and dropped it into his coat pocket. The coveralls and hard hat he stuffed into a canvas airline bag along with scrambler phone and flag.

He opened all the doors of the BMW and waited while the residual fumes cleared. Then from each of his nostrils he extracted a filter plug. He sealed them in another zip-lock bag that went into the same coat pocket. He climbed into the BMW, started the engine, and turned it around, then drove back down the wooded road, heading for Seattle. Saxon's BMW would soon be back in its usual slot on the A level of the central campus underground parking garage.

Melissa was sure she wasn't lost. But she was kind of turned around, and the trees all looked the same. She tried to remember how she had come here. . . .

This morning had been fun. After climbing down from the treehouse, they'd gone exploring together in the forest. They'd seen many peculiar insects and some very strange birds that were eating berries in a bush. They could hang in midair when they were eating, and they all had two pairs of wings. David had said there must be two kinds of birds here: those with four wings like the berry eaters, and those with four legs like the treebirds.

They had collected berries and mushrooms into plastic bags for the food supply. David had brought the big black gun along. For protection, he said, against big animals. But the only animals they'd seen were the birds eating berries, some other birds high in the trees, and a few of the shy six-legged squirrels that could change color.

The problems had come after lunch. David had set up a work table under the tree and had began to work with some papers and things. She and Jeff had an argument then, and David had yelled at her. It was so unfair! It had been Jeff's fault . . . he was being a brat, but David had blamed her. She was the oldest, he'd said, and should have better judgment. So she had decided to go off by herself in the forest to collect some more of the sweet pink berries they'd been eating since this morning. She'd left without telling David and picked a time when Jeff wasn't watching.

She had found quite a lot of the berries, two plastic bags full. And she'd seen some interesting rabbitlike creatures. But now she realized that she didn't actually know quite how to get back to the treehouse. A knot of fear tightened in her stomach. What if she had to spend the night outdoors? She remembered David's warning about the dark things that flew at night and the large bearlike creature he'd seen last night at the base of their tree.

Taking a deep breath, Melissa looked around. She musn't panic. She was pretty sure the treehouse was in this direction, but the brown-orange forest floor didn't look quite right. She walked on. Then through the trees she saw a sparkle of reflected light, something that was silvery. She walked toward it.

It was a small pool of water. Cold, clear water was trickling from some green mossy rocks on one side of it, and on the other a small stream ran down the hill. The forest here was very still and quiet except for the small sounds of running water.

Melissa knelt next to a big rock beside the pool, studying the ripples on its surface, then looking down into its clear depths. Small jewel-like swimming insects scurried about in patches of sunlight near the pool's edges, but its center was clear and deep. She reached out and dipped her hand there, bringing to her mouth a cupped palm of cold water. She was thirsty, she realized. The cool water tasted wonderful. She drank more.

She recalled getting a drink of cold water from the refrigerator at home and felt suddenly very sad. Mother had told her never drink out of the bottle, always get a glass. She thought of her mother then, and her father. They'd be upset now because she hadn't come home last night. Mom always wanted her in the house before dark. They must think that she and Jeff had run away or were lost or kidnapped or even dead. She pictured her mother in the back yard, calling and calling for Melissa, and no one came. A tear slid down her cheek and dropped into the water.

She studied the ripples in the pool. As the reflection cleared she saw another face in the water. She looked more carefully. It was the face of a small brownish creature, reflected in the water. It must be behind the big rock at her side. Melissa drew a quiet breath and kept very still as she watched the creature. It sat at the water's edge and drank, lapping up the water with its pink tongue. Then its light brown forepaw darted into the water and emerged with a wriggling minnow held between tiny fingers. Through the ripples Melissa could make out that the creature delicately placed the minnow into its mouth. She giggled.

When the ripples cleared again, the creature's calm violet eyes were looking directly at her in the water. It stared at her for a long time. She noticed that it had big pointed ears, brown fur that now looked darker than it had before, and a long, flexible, bushy tail. And it had six legs—or perhaps four legs and two arms was more correct. It stood on the four back legs rather like a cat, but its body was longer and curved upward near the front, where the other two legs were more like arms ending in little six-fingered hands. It flicked its ears forward in a funny way, making Melissa laugh again. Then the creature scampered around the rock and ran slowly toward the forest to disappear behind a tree.

Without thinking about anything but the little animal, Melissa followed it. It ran from tree to tree. She noticed that it was an orange-brown now, close to the color of the dead leaves on the forest floor. It did not seem afraid, but it always kept a short distance ahead of her. The woods looked more familiar here. The little animal's fur changed to a lighter shade of brown as it climbed a tall tree. Melissa walked all around the tree, but could see no sign of the animal. However, very high up in the crotch of one of the larger branches was what might have been a nest.

Finally, Melissa gave up searching for the little creature and looked around her. She was in a part of the forest very near the treehouse, she realized. . . .

Melissa, feeling very excited, walked up to David with two plastic bags full of pink berries. He was sitting on a big rock, working at the table he'd made from a piece of plywood and some branches. She saw that he was staring at a large piece of white paper with lots of colored lines drawn on it. It was unrolled on the tabletop, and he'd put rocks at the corners to hold it down.

David suddenly smiled and quickly copied something from the big drawing to a pad of paper in his lap. Then he frowned. "Damn," he said, and drew a line through what he'd just written. Looking up, he seemed surprised to see Melissa there. "Hi," he said. "What's up?"

He didn't seem to be mad at her anymore, and he hadn't noticed that she'd been gone, she thought. Good. "David," she began, "I saw a new animal in the forest!" As she talked, she added the pink berries she'd collected to their small store of food.

David frowned. "What kind of animal?" he asked. "How big was it? Maybe it was a relative of that bear-creature I saw last night." That bear must worry him a lot, she thought.

"No," she said, "it was little and cute, like a brownish-colored kitten." Melissa smelled something interesting and realized that she was hungry.

Jeff was standing by the fire, stirring a big pot of the mushroom soup, half instant mix and half native mush-rooms. She ignored the face that Jeff made at her when David wasn't looking and took the white Styrofoam cup with her name on it. She removed the rock that kept it from blowing away and helped herself to some of the soup.

"We must be very careful here, Melissa," David said. "We know very little about the animals that live in these woods, and even the smallest ones could be dangerous. But I guess it's good that there are more animals around. Our instant soup and peanut butter are running pretty low. We're going to have to get more of our meals from the local plants and animals. Do you think maybe we could trap your critter? Is it big enough to make a meal of?"

Melissa abruptly swallowed the hot soup that had been cooling in her mouth. "No!" she said, louder than she'd intended. "This one isn't to eat, David! It was like a little brown kitten. It had big round eyes that were a sort of violet color, and cute pointed ears, and a long furry tail . . . and it had hands, David. Little hands with six fingers. It likes minnows, too. I saw it eat one. It seemed smart, like it was just about to talk to me. I want to get it to come here so I can play with it, not eat it." She smiled her most charming smile, hoping to win him to her point of view. "Please, David, can I?" she begged.

Towering above her, he looked down, a worried expression on his face. "Melissa," he said quietly. "You must understand something. We're in a very difficult situation right now. I'm trying to figure out how to get us back home, and we must have enough food to live on until I do. When we're safe and have enough food to take care of your own needs, then maybe we can think about having pets. But not now, Melissa. Not now.

"Remember, this is October. Winter is coming soon. Unless we can find good sources of food and water, we're going to starve." He paused for a moment, and seemed to be making sure she had heard him. "And although it may have looked like a sweet little kitten," he went on, "it's a wild animal, and it could be dangerous. Animals, even little ones, can scratch and bite. It could hurt you if you got too close or tried to pick it up. So, no pets for now." He looked stern.

Instead of answering him directly, Melissa told him about the pool of clear water she'd found. David became very excited at the news. Then Melissa led Jeff and David, who brought along the big gun, back to the spring. David also brought a Styrofoam cup to leave there, and they all used it to take long drinks of the delicious cool clear water.

When they returned to the treehouse, David explained that they could make the best use of the new source of water by building a cistern against the side of the tree, in a place where it curved inward. He said they would make a wall of rocks and dirt that extended the curve of the tree into an oval basin. They would put a sheet of plastic inside to make the cistern watertight. It would hold the water they carried here from the pool, and it would also catch rainwater. He assigned the two of them to look in the forest nearby and find the biggest rocks they could carry to the side of the tree. While the children collected rocks, David returned to the table with the drawing.

"Mine's better than yours," said Jeff as Melissa dropped

her rock in the pile. He was being a brat again. She turned to go back to the rocky area she had located, and Jeff ran ahead of her. He kept bragging that the rocks he found were bigger and better than hers, and about how he liked to squash the squirmy things he found underneath them. He wouldn't go off and look for his own rocks. Instead, he'd run ahead in the direction she was walking to find the best rocks before she could get them. It made her so mad. . . .

She was older and should have better judgment, David had said. Melissa decided to ignore Jeff. She picked up rocks where she found them and thought about the little brown animal. She'd been lost, she realized. She'd been wrong about the direction of the treehouse when she came to the pool. The little animal had led her back here. Had it somehow guessed that she needed help? She couldn't mention this to David without admitting that she'd been lost, but she was sure the brown kitten had understood her problem and had been trying to help her.

She looked carefully in the forest all through the afternoon and into the evening. Sometimes she felt sure that something in the trees was watching her, but she saw no more small brown animals in the woods that day.

19

FRIDAY AFTERNOON, OCTOBER 15

Victoria was sitting in her basement bedroom before her ancient Macintosh 512E, typing intently, when William arrived back from another day at Theodore Roosevelt High School.

"Whew, thank God it's Friday-o," said Flash, putting down his school notebook. "Hey Sis, whatcha doin'?" He peered over her shoulder.

She turned to him, trying to block his view of the screen. "I just came home for some lunch and to get a book I needed for a design problem," she said. "William," she added, attempting to sound casual, "how did you manage to get into Professor Saxon's files the other day?"

"Why, Sis!" replied Flash with heavy mock chagrin, "I thought that only naughty hackers concerned themselves with things like that. You wouldn't really want me to disclose clandestine methods for callously invading another person's sacred privacy, would you? That might allow someone to pry into intimate personal files and read lurid private correspondence. You want to do that? My goodness gracious, I'm shocked! My own sister wants to become a hacker! Whatever is this world coming to?"

"Cut the crap, dammit!" said Victoria, feeling warmth as her cheeks grew redder, "I told you what happened at the lab on Wednesday. Yesterday Allan was acting very devious, as if he were hiding something, and today he's gone off somewhere. He disappeared without telling anyone where he was going. Even Susan, his secretary, doesn't know where he is. I need to look in his protected files on the VAX for clues to what's going on. This is important, William.''

"Hmmm," said Flash, "this might actually be a bit of the old El Fun-o. I've always wanted to hack in a Noble Cause. OK. Move over, Sis, and let's see what we can find out about Herr Doktor Professor Saxon.'' He beetled his eyebrows. "We have our ways of making computers beg to confess,'' Flash said, faking a German accent. He pulled a second chair up to the Macintosh keyboard and started to type.

Suddenly he stopped, looking down at the table beside the computer. There was the small white business card of one Agent Bartley of the FBI, Seattle Office. He looked at his sister suspiciously. "What's this, Sis, a setup? Did you tell the FBI that I was on the Physics HyperVAX the other day?'' His eyes narrowed.

She smiled and patted him on the shoulder. "Your guilty secrets are safe with me," she said. "This person came to the lab the other day to ask about the disappearances, and he gave me his card. I was thinking of calling him to suggest that Allan Saxon knows more than he's telling, but I decided I'd better get more information before doing anything like that.''

Flash paused a moment longer, then nodded and rapidly typed instructions to the VAX. "Guess we'd better see what's in those encrypted files then," he said.

"Can you actually read encrypted files?" she asked. "I thought it was supposed to be impossible to break modern encryption codes.''

"We'll need some help and some luck," said Flash. "There are so many possible combinations that you can't just guess at random. In a reasonable time it's impossible to check every guess, and it's sure to tip off the system manager if you try. But we have a little helper-o. See, the system manager on your HyperVAX is very security conscious. He's activated a VMS system surveillance option that makes an entry in an accounting file every time there's a bad log-in and every time a bad input generates a system error. It's intended to help him catch hackers. These security freak-os sure make things easy. It's set up so it doesn't record things like good passwords and encryption keys. But if someone mistypes something, it goes right into the file-o. Here's last month's accounting file. I'll copy it into your area, and we'll see what we can find.''

"How can you just copy that log file?'' asked Victoria. "Isn't it protected?''

"It should be,'' said Flash, "but it wasn't automatically protected in some versions of the system software. There's a mandatory patch that your VAX manager was supposed to have installed to make this file unreadable, but I guess he hasn't gotten around to it.'' He grinned. ''A busy fella like him can't remember everything.'' After the **$** prompt he typed: **COPY SYS$MANAGER:ACCOUNTING. DAT[ ].** Then he called up the editor and went to work on the **ACCOUNTING.DAT** file.

"See, first I'm searching for incidents that involved Saxon's user code or where the user name before the password was **SAXON**. Here's one where he tried to do a log-in but screwed the dog-o. That's supposed to be his password, but it was mistyped. And see, here's the same thing a couple of days later. And here's another one. The mangled passwords are 'DAVISS,' 'VIS,' and 'DASVIS.' What do you think he was trying to type?''

"It must have been 'DAVIS,' '' said Victoria. "That's Allan's middle name, now that I think of it.''

"Connect-o!'' said Flash, and wrote something on a pad. "Now, we search on errors that involved the system encryption utility. He uses it more than anyone else. Ah, here's one. See, he typed 'HOLOSDPINWAVE.' The entry was supposed to be a maximum of twelve characters and he'd typed thirteen, so it was logged as an error.''

"You can stop there,'' said Victoria. "His encryption key has to be 'HOLOSPINWAVE.' That's the area of condensed-matter physics he's been working in for the last several years. I guess his finger made an extra 'D' when he typed the 'S.' '''

"Great!'' said Flash. "Now, Victoria my dear, we can delve into your Professor Saxon's innermost secrets. He is now com-plete-ly in our pow-waaa! Ain't hackin' fun-o!'' He grinned.

* * *

David sighted up through the forest canopy. Late-afternoon sunlight slanted through the cover of branches and leaves overhead. He could see blue sky, with a few clouds sliding slowly by in a direction he judged to be north. There was a south wind. He could feel it cooling the light beading of sweat on his face and neck. At home in Seattle a south wind usually meant that bad weather was coming, that a low-pressure area parked out in the Pacific was spiraling a storm front in from the south. David wondered if the topography of this planet was similar enough for the same weather rules to work. If a storm front was on the way, their new cistern would soon be ready for it.

He picked up the makeshift shovel again, an aluminum plate clamped with a lever-jaw wrench to a piece of pipe, and lifted more dirt from the floor of the scooped-out area, spreading it against the rough rock wall. Beside him Jeff was smoothing and packing the dirt in place against the wall with his hands.

"David," said Jeff.

"Yeah," David answered as he worked the shovel blade into the dirt again.

"I think I know where those colors on the ground come from," Jeff said. "You know, the ones around the tree that are all in a line."

"Yes," said David. "So where do they come from?"

"Those colors're treebird poop," Jeff said, then giggled.

David stopped and looked at the boy. "How do you know?" he asked.

"This morning I was dragging a big dead branch up for the fire, and when it dragged across the line of colors, I noticed that it kinda rubbed them out. I didn't think much about it until I saw the treebird fly down from the tree and land just where I'd dragged the branch. It kinda walked around, pecking at the ground and scratching it with its front claws. Then it sorta did a waddle dance along the line, and I noticed that it was making poop on the ground. David, it can poop in colors!"

David looked at Jeff, then speculatively up at the tree. He could see the green treebird at work, busily grooming the bark along the broad wall of the trunk. "The line must be a border," he said.

"You mean like countries have?" Jeff asked.

"Yeah," said David. "It's to mark and claim territory. Have you noticed how each tree has only one treebird? It must be that they mark off their territories with those colored lines, surrounding their own tree with a color-coded circle to warn other treebirds that this tree is taken and off limits. On Earth, birds make birdcalls in the morning for the same purpose. In this world Nature seems to have found, er, another method."

Jeff nodded and began again to pat the dirt into the wall. Melissa was leveling the dug-out floor, stamping it down with her feet. There was a kind of logic to it, he thought. The healthier and more successful the bird was in its ecological niche as tree groomer and insect eater, the more vigorously and distinctly it would be able to mark off its territory and discourage intruders. David paused to survey their own border-work, a curving rock wall delineating the wide dirt-lined basin against the side of the big tree. He swatted ineffectually at a blue flying insect that seemed interested in him.

"That will just about do it, kids," he said, smoothing the dirt he had just shoveled. "I'll go up and get the plastic liner and some tools, and you two can finish the smoothing over here."

"OK," said Jeff, patting more dirt with his hands. He seemed to be enjoying himself.

"Oomph," Melissa grunted as she stamped, "I'm glad we're almost done." She lifted a pink jewel-headed worm from the loose dirt and tossed it over the wall. Then she stamped again.

David vaulted the low rock wall and walked to the foot of the ladder hanging from the treehouse door-hole. He started upward. As he climbed, something flickered at the edge of his peripheral vision. There might have been a brown something moving in a nearby tree. He turned toward it, but there was nothing. He blinked, then continued the climb to the treehouse. At the door-hole he tied a long wire around the folded sheet of five-mil black polyethylene he'd placed there and lowered it to the ground. Then he gathered hammer, nails, wood strips salvaged from the old Helmholz coil supports, and a few other items, and climbed back down.

The rest of the construction went swiftly. Against the tree he secured one edge of the plastic sheet, now sandwiched between the wood strips, driving long nails through wood and plastic into the upthrust scales of the bark. The remaining sheet was unfolded to form a watertight lining for the rock and dirt basin. The edges of the plastic sheet were folded down over the cistern's rim and secured against the outer wall with sharpened wooden pegs. A second sheet of black plastic formed a lid stretching over the top of the cistern. It was pegged into place at the rim, one unsecured edge butting loosely against the back wall near the tree. Wings attached to the tree extended outward and upward to catch additional rainwater, while the central cover would reduce evaporation of the water already collected. It would also be lightless inside, so that algae and slime mold would not grow in their water supply.

David stepped back, inspecting their handiwork. It looked good. There remained only the matter of the water to fill it. He looked across at the children. "You two have been working very hard," he said. "Time for a break now." Jeff nodded and smiled. Melissa wiped her hands and looked down at her clothes. They were all rather dirty, David thought. When they had more water, he would use their limited soap supply to do something about that.

They sat in a row, relaxing with their backs against the tree. "Have you two ever seen the old Disney movie *Fantasia*?" David asked.

Jeff looked doubtful, but Melissa said, "Yes, Daddy took us to see it when it was shown again last year. I liked it. It had dancing flowers and fairies and witches and centaurs and flying horses. It was lovely. I liked the music, too."

"Yeah," Jeff spoke up, "and I liked the dina-sawer fight."

"Yes," said David, "I saw it first when I was about your age. Do you remember the sorcerer's apprentice part, where little Mickey has to carry water for the wizard?"

"Yeah!" said Jeff. "That was nice too." Melissa nodded agreement.

"Well," said David, "I want you guys to pretend that I'm the sorcerer and you're my apprentices. Here's a big plastic jug for each of you. I want you to go to the spring, fill the jug with as much water as you can easily carry, bring it back here, and pour it into the cistern. That will give us a water supply even if it doesn't rain soon." Melissa looked thoughtful. He wondered what she was thinking. Perhaps she was remembering the movie.

She stared off into the woods, then smiled and picked up one of the jugs, walking off in the direction of the spring. Jeff followed. David wiped his hands on his jeans, sat down on the big rock before the crude table, and picked up a pencil. He wasn't doing too well as the sorcerer, he thought ruefully. The daylight wouldn't last much longer, but it hardly mattered. The more he studied the circuit drawings, the more impossible it looked to use the equipment he had to make a twistor field.

As if returning from a long way off, Allan Saxon came slowly awake with daylight filtering redly through his closed eyelids. Ugh. His head felt terrible, there was a ringing in his ears, his tongue was numb, and there was a vile taste in his mouth. He struggled to remember. It must have been some party. . . .

No! He had not been drinking. The recent events snapped into register. He had driven across the lake on 520 and taken the usual exit. There had been a flagman on the road, then . . . nothing? Something cold and wet had struck his face, something with a taste like . . . oysters? He couldn't remember anything else.

He tried to move and failed. His arms felt oddly constrained. He opened his eyes, then waited while they focused. He was in a room with white walls. Slanting sunlight was filtering through gauzy white curtains. The foot of the bed was brown particle board and had an institutional look. Beyond it was a closet. A plain chair and table were beside the bed. There was no other furniture in the room. Opposite the window was a brown wood door, presently closed.

Looking down at his own body, he discovered the cause of the curious immobility of his arms. He was wearing a canvas straitjacket, his arms strapped across his chest.

Straitjacket! A wave of fear swept through him. Was this a mental institution? Had he had some kind of breakdown? Was he crazy? "Help!" he yelled. "Let me out of here!"

He heard approaching footsteps. The door opened and two men came in. One wore fairly ordinary clothing: brown slacks, white dress shirt, dark red tie. Only one thing was odd: the man was wearing a ski mask. A terrorist? The other man was much larger, and had to stoop a bit when he came through the door. He was also wearing a ski mask, which stretched tightly over his large head, and where one of his hands should be there was a white bandage. Saxon remembered the blood in the laboratory and wondered.

"Ah, Professor Saxon," said the man before him. "At last you're awake." The voice sounded crisp and professional, slightly muffled by the wool.

"Where am I?" Saxon asked. "What time is it?"

"This is Friday afternoon," the man said. "You were out for over twenty-four hours. Our dose level was a bit high, I'm afraid."

"Why am I here?" Saxon's voice rose. "And who the Hell are you?"

"I'm afraid I can't answer your questions, Professor," the man said. "I can only tell you that this is a matter of national security. We work for a special secret agency of the federal government. It would be very dangerous for you to know too much about us. That's why we've concealed our identities with these masks. It's for your own protection."

Saxon felt a sinking sensation in the pit of his stomach. Oh shit, he thought, it's about the missing card from that military computer. They've found out somehow. "Look, goddammit," he said, more aggressively than he felt, "I'm cleared for secret information. I've had my loyalty checked eight ways from January. I hold top-secret clearances for consulting at Livermore and Los Alamos, and I've served on presidential commissions and DOD panels. Don't pull that secrecy shit on me! Where do you bastards get off, kidnapping me and tying me up like this. Release me immediately!'' He felt the itching sensation at the rear of his scalp. Blood pressure too high. He took deep breaths, trying to remain calm.

"The straitjacket was only for your protection, to prevent you from doing anything rash before we could advise you of the situation,'' the man said. "We'll take it off now.'' He gestured to the big man to undo the straitjacket's straps, then apparently decided to do it himself instead.

The big man must have lost the hand only recently, Saxon concluded. Interesting. He shrugged out of the canvas sleeves and sat up, rubbing his arms. He saw that underneath he was wearing a white hospital gown. "What the hell did you use to knock me out?'' he asked. "I feel awful.'' He massaged his forehead and groaned.

"It's a selective nerve-blocking protein combined with a penetrant agent, strictly nonlethal,'' the man said affably. "Comes in a nice little aerosol can. The government finds many uses for it. Didn't kill you, did it? Believe me, you'll feel better soon.''

"OK, enough of this,'' Saxon said. "Show me your federal agency IDs now, please.'' Perhaps these bastards were on to him, he thought, but he must continue to act innocent and offended.

"Sorry,'' the man said, "I told you the secrecy is to protect you. Sure, we could produce any ID you'd care to believe, but there's no need for such games, is there, Professor? We've got more important business. We have lots of talking to do.''

Saxon's head hurt. He tried to shake it clear and instantly regretted the move. "What talking? What do you want to know?'' he asked.

The man placed a little digital disk audio recorder on the bedside table and depressed two buttons. "For starts,'' the man said, "tell me about everything you've done in the past month. . . .''

Victoria was disappointed and impatient. Decrypting the files in Saxon's most protected subdirectory was taking a long time. She had wanted to get back to the university before Sam left for the day. The decryption process itself was time consuming, even on the HyperVAX, and the decoded files concerned irrelevant items: personnel evaluations, salary lists, and rejected NSF and DOD proposals.

"Hmmm, this looks more interesting," said Flash. He was working on a file with the unpromising name of **MCEVAL.TEX.** Vickie read the text over his shoulder. The document concerned the evaluation of a classified military control computer. The work had been done for the Megalith Corporation of San Francisco, California. What was Saxon doing evaluating secret military hardware? Then Victoria remembered that Megalith was the outfit that had loaned Saxon money. "William," she said, "what do you know about the Megalith Corporation?"

"Hmm, Megalith . . ." Flash mused. "Yeah! You're talking el big bucks-o. Those guys have supercomputers all over the place, big mainframes, top-of-the-line IBMs, HyperVAXes, Suns, Crays . . . lots of networking, lots of military work-o. Some of the more talented of my former associates cracked their big systems a few times just to show it could be done. But Megalith has real heavy security. The cracks never lasted more than a coupla days.

"And Megalith has the rep of being a bad outfit to mess with. Two of the guys 'visited' a Megalith mainframe and bragged about it on the net. Not long after that some big mean guys showed up at their place. Got their heads broken and their systems trashed. The word is: Leave Megalith A-Lone-O."

Quitting time, Sam Weston thought, walking back to the electronics shop. As he passed the large basement storage room, he noticed that a light was on inside. He halted and peered inside. Everything looked the same as usual: metal and plywood racks reached from the bare concrete floor to the low ceiling, groaning under the accumulated burden of obsolescent electronic equipment from the physic's experiments of yesteryear. This was an instrumentation boneyard where old equipment from departmental research or the federal surplus lists was brought when it was too old or unreliable to be of use but too valuable to throw away.

Every spring Sam would cull the most useless items from the collection and direct some work-study students to strip them down for parts. He glanced around. There were some real memories here, he thought.

The grating sound of a moved chassis echoed from the back of the room. "Who's in here," Sam called, his reverberating voice sounding hard with authority.

A shock of coppery red hair shone through a gap between boxes, then a pretty face peered out from behind the rack. "Just me, Sam," Vickie said. "I didn't see you in the shop."

Sam walked around the rack. "Whatcha doin', honey?" he asked. "Lookin' for more stuff to make into big wood marbles?"

She smiled like the sun coming out. "As a matter of fact, Sam, that's more or less what I am doing." She described her meeting with the chairman yesterday. "So Weinberger gave me the OK to build what I want, as long as there's no impact on departmental funds or technical services."

Sam nodded. "And now you're in here scrounging parts," he said.

"Right," she said. "I particularly need power supplies and anything that will drive high-power RF." She gestured at the heavy chassis that she'd been removing from the rack. "What do you know about this kludge?"

He shook his head. "You don't wanna have anything to do with that one, honey," he said. "Has an intermittent power transformer. Works fine when it's cold, but as soon as it gets hot the juice goes off. Took the Penning trap guys weeks last summer to find out that dang thing was their problem. Their trap would dump its antimatter load in the middle of the afternoon like clockwork. It was too hot to work days in their lab then, what with all the power they were dumpin' and no air conditioning, and they were home sleeping for the next all-night marathon. They thought for a while somebody was sneakin' in to sabotage their experiment. You don't want it."

Vickie nodded and shoved the chassis back to its place on the shelf, a discouraged look on her face.

Sam thought for a moment, weighing alternatives. "Can

you keep a secret, honey?'' he asked finally.

"Sure, Sam,'' she said. Her raised eyebrows made twin arches.

He walked to the rear of the room, fishing in his pocket as he went for the big key ring. "I have a place,'' he said, "where I keep some of the better items.'' He produced a key and inserted it in a round brass lock plate in a panel. The inconspicuous wooden panel, painted the same color as the wall and half concealed behind an adjacent rack, swung inward. "You see,'' he said, "when the good stuff comes in from the surplus lists and nobody has an immediate use for it, I kinda put it in here for safekeepin'. If I left it out on the racks, no tellin' what might happen to it.''

Vickie smiled. "Right,'' she said, peering into the dark opening, "no telling . . .''

Sam flicked a switch inside. New-looking power supply units bearing military stamps were stacked in neat rows. Several high-frequency radio transmitter racks were just behind them. The little alcove was quite deep, and it was nearly full.

"Wow!'' she said, "This is a treasure trove! And it looks like just what I need. How much of it can I have, Sam?''

"How much can you carry away, honey?'' he asked. "Business has been kinda slow lately.''

Allan Saxon was frightened. The man who claimed to be a federal agent had questioned him closely all day yesterday. Saxon had managed to avoid the matter of the circuit board, but he'd told them everything he knew about the disappearance of the twistor apparatus. He'd explained that Harrison must have taken the equipment to a shadow universe, and that only by building new equipment could they get the old equipment back.

But this morning the cooperative and even cordial atmosphere of yesterday was gone. The man had new orders, he said. The two of them, still wearing ski masks, had taken off all Saxon's clothes and tied him in this chair. The man who did the talking had set up a suitcase-mounted machine that had many wires. He'd attached flat electrodes at the ends of the wires to various parts of Saxon's body with adhesive tape. The wires were connected to his hands, feet, head, and genitals. They'd used a kind of gray paste. The man said it was silver, that it prevented telltale arc burns.

"This machine," the man said, "is the result of years of development by intelligence agencies around the world." He patted the controls. "It's constructed to deliver strong and controlled electrical shocks to the human nervous system. I have complete control over the strength of the shocks. They can be made very painful . . . so painful that no one has ever been able to resist telling me what I want to know."

He looked steadily at Saxon. "If you cooperate now, I won't have to use this machine. But you must tell the whole truth, not lies, as you did yesterday."

"I told you everything—" Saxon protested.

"No!" said the man. "We have infrared and ultrasonic sensors in this room." He looked upward to a little box mounted near the ceiling. "We can detect lies. I know you were lying yesterday. If you don't fully cooperate now, I'll have to use this machine. I'll create unendurable pain until you talk. Surely you don't want that."

"But I wasn't lying!" Saxon protested again. At least, not much, he thought.

"I don't like creating pain," the man said grimly. "I hate it." His voice hardened. "If I must use this equipment, it's your responsibility. As a professional, I do what is necessary."

He started the little digital disk recorder again and began to ask questions.

Saturday night was now almost Sunday morning. Flash had been working at it all day, and now he was feeling tired and discouraged. He was rusty, no doubt about it. His "good behavior" in the nine months after his bust had cost him all of his good contacts. The hacker boards he'd used so frequently just last year had either vanished or would not accept his old passwords.

His only hope now was to try to reestablish some of his contacts on the public nets. He'd struck out on CompuServe and BIX and GEnie, and now he was just cycling through them. It was frustrating. Nobody would answer his E-mail.

He dialed into GEnie again. He'd seen a public message there signed by one "Albert Alligator," a 'nym he recognized from his prebust days. An hour ago he'd left a private E-mail message that only the real Albert-A would recognize. The GEnie prompt said that he had private E-mail. A score-o!

He read the message, a warm greeting from his old friend Albert. It gave a voice number to call. Flash disconnected and dialed the telephone, smiling. He was about to reenter the hacker community.

20

SUNDAY MORNING, OCTOBER 17

The balding man sat in the paneled living room, typing rapidly at an elderly VT–220 computer terminal linked by telephone to the VAX at his office. Outside the barred window he could see a broad swatch of Lake Washington through the trees. He was informing Broadsword of their progress in the interrogation of the subject, Allan Saxon. The news was not good.

The old "federal agent" scam had gone well at first. The subject had told them a story that checked with every aspect of the recordings from the university. He'd given every appearance of cooperation. But the sensor equipment had shown evidence of lying. Yesterday they had used the electrical equipment. That seemed to work better. The subject had confessed to some caper with a military computer and seemed to believe he'd told them what they were after. But when it came to the information Broadsword wanted—the details of how the twistor apparatus had been removed from the laboratory and the secrets of how it worked—the subject had claimed ignorance and stuck to a bizarre story about "other universes." Even when they threatened him with federal prison for his "crimes," he wouldn't change his story.

Now they were at a branch point. They couldn't proceed further without advice from Broadsword. They could drop the whole thing here. If the business with the military computer checked out, they had the Saxon creep by the balls. They could put the fear of God into him and let him go, and he wouldn't dare complain to anyone.

On the other hand, they could dig deeper. Some recombinant DNA research at one of the secret DOD labs had produced a remarkable new drug, neurophagin. It was a monoclonal antibody that attacked a particular part of the central nervous system, the nerve bundles that acted as censors for the brain. The right amount of the stuff and it was literally impossible to conceal anything, yet the higher mental processes were relatively unimpaired. The subject would talk his head off about anything he was asked, with his rational processes doing their best to provide all the answers.

Trouble was, the treatment was irreversible. The antibodies worked by labeling nerve cells for destruction by the body's own immune system. The subject was placed permanently in a state not unlike some of the more lucid phases of Alzheimer's disease. It was not a nice treatment, even for this slimy creep. But on the whole it was preferable to the torture methods they'd used yesterday. There was much less screaming.

The balding man completed the message that spelled out the possible alternative procedures, then hit RETURN. Now he had only to wait for Broadsword's reply. He went to the refrigerator for a beer.

It was perhaps two hours later when the terminal beeped and the VT-20 screen read **You have 1 new mail message.** He quickly decrypted the new message from Broadsword.

It read: **Advise you proceed with neurophagin treatment.**

Victoria Gordon closed the door of room 103, the seminar room next to the lab. This was Sunday morning, with hardly anyone in the building, but she wanted to keep the meeting private. She needed a low profile. The room was smaller than the usual classroom. It was intended for meetings and the interactive discussions of small seminars. High windows facing the library filled the wall at the far end of the room. A blackboard on one long wall was covered with arcane symbols and diagrams left over from some seminar on Friday. Most of the vinyl-tiled floor was occupied by a long table and a few dozen chairs.

Seated around the table were Paul and Elizabeth Ernst, Rudi Baumann, George Williams, Jim Lee, and Sam Weston. In chairs along the long blank wall sat three women grad students, friends of Vickie's from other departments.

"OK," Vickie said, "I guess we'd better get on with it. This is the first meeting of the Twistor Working Group. I want to thank you all for coming in like this on a weekend. Since some of you don't know one another, I'll start with introductions." She introduced each person in turn.

"You all know the story and understand the problem," she began. "Each of you is here because you've agreed to help me construct a second-generation twistor generator. It's going to take a lot of work, and we don't have the usual advantages of the departmental shops. Professor Weinberger gave me authorization to go ahead with this the assurance that there will be no use of departmental funds or technical services. I intend to honor that commitment. We can use the machine tools in the student shop, but that's all."

Sam raised his hand. "I want everybody to understand," he said, "that I'm one of the resources you ain't supposed to be usin'. I'm here, as the army says, strictly as an observer. The work I do on this project will be to fill in the gaps and help Vickie with debugging. It'll be after hours on my own time, like today. OK?"

Vickie nodded and turned to survey the group. "I want to break this group up into smaller teams that will have responsibility for pieces of the project. The teams I have in mind are mechanical construction, electrical wiring, electronic construction, and supply/transportation. First, who knows how to use machine tools like lathes and milling machines? We'll need someone using the tools in the student machine shop to make things for us."

Vickie was surprised when Rudi Baumann put up his hand. He was supposed to be a theorist. "While my friend here," he said, patting George on the head, "was playing football and thickening his skull by colliding it with others, I was working after school in my uncle's *Maschinenfabrik*, er, machine shop, in München. I could earn a living that way now, if it was necessary. I would enjoy the smell of hot steel chips and machine oil again. It would be almost like coming home." He smiled.

Denise Sonneberg, a grad student in botany, raised a hand. "I had a good machine-shop course in high school, and I did pretty well," she said. "I could help him."

Rudi turned and smiled at her. "You're hired," he said.

"OK," said Vickie, "how about heavy electrical wiring?"

Paul Ernst raised his hand. "I've done some electrical wiring," he said. "After we bought our house, we rewired it ourselves. I even replaced the old fuse box with a breaker service panel. I think I can do your wiring, Vickie."

"I can help," said Elizabeth. "I helped when we did the house." Paul nodded.

"OK," said Vickie, "next is circuit-board wiring. Who knows how to use a soldering iron and follow a wiring schematic?"

Jim Lee and the two other graduate students indicated that they did. Vickie described the circuit construction problems they would face.

"That leaves supplies and transportation," said Vickie. "Somebody has to chase around town finding bits and pieces of hardware and circuit parts as we need them."

"Guess that's me," said George. "I've got a station wagon and a strong back." He grinned at Rudi.

In the next hour, Vickie, assisted by Sam, went over the lists of work that needed to be done. By lunch time everyone had his or her first assignment, and Vickie was feeling quite optimistic about rebuilding the equipment.

David had discovered the creek. He'd followed the small stream from Melissa's pool along a meandering path through the forest and found that it joined a larger flow not far away. The creek, brushy at the banks and with few of the big trees growing very close, produced a gap in the forest canopy. For the first time since their arrival here David had been able to view a broad stripe of unobstructed sky. The clouds were still streaming northward, he noticed.

Walking along the creek, he had come to a deep pool. Dark shadows could occasionally be seen moving in its depths. He guessed that there might be fish in the depths of the pool.

Back at the treehouse he'd spent the remainder of the day manufacturing fishing equipment. At first he'd tried, with little success, to make fishhooks from salvaged springs. Then he thought of fish spears. He'd heated large nails in the fire, then hammered and filed them into barbed steel points. These he drilled and pinned into long thin shafts of white PVC pipe.

Today, during the first hour of fishing they'd thrust their spears into the water many times but had nothing to show for it. Then Melissa had speared a large fish.

It was quite a strange-looking fish, and rather pretty—blue with orange highlights, and three pairs of fins instead of the usual two. The front fins were not in the usual place but directly under the gills. They were long and projected downward and forward, almost like forepaws. David guessed they might be useful for feeding as well as for swimming.

Melissa's fish was the last one they caught for another hour. Then, just when David had decided to call it a day, the fish from the depths had begun to feed on blue insect-creatures with long abdomens that were flying in swarms near the surface. The fish spearing became easy.

Melissa was particularly skillful at it. As they added to their catch, she had repeatedly described the wonderful fish dinner they were going to have this evening. The daylight had begun to fade, but they had not wanted to stop.

The storm had struck like a physical blow, taking David quite by surprise. Big raindrops hit him hard in the face, and a darkening gloom descended on the forest. "We'll have to make a run for the treehouse," he called to Jeff and Melissa above the sound of the wind.

"Eee, it's cold!" Jeff cried. He tried to brush the icy rain from his face. David gave the remains of their lunch to Melissa to carry and gathered their catch into a plastic bag. Jeff carried the fishing gear. The three of them set out at a jog, Melissa first, Jeff in the middle, and David behind them. Jeff slipped in the mud once and skinned his knee. After that, David carried the fishing gear too. It became darker, and he gave Melissa the flashlight. He kept the big gun ready under his coat, out of the rain but there in case they met a large carnivore in the dark.

They finally reached the treehouse cold, wet, and nearly exhausted. The fire left smoldering in the rock-lined pit was drowned, the pot of soup had been overturned by a blown branch, all the firewood was wet, and everything that had been left outside on the ground was drenched. David shined the flashlight beam into the cistern. At least it was filling nicely. They would have to carry no more jugs of water for a while. Gathering various soaked items from the ground, they climbed the ladder to the treehouse and were finally out of the wind and rain.

They all sprawled dripping on the floor. David attended to Jeff's knee with antibiotic cream and an adhesive bandage from Sam's toolbox. He wondered if the bacteria of this world liked people and if they responded the same way to antibiotics. After Jeff's knee had been treated, David insisted that the children get out of their wet clothes and into their sleeping bags. He pulled up the ladder and blocked the door-hole against some of the wind and rain. Then he rigged a clothesline across one end of their compartment and hung their soaked clothing to dry.

"I'm hungry," said Melissa from her sleeping bag, still shivering. "When can we eat the fish, David?"

"No fish dinner tonight, I'm afraid," David said. "We aren't sure if this kind of fish is OK to eat. I'll have to test them first. Since we don't have a fire, I guess I'll eat some raw fish tonight."

"Ugh," said Jeff, "raw fish is yukky."

"I'll pretend I'm at Nikko's Sushi Bar in Seattle," said David. "We'll cook the rest of the fish tomorrow when the rain stops. But for tonight, I'm afraid you're going to have to make do with raw mushrooms and pink berries.''

Melissa looked longingly at the fish, then pulled her head inside her sleeping bag.

The night was as cold and damp and miserable as David had expected, and the fish smell from his partially washed hands permeated everything.

By midnight Sunday, Flash was back in the hacker business. He rubbed his neck as he set the ancient Mac to dial a southern California area code at 4800 baud. His back was getting tired. Vickie had said it was OK to run up her long-distance bill, so he didn't even have to ''phreak'' it, as he'd done in the old days, for free long distance with bogus access codes on MCI and Sprint. That saved some time, at least.

The Mac screen registered a **CONNECT**, followed by:

```
    < ——————————— >
    < Welcome to the gangplank >
    <     of the Starship Orion.   >
    < ——————————— >
```

This is a public bulletin board intended primarily for the use of the fans of that fabulous TV series, "Hunt of Orion." Admiral Robert J. Hunt at the helm.

Please sign in:

''Ugh! The lowest of life forms, sci-fi video freakers,'' said Flash aloud. He responded with the borrowed 'nym he had been given: ''The Deviant.'' The system responded with the prompt **Password:** and Flash responded with BLOWJOB. The system then proceeded through its normal spiel:

```
<  ———————————————————  >
<  Welcome aboard the Starship Orion  >
<  Admiral Robert J. Hunt commanding  >
<  ———————————————————  >
```

**This is a public bulletin board
intended primarily for the use of the
fans of that fabulous TV series, "Hunt
of Orion."**

**DISCLAIMER:
Any posting of telephone numbers,
access codes, or credit card numbers
intended to facilitate unauthorized
access to computer or telecommunication
systems is strictly forbidden. The
SysOp disclaims any responsibility for
such activities and will delete the
posts and cancel the access of any user
engaging in such activities.**

The Deviant has no mail waiting.

Command (Menu=?):

This was the point that Flash had been waiting for. According to his informant, the system so far had been just window dressing, a carefully crafted disguise intended to conceal the true nature of the board. He typed ROCH-ESTER.

The system made a beep and responded with **Invalid response! Hit RETURN to continue:**

"Sure, sure," Flash muttered. This was part of the cover. He typed BUFFALO.

And was in:

```
<  ———————————————————  >
<  CONGRATULATIONS! You have gained  >
<     access to the Hacker's Haven BBS  >
<        operated by The Investigator.  >
```

```
<         ————————————————         >
<      ***EQUAL ACCESS FOR ALL!***    >
<    **POWER THROUGH INFORMATION!**  >
<         ————————————————         >
```

NOTICE: If you are an employee of a
law enforcement agency or a tele-
communications company or are related to
such a person, you are not authorized to
use this system. Please hang up
immediately or you will be in violation
of state and federal law.

Command [T(itles), R(ead), Q(uit)]:

The standard el bullshit-o, Flash thought. He turned on
the Mac's elderly Image Writer II printer to get a hard copy
of what followed, then scanned the message base for likely-
looking entries. As usual, the messages were a random mix
of telephone numbers, access codes, and a few credit card
numbers, mostly of no interest. He had almost decided to
give up on the message base and post some E-mail to likely
hackers when he came to message number thirty-seven:

Message #37: New TeleNet Codes
(Spacebar quits message)
Posted by: The Electron Terrorist
Date: October 17 @ 02:24 EDT
Good News! I just cracked the
TeleNet user file. Here are a few
Addresses and Passwords for their big $$$
customers:

There followed what looked like a list of the Fortune 500
companies, with a network address and password for each.
Flash whistled. Scanning down the list, he came to the entry:

Megalith Corp. MEG3592 AMBIANCE

Flash turned to Victoria, seated on the bed across the room, a multicolored circuit diagram spread out before her, an integrated circuit catalog in her lap. "Hey, Sis!" he yelled, a note of triumph in his voice. "We now have a way to crack Megalith!"

Flash, seated at the Macintosh in Vickie's bedroom, had just entered his fourth Megalith super-mainframe. Things were going better now. After school he had tried his first assault on Megalith, and it had been a near disaster. He'd used the University of Washington HEPNet link, and a system manager on the first Megalith system he'd entered had spotted his activity and demanded to know who he was and how he'd gotten onto the system. He'd disconnected instantly. Then he had to crack the UW system's logging files to erase his tracks before Megalith security could backtrack.

Over dinner he'd thought about the fiasco and decided that this was no time for sloppy work. He was dealing with the big time, and he was going to have to be much more careful to bring this one off. He'd developed an indirect and untraceable routing through a Canadian university computer. Then, using the access codes posted by the Electron Terrorist, he had networked into another Megalith system. This system was a very large IBM mainframe.

He had found a user with a high activity level but, on the basis of the files in his directory, no evidence of computer sophistication. The owner was clearly a plodder. Flash had boldly assumed the identity of this user. Pretending to have program problems, he'd asked the system manager to help him and was able to pull off the old Trojan horse scam, which he knew from experience was still workable on IBM operating systems. The system manager had run the innocent-appearing program in question in the system manager's own account and under the blanket of the system manager's own privilege levels. It had been a deceptively simple little program that, among other things, had awarded Flash's account SysOp privileges. He'd then been able to determine that this system was part of a local area network that linked it into other IBMs and a Cray, all located in the San Jose area and used by Megalith engineering groups.

Soon Flash was the master of all these systems. On the second IBM he'd found a lightly protected file belonging to a word-processing group. The file contained the current network addresses, access codes, and telephone dial-ups for all of Megalith's major computer sites. In this list Flash found a promising DEC HyperVAX located in the corporate headquarters in San Francisco. He dialed in to the VAX, quickly determined the name of the system operator, and logged off. Then, establishing an account in the same name on one of his captive systems, he came back in through DEC Net and found that, as expected, he had captured all the privileges of the VAX SysOp. Essentially, he was wearing the SysOp's skin.

Scanning the user list, Flash spotted a familiar name: Pierce. Yes! Saxon's reports were addressed to that guy. Pierce should be into some interesting things. His directory was super-protected, set up to be airtight. Even the SysOp was locked out. Well, there was more than one way to skin a snake. Flash typed in a short program written in the language C, composing it from memory, and compiled it. Checking to make sure that Pierce wasn't using his terminal, he allocated the unit and connected his C program to it.

Then he waited, a spider with its web arrayed neatly in position. It didn't take long. It never does, when you're on a roll.

Martin Pierce sat at his desk in his San Francisco office, cradling his head in his hands and contemplating his problems. Things were not going well. Before returning to San Francisco, he had arranged for the lease of a secluded lakefront residence near the University of Washington in the fashionable Laurelhurst area. The house he had selected was isolated from nearby residences by distance and large shrubs, was furnished, had a large garage with automatic doors through which unobserved arrivals and departures could be arranged, and even had its own boat dock complete with motorboat. That could prove useful, on the off chance that some disposal work was needed.

Mandrake and the PSRS personnel had taken Saxon to the house for interrogation. A cover story detailing Saxon's "emergency trip to Switzerland" had been carefully fabricated. A meticulously constructed trail of Saxon's BitNet communications, airline tickets, and border crossings led from Seattle to Zurich and vanished there.

At first, Mandrake's reports to Pierce on the progress of the interrogation implied that Allan Saxon was being obstinate in refusing to reveal where the missing equipment had been hidden, how the disappearance trick had been done, and the technical details of the twistor effect. Mandrake had even felt admiration for Saxon's great strength of character in resisting their initial methods of persuasion. It soon became clear, however, that there was another problem. Drugs like neurophagin have proved to be completely reliable in these matters, and against these no strength of character can prevail.

It was no longer possible that Saxon was faking ignorance of the location of the equipment or the details of operation of the twistor effect. He truly was ignorant of both, except at the most superficial level. And he seemed to truly believe some bizarre story about shadow universes, perhaps a delusional side effect of the drug. Saxon was worthless as a source of information, but it would still be necessary to keep him out of circulation for a while.

At the proper time they could drug him, fill his stomach with cheap wine, and dump him in a doorway on a skid row in some eastern city. If and when he was finally identified, it would probably be assumed that he'd suffered a mental breakdown. It was an excellent cover. Even if the irreversible effects of neurophagin left Saxon with enough of his faculties to make accusations, these would be dismissed as paranoid delusions.

Pierce gritted his teeth with resolution. He had already exceeded his mandate by a considerable margin. The Megalith board always favored aggressive actions with a profitable bottom line, but there must be no hint of some cowboy operation that was out of control. He must be very careful.

With determination, resolve, and the proper strategy, this enterprise could still be brought to a profitable bottom line. The surveillance recordings indicated that only two people understood the intricacies of the twistor effect: David Harrison, whose disappearance had caused all the present problems, and Victoria Gordon. Since Saxon knew nothing about how the apparatus had been snatched from Pierce's grasp, and since Harrison was missing or hiding out, Gordon was next on the list.

Last week Pierce had arranged for a Megalith campus recruiter to approach Miss Gordon with an extremely attractive job offer. The strategy had been to get her attention focused on the large salary, then reveal the side condition that she must go to work for Megalith immediately. It had failed. The recruiter had reported that as soon as Gordon discovered the offer was from Megalith she had told him she was definitely not interested and had stalked out. So be it. There were other ways.

Pierce raised the flat color-graphics screen from its recess in his desk. It was time to discover what could be learned from Miss Gordon by more direct methods. He initiated his standard log-in procedure. Curiously, it took a bit longer than usual for the system start-up messages to appear. But soon he was into the system and uploading detailed instructions to the PSRS VAX for the initial phases of the Gordon operation.

Victoria hoisted her bike up the ancient wooden stairs of the old house on Densmore and clicked the chain lock around a weathered post. She was tired. The teams she had organized yesterday had been busily going about their tasks today. But everything else depended on her providing a design for the new twistor hardware. That was moving with frustrating slowness.

It had been a warm day for October, and the sagging front door was ajar. She squeezed past it, walked through the house to the kitchen, and clopped down the worn basement stairway. It was cooler down here. In her bedroom her brother was seated before the dim screen of her Mac. "Hi, William! What's up?" she asked.

Flash glanced up. He had an underfed, hollow-eyed look but he was clearly happy. "El progress-o! Our most important product!" he said. "I'm getting damn close, Sis. Remember those letters from Saxon to a guy named Martin Pierce at Megalith? Well, I've cracked the system that Pierce uses. It's in San Francisco, and he's got his area protected up the wa-zoo, but I slipped a port feedthrough decoy into the system. I've already got both of Pierce's passwords and one encryption key."

"That was fast," said Vickie. "How'd you manage it?"

"Well," said Flash, "Pierce always uses the same terminal port to connect to the computer. It must be hard wired. I got myself SysOp privileges on his system and planted a decoy program in the system that's sitting right on his port line. Whenever Pierce types into his terminal, he's talking to my program, not the system. When he tried to log in, my program creates a new process and logs him on, just as requested. Whatever he says to do, the program passes it along. The only difference is that it makes a file on the disk that records everything he types and everything he reads: passwords, encryption keys, access codes, the works. He's already used it twice today. I checked. Later tonight I'll go into the system again and fetch the full records back here."

"William, is there any sign that anyone might have detected your messings-about in their system?" asked Victoria, remembering the stories about Megalith security.

"Nary a ripple-o," said Flash. "I got off to a bad start, but since then I've been very careful, Sis. No flashy stuff, just smooth subterranean hacking. The program's invisible unless the SysOp is specifically looking for it, and anyhow there's no way my network linkups could be backtracked here. And we're almost in the clear. I've already downloaded lots of Pierce's suspicious encrypted files to the Mac, so I only need to go into his system one more time. I've got three floppies full of his files, a few megabytes' worth. We can decrypt them right here and read them. But not 'til I get that one last encryption key. Then we'll see what foul deeds Mr. Pierce has been up to." He smiled.

"OK, come on, Hacker Hero," she said, patting him on the shoulder. "Put your toys away and get dressed. I'm taking you over to the Pizza Haven in the Broadway district for one of those loathsome pepperoni-and-anchovy pizzas you're addicted to. You deserve some good old R and R. And I'll stand treat for the arcade games and pinball, too.''

Flash shut down the Mac and headed for the door.

When Vickie and Flash returned from the Broadway district much later that evening, a nondescript panel truck was parked nearby on Densmore next to a utility pole. There was nothing about the truck that would have drawn the attention of a casual observer. But if one had been able to see in the near infrared region of the optical spectrum, as certain insects can, thin beams of IR light would have been visible linking the truck with inconspicuous reflectors on several windows of a nearby house and with a small gray module attached to a telephone terminal box high on the utility pole.

21

WEDNESDAY, OCTOBER 20

Victoria got up at six forty-five, showered, dressed. She burned her finger cooking the bacon for breakfast. William had been hacking until quite late and didn't want to get up at all. She had to pull the covers from his bed and threaten him with a drenching if he didn't get up immediately. They'd eaten breakfast quickly, and he had to run to catch the school bus.

She unlocked her bike from the porch. It was raining hard, she realized, and went back into the house for her rain gear. Finally, slicker clad, she eased her bicycle down Densmore.

She'd just reached the Burke-Gilman Trail when she noticed that her rear tire was going flat. She always carried a spare tube and a set of mounting levers in her pack. But dismounting the tire, locating the nail, mounting the new tube in the old tire, and inflating it with her hand pump, all done in the wet semidarkness and rain while squatting beside the trail, was not a pleasant experience. Morning bikers dinged their bells and splashed her as they went by, and the joggers made misguided attempts at humorous commentary.

By the time she arrived at Physics Hall, the fast oscilloscope she needed had already been borrowed by another group, and the CAD/CAM design computer hooked up to the NC mill in the student shop was already in use and had grown a long waiting list.

She washed the stale residue from her coffee cup, refilled it from the coffee pot in the machine shop, and went to the basement room that her group was using to assemble the new twistor apparatus. No one else was here yet. It had been a low-ceilinged storage area, practically a broom closet, but she'd prevailed upon Sam to relocate its contents so her group could work here. There wasn't really much room to work. Surplus equipment, parts, and components were stacked everywhere. Two vertical racks holding electronics chassis occupied the center of the room. Their many empty slots, a smile with missing teeth, were a silent reminder of problems yet unsolved.

She consulted the long MacProject III task chart taped along one wall. Many of the tasks were checked off as done, but too many in critical places along the path lines were lagging. Most of these involved designs that she had yet to complete. There were just not enough hours in the day. Her helpers were very conscientious and hard working so far, but she was the only one with the experience to tell them what to do. And often it required more time to give detailed instructions and then correct mistakes than to do it yourself. She had the feeling that all the burdens of the world rested squarely on her shoulders. She took a deep breath.

Once more she thought of David, stranded in another universe, perhaps dying . . . She got to work.

David, standing at the makeshift table at the base of their tree, poured the steaming milk-white liquid into the first of a row of white paper tubes. A stick across the top of each tube supported a thick string hanging down the center line. "Cross your fingers, Jeff," he said. "We may soon have ourselves a new light source." Yesterday Jeff had discovered some waxy white berries growing on one of the bushes near the pool. He'd brought them to David, saying that they smelled like candles. David had found that their waxy outer coating melted when heated, hardened when cooled, and burned smokelessly when soaked into paper.

This morning both children had gone berry picking and come back with a surprisingly large quantity of the "candleberries." David had heated their harvest over the fire in an old coffee can and was now pouring a milky stream of melted berry-wax into a makeshift mold. So far, so good. The liquid filled the first paper tube to the top. David moved on to the next tube in line. After the candles cooled, he and

Jeff would see if the things actually burned like candles.

Another experiment was in progress by the fire pit. Melissa was smoking fish. Monday had dawned cool and clear after the storm of the night before. They had cooked their first catch, and, for the first time since their arrival, they'd had enough to eat.

Now there was even something of a fish surplus, and Melissa was experimenting with preserving the catch by suspending fish fillets inside a wire-reinforced, aluminum foil "umbrella" over a smoky air-starved fire. The technique seemed to be working, and as an added bonus the swarms of small blue insect-creatures that had been attracted by the fish smell were driven away by the smoke.

When the last tube was filled with wax, David put down the can and aimed the CCD camera, recording Jeff with the candles and Melissa at work with the fish. This morning he was feeling more optimistic. The children were, for a change, getting along and working well together. He wondered why. Perhaps the stress of their new situation was diminishing, and they had interesting work to keep them occupied. The basics, thought David. They had structured work, preserved food, nearby water, a latrine, a source of illumination at night, a dry place to sleep.

It was likely they would survive for now, if nothing went seriously wrong and the winter was not too severe. The animal life and edible plants in this world were abundant enough that, at least for the moment, they could live off the land. But there were certainly differences here.

Opening Melissa's first fish to clean it had been a great surprise. Superficially, it had seemed an ordinary fish. There were too many fins in the wrong places, perhaps, but on the outside it was still just a fish.

Inside was another story. The internal organs had completely different structures and organization. There were two stomachs, no identifiable liver, the intestines were organized as a network rather than as a folded tube, and there was a bewildering array of other organs with functions David couldn't even guess. He wished he could recall more details from that messy biology lab he'd taken in college.

And the birds. He glanced up to where the treebird was

working its way along the tree trunk. The birds seemed to come in two groups. Those like the treebird divided the basic six-appendage body design into two wings, two walking feet, and two manipulator feet used for food gathering and perhaps also for fighting and defense. So far these were all large pelican-size birds, few in number and quite territorial.

He looked higher, to the flyer activity at the forest canopy. Up there were the four-wingers. Their design involved two pairs of wings with a muscle structure that made one pair of wings go up while the other pair went down. That counterbalanced wing movement seemed to be a very efficient design. Birds as large as robins were able to hover like hummingbirds. They were fascinating to watch. Perhaps he'd set up a bird feeder near the treehouse so he and the children could study them more.

He was still very concerned for the children's safety. Many times a day they had to climb to a dangerous height to get to the treehouse, they were eating plants and fish with unfamiliar characteristics that might contain toxic biochemicals, and there were large and dangerous carnivorous animals in the forest.

There was now some evidence that the big carnivores hunted only at night. They'd been here for a week now, and in that time David had seen the large bearlike animals only at night. But he still carried the gun whenever they explored new parts of the forest.

David had had some initial misgivings about his capability for dealing full time with the Ernst children. He was much relieved to find that he was able to take care of them without major traumas on either side. He was glad they were with him, actually. They could do useful things, and they were good company. Looking after them kept him from devoting too much time to brooding about their biggest problem: to find a way home.

It was ultimately a problem of electrical power. They had all the complex apparatus, the microprocessors and power supplies and multi-pole coils, needed to operate the twistor apparatus and return them to their proper universe. David had everything but the hydroelectric dams, the transformer stations, and the transmission lines to deliver electrical power to the university to feed the breaker boxes to power the equipment to make the twistor field to take them home. The big sources of electrical power now lay a universe away. And the twistor equipment required many kilowatts of power.

When Melissa discovered the pool with its natural spring, David had considered the possibility of building a dam and installing a small electrical generator turned by a millrace. But the problem of scale defeated him. Even if he could convert one of their electric pump motors to an efficient electric generator, which was by no means certain, a twistor field large enough to transport them back required many times the power that such a setup might conceivably produce. He'd also considered trying to convert one of the mechanical vacuum pumps to operate as a steam engine to turn the hypothetical electric generator. But that too was impractical; there was not enough metal to make a boiler, no way to shape the needed metal into a closed vessel, no way to seal the vessel well enough to hold steam pressure. Making a bank of large liquid-cell batteries was perhaps a more realistic low-technology alternative, but even that required quantities of electrolytes and electrode metals that were simply unavailable here.

It looked as if they might become permanent residents of this universe. At best it would take many years to relearn the old skills of smelting and forging metal, making copper wire and magnet steel and battery zinc and acid, producing boilers and bearings and chemicals, the products of a whole technological civilization. And until that technology was reinvented, their only electrical power sources were a few puny flashlight batteries and solar cells that would not last forever. If only it didn't require so damned much energy to produce a twistor transition. . . .

An elusive thought flitted at the periphery of David's consciousness, evading his grasp, just out of reach. He snatched at it—

He smiled. Of course! Rescale the energy! The power for the twistor field goes as the cube of the field diameter; a doubling of the field diameter requires an eightfold increase in the power. That means that a big field size requires a huge amount of power. But it also means that a smaller field takes a far smaller amount of power. A small enough field could operate on a few flashlight batteries!

David rapidly calculated how big a field one could make using several flashlight batteries as the power source. The answer came quickly. About the size of a baseball or perhaps a grapefruit. Small. Not enough to send people anywhere. But enough to send messages, to establish contact, to let those on the other side know that they were still alive and well. A bottle in which to float a message from castaways to the distant shores of home.

His mind racing, David strode to the ladder and began to climb rapidly up to the treehouse. He would make a prototype. There was work to be done.

As soon as David was out of sight, Melissa selected a choice fillet of fish from the bucket of those waiting to be put into the "smoker" and walked around behind the big tree. "Kitty?" she called softly. "Here kitty, kitty, kitty!"

A small brown-orange figure darted from behind a nearby tree and scampered across the carpet of leaves. It took the fish fillet in one tiny hand, paused to taste it, and then vanished into the forest.

Melissa smiled.

Flash returned from school at 3:37 P.M. There were some leftovers from last night's pizza still in the upstairs fridge. He gave it a quick nuke job in the microwave and carried it downstairs to snack on while he started up the Mac. The anchovy flavor was even better after sitting overnight. He'd noticed that before.

He activated the modem and began to weave a convoluted path through the net. In a few minutes he had arrived at his destination in San Jose and DECNetted across to the Megalith VAX in San Francisco. Quickly he downloaded the day's collection from his decoy file, watching it as it went into the Mac. Good, the second encryption key was there in Pierce's recent dialogue. They were in business.

He disconnected the decoy from Pierce's port, deallocated it, deleted the program, and wiped away all evidence of his

snooping. Briefly he considered doing some mischief as a
parting shot. Perhaps he should delete all of Pierce's files
and backups, or maybe send obscene mail messages in
Pierce's name to the receptionists and secretaries of all the
Megalith vice presidents. Or he could order in Pierce's name
the issuance of Megalith payroll checks to selected worthy
dudes and causes. . . .

But no, that was kid stuff. He was now an ethical "professional" doing honorable work. He backed out of the Megalith systems one by one, erasing all evidence of his
intrusions, folding the net behind him, and then switched
off the modem. He was home free. He hadn't lost the old
touch-o.

Flash fetched a Coke from the fridge and set about decrypting Pierce's files. It was going to be interesting to learn
what secrets lay beneath all those layers of protection.

The balding man had just established a link from the van
where he was sitting to PSRS headquarters. He placed the
encrypted file he had prepared in the [**BROADSWORD**]
area of the PSRS VAX. How long would it take for his
client to read it and reply, he wondered.

He had been monitoring the Gordon subject's telephone
line this afternoon when data communications at 4800 baud
had come on the line. PSRS was, of course, set up for
interception of data communications as well as voice recordings. He had watched with interest as the subject using
the line wove a network path from one computer system to
the next. The subject clearly knew what he was doing and
was up to something.

Since the primary subject, Victoria Gordon, had been
observed to leave the site early this morning, it was likely
that the communications were initiated by her brother, William Gordon, who had a police record for computer-related
crime.

In rapid succession the subject penetrated several computer systems of the Megalith Corporation and finally downloaded a data stream of terminal dialogue that seemed to
involve some decryption on a [**PIERCE**] account of a Megalith Corporation VAX system located in the San Francisco

area. The balding man had recognized the message as one
that he had previously sent to Broadsword. He had duly
included this information with his encrypted report to
Broadsword and inquired if this activity was of any interest.

The old VT-220 terminal beeped and the message **You
have new mail!** appeared on its screen. That didn't take
long, he thought as he fetched the MAIL message:

To: **MANDRAKE**
Subject: **GORDON SURVEILLANCE**
Text: **Urgent you apprehend BOTH Victoria
Gordon and William Gordon and hold both
for immediate questioning. Also retain
all data recording media found in the
possession of William Gordon and hold
these for further instructions. Under
no circumstances are any files on these
media to be read or decrypted.**

The balding man rubbed his chin. The subject's hacking
had clearly touched a nerve. There was indeed a connection
between Broadsword and the Megalith Corporation. That
information could prove very useful. After they nailed the
Gordon kid, he'd have to have a look at those files, maybe
make backup copies for insurance . . . can never tell when
a bit of leverage with Megalith might be useful.

He would need some help with this operation. He reached
for the telephone.

Too much still to do, Vickie was thinking as she counted
the empty spots in the twin electronics racks. She looked
at her watch. Six P.M. It was too early to be this tired and
hungry and frustrated. At the group meeting over lunch
she'd had a big argument with Paul. He still wanted to make
a deal with Allan Saxon to get his company's help with the
project. Dumb! And now Jim Lee, who'd signed up to her
help her this evening, had just begged off, pleading a do-
mestic emergency and leaving her with no help for tonight.

She scribbled a few updates on the project time line taped
to the wall. It was going to be at least a week before they

could try any twisting. She thought about that. The first test would be to see what a half-meter twist into the target universe produced. Maybe another "wooden marble." Maybe a ball of dirt or water. This basement room was lower than the lab upstairs, but the she had so way of knowing if it was above or below ground level over there. If the twist produced only air, they'd twist a camera through and take a look. She wondered what David was doing now.

The wall phone rang. She walked across and answered it. It was William. She wondered how he'd found this number. Probably found the departmental phone book on the HyperVAX.

"Sis!" he said, excited. "I just read the Megalith files. That Pierce creep ordered some guy named Mandrake to do a snatch on you! You're supposed to be kidnapped! Get out! Quick! I think our phone's tapped, too. They know. Get to a safe place. If you can, meet me at midnight tonight for anchovies. *Go! Now!*" He hung up.

Anchovies? she thought, then remembered last night's pizza at the Broadway Pizza Haven. She struggled into her jacket and opened the door to the basement hallway. Two men were standing just outside the door. The one in front was quite large. She noticed his right hand was missing as he grabbed for her.

With a skill acquired over several years with the Tae Kwan Do Club at CalTech, she kicked the big man expertly in the crotch with her toe, then deep in the stomach with her instep. He was doubling over as she whirled to meet the other man.

A mist of aerosol droplets drifted over her from a little spray can the man was holding. She tasted oysters, then . . . darkness.

As Flash put down the phone, he heard one car door slam outside, then another. He shoved four diskettes into his pocket. The FBI man's card was still on the computer table. He took that also. As he was walking down the hall to his room, he heard a loud knocking on the front door above, then heavy footsteps in the upper hallway. A rough voice above said something about "Gordon."

He was prepared. None of the el bust-o. No more up-against-the-wall-turkey for The Flash. Moving quickly, he closed the door and turned the key twice in the lock, then put a steel rod through it wired to the doorknob so it couldn't turn. He rolled the heavy chest of drawers to a position blocking the door and flipped down the latches on its oiled casters, locking them. Moving to the window, he freed the carefully cleaned and modified window latch and slowly pushed the bottom of the window outward so that the ivy vines growing over it at ground level moved silently outward like a tent. Fitting his legs into the gap formed by the ivy, he slid outside and pulled the window closed. He found the Allan wrench he had taped over the windowsill, slipped it into the small hole he had drilled in the window frame, and relocked the "doctored" window latch from the outside.

Flash slithered down the ivy-covered passage to a point where he could exit hidden from the street. In the six-o'clock twilight he darted across the gap between the houses and down the side basement steps of the old house next door. Fitting the key taped over the doorsill into the lock, he let himself in. As he closed the door, he heard banging noises coming from his rooming house. He locked the heavy basement door from the inside, pocketed the key, and made his way through the darkened basement to a little-used cupboard at floor level near the old furnace. Crawling into the opening, he pulled the door shut and crawled into the long space behind stacks of old magazines.

Flash had read that the best strategy for a fugitive was to "go to ground" and stay in quiet hiding for as long as possible, especially when there were searchers nearby. He'd made his plans accordingly. He located the plastic bottle of "borrowed" sleeping pills that he'd taped in the corner. They were the new controlled-duration type with a calibrated sleeping period. He shook out two of the green ones, the five-hour kind, and swallowed them. Briefly he imagined the Megalith muscle trying to deal with the "locked-room" mystery he'd left for them, and he smiled. But soon he slipped into a deep and dreamless sleep.

* * *

Another afternoon storm was in full force in the world beyond the treehouse door-hole. There were pounding gusts of wind, and it had been raining hard for the past few hours. The tree groaned faintly in the wind. David had worried that the spherical hole carved by the twistor field might have weakened their tree to the point of collapse. But on consideration, he realized that the width of the treehouse cavity spanned less than a third of the tree's full diameter and took away a maximum of ten percent of the tree's cross section. It was probably OK.

When the rainstorm had blown up after lunch, they had quickly moved anything up into the treehouse that might have been damaged by wind or rain. After that, except for brief trips to the latrine, David and the children had stayed in the treehouse. They were relatively warm and dry, and a few lighted candles provided dim illumination. They'd eaten an early dinner, feasting on some Melissa's smoked fish while it was still warm. But now the children were growing whiny and getting on each other's nerves again. And certainly on David's.

David sat at the big worktable. In the reflector-enhanced light from one of the new candles, the circuitry of the new mini-twistor prototype was slowly taking form. He was making wirewrap connections between small scavenged components, IC circuit chips, resistors, and small disk capacitors mounted on a rectangle of perf-board, perforated brown plastic that stood on four corner screw-legs.

He stopped. Consulting his crudely penciled circuit diagram, he realized that his last four wirewrap connections had been off by one pin. Damn. They'd have to be clipped out and rewired. He put the breadboard down on the table and rubbed his eyes. Time for a break.

"Hey!" he said, turning to the children. "I think we've worked enough for now. What can we do that's fun? How about some songs?"

Jeff immediately turned from his argument with Melissa and walked over. "What's today, David?" he asked.

David looked at his digital watch. "Today's Wednesday, October twentieth, and it's six-thirty-two P.M. and twenty-three seconds, Pacific Daylight Time."

"Then this is the day for our story," Jeff said seriously.

"Yes, you should tell us more of the story about Ton, David," Melissa added.

"You're absolutely right," said David, "this is story day." They ranged themselves in a circle, the children perched on their sleeping bag and David sitting on the floor in front of them.

"OK," he said, "do you remember Ton discovered how to make the Urorb work?"

Two heads nodded.

"Well," said David, "Ton next picked up the strange pointed weapon, the Pricklance, and examined it. The book had implied that it was to be used with the Urorb. He thought about this, trying to imagine how that might be done. Then he lifted the crystal sphere with his left hand and looked into it. Ton was growing increasingly hungry, and he thought of the wonderful red apples that should now be ripening on the large old tree behind his father's forge. The tree, laden with apples, appeared before him in the Urorb. Almost reflexively, Ton lifted the pointed rod and made as if to spear an apple on its tip. He felt the weapon grow heavier, and when he looked, there was a beautiful red apple skewered on its pointed end.

"When he placed the weapon on the rug and touched the apple, he found that it was not the illusion he was expecting. Instead, it was quite real. He wasted little time in eating it, core and all, before continuing with his investigations. After a few more apples had been speared and eaten, Ton decided on a broader menu. He recalled the many trips that he had made with his mother to the vendor stalls of the local village market. He concentrated on his memories until he could see the village marketplace in the Urorb. It was late afternoon and most of the vendors had left for the day, but one persistent old peddler was still hawking broiled sausages. Ton speared two of them, promising himself to repay the old man when next he had the opportunity. He completed his 'shopping' expedition by carefully snagging the tie-strings of a leather sack of goat's milk. Shortly thereafter, his stomach pleasantly full, he took a nap."

David studied his audience for signs that they might follow Ton's example. They were now lying on their sleeping bag, but appeared wide awake. He swatted at one of the blue flying insects that had taken up residence in their treehouse. It was a clean miss.

"Ton wasn't sure how long he had slept. When he awoke, he found that the Urorb would give only dim light, and he feared that he had worn it out with his 'shopping expedition.' But when he visualized his mother's kitchen, now lamp lit, the Urorb's light became reasonably bright. He realized that it was night in the outside world. The dimness of the Urorb mirrored the darkness outside.

"Ton tried to visualize the cottage of Zorax but could see only dimness, and he concluded that it was dark within and that no one was home. Then he remembered his brief exchange with Elle, the girl in the tower. He had never seen her face, but he remembered the lower part of the tower quite well, and presently through the Urorb he could see it faintly in the starlight. There was a light in an upper barred window. Through successive visualizations which made his head hurt behind the eyes, he was able to approach the window, to see inside, and finally to pass his viewpoint through the bars and view the room.

"Elle was there, and she was crying. It was the first time that Ton had actually seen her. He realized that she was very beautiful. He felt himself falling instantly in love with her and longed to speak to her. But though he called to her, it was in vain; she didn't hear him. He examined the steel-banded door of the tower and concluded that he had no way of opening it for her with his weapon. Finally he had an idea. He tore a blank page from the back of the leather-bound book. Using his own blood for ink and the point of the weapon as a pen, he wrote a brief note identifying himself and telling her that he was watching over her and would save her if he could. He folded the note, skewered it on the tip of the weapon, and, using the Urorb, he dropped it in her lap.

"He watched as she read the note and was delighted that she seemed to understand and to look around the room, smiling. Most of the rest of the night Ton watched over Princess Elle while she slept."

David surveyed his audience again. This time they were, like Princess Elle, asleep.

It was eleven P.M. and very dark when his watch alarm awoke Flash. He was kind of groggy from the pills, but it wasn't too bad. Their time-released stimulant component made him feel fairly alert. He had just an hour before attempting the meeting with Vickie. In the darkness he slipped out the back entrance of the old house and headed west toward Fremont, putting distance between himself and Wallingford. He crossed over the Ship Canal on the Fremont Bridge, then ascended Queen Anne Hill using side streets and alleyways until he reached Aurora, six lanes of fast north-south traffic. There he connected with a bus to downtown, then transferred to another bus that dropped him off in the Broadway district.

Circling around through a parking lot on Tenth Street, he entered the Broadway Arcade by the rear entrance next to the Washington State Liquor Store fronting on the parking lot. He climbed the back stairs to the upper level, a balcony mezzanine containing vacant shop space relieved by a record/video store, a hair stylist, a travel office, and a law office. At midnight these were all closed, and he was able to look down unobserved on the Pizza Haven at the first-floor rear of the Arcade.

His sister wasn't there, but neither was anyone who looked like Megalith muscle. Flash settled down in a shadowed doorway to wait. The pizza smells from below pulled at his empty stomach, but he dared not go down to buy any. He sat listening to the exotic sounds from the arcade video games just below him and for a while imagined that he was playing the games himself.

He was really worried about his sister. After his mother had died of cancer when he was ten, Vickie had been the closest thing to a mother he'd had. He should have taken care of her. Those Megalith guys were nothing to mess with, and if they had snatched Sis . . . He shuddered. He was responsible. He had known they were trouble, and he should have talked her out of her crazy idea. But instead he fell in with the game of cracking their system like some little kid playing a video game. And now they had Sis. His mind whirled, constructing absurd baroque schemes for heroically rescuing his sister, for destroying the Megalith Corporation. He wiped a bit of moisture from the corner of his eye. This was real life, and he was just a kid. What could he do, really, except run away and hide out? He felt very low, depressed.

When his sister had not appeared at the Pizza Haven by one A.M., Flash decided to give up. His head felt like it was filled with mud. He walked to the opposite end of the arcade's balcony and waited by the big upstairs window until he could see a number 9 bus at the traffic light two blocks to the south, heading north toward him along Broadway. Then he sprinted to the pay telephone in the corner near the men's room and dialed 911.

When the emergency operator answered, Flash said, ''Please don't interrupt. My life's in danger, and I can't give my name. I have information that people working for a Mr. Martin Pierce of the Megalith Corporation have kidnapped Victoria Gordon, a UW physics graduate student, at about six P.M. today. This kidnapping is related to the disappearances of Dr. David Harrison and the Ernst children. Please notify Agent Bartley of the FBI, Seattle office. Goodbye.''

He hung up and ran down the stairs and out the front of the building, stepping onto the bus just as the door was closing. He showed his bus pass and scrunched low in a seat as the bus headed north, wondering where he could spend the night. In the past six weeks as a new kid at Roosevelt High he hadn't made any friends whom he knew well enough to ask for help. He had many good friends on the boards, but he didn't know their addresses or even what they looked like.

The bus angled downhill beside and under the I- freeway to where Eastlake crossed the Ship Canal, then halted at the University Bridge as the red-and-white barriers went down. The bridge operator, who Flash could see in his little brick tower, was raising the bridge for boat traffic. The span began to lever upward.

Hey, David lives around here, Flash remembered. He

walked to the front of the bus and asked the motherly bus driver if she would please let him off, that he'd fallen asleep, missed his stop, and would have to walk a long way back. Looking straight ahead, she explained that Metro regulations did not permit passengers to exit between bus stops. Then she looked across at him, smiled, and the door opened. "Oops, must have hit the wrong button," she said.

Flash smiled, waved his thanks, and exited. He threaded his way to the walkway through the stalled traffic waiting for the bridge.

He walked south along the bridge walkway, watching the sailboats go past, and then turned east to walk down through the parking lot of the Red Robin hamburger place next to David's apartment. Circling around back, he climbed through the steep brushy slope to David's well-remembered deck that faced north across the Ship Canal to the U-district. As he'd expected, the deck door was locked.

He removed the long wire-thin Allen wrench that he always carried in his billfold and expertly picked the lock of the sliding glass door, letting himself into David's apartment. It was dark in the apartment, but he remembered the layout from their visit last month. He headed for the small kitchen.

When he opened the refrigerator door the light inside came on, and he could see that David had a good supply of food. He selected a butter plate, half a carton of milk, a package of salami, a jar of dill pickles, and a chunk of sharp cheddar cheese from the shelves, then turned to put the food down on the kitchen table behind him.

He almost dropped the load of food when he saw the thing on the table. It was a white paper, official-looking with a seal and "FBI" in bold letters across the top. Putting the food down carefully, he studied the paper in the pale light streaming from the open refrigerator. The document stated that the apartment had been legally entered and searched by agents of the FBI in pursuance of an authorized investigation. It said that they might return, and it gave a telephone number to call for more information. Spaces for the code number of the search warrant and the case number were filled in with blue ball-point at the bottom of the page, and the document was signed by one Agent Cooper.

Flash felt scared. This was the one place he'd considered safe, and it had already been searched by the FBI. And they might be back. His mind raced. Would they come back? Only if there was reason to believe they'd missed something, or if there was something new to look for. It was probably OK for him to stay here, at least for a day or so. Until the food ran out. He made himself two sandwiches, ate them quickly along with three of the pickles, and finished off the milk.

He used the toilet without flushing it. Then he flopped on the bed still wearing his clothes and was immediately asleep.

Vickie came suddenly awake. Where . . . Then she remembered the phone call from William and the men who'd been waiting outside the door of the basement workroom. Her head hurt, and there was a bad taste in her mouth.

She opened her eyes and looked down. She seemed to be trussed up in a straitjacket. She wiggled erect and put her legs over the edge of the bed. Well, she could still kick. She studied the room. Bare, hospital-like, with a table, chair, and bed. The room had a window, a doorway to what looked like a bathroom, and another closed door. High in one corner was a small box. She wondered what it was.

She eased off the bed. A bit shaky, but she could walk. She went to the window and nudged the curtains aside with a knee. She saw barred windows and a frosted pane circled by aluminum alarm tape. She considered whether it was possible to break the window and saw through a strap with broken glass before the alarm brought interference. Probably not.

She moved her arms inside their canvas cocoons. How was it stage magicians were always able to escape from these things? She had seen it done, tried to remember how. Loosen one arm, put it over the head, same with the other, then shrug out of the thing. Trouble was, the magician always tensed his body when he was being strapped in. She'd been unconscious and fully relaxed, and the straps felt tight. Still . . . For the next ten minutes she worked to develop some slack in her right arm. Not much progress. She walked to the bathroom and looked in. There was a toilet and a wash basin. Her clothes were hanging from a hook on the wall, undies and all. She looked in the mirror over the wash basin. Below the canvas edge of the strait-jacket, she could see she was wearing a hospital gown. Those bastards, she thought.

She walked over to the closed door. Leaning a shoulder against the wall, she turned the knob slowly with her bare foot. The knob felt cold between her toes. It turned freely, but the door didn't open. Locked from the outside.

Then she heard approaching footsteps. Quickly she got back into the bed and tried to simulate an attitude of un-conscious sleep. She heard the door open and footsteps entering the room. She kept her eyes closed.

"No use playing possum, Miss Gordon," a voice said. "We've got a Doppler sensor on this room, and it showed you moving around. We know you're awake."

Shit, thought Victoria. She opened her eyes. A man wear-ing a ski mask was looking down at her. "Must be cold out there on the slopes to make you wear that thing," she observed. "Is there much powder on the runs today?"

He laughed. She noticed that another man was behind him, also wearing a ski mask. The missing hand was un-mistakable. He was the big one she'd kicked in the groin. She wondered now if that had been wise.

"Miss Gordon, we're here on a matter of national se-curity," the first one said. "We work for a special agency of the federal government. It would be very dangerous for you to know too much about us. That's why we've con-cealed our identities with these masks. It's for your own protection."

"Of course it is," Vickie said sweetly. "You're very special federal agents who just happen to go around kid-napping people whenever Mr. Martin Pierce of the Megalith Corporation gets on his computer and tells you to. Is that the story you want me to believe, Mr. Mandrake?"

The man paused. Vickie watched the masked face closely. Gears seemed to be spinning just behind the wool covering.

He hadn't expected me to confront him like that, she guessed.

"Miss Gordon," he said finally, "we're well aware of your brother's criminal activities in illegally gaining access to certain commercial computer systems. He's in custody now and has made a full statement. We'd like you to cooperate also."

Vickie blinked. Did they have William? Should she believe them? Probably not. If they *said* that they had him, it probably meant that they didn't. Now it was her move. "Yes, of course, Mr. Mandrake," she said in a sarcastic tone. "You clowns have probably also kidnapped the whole physics department and the UW women's volleyball team by now. Right?"

It was Mandrake's turn to blink behind the ski mask.

"Come on," she continued, "let's stop playing these silly intimidation games, shall we? I know exactly who you are and why you kidnapped me. Kidnapping directed across a state border is a federal crime, you know. Now just why is it that you and Mr. Pierce are willing to risk the consequences of something like that? Just what does the Megalith Corporation have to gain that makes the stakes so high?" Vickie looked closely at the man. Perhaps her strategy of forthright challenge was paying off. He was still off balance.

Mandrake sat heavily in the chair beside the bed. "Miss Gordon," he said, "you're clearly a highly intelligent person. I'm sure you know what my employers, whoever they may be, want. I take it from your tone that you might be willing to cooperate, if the price is right. Just what is your price?"

She looked directly into the eyes behind the mask. "You've been listening in on us all week, Mandrake. You know the score. My colleague David Harrison and I have made a marvelous discovery. It's something that might happen to a physicist only once in a lifetime, if she was very lucky indeed. But because of your meddling, David and two innocent children are either dead or in a life-threatening situation. My price? My price is that I want to be able to follow up on our discovery without any further interference from you and your goons. I want to try to get those three people back. When that's accomplished, I'll be glad to tell Megalith anything they want to know about the twistor effect, provided I can tell the rest of the world at the same time. What you and Mr. Pierce already know ought to give you a head start in exploiting the effect, and that should be sufficient. On the other hand, if you don't let me go, you'll never be able to learn enough to even recoup your losses. So that's my price, Mandrake. Let me go now and stay the Hell out of my way.''

Mandrake stood up. He unbuckled the straps on her strait-jacket. "You can take that off now," he muttered. "It was only to keep you from doing something stupid. You're on your honor not to try to escape. You couldn't anyhow, but you could cause us some trouble. I'll communicate what you've said to my employer. I don't know if he'll buy it, but I'm willing to treat it as a legitimate offer and try.'' The two masked men left the room. The door clicked shut, then there was a second click from outside.

Removing the straitjacket, Vickie hurled it angrily at the box near the ceiling. It missed the box and fell to the floor with a klunk. She felt very alone, very vulnerable.

Something was bothering her. Why had Mandrake un-buckled the straitjacket, she wondered. Was this really a process of rational negotiation? Was it some kind of good-guy/bad-guy trick? Or was it only that this way they avoided having to assist her in eating meals or using the toilet? She moved toward the bathroom. Perhaps she'd feel better wearing her own clothes, she decided.

Mandrake, still wearing the ski masks, returned after a few hours. "Sorry," he said, "no deal. You're not, as you seem to think, holding a winning hand. My employer instructs me to make you aware of certain facts and techniques.'' He described the drug neurophagin and its effects on the nervous systems of those to whom it is administered. He explained that they would have to use it on her unless she elected to cooperate.

"That's a frightening and disgusting story," she said. "But I don't believe a word of it. It's just another technique from your bag of interrogation tricks. If it were true, you wouldn't tell me about it unless you planned to kill me sooner or later.''

"It leaves no traces," said Mandrake, "and no one would believe you. Any doctor would testify the syndrome was a premature case of Alzheimer's. But you do have a point. It would be pointless to tell you about neurophagin unless we could demonstrate its effects.''

He opened the outer door of the room and led her down the hall to a second doorway. The large man followed silently. Mandrake produced a bundle of keys and unlocked a deadbolt lock mounted on the outside of the heavy door. They entered a room much like the one they had left. On the bed lay Allan Saxon, smiling placidly and talking quietly to himself.

"There are people coming into my room now," Vickie heard Saxon murmur. "Oh, there's Vickie. She's such a pretty girl. Nice legs. I wonder if she fucks.''

Vickie was shocked. Was this really Allan Saxon?

He sat up in the bed. "The trick is to gain control, dominance," he murmured. "I'll speak to them in a loud voice, and perhaps they'll do what I want." He paused. "Gentlemen, it's time for me to leave! Please accompany me to my car." He stood beside the bed. Vickie took a step backward.

"Not just yet," Mandrake said. "But soon, sir, soon.'' He gently put his hand on Saxon's shoulder.

"I wonder if he's lying," said Saxon. "He always lies, doesn't he. I always lie too, when I can get away with it. Am I lying now? I like to lie to women. I like to lie with women. I wonder if Vickie would lie with me. Should I ask her. No, the men might hurt me again. I never knew that it could hurt so much. But I didn't lie to them. I told them the truth, but they wouldn't believe me. I told them that David had gone to a shadow universe. The shadow knows what evil . . . Poor David. He's only a shadow, now. Just he and his shadow . . .''

Mandrake looked at Vickie. "Seen enough?" he asked.

"I've seen many things," Saxon said. "I've seen an atom alone in a trap. I saw a rat in a trap, once, but it was dead. It had yellow teeth and a long scaly tail . . .''

Vickie nodded, retreating from Saxon, and they quickly left the room. Mandrake relocked the door, then led her into her own room. She sat on the bed. Mandrake sat on the chair, and the big man stood by the door.

"That's horrible!" Vickie cried, her face in her hands. "How could you do that to someone?"

"I could demonstrate," Mandrake said.

"Look," said Vickie, "you're not thinking this through. You don't need another zombie, you need my cooperation. If I were in that condition, you'd never learn what your friend Pierce wants to know."

"I agree with you, Miss Gordon," Mandrake said, "but my employer doesn't. By the time he realizes his mistake, it will be too late for you. So your only alternative is to cooperate." He put a little digital disk recorder on the table and activated it, then asked her a stream of questions.

She answered the questions truthfully, as long as they didn't reveal certain key techniques needed for the twistor effect. And the questions were mainly about where the twistor apparatus "had been taken." She carefully explained to Mandrake what she thought had happened to the apparatus. She described the physical evidence that supported her views. The questioning took a long time. Mandrake was noncommittal at the end, but she felt that he hadn't believed her. Finally, the two masked men left her alone again.

About half an hour later the large man came back alone. He had something to tell Vickie, he said through the ski mask stretched tightly over his face. It was about sex. He sat in the chair by the bed, his hands in his lap, and spent a seemingly endless time telling her in great and graphic detail what he planned to do to her and with her. Some of it involved his arm stump. It was almost as if she were not in the room, or perhaps as if he were confessing to a priest. He told her about the prostitutes he'd "snuffed," about the things he'd done to them first. . . .

He was clearly psychotic. She wasn't sure that some of the actions he described were physically possible. Mandrake must have sent him in to scare her. He had succeeded; she was completely and profoundly terrified, afraid to even look at the man. Finally he left, locking the door behind him.

* * *

David sat back from the worktable and placed the pistol-grip wirewrap tool on the candle-lit surface. One of the blue flying creatures buzzed near the candle flame, and he swatted at it. Then he examined the object on the table with satisfaction.

The twistor prototype was done. Mounted on the perf-board surface were a jumble of capacitors, resistors, IC chips, transistors, and diodes. Some of the components were crudely tack-soldered together, while others were enmeshed in many-layered zigzags of pale red wirewrap connections.

It was not very neat, but after all this was only a test prototype, to see if a small twistor field could be generated on battery power. At the edges of the perf-board dangled about a dozen silvery potentiometers, three wires leading from each to the prototype while their shafts rested on the table top. The function of each pot was scrawled in black letters across its shiny back surface.

David connected wires from the prototype to the bank of flashlight batteries he'd assembled. Then he quickly did some power-up checks using dummy loads for the twistor coils and observing electrical wave shapes with Sam's small LCD oscilloscope. He noticed an interesting effect. When the feedback loop gain of one of the operational amplifiers was set slightly above its proper value, it tended to oscillate. This had the consequence of making the twistor rotation sequence advance continuously. He'd seen the effect before. It had been responsible for their first "vacuum improvement" indications of the twistor effect.

He considered. For the gadget he was planning to build, this bug might actually be a feature. It might, with luck, allow him to "peek" through the field sphere, seeing light and perhaps even hearing sounds from the other side. David scribbled some changes on the circuit diagram, adding two integrated circuit chips and another switch to the design. He continued with the power tests until he was satisfied. It was looking very good. He cut power.

Then he connected the twistor coils he'd carefully wound and set in epoxy the day before. They were curved sections of spherical surfaces, scaled-down versions of the useless big ones that still stood in the center of the room on their large wooden supports like some inept attempt at postmodern sculpture. He reconnected power and pushed a red button mounted on the perf-board. Nothing.

He'd screwed up, cut too many corners in the design, he thought ruefully. Or perhaps . . . perhaps he just needed to increase the positive feedback coupling. He twitched the feedback potentiometer clockwise and made a note in the open lab notebook beside him, then made two measurements with the ohmmeter and noted them.

He reconnected the batteries and repeated the earlier checks. He pressed the red button and watched the candle flame through the little coils. The region between the coils might have wavered infinitesimally, creating the illusion of a very slight dimming of the candle flame beyond. Good! He turned another potentiometer clockwise, watching the faint darkness between the coils near the flame as it deepened, then lightened, then grew very dark indeed. He smiled and disconnected the batteries, made more notes and more ohmmeter readings. He would need this information if a portable unit was to be built.

Finally he reconnected the battery bank, pushed the red button to verify that the darkness still came, and reduced one of the pots until a black mark on its shaft matched a similar mark on its threaded sleeve. He inhaled and pressed the red button. There was a quite audible *pop!* sound.

David quietly disconnected the batteries again. He stood up, stretched, and looked down again at the untidy prototype. The damned kludge actually worked! He had a functioning twistor device. He stood quietly for a time.

Then he yelled "*Yaa-hoooo! Yee-haaaaaaaa!*" and jumped up and down. Sound completely filled the treehouse echo chamber.

Melissa, who had been asleep for hours, sat up and looked at him in amazement. Jeff turned toward him and stared.

David hugged them and told them that everything was OK, that everything was wonderful, that he would tell them in the morning.

They went back to sleep. David, weary but happy, curled

up on his mattress too, thinking what he'd do if they returned. *When* they returned.

Jeff needed to go to the bathroom. David had arranged a plastic garbage can behind the gray cabinet as a "nightjar," but Jeff didn't approve of this substitute for sanitary facilities. He decided that, although David had warned them that dangerous animals might be outside at night, he would use the new latrine David had made behind their tree. Quietly he took the small flashlight David kept on the table, walked to the door-hole, and unfastened the cover. The rain had stopped and a half moon was out between the trees, low in the southwest. It was a funny moon, about the same size as the one he remembered at home. But it had two big dark craters just above the dark part that were like eyes, watching him. It made him feel a little scared. He silently lowered the ladder, climbed down, and walked through the slanting moonlight to the latrine behind the tree.

As he was finishing, he heard a rustling sound. It was coming from the bushes on the left. Jeff shined his little flashlight in that direction. Two yellow eyes, large and very widely spaced, looked back at him. The rustling sound increased, and Jeff could see that below the large eyes there was something else . . . long red and pink worms were hanging down, thrashing furiously in the underbrush. Then there was a growling noise that rose in both loudness and pitch. Jeff backed away around the tree.

His retreat was a signal to the animal. It broke from the bushes with a loud crashing of branches. Jeff screamed and ran for the ladder. He climbed very fast. When he was about halfway to the door-hole he looked down to see an enormous bearded animal standing below, bellowing out an unearthly wail in his direction. A very large forepaw reached for him, and he saw, as if in slow motion, one curving black claw cutting a piece of rubber from the heel of his lower sneaker. He was terrified. He climbed very, very fast then, plunging into the door-hole screaming. He could hear the scraping, scrabbling sounds of the animal as it climbed the tree behind him.

As Jeff ran across the floor, an enormous head, outlined

by moonlight, swept aside the Fiberglas batting that hung over the door-hole. Jeff, screaming, huddled behind the gray cabinet and shined his light backward. It was horrible, with big yellow teeth and pink and red wormlike things crawling around the edges of the great gaping mouth, beckoning him to come inside. The great fangs and writhing mouth were joined by an enormous clawed paw that reached through the hole and extended in his direction. Jeff retreated further, shrieking as he went.

A red spot appeared between the eyes of the large head. There was a shot and an answering explosion. The head jerked and twisted sideways. There was an unbelievably loud roar of outrage. The red spot moved again and there was another shot and a bright explosion at the center of the large head. Then three shots more in rapid succession. The final one pierced a huge eye, and there was a muffled explosion from inside the great head itself. It recoiled backward and disappeared, replaced by silvery moonlight. David stood and walked to the door-hole, the black pistol in one hand and a flashlight in the other. Jeff joined him at the door-hole, standing very close to David. Then, gathering his courage, he put his head out through the hole and looked down.

David shined the light down on the sprawled shape of the large animal twitching on the ground below. "Well, Jeff, it looks like we'll have a supply of meat for a while. I was getting tired of fish anyhow. Are you OK, Jeff?"

Jeff nodded. He was very glad that David was there. He put his arms around David's legs and held on tight. After a while he felt better. He resolved always to use the nightjar after that.

22

SATURDAY, OCTOBER 23

David sat on the huge branch near the door-hole of their treehouse, his back against the trunk of the tree, one leg dangling. The birdcalls from above attracted his attention. Sunlight filtered through the overhead leaf canopy. High on the tree trunk David could make out the green shape of the treebird, busily rendering its services. The air smelled fresh and wintry now. Only yesterday it had reeked of "shadow-bear" carcass. . . .

After photographing Jeff with his large friend, David and the children had spent most of the previous day in skinning and butchering the animal. It wasn't actually a bear, of course. Its bearlike similarity was ruined, for example, by the ruff of long thin tentacles that surrounded its mouth, a pink-and-red fringe that gave the animal a bearded appearance. The tentacles might be useful, he suggested to the children, in foraging for food.

David had planned to provide an anatomy lesson for Jeff and Melissa while he was butchering the bear, but the organs were like nothing he had seen before or could have imagined. The smells given off by some of the strangely shaped innards were equally unimaginable. Blueflies, the blue flying insect-creatures, had particularly appreciated the more odoriferous items. He had salvaged all he could from the carcass. Then, using a system of levers and pulleys, he had dragged the massive remains some distance into the forest. He wanted to avoid attracting scavengers to their campsite.

After the butchering and dragging, David made a partially successful attempt to wash the bear-juices from his skin with cold water from the cistern. There was no shortage of water for now. The cistern was nearly full from the recent rains. But they were running low on soap, and David found that he still smelled a bit like bear, even to himself. He swatted at a bluefly. How well, he wondered, could one make soap from bear fat and ashes? He must start experimenting soon.

David looked down. Below, Jeff was stirring a nice shadow-bear stew that bubbled on the cook fire, and he occasionally turned the strips of shadow-bear jerky that were smoking under the aluminum foil hood. It was probably good therapy. Jeff had awakened screaming from a nightmare the night of the incident, but last night he had slept peacefully. It probably soothed the psyche to dismember and eat the things that scare you.

David glanced at the objects in his lap. He'd been sitting in the sunlight working on a smaller, portable version of the prototype twistor generator. It had been only late yesterday afternoon that David had been able to resume work on it. He held up the board. Not bad, he thought. The clutter of the prototype breadboard had been simplified and concentrated into a single narrow rectangle of perf-board, dense with small op-amp chips and larger digital LSI bugs, their little legs poking through the perf-board holes to be laced together underneath with many-layered zigzags of pale red wire. At the edge of the board a row of small in-line potentiometers were arranged neatly.

He tested the fit of the circuit board to the length of gray PVC pipe that was to be its housing. The fit was neat, and the row of holes in the pipe lined up nicely with the pots. David checked the contacts of the four power transistors set in horned heat sinks studding one side of the pipe. No problem there. He took a black Sharpie pen from his shirt pocket and, bracing an arm against the tree, inscribed in minute letters a neat label at the right of each hole. Just a bit more work and the thing would be ready to test.

Below, Melissa walked around the side of the tree. She'd been acting rather mysterious lately, David thought. She was carrying something dark. "David!" she called. "Come down! I want to show you something."

He descended the ladder. As he turned at its foot, Melissa

approached him. "Whatcha got, Melissa?" he asked.

Melissa extended her hands, holding something out before David's face. Sitting pertly in the bowl her hands formed was a small brown animal with big pointed ears and two oversize violet eyes. It's cute, David realized.

"This," she said, "is a shadow kitten. His name is 'Shadow.' He likes fish. He eats shadow-bear meat too, but he prefers fish." The small brown creature, its hind legs and tail folded under it, sat propped on its middle pair of legs. It showed its pink tongue and held its little brown forepaws upright. They ended in two tiny six-fingered hands. Except for the extra finger, the hands might have belonged to a human baby.

A bluefly buzzed near David's nose. The brown creature's hand darted, so fast that it appeared before David's face without seeming to have moved there. The bluefly was held firmly between the brown thumb and the first small finger. Then Shadow delicately separated the large blue abdomen from the bluefly and extended its little hand, offering it to David. David backed away, shaking his head. Shadow blinked, then placed the morsel delicately on its own pink tongue and swallowed. With its other hand it casually tossed away the head and thorax of the bluefly. The expression on its small face might have been interpreted as one of amusement and satisfaction. Like a shrimp, David thought. You eat the back part and throw away the rest.

"Shadow catches minnows like that, too," Melissa said. "He's very quick."

Solemnly David extended an index finger, which was duly gripped by the little hand. "Hello, Shadow," he said as the creature squeezed his finger. "I'm pleased to meet you." He had a feeling of unreality as the small creature nodded its head, made a high-pitched chattering squeak, and changed its color from brown to green. He had the distinct impression that Shadow was pleased to meet him also.

It was getting late, David thought, looking across to where the children were sleeping. The little brown animal was awake, however. Shadow was seated on the work table near the reflector-hooded candle, watching with untiring attention as he worked.

David looked at his watch. After 1:00 A.M. But the mini-twistor unit was about ready to try. He clipped the small digital ohmmeter to several spots on the perf-board strip and adjusted the resistance of each pot to the nominal values he'd taken from the prototype. Nothing left but final assembly.

He slipped the electronics-laden strip into its PVC-pipe jacket, then fitted the pipe into the modified barrel of the big four-cell flashlight. The gray PVC extended the cylindrical shape of the flashlight for another twenty centimeters beyond the point where the flashlight lens would normally go. On one side of the flashlight's on-off switch, which retained that function, were mounted three small red push buttons which David had labeled PEEK, TALK, and TWIST. At the other end of the PVC pipe a cup-shaped array of curved copper coils, about the size of half a grapefruit skin, had been fixed in place with clear epoxy. The result was an impressive gray-and-silver macelike object half a meter long with a coppery cup at its business end. David took a breath. It was time for the smoke test.

He slid the on-off switch forward. A green LED labeled POWER lit on the gray barrel. Nothing else happened. OK. He sniffed at the row of holes, but smelled only cedar and curing epoxy, not burning parts. Good. Like a priest kissing a sacred object, David touched his lips to the line of external power transistors. They had now warmed to about body temperature, but no higher. Fine. He squinted across the cup at the candle flame and pressed the small red TWIST button on the left. Nothing. He frowned.

Maybe the feedback coupling had drifted off again. Switching off, he inserted a screwdriver in the third hole and gave the trimpot behind it a half turn counterclockwise. Then he switched on and tried it again. There came the satisfying *pop* sound.

At the sound, the little animal looked startled. Standing on its four legs, arms against its chest, it looked around. Then, satisfied, it settled back down to watch David again.

David used the screwdriver to trim the tuning control,

resetting the frequency for "home." Except for final calibration the thing was finished. He felt a glow of satisfaction. He preferred electronic innards to bear innards any day. He stood, walked over to the door-hole, and pulled aside the Fiberglas cover. It was dark outside, and fairly cool. Leaning forward on his knees, he extended his torso through the door-hole, the new device held before him. He brought the cup of coils at the end of the device close to his eye and sighted to the right along the curving bulk of the tree.

He'd learned from the prototype that when he made the field driver "tumble" in a repeated transition, then detuned the transition field slightly, an interesting and useful thing occurred. Photons of light were diverted from one universe to the other while matter was left undisturbed. This made the device safer to use, because he didn't have to worry about sending his nose into another universe. This was what he now called the PEEK or photons-only mode. When the PEEK button was pushed you could look but not touch.

A second button, which tumbled a properly tuned twistor field, was labeled TALK. It wasn't tested yet, but David estimated that it should transmit enough sound vibration via the air passing through the continuously rotating twistor field to allow speech communication between universes. If that worked, it should be useful. The third button, labeled TWIST, produced a single twistor transition. David had carefully tuned the unit to link with the universe from which they'd come.

He peeked. Through the hazy sphere hanging over the coppery cup, light from the hallway could be seen coming through the frosted glass door panel of his deserted laboratory in the other universe. A huge sphere of wood occupied most of the space behind him: the treehouse cavity. He was surprised that so much weight could be supported by what was left of the floor structure.

David had prepared a note that described their present situation. He placed the slip of paper into the coil cup and pushed TWIST. The paper disappeared from the cup, and, using the PEEK button, he watched it drift to the floor of the laboratory. Then he switched the unit off. Perhaps someone would find his message tomorrow, a note from castaways stranded on a distant shore.

He would leave more notes around the building to ensure that Vickie and Paul and Elizabeth knew that he and the children were still alive. He wondered how others in the department were taking the recent events. The wooden ball must have caused quite a sensation. He wondered how much longer the batteries in this unit would continue to operate.

Batteries: that suggested something to David. Besides leaving notes, there might be another use for this little device if he could find the right places to use it. That might require acrobatics done best in daylight. . . .

"Pull!" David yelled. Melissa and Jeff, below on the ground, pulled on the long guy wire that was tied to his waist. He sighted through the hazy sphere at the end of the twistor device. "More this way!" he shouted, gesturing to the right. The children shifted their positions, changing the angle of the pull wire to swing him in the indicated direction. Jeff stepped on Melissa's heel and she dropped her grip on the wire to turn and glare at him. Jeff, still holding the wire, was pulled forward, and David's position changed in the wrong direction. Dangling from a heavy wire dropped from a large overhead branch, David was suspended perhaps six meters above the ground. This wasn't working. . . .

He'd set his watch alarm for five-thirty, rousing the children at first daylight to come out with him on this "energy hunt." Jeff, still not quite awake, and Melissa, with Shadow in her lap, had sat against a tree and watched without comment as David had gone through a strange ritual, climbing a short distance up one tree trunk, sighting through the fuzzy sphere that formed in the coil cup of the new twistor device, then climbing another tree and sighting again.

He'd moved erratically through the forest in this way, mapping the location of Physics Hall in another universe and finally zeroing in on the electronics storeroom in the basement. The location he needed was, unfortunately, out of reach. It was too high above ground level to be reached from below, too far down to be reached from a high branch, too far away from any tree trunk. David considered collecting enough rocks and wood to build a tower under the spot, but then he had a better idea.

He'd marked the location, then returned to the treehouse for a big roll of the heavy electrician's wire. He had secured a length of it from an overhead branch, then fashioned a sort of sling seat that allowed him to lower himself from the branch to any desired elevation. He attached a guy wire to his waist, to be pulled on by Jeff and Melissa until he was at the proper location. He'd worked with Melissa and Jeff, showing them how to pull the wire tight, how to stop him from swinging back and forth. He tried to make it seem like a game. His strategy worked, up to a point. The children were enthusiastic about pulling him around as he dangled from a tree branch, but their actions were not coordinated. They kept bumping into each other, and they were too easily distracted. They moved him in random directions to random places that bore no correspondence to his shouted directions, not at all where he wanted to be.

It was damned frustrating. He was so close. Through the twistor sphere he could see the shelves of batteries and electronics components in the storeroom. But his position was wrong. What he needed was still far out of reach. He looked up at the branch from which he hung suspended. Shadow sat on it, looking down at him with an expression of amused curiosity. David turned to the children below him. The problem lay in coordinating their pulls on the guy wire. He thought for a moment. Perhaps there was another approach. "OK, listen," he called to them, "we're going to try something else. Melissa, you let Jeff hold the wire all by himself. I've got another job for you."

"OK, David!" she called back. She let go of the wire she was holding and stepped back.

"Good," said David. "Now, Jeff, I want you to pull the wire tight and bend it around the base of that bush over there. Hold the wire and walk around the bush until you can feel it begin to pull, just a bit. Now I want you to pull back on it, hard. Melissa, help him pull . . . that's right!" The wire from his waist to the bush stiffened, and the wire supporting him from above swung out to a large angle with the vertical. "Now walk back the other way around the

bush," he called to Jeff, "so the wire winds around it and
friction holds me here. That's good, Jeff. Stay right there."
David was now hanging about a meter from where he needed
to be.

"OK, now Melissa, get that extra length of wire on the
ground over there and bend it in half." She walked to where
an extra piece of wire lay on the ground and picked it up,
bending it double. "Fine!" he called to her. "Now hook
it over the wire that goes up to me. Right. Now pull sideways. No, sideways the other way! That's right! Just a little
more. Good! Try to keep me right here."

Her sideways force on the guy wire moved David in the
correct direction, bringing him to the desired spot. He
hooked a leg over the guy wire and levered himself the last
few centimeters. He sighted through the fuzzy twistor
sphere, then shifted it slightly. He could see that it was
positioned directly over several black-and-gold Duracell D
cells. He held his breath and pressed the TWIST button.
Black-and-gold shapes plummeted to the ground, making a
soft *crunch* when they hit the leaves below.

The children, seeing the batteries tumble into the leaves,
dropped their wires and ran over to find them. The wire
from David's waist snaked around the bush, and David
swung helplessly back and forth in a long pendulum arc,
cursing as he swung.

"No, dammit!" he called down to the children as a swing
placed him momentarily over their heads. "Never mind the
batteries," he shouted, "leave them there! Go back to the
wires!"

Jeff ran back, grabbed his wire, and was immediately
pulled off his feet as David swung away from him. Melissa
came to help, and together they managed to bring David to
a stop. Positioning David was easier the second time. Jeff
and Melissa, working together, used the bush as a bollard
and pulled David out to the appropriate angle, then bent the
wire sharply around the bush base. Then Melissa pulled
sideways with the doubled wire and moved David the last
small distance.

More disks of shelf-wood, black-and-gold batteries, and
chopped-off pieces of batteries cascaded into the leaves.

Then under David's directions they shifted positions, and he went to work on Sam's stock of power transistors. It was exhausting work. By the time the point of diminishing returns had been reached, certain areas of the electronics storeroom resembled a war zone. David left a scrawled note of apology amid the devastation, then lowered himself to the ground to collect the loot.

He looked at his watch. It was still early. Maybe they should visit some other establishments as well, now that they'd established the technique.

Sam Weston was furious as he surveyed the wreckage of the electronics shop storeroom, discovered when he arrived this morning. In his years with the physics department he'd learned to live with the Monday messes left in his shop by the weekend forays of graduate students and professors trying to fix or improve their equipment or to scrounge for parts.

But this was different. Over the past weekend the shop had been vandalized. The stock of batteries was nearly gone. And most of those batteries that were left had been sliced to pieces. Big holes had been cut in some of the wooden shelves. The power transistor stock had been singled out for particular mayhem, with whole drawers of the biggest transistors gone and cavities cut in other drawers. Drawers containing some types of integrated circuit chips and power resistors had been similarly vandalized. But the capper was that the vandals had the audacity to leave a crudely forged note in the mess bearing the signature of the vanished David Harrison and saying that he'd "had to borrow a few things."

The campus police officer surveyed the destruction and made notes in his book. "Maybe this is some new student fad," he said to Sam. "The Radio Shack store and the Safeway over in U-Village reported some similar problems early this morning. At the Safeway some canned goods had been stolen. Mostly small cans, for some reason. There were big holes cut in their shelves too, and a lot of the cans had been cut in half and dumped. A real mess."

"You think it might've been the same people?" Sam asked.

"Mebbe so," the policeman answered. "The vandals, whoever they were, went after batteries at both places. And a nice king salmon in the Safeway meat department had several big round pieces cut out of it, but the rest of the fish was still there, hardly disturbed. No sign of how it was done. It's a twenty-four-hour store, but none of the employees saw anything suspicious 'til they noticed the mess about seven-thirty A.M."

"Real weird," said Sam.

"Yeah," the policeman answered. "Whatever you've got, Mr. Weston, it's goin' around."

After the policeman left, Sam sat at his desk staring at the note and considering the strange events of the previous week. He glanced at the smooth, knife-sharp edges of the holes in the shelves. Like the wood sphere in Vickie's laboratory. David and the children, then Vickie and Professor Saxon had disappeared. Then his shop had been raided. Was this vandalism a coincidence, or could there be a connection? Couldn't hurt to play it safe, he decided.

He took the departmental truck to Central Stores for more batteries, then to Radar Electric for replacement ICs and transistors. When he returned to the shop, he repaired the damaged shelves with new plywood. The new supplies he elevated on empty cardboard boxes so that they were well above the level of the new shelves. On top of the pile of batteries he left a note addressed to David, asking if there was anything else he needed. He was like a little kid leaving notes for the Tooth Fairy, he thought.

David sat at the big worktable inside the treehouse, the loot from the morning's raids making several large piles before him. He felt a bit guilty about what he'd done to Sam's storeroom. His control had been poor, and he'd made rather a mess. But they had *batteries* now.

The treehouse was now illuminated by the portable fluorescent-tube flashlight suspended over the worktable. At his elbow sat Shadow. The creature seemed to be fascinated by the useless beige telephone that still sat on the worktable. He held the receiver in his hands, turning it over and over, sniffing it, and poking at the holes in the earpiece with a tiny finger.

"Shadow's amazing," David said to Melissa. "He gives the impression of understanding English. He seems smarter than the gorillas and chimps I've seen. You know, there are supposed to be biological limits on how intelligent an animal of a certain size can be. Our intelligence is supposed to be because of our big brains. But I'm not sure those rules work in this universe. I noticed when I was butchering the bear that a bullet had blown a big hole in its skull, so I poked around inside. The bear's brain case and the stuff inside were really small compared to those of an Earth bear, and its nerve structure, if that's what I was looking at, looked very odd. I'd bet Shadow's nervous system is similar. Maybe that's how there can be so many smarts in this guy's tiny little head." He stroked Shadow.

"The bear wasn't smart to poke his head in our treehouse," said Melissa. "But you're right about Shadow. He understands English. Watch this." She turned to the small brown creature. "Shadow, bring me the number-two battery there." She held up two fingers and pointed to the line of black-and-gold D cells along the edge of the table.

The small brown head raised and rotated clockwise. The oversize ears pricked up sharply. Shadow put the telephone receiver back into its cradle and walked, centaurlike, over to the line of batteries. He selected the second battery in the line and brought it to Melissa.

She smiled, patted the little head. Then she gave him David's little red Swiss army knife, with the knife blade out. A bluefly buzzed nearby. Shadow struck lightning fast with a tiny finger and thumb, snaring the blue shape out of the air. With David's knife he sliced off the insect's abdomen and popped it into his pink mouth. Catches on fast, David thought.

Then Shadow jumped, knife in hand, to the next table, where he delicately sliced a hunk from the pink-red sphere of king salmon meat lying there. He put the knife on the table and held the small slice of salmon in his delicate little hands while he ate it.

David had recorded the events with the CCD camera.

"Hmmm," he said as he recaptured his knife and wiped it off, "that gives me an idea." He picked up the twistor unit, placed it between his knees, and put a cut-out circle of shelf-wood, one of many on the table, into the cup. Then he lifted Shadow and put him on the wood surface in the cup. "Yes," said David, "he fits nicely. Stay there, Shadow." He lifted the twistor cup to eye level with Shadow balanced in the bowl, flicked the switch on, and pressed the right button. Shadow's image darkened, and he could be seen within a fuzzy sphere. David pressed the left TWIST button. Shadow disappeared, to be replaced by a wooden sphere. David removed the wooden sphere from the cup and put it on the table.

"Oh!" said Melissa, "David! Where's Shadow? Did you turn him into a ball? What did you *do* to him!"

"Don't worry," said David, "he's perfectly all right. He's presently inside an air-filled cavity in the big wooden sphere in my laboratory, back in the 'normal' world. Watch!" He pressed the right PEEK button and a dimmed image of Shadow appeared in the cup. David adjusted the position of the field slightly to match the walls of the wooden cavity in the other universe, and pressed the TWIST button.

Shadow was in the cup once more.

"How'd you like our universe, Shadow?" David asked, grinning. Shadow's big violet eyes looked at David. David had the distinct impression that the shadow-kitten was amused, too. It looked closely at David's thumb as he placed the little creature back on the worktable.

"Now, Shadow," David said, turning to the telephone instrument on the table, "it's about time a smart guy like you started getting a real education. Come over here. You're going to learn how to dial the operator."

Vickie squirmed against the ropes once more. Her arms and legs were tied securely to the straight-backed wooden armchair and there was a rubber gag in her mouth. She was very frightened.

For most of the past week the Mandrake person, always wearing the ski mask, had come to her little room to ask her questions. He had been pleasant and professional, and she almost liked him. Then this morning he' had come in with the large man. He was carrying a little black case. He had put the case on the table beside the bed and opened it. Inside was a hypodermic syringe.

The large man had held her arms, and Mandrake had explained that his employers had ordered the use of neurophagin. Vickie had begun to scream at them. The big man had silenced her with a foul-tasting rubber gag. It had been like an obscene rubber tongue intruding into her mouth. Mandrake had expertly filled the syringe and approached her.

When she judged the moment was right, she had kicked him in the knee, then the crotch, then struck hard against the hand holding the syringe. The plastic tube had crashed hard against the wall and broken open, leaking amber fluid on the floor. Mandrake had collapsed to his knees and remained there for a minute or so. Finally he had risen, apparently still in pain, and had struck her hard in the face twice. He was very angry. That was the last of their neurophagin supply, he raged, and it would take half a day to get more. They had tied her to this chair, gagged and helpless. Mandrake had collected the broken syringe parts in the black bag and the two had left, locking the door behind them.

Now her mind kept endlessly cycling over the same ground, looking for a tool, a gimmick, a way out.

Flash sat at the teakwood desk by the big deck window, a book in his lap, waiting for David's Macintosh III to decrypt another Megalith document. He looked out the broad window across the Lake Washington Ship Canal at the towers, peaked rooftops, and squat rectangles of the university in the distance. He wondered where Vickie was now and what was happening to her. He was really worried. For the past five days he had been using David's Flat-Mac to decrypt a large number of the Megalith files that he had brought with him. David's machine, a small briefcase unit with a hi-res color flat-screen built into its lid, had ten times the memory of Vickie's Mac and a much faster CPU. But this was still slow going because the decryption algorithm took lots of CPU time, and there were so many of Pierce's communications to sort through.

The degree of corporate ruthlessness the files revealed was very disturbing, painting a picture of a high-tech rogue corporation that routinely used theft, fraud, and violence to achieve its goals. And they had Sis. . . .

At the end of each day Flash had made hard copies of the previous day's decrypted files with David's laser printer. Then he'd taken the number 9 bus to the Broadway post office and mailed them to the Seattle office of the FBI. That was his insurance in case he was nabbed by the kidnappers before he was finished. When the decrypting and printing of all the files was complete, he planned to take them personally to FBI headquarters and confess his recent hacking of Megalith. He was very worried about his sister, but he couldn't think of a better scheme to help her.

The program signaled completion and Flash studied the newly decrypted document. It indicated that the day after David and the children had disappeared, Pierce had arranged for Megalith to very indirectly lease a house in Laurelhurst for $4,500 per month. There was an inventory of furniture and even a boat. It sounded quite fancy.

Why would Pierce do that, Flash wondered. Could they be holding Vickie there? Perhaps he should go out and phone in an anonymous tip to the police . . . Couldn't do it on David's phone or they'd backtrack him. He looked at the little time display in the upper right corner of the Mac's display. A little after eleven. In maybe an hour he'd make another trip to the post office and use a pay phone at the same time.

Flash started the program decrypting another of Pierce's files and turned back to the book in his lap. In the three days he'd been here, while he was waiting for the computer to complete decryptions, he'd read through a good chunk of David's collection of hard science fiction hardbacks. He'd done one Niven, a couple of Benfords, a Brin, two Bears, and a Hogan. Now he was working on *The Shadow of the Torturer*, the first volume of Wolfe's *The Book of the New Sun*. Nice stuff. He couldn't understand why some people thought it was a fantasy, though.

There was a sound from the bedroom, then another. Flash crept across the carpet and peered through the door, his head low in the door frame. A small brown animal stood on the walnut dresser next to the telephone. It had four legs and two arms, like a miniature centaur. A voice that sounded like David's said, "Shadow, pick up the receiver." The creature responded by lifting the telephone receiver and placing it carefully on the dresser, mouthpiece up. The dial tone from the receiver made it back away. Distracted, it walked across the dresser and sniffed at the bottle of after shave standing there. "No, Shadow, come back," said the voice, "back to the telephone." The creature stood for a moment, then walked back across the dresser to the telephone instrument. It still seemed wary of the dial-tone sound. "That's right, Shadow," said the voice, "push the 'O' button. Push it now. That's a good fellow. Go on, push it now . . ."

Almost reflexively, Flash called out, "David, is that you?" The little animal jumped off the dresser, scrambled behind it, and peered up from underneath with large violet eyes. Flash noticed that now it looked the same gray color as the bedroom carpet.

A dim sphere that was hanging in midair near the creature moved toward him and flickered. "Flash!" said David's voice. "What the Hell are you doing in my apartment?"

Flash told him.

23

TUESDAY NOON, OCTOBER 26

David was exhausted. He had been running through the forest for nearly an hour. It had been quite strange to walk over the waters of Union Bay and along Lake Washington with dry feet like some Biblical figure. He stopped again to take a bearing. Holding the twistor unit at eye level, he pressed the PEEK button. A black sphere formed in the coil cup at the end of the device. Nothing could be seen within it. He was below ground level here.

He switched off the twistor unit and shoved its long cylindrical body through a loop of his belt. The silvery flashlight barrel projected behind him almost like a short sword, he noticed, and the cup at the other end was like a rounded handguard. He stepped across the brightly colored line surrounding a nearby tree and began to climb its broad trunk, using the large upthrust bark scales for hand and footholds. The green treebird higher in the tree squawked a threat down at him but did not approach.

Shadow scampered up the tree ahead of David. He seemed amused at his companion's lack of native climbing ability. When David was about four meters off the ground he paused and PEEKED again. He'd been traveling parallel to the Laurelhurst lakeshore. In the scene visible through the field sphere, he was just above the lake level and opposite a boat dock. A fast-looking motorboat was tied at the dock, and a house number was nailed to the edge of the pier. It was the address he'd been looking for. He descended and climbed uphill toward the place where, in another universe, a large house had been built on the shore.

The house, David was relieved to find, was on about the

same level as the forest floor. Seattle is built on many hills, and this universe had sizable hills of its own, but the topography had rarely corresponded during David's journey here. If the house had been at a level much higher or lower than that of the forest, reaching it could have presented a serious problem.

He walked "into" the house, pressing the PEEK button and watching as he passed through an outer wall and into the kitchen. Empty. He pressed TALK and put his ear near the sphere, listening through the low hum of the cycling twistor field. His ear felt cool as a flow of air passed from his universe to the other, caused by the pressure difference that he'd noticed before. Male voices came to him through the hum. He chose a direction that should take him through one of the kitchen's interior walls, walked a short distance, and PEEKED.

Two men were seated in the living room. David recognized them as two of the three "movers" who had invaded his lab. The balding man, the one who had done all the talking, sat in a large armchair. There was a brightly colored ski mask on the armrest beside him. The large ugly man sat opposite him on a sofa. He was the one who'd pointed the gun, and now David noted that the man's right hand was missing, the stump covered by a sort of tan sock.

David walked to a corner above their heads and just behind them, well out of their field of view. He pressed TALK again, and listened.

The large man was feeling impatient. "When'll they be back?" He looked across at his boss.

"In maybe forty-five minutes, an hour," replied the balding man. "We used up most of the neurophagin on the old guy, and the bitch trashed the rest. So I sent 'em over to Harborview for more. The docs there are using it for tests on some loonie cases. The DOD supplies the junk and pays for the research. One of the duty nurses there's a junkie and a friend of mine. She works the psycho ward and gets me some real good junk for this kind of work. They watch the hard drugs pretty close there, but who'd want to steal neurophagin? Its side effects are supposed to be a secret, but all the nurses know it's bad shit. Causes permanent brain damage.'' He smiled.

"Then we juice the chickie?" the big man asked.

"Then we do the girl," the other answered. "Ya know, she's got a good kick."

"How're the old family jewels doin'?" the big man asked. "She whammed you a good 'un." He chuckled appreciatively.

The balding man looked annoyed. "I wasn't expecting it," he said. "She'd seemed so cooperative. I should've remembered what she did to you when you guys snatched her."

The big man scowled. "When do I get her?" he asked finally, looking wolfish.

"Soon," said the balding man. "After we use the neurophagin it'll take maybe a day or two more of questioning. Then, if Broadsword says it's OK, you can have her for a while. Guess we'll have to use the boat to sink both of 'em pretty soon anyhow."

The big man smiled in anticipation, then frowned. "Hey, there's a draft in here," he said looking around. "And do you smell somethin' funny?" He thought he saw something flicker at the edge of his vision, but when he turned toward the corner nothing was there.

The balding man sniffed. "Just fresh air," he said. "Smells like cedar trees or somethin'."

The big man frowned, recalling the strong cedar smell in that room at the university and the weird happenings when he'd lost his hand. It'd been a shock, losing the hand. He'd decided that he was going to get a sharp hook, like a pirate's, to replace it. In his kind of work a hook like that'd be a definite asset. And it would have other interesting uses, too. The cedar smell came again. "I don't like this old place," he said. "It's kinda spooky." He put his left hand in his pocket to rub the rabbit's foot that he always carried.

"Funny you should say that," said the balding man. "When the real-estate broad at the Scott office gave me the keys, the guy at the next desk asked, kinda jokin', if this house was the haunted one. I asked what the hell he meant. The lady told him to shut up, but he said they already had the lease money so there was no harm in telling.

"He said that a rich old lumber guy had owned this house, and one morning he shot his wife and daughter and grandkids and then hung himself in a tree out in the yard. S'pose to be their spooks, still here, is why they're rentin' now instead of sellin'. They wanna let the rumors die down first. It's sure a creepy old place all right, but I haven't seen any spooks." He paused. "Hell, I need a brew," he said, getting up and moving toward the kitchen.

As soon as the balding man had left the room, the big man felt a cold wind near his ear. He looked around suspiciously but saw nothing. Then, very close by, he was startled by a crazy-sounding voice that whispered to him. "We're coming for you," the voice said. "We are. We'll make you one of us. You'll be part of our house . . . always."

The big man screamed, jumping up from the sofa and looking around. Nothing was there. He was sweating and his heart pounded. The other man came back into the room at a dead run. "What th' Hell?" he demanded. "Why'd you yell?"

The big man turned slowly. He couldn't tell his boss. "Nothin'," he muttered. "I just bit my tongue, and it hurt." He grinned sheepishly.

The other man looked disgusted. He turned without a word and stalked back toward the kitchen.

The big man stood up and paced. He'd heard it. It couldn't have been his imagination. He rubbed his rabbit's foot again. The old stories came flooding back, the ones his grandma would tell to scare him when he'd been bad. And the nightmares that had followed. In the stories the guys never had the sense to leave, to run, and the horrors always got 'em. He felt the wind again, and looked around. Nothing. Then the voice came again. "We'll eat off your other hand," it said, "and then your balls, and then your nose, and then your eyes. . . ." He repressed the scream this time, but ran to the bathroom, closed and locked the door, and leaned against it, trembling.

There was a terrible shit-smell. He'd fouled his pants, he realized. Shaking, he cleaned himself as best he could. Then he vomited his breakfast. He was scared, shaking. He wasn't ever going to leave the bathroom, to go out there.

Then the cold wind came again. He hadn't locked them out. The crazy voice said, "We are very very hungry. We need your flesh. Give it to us . . ." There was a sharp pain in the fleshy part at the edge of his left, his remaining hand. When he looked down, a circular wound was there, like a bite.

He erupted from the bathroom, a reddening towel wrapped around his hand. He fumbled with his keys at the front door, got it open, and ran. He ran and ran. He was still running when the police car stopped him a long time later.

David was PEEKing as the balding man, bottle of beer in hand, cursed as he locked the front door. He turned, walked to the living room, and put on the ski mask. Then he walked up the stairs, still muttering to himself. Damn, thought David, he's going to be out of reach. And the bastard's planning to do something to Vickie. From where he stood he could only reach to the high ceiling of the first floor.

David stuffed the twistor unit through his belt again and climbed a nearby tree. Its treebird owner glowered down at him from a high branch. Shadow led the way as usual. They stopped on the lowest limb. David removed the twistor unit from his belt and PEEKED through the field sphere. An empty room. He moved farther out on the branch and sighted again. He was looking down from a point near the high ceiling. He drew a sharp breath.

Vickie was there. She was tied in a chair, some pink rubber thing wrapped around her mouth. She was awake and looked very frightened. She was struggling against the ropes, and David could see where they had rubbed her wrists raw. He felt a rush of helpless anger and frustration. The balding man, now wearing a ski mask and still holding the beer bottle in his hand, was standing in front of her.

From his precarious perch on the tree limb David lacked the control to do the ghost routine again, and the balding man looked to be more difficult to frighten. His mind raced.

He decided on another approach. He pressed the TALK button and spoke into the sphere in a loud commanding voice. "All right, you're all finished here, fella. This is the police. The house is surrounded now, and there's a sharpshooter with a rifle pointed right at your heart. If you don't wanna get hurt, untie the lady. Now! Move!"

The man jumped and looked around. Then he took a small white-handled pistol from somewhere behind his back and walked over to Vickie. He pointed it at her head. "I don't know where you are or how you're doing that, buddy," he said, "but you're obviously not the police. You sound more like that smartass at the university. I have a nice hostage here, a good friend of yours. Show yourself now, or I'm going to put a nice round hole right through this lady's head." His thumb clicked the pistol's safety off.

David realized that his police routine was not going to work. He spoke once more into the sphere. "This is your last warning, fella. Untie the lady now, and you won't be hurt. Otherwise, we're going to have to kill you." He looked back at the man. Stubborn bastard.

"C'mon," David said through the sphere, "you look like a reasonable guy. Why take chances, when you don't know what you're dealing with. I don't want to kill you. Let her go. Now!" Then he edged out on the limb to a spot right over Vickie's head. He tied a length of climbing wire around the limb, slipped into his sling seat, and lowered himself until he hung sideways just above the man with the ski mask. "Last chance," he whispered near the man's ear. The man jumped and shoved the gun tight against Vickie's head. David was close enough to see the man's finger tightening on the trigger. There was no time left, no choice. He might shoot her. And even if he didn't, the others would soon be back with the drug. It was now or never. Dangling upside down now, David struggled to position the hazy twistor sphere at the rear center of the man's head, the muscle-control area. His hand trembled as he pressed the TWIST button. A reddish-gray lump of hair, skull, and nerve tissue dropped to the forest floor, making a soft *plop* as it landed among the leaves below.

In another universe the man in the ski mask collapsed to

the floor, a gaping wound at the back of his head. Bright red blood flowed out on the wooden floor in a spreading pool. Vickie peered down at him, her eyes wide, then looked around. "Mmfff!" she said through the rubber gag. "Mmmmmmfff!"

David felt sick. He'd just killed a man, another human being. He pulled himself back upright and sat for a moment, fighting the waves of nausea. Finally he leaned over and spoke into the sphere. "Vickie!" he called to her, "It's me, David. The kids and I are OK, but we're still in this shadow universe. We can't get back, yet, but I've got a small portable twistor unit working. I was using it on your friends. You're safe for the moment, but some more of those guys will be coming back very soon."

She turned in the direction of his voice and nodded.

"I'm going to send a little friend of mine to help you. His name is Shadow. You'll like him." Then David took out his little red Swiss army knife, opened the knife blade, and reminded Shadow how to cut rope with it. Then he moved to a point on the limb which would put him next to the curtained window and sent Shadow through. He watched as Shadow went through, caught the curtains, descended, and strode centaurlike over to where Vickie was tied. He seemed very interested in her, and sniffed her thoroughly. David directed Shadow with the voice commands he'd been trained to follow, and soon the little creature was sawing away at the ropes.

As Shadow worked, David explained to Vickie where she was and what Flash had told him. He suggested that she call the police as soon as she was free. As he was talking, he noticed that the view through the sphere seemed to be washing in and out. He put his fingers on the power transistors along the side of the twistor unit. Five of them were cool, but one was quite hot to the touch.

"This damned thing's going out on me!" he yelled through the fading field. "Be—" The dim sphere in the cup abruptly winked out. "—careful!" He switched off the power, spat and blew on the hot transistor to cool it, then tried to produce the field again. The copper cup had no dark sphere inside. "Shit!" said David. The only power transistors in this entire universe were back at the treehouse.

He climbed down from the tree and headed back there at a dead run.

The doorbell rang. Flash carefully opened the door of David's apartment, keeping the chain latch on. Two men stood on the doorstep. One was very large. Flash looked out at them, ready to bolt. Somehow they didn't look like Megalith goons or FBI.

"Hi, I'm George Williams," the big man said, "and this is Rudi Baumann." He indicated his companion, smaller, darker and with ruddy cheeks. "Paul Ernst sent us over when you called. We'll take you to get the stuff on your list. We're friends of David and your sister, and we want to help."

"Great-o!" Flash said, taking the chain latch off and opening the door wide. It was wonderful to be with real human beings again after almost a week of isolation. Before David, or at least the voice of David, had taken the little animal back and gone to investigate the house in Laurelhurst, he'd dictated a long list of items for Flash to buy. He'd sent through credit cards and a bank card, given Flash his bank access code number, and told him to use those for the purchases. Then, almost as an afterthought, he'd suggested that Flash try calling Paul Ernst at the university to get help.

Flash, not wanting to run the risk that the calls could be traced to David's telephone, had slipped out over the deck and walked across the University Bridge to a pay phone. There he'd called Paul. He'd also called 911 to declare that kidnap victim Victoria Gordon was being held at an address in Laurelhurst that he gave them. George and Rudi had been at the door within fifteen minutes after Flash arrived back at the apartment.

They all got into George's station wagon, which was parked outside. "David suggested that I go out on Aurora Avenue North," Flash said. "Most of the stuff on the list should be available at Sears or the big discount stores out there. But first I'm gonna need some of the el cash-o."

"No problem," said George. "Paul Ernst is bankrolling

this. Wants his kids back, I guess." They crossed the Ship
Canal, then headed west.

Victoria, with Shadow nestled in the big pocket of her
jacket, was at the front door ready to leave the house.
Shadow still held David's little red knife in one tiny hand.
After her new friend had freed her from the chair, Vickie
had been able to remove the gag and run downstairs. She
had tried to call the police, but she couldn't make the telephone work. The front door wouldn't open. She examined
the deadbolt lock mounted on it. It had no knob, and couldn't
be opened without a key. She checked the back door and
the door from the kitchen to the garage. They were all the
same.

Frustrated and feeling desperate, she climbed the stairs
to the bedroom where she'd been held captive for almost a
week. Mandrake was still on the floor, his head and shoulders in a large pool of dark blood. His eyes were open.
Could she make herself touch him? Her stomach churned.
It was the only way.

Steeling herself, Victoria walked to the side away from
the pool of blood and searched Mandrake's pockets. The
bundle of keys was in his trousers. In his jacket pocket she
found the little disk recorder and several used disks. She
took them all. She considered also taking the white-handled
gun still clenched in his hand, but she was inexperienced
with such weapons. She kicked it under the bed instead.

As she stepped from the bedroom into the hall, she heard
low rambling speech. Allan Saxon! Sorting through the
keys, she selected a likely candidate and inserted it in the
lock. The lock clicked open. She entered the room.

Saxon was on the bed just as before. He stared at the
small brown creature peeking at him from her pocket. "It's
Vickie again," he said, "and she has an animal. What kind
of animal is it. It's brown. It has hands and a knife. I wonder
where she got it."

"Allan," she said, "we're leaving this place. Come on!"

"I'm going to leave," he said. He put his feet on the
floor. They were bare, and he was wearing a hospital gown
that exposed a stripe of bare flesh down the back.

Vickie looked in the bathroom and found some clothes. She gave him shoes, trousers, and a coat. "Put these on quickly," she said. "Keep the gown on and don't worry about socks."

"I won't worry about socks," Saxon said as he moved to obey her. "I never worry about socks. I don't worry about anything anymore. You put one leg through the hole and then the other. The whole is the sum of its parts. Some of the parts are shoes. Are these shoes on right? One is right and the other is left. One is the mirror image of the other. Which is the real one and which is the image? I never could work that out. Out is where we want to go. Let's go out now." He stood.

As they reached the foot of the stairs, Vickie heard the crunching sound of tires on the gravel driveway outside. Saxon followed her to the back door, muttering as he went. "What's that sound? Are the men coming back? They like to hurt me. Vickie, I feel afraid." He looked afraid, too. She heard the sound of the electric door opener working in the attached garage.

She fumbled with the big key ring, searching for a key that would match the deadbolt lock. Finally she found it and they walked into brilliant sunlight. She turned and closed the door quietly. As she did, she heard a key snick in the lock of the door leading from the house to the garage. She looked around. There were high walls on both sides, blocking access to the front yard and running downhill to Lake Washington. She led Saxon that way.

"We're outside now," he said. "It's good to be outside. There is sunshine and water. We can swim in the water. It's cold and wet. When you wet the bed, first it's warm and then it gets cold. But I didn't wet the bed. Joyce did it."

Victoria wondered who "Joyce" was. She saw a boat dock on the lakefront and an inboard motorboat nestled against a piling. As they reached the dock, she could hear shouting from the house.

She helped Saxon into the boat, undid the front mooring rope, and climbed in herself. Shadow leaped to the seat beside her. Saxon sat erect in the rear seat, still talking to himself. "We're going for a boat ride. I like boat rides. I went on a big boat once. It was the *Queen Elizabeth II*. The food was good. I screwed five different women. There's something about a boat trip that makes them want to fuck. It was nice."

Fumbling with the ring of keys, Vickie found one that might fit the boat ignition. It did fit. She started the engine, let it idle quietly, and eased the boat away from the dock. There were more shouts from the house, and two men emerged from the back door. There were guns in their hands.

The boat lurched and stopped. Victoria looked back. A rope at the stern was still tied to the dock! Leaving the engine to idle, she crawled over the front seat to the rope, only to find that at this end it ran through a bracket eye with a loop secured by three crimped metal rings. It could not be untied. She would have to get off the boat, and there was simply not enough time. The men were hurrying down the long back yard toward them now at a dead run.

She felt something and looked down. Shadow was at her side, offering her the little red knife. She took it and sawed at the rope. It gave a little. She sawed harder. The rope parted, and they were idling slowly away from the dock.

Vickie vaulted the seat, grabbed the wheel, gunned the engine, and they were off. At least now she couldn't hear Allan's ramblings over the sound of the engine. Sounds of gunfire came from behind them. She steered from side to side to spoil their arm. Looking back, she saw the two men, legs spread, arms locked and extended, firing at them from the dock. Bullets made splashes on the water beside the boat. Shadow had joined her in the front seat now, and seemed to be enjoying the ride enormously.

Soon they were out of range. Vickie, with Shadow on her lap, steered the boat straight across Lake Washington at top speed, heading for Kirkland, a suburban town on the east shore. She picked the target of the old *Lightship Relief* to steer for, a red-painted relic permanently anchored near the Kirkland pier. When she was close enough, she slowed the boat to a crawl and edged up against the Moss Bay Public Pier, then tied up the little boat at the broad dock. As she was climbing out with Shadow to stand on the pier,

she looked back at Allan Saxon. He had not moved since
they left the Laurelhurst dock.

The bullet's exit hole was like a red rose decorating his
broad forehead, the red and gray stem of the flower branch-
ing down his face.

Flash looked at David's list. There was a check mark by
every item. It had all worked out pretty well. First, George
had driven to the Aurora branch post office, and Flash had
mailed the fat envelope containing the latest installment of
juicy and incriminating items from Pierce's files to Agent
Bartley of the FBI. Then they'd hit the discount stores. At
Price Savers he'd purchased four compact and powerful
gasoline-powered electric AC generators. At Pay'n Pack
he'd added two rolls of duct tape, several short plastic garden hoses, a coil of rope, and many coils of wire. At K
mart he'd bought some dryer ducting and four two-gallon
plastic gasoline containers carefully measured to be within
David's specifications. He filled the gas can with regular.

David's apartment was the agreed-upon rendezvous point.
They'd returned there with the loot, and the three of them
had lugged it inside. After the hauling was done, George
and Rudi had to return to the U. George said he was sched-
uled to present an astrophysics seminar on "the more mun-
dane world of quantum cosmology." They promised to
return later with Paul.

All the stuff occupied a good fraction of David's living
room. Flash began the lengthy process of stripping down
the generators, removing all unnecessary parts, bases, shock
mounts, mufflers, and gas tanks to make them as compact
as possible. Then he packed most of the other items into
compact bundles of carefully measured dimensions.

Later, as Flash was finishing up, he happened to check
his watch. It was 5:33 P.M. He decided to catch the evening
news and flipped on David's wall-mount TV flatscreen. The
lead news item, already in progress, surprised him.

The announcer was doing a voice-over of a scene showing
a white-draped figure being loaded into an ambulance. He

was saying that Professor Allan Saxon had been killed while
he and his student, Victoria Gordon, were escaping in a
motorboat from kidnappers holding them in a house in the
Laurelhurst area of Seattle. One of the kidnappers, a Seattle
private investigator, had also been killed, and three other
men had escaped. The police had apprehended one of the
kidnappers, a large one-handed man, a few hours later. Miss
Gordon had provided digital recordings related to the kidnapping and murder and was now assisting the police and
FBI in apprehending the remaining fugitives. Flash cheered.

The coverage switched to a downtown fire. He tried other
channels. The kidnap/murder was covered on other local
stations, but none provided any new information. On CNN,
however, there was a report of an FBI raid on the San
Francisco headquarters of the Megalith Corporation. The
camera showed workmen carrying boxes of seized files and
laser disks out of an office building. The voice-over said
that several Megalith executives had been arrested or were
being held for questioning.

Flash stared at the wall screen for a long time after that,
not seeing the picture.

"Flash! Wake up!" the voice said.

Flash sat up in bed and looked around. The venetian
blinds were closed tight, the curtains were drawn, and the
room was dark. He could see no one in the dimness. Then
he noticed a faint, glowing sphere floating near the head-
board. "David?" he called.

"Yes, it's me," David said. He sounded out of breath.

Flash yawned. "What time is it, anyway?"

"It's seven thirty-five," said David. "The sun's been up
for almost an hour. Flash, what happened? Is Vickie all
right?"

Flash told him that Vickie was fine. He described what
he'd seen on the TV news the previous evening, including
the Megalith arrests.

"That's wonderful!" David sounded relieved. He told
Flash what had happened at the house in Laurelhurst.

"I was expecting you to show up again yesterday," Flash

said. "Paul Ernst and his wife came over, and later George
and Rudi showed up again. We waited for you a long time.
They helped get the stuff ready, and they didn't leave 'til
after midnight. I talked to Vickie on the phone last night,
but I haven't seen her yet. She's still busy with the police
and the FBI. They're still looking for two of the kidnappers.
Oh, and she asked about you. Said to tell you to hurry
home. Why'd you take so long getting back here?"

"I got lost trying to find my way back to the treehouse,"
David admitted sheepishly. "I've been using the twistor
unit to navigate, peeking into your universe to look for
landmarks and read street signs for orientation. But the damn
thing blew a transistor while Shadow was untying Vickie.
Without Shadow or the twistor unit to help, I wasn't sure
where I was. I walked west and a bit south, hoping to find
a place that looked familiar. That didn't work. It got dark,
and I still hadn't found the treehouse. When I saw a big
animal in the bushes, I climbed a tree and stayed there for
a while. Had to fire a warning shot to discourage the critter
from joining me up there.

"I was lucky there was a nearly full moon last night. If
it hadn't been for the bright moonlight, I might still be
wandering in the woods. Finally I stumbled on a creek that
looked familiar and followed it back to the spring we've
been using. I didn't get back to the treehouse 'til very late.
I was damn lucky to find it at all."

"Did you get the twistor thingie fixed OK?" Flash asked.

"Sure," David said, "otherwise I wouldn't be talking to
you, would I? It only took a few minutes to put in a new
power transistor. Then I gave up for the night and went to
bed. I didn't sleep very well, though, and as soon as there
was a little daylight I went back to the Laurelhurst house.
There were police barriers in the yard and all over the house,
and there was a patrol car outside. But no one was inside.
So I hiked over here to find out what'd happened."

"Glad you're back," said Flash. He called Paul to tell
him the situation. Then he dressed and showed David the
loot they'd collected yesterday. There was much work yet
to do.

* * *

David and the children pulled on the Indian-style travois, dragging the last load of equipment up to the base of the tree. The equipment made quite a large pile. They had spent most of Wednesday moving the generators and gasoline. David thought ruefully that if he'd been more patient and clever, he and Flash and the others might have been able to set up a transfer site closer to the university. But any place near the university seemed to be several stories above ground level here, while his apartment had the convenient advantage of being at ground level in this universe. The brute-force approach had won out.

Bringing the bulky electric generators through the twistor field had posed a difficult technical problem for David. Even stripped of nonessentials they were too big to pass through the small twistor field in one piece. David had solved the problem last night by constructing a powerful booster amplifier using some of Sam's large high-frequency power transistors. This unit was energized by many batteries, some newly acquired from Sam's shop, all soldered together in a makeshift series-parallel configuration. For the field itself, David had carefully wound a new set of half-meter twistor coils, consuming most of his stock of insulated wire in the process.

Then, connecting the booster amplifier to his portable unit, David had run long power co-ax leads to the new coils, now forming a white inverted cup in the center of a clearing, held in place by a crude tripod of cut saplings. He'd set the drive unit for a half-meter field diameter, the largest field the booster amplifiers would handle. Flash had suspended one of the AC generators by a rope from a wooden plank between chairs on David's deck. They had measured everything several times to get the height right. Then David pushed the TWIST button. The generator appeared and dropped a dozen centimeters to the ground, falling into the pile of leaves David had arranged as a catcher. At the arrival of the first generator, the children clapped with excitement and danced around.

Flash had set up the next load, and the operation was repeated six more times. Finally all of the generators, their gas tanks, and miscellaneous small parts had been successfully transferred. Then, one by one, they had brought across the containers of gasoline.

Now it was all collected here at the base of their tree, and they sat resting, leaning against the pile before the final work of hauling it up to the treehouse.

"David, look at that," said Jeff. David turned to look where the boy was pointing. The treebird was waddling across the ground, leaving a brightly colored line in its wake. But no, it wasn't their treebird, for with an outraged screech that creature dived from high in their tree. As it passed over them, a trail of colored excreta intersected their resting place. David felt wetness on his arms.

"Ugh," said Melissa, "the nasty thing. It messed on us." Jeff giggled, then looked unhappily at the bright colors decorating his jeans.

"It's marking its territory," said David, wiping at his shirt front, "and it must consider us part of its territory." He walked to the cistern and began soaking a rag for the cleanup.

The diving treebird threw its body, all four claws forward, at the green intruder. The invader ceased its waddle and jumped aside at the last moment, barely avoiding the clawed onslaught.

"Damn," said David, realization dawning. "We rubbed out the treebird's border line when we dragged all this stuff across it. I'll bet they're genetically programmed not to cross a border line, but when one is erased, invaders can enter. I'm afraid there's going to be a fight for possession of this tree." He wiped with the wet rag at the colorful mess on their arms and clothes. It came off their skin readily enough, but on their clothes the water only seemed to spread the colorful blotches.

The battle for dominance and possession was now reaching its peak. The green shapes circled, foreclaws extended, feinting and screeching. Their own treebird was slightly larger than the intruder, allowing them to distinguish one from the other. The children cheered for their bird whenever it scored a hit on the intruder. David noticed that, despite the menacing foreclaws each opponent thrust at the other, the battle was made up more of posturing and threats than of wounds. A few green feathers were detached, but this was clearly a conflict ritual, not a fight to the death. The birds continued to circle and squawk and strike for a long time.

Finally, after a hit from their treebird produced a puff of green plumage, the intruder became discouraged and retreated into the forest. The winner waddled in a triumphant victory dance along a complete circuit of the border line, reasserting his dominion over his own true territory. Then he flew to a high branch, trumpeted out a raucous victory call, and resumed his duties of grooming his tree.

David and the children, now rested, entertained, and colorfully decorated, began the final work of moving their loot into the treehouse.

The generators, containers, and other items occupied a considerable area of the treehouse floor. The familiar smell of gasoline was everywhere even though the gas containers were tightly sealed. Much assembly work remained to be done, but it could not be done in semidarkness and must wait until morning. There was only one candle burning at the moment. David had used up most of their supply of candles last night while he was building the amplifier, and there had been no time to make more. It would have been clever, he thought with the wisdom of hindsight, to include a gasoline lantern on Flash's list.

"David," Melissa said in a tone of voice that David had heard before on occasion, "today's Wednesday, isn't it?"

"Yes, I believe it is," said David.

"Yeah, it's story time, David," said Jeff.

"All right," David said, "I can't do any more work tonight anyhow. Do you remember what happened last time? You kinda dozed off at the end. Ton figured out how to make the Pricklance work by poking it through the Urorb, and he used it to send a note to Princess Elle."

Both heads nodded. "I wasn't really asleep," Melissa said.

"OK," said David, "now settle down in your sleeping bag and I'll tell you what happened next.

"In the morning, when Ton could use the light from the

Urorb to read, he again studied the old book. Now that he understood how to use the Urorb and the Pricklance, the part about the Surplice made more sense. One was supposed to wear the Surplice like a coat. The user put it on, visualized the place where he wanted to go with the Urorb, extended the Pricklance through the Urorb, and . . .

"He read the words again. There was something missing. The text said that the golden sash of the Surplice must be tied to the base of the Pricklance. Ton turned the ruglike object over and over, searching for pockets or hidden recesses. There were none. And it had no golden sash, although there were loops where one might have been attached.

"Ton put on the Surplice, tying a length of rope around the garment in place of the sash and tying one end of it to the Pricklance. He focused on his mother's kitchen and followed the book's directions. Nothing happened.

"Ton was very disappointed. He had almost believed that his problem was solved, that the Surplice would provide a way of escaping this underground prison and returning to his home. But one crucial ingredient was missing. There was still no way out. Miserable, Ton lay on the Surplice and wept. And after a while he fell into a deep sleep.

"He dreamed. He was back at the cottage of Zorax, cleaning up the residues of a particularly messy experiment. The old man was sitting in the corner, and he was laughing to himself. That was odd, for he almost never laughed. Zorax was holding something. Ton knew better than to look around, for what would surely bring a beating, but in the corner of his eye Ton thought he could discern the yellow glint of gold—

"Suddenly Ton came wide awake. The dream was very vivid. It had seemed so real . . . Then he remembered that the scene had actually occurred about a month ago, just after Zorax had been away for several days. He remembered some of the event. But had there been a golden object in Zorax's hands? Ton could not remember. He certainly had not noticed it at the time. Still, it could be true. . . ."

David glanced across at the children. They weren't sleeping. They looked quite wide awake and interested. He, on the other hand, felt bone tired and rather drowsy. He yawned, then continued the story.

"Ton picked up the Urorb and concentrated on the cottage of Zorax. It was empty, as before, but it was now day in the outside world, and he could see well enough inside from the daylight coming in through the greased parchment of the windows. He surveyed the room. Where would the old man have kept the scarf? In the dream, Zorax had been sitting near the fireplace. Ton looked there. The fireplace was constructed of rough stone, and there was a long shelf above the hearth. Several niches were cut at odd places in the broad upper part.

"Ton examined the shelf. There was a clutter of miscellaneous objects there: vials, crystals, a brass coin inscribed with an incredibly ugly face, a dried toad, papers, the paw of an animal—perhaps a fox—an iron rod like a great needle, pointed on one end and with a circular hole at the other, books and papers in an unstable stack, a half-eaten apple, and many other objects that Ton could not readily identify. Then he studied the niches. One held a cracked black sphere; in another there was a human skull.

"On the highest of the niches was a small steel-bound box. Considering Zorax's habits, Ton decided that this might be a likely place to look. He grasped the Pricklance and poked through the Urorb at the box. It fell to the floor and burst open. Inside was a golden-colored strip of cloth. The sash!

"At that moment the door of Zorax's cottage burst open and the magician himself walked inside. Ton considered whether he had time to wind the scarf around the Pricklance and retrieve it. He decided that he did not and shifted his point of view to regard the magician. It came as a shock to realize that he was not invisible to the old man, who seemed very much aware of his presence. Zorax strode forward, but did not, to Ton's surprise, reach for the scarf. Instead, he took the pointed iron rod from the fireplace shelf. Ton could see the old man's lips move, and suddenly a tongue of green flame erupted from the tip of the rod and came straight at him. He struggled to shift his viewpoint, but before he could do so the flame came through the Urorb and struck him squarely in the face. He screamed.

"From a corner of his mind, he realized that he was in great pain and that he could not move at all. He was paralyzed and dying. He slowly sagged sideways, and in doing so his hand touched the little book. At the instant of contact his perspective shifted. He was still in pain, still dying, but somehow he was in control of the flame. He pushed it away from him, and it retreated. Its flow reversed, and now it was not attacking him but Zorax. The great pain was diminishing, and he could see the old magician writhe as the green fire ran from the rod up his arm to cover his body. The form of the old man seemed to wither and turn brown like an autumn leaf. His height diminished, and he looked thinner, like a dry branch. Abruptly, the green flame disappeared and the iron rod fell to the floor.

"Ton shifted his viewpoint and looked. There on the floor were the clothes that Zorax had been wearing. Nothing else remained. He turned his view to the fireplace. The golden cloth still rested on the floor, glittering in the light from the windows. With the Pricklance he pierced a corner of it, then wound the cloth around the end of the weapon and pulled it back.

"He had the golden scarf!"

David looked again at his audience. They were fast asleep now. He blew out the candle and lay down. It had been a long day.

David, broom in hand, was sweeping away the colored border line. He would clean up the forest floor, erase the boundaries. He worked on with the heavy broom until the line was gone.

A bright green treebird waddled from the forest and crossed the place where the line had been, leaving a new brightly colored line in its wake. Two more treebirds followed it. Then more. Soon the ring beneath the tree was solid green with them.

They flew and squawked and clawed and pecked at each other. This was no confrontation ritual, it was a fight in deadly earnest. The green plumage began to run with bright red blood, and soon the forest floor was littered with green bodies. The few survivors continued their attacks until all was quiet in the forest and red and green death lay everywhere.

David came awake with a start, shaking green wisps of the dream from his consciousness. He pushed the backlight button and read his watch. It was three A.M. An urgent problem had been pressing at the edges of his mind, he realized . . . territory.

Tomorrow, if everything worked out, they would be returning home. He tried to picture what would happen then. He'd be very happy to reunite the children with Paul and Elizabeth, and it would be wonderful being with Vickie again. But the twistor effect itself was going to be a problem.

The twistor genie was out of the bottle. He'd inadvertently demonstrated to the authorities how the twistor effect could be used as a surveillance tool and a weapon. And they had discovered a whole new planet on which no one—no one but Jeff—had yet made a claim. Many power groups and nations of the old world would compete to stake claims in this new one. The genetic psychoprogramming of most of the human race compelled men, no less than treebirds, to claim and hold territory. And that programming was about to be reactivated in the biggest territorial scramble since Columbus. The twistor effect might spark devastating wars of territory, nuclear wars that could bring the end of civilization.

David thought back to his days at Los Alamos: the security checks, the classified documents, and the secret research labs. The government would surely want to classify everything about the twistor effect they could, to seal it in a wall of secrecy. That was almost inevitable.

He was certain it was the wrong thing to do, that in the long run such a policy would lead to disaster. It was like trying to seal a vessel of heating water to keep it from boiling. It worked for a while, and then there was a big explosion. It was far better to dissipate the force of the steam over the largest available volume than to try to keep it pent up. The twistor effect was no secret to Megalith, the people in the physics department and a few others. Word of the secret effect and the access it opened to shadow universes would spread.

Once a thing is known to be possible, its secret will soon be rediscovered. Attempting to monopolize knowledge is a fundamental mistake. When knowledge is shared, it's quantity isn't reduced or diminished. On the contrary, when more minds work with the knowledge, it grows and flowers, and everyone gains. New information is misused when it's hoarded and protected. It must be distributed as widely as possible, particularly when it is coupled so directly with the opportunity for new territory.

There had to be a way to defuse this bomb before it exploded, to safely dissipate its energy. But how? He lay for a long time, turning the problem over in his mind.

He twisted on the sleeping pad, realizing that he wasn't very comfortable. A lump under his hip was pushing against his side. Reaching down, he found that he was lying on the cut-off cord of the telephone.

An idea exploded into his consciousness, dazzling him with its simplicity. There was a way! For the rest of the night, David dozed fitfully, plans for tomorrow swirling in his head.

24

THURSDAY, OCTOBER 28

David looked around the room. They were all set. In the treehouse, four gasoline engines were driving generators, each powering a bank of twistor drive units in the big rack. Sections of plastic garden hose from the generators were joined by a ball of duct tape to the gray spiral tube of dryer ducting, leading the engine exhausts out the tree-hole. David powered up the little control computer. He was pleased to see that it functioned normally on this makeshift power. The familiar icons of the control program filled the screen. Jeff and Melissa sat beside him at the console, watching with fascination.

David moused up the file containing the settings from the transition that had brought them to this universe. He changed the signs of several parameters to reverse the direction of the twistor transition. He moved the mouse to the (ACTIVATE) control on the computer screen and clicked. The synthesized voice of the control program began the down-count: "*Five! . . . Four! . . .*"

"It's talking again!" said Jeff, delighted.

"Yes, it is," said David. "Isn't that great?"

"*Three! . . . Two . . . One!*" said the synthesized voice.

"David, are we really going home?" asked Melissa.

"*Activating!*" said the voice.

The Seattle Convention Center was a sprawling free-form building that extended its domain from a fringe of downtown hotels to spread directly over the I-5 freeway bisecting downtown Seattle. Inside, Gil Wegmann was covering a medical technology convention for *Newsweek*. He'd just been interviewing a biotech magnate who was pushing a new, FDA-approved, bio-tailored virus. The virus, it was claimed, would on command attack human fat cells and only fat cells. The bio-tekkie expected to be very rich very soon.

Gil's beeper summoned him to the nearest telephone. His boss in New York had received a hot tip that something was up at the University of Washington. He wanted Gil to get over the UW physics department in a hurry, because something very big was about to break.

Wegmann, who had for the past year been trying to get transferred out of the sinkhole of being a science reporting understudy at *Newsweek* and maneuver his way into the foreign news department, was considerably less than pleased. As far as he was concerned, "hot physics news" usually meant that someone who was not at all photogenic and who showed serious personality defects had discovered something unpronounceable that couldn't be explained in simple terms and had no discernible practical applications. Gil liked covering medical stories better; at least with medicine you could always imply that it was a possible cancer cure.

Nevertheless, he dutifully flagged down a taxi in front of the convention center, and, after a few mishaps, he and the cab driver had managed to find Physics Hall. In the rear parking lot were several vans painted with logos of the local TV stations. That made it easy. He walked to the back door, followed the extension cords and the small groups of curious students and faculty to the bright lights, and there they were, all crowded into a long room. The university police officer guarding the door admitted Gil after seeing his press card.

The room was unusual for a physics laboratory. It was occupied by a huge dome of polished wood. A planetarium? No, that was astronomy, not physics. He wondered what the thing was for and how they'd gotten it through the door. The near half of the room was crowded with cameramen, TV cameras, lights on stands, and numerous people. Gil picked a "suit," a distinguished-looking guy standing to one side near the door, identified himself, and asked what was happening here.

The suit turned out to be one Professor Ralph Weinberger, the physics department chairman. He described what had been happening, and mentioned Victoria Gordon's kidnapping. He pointed to a beautiful redhead in a light blue dress who was standing in front of the wooden dome. Gil had assumed she was a TV reporter; she'd been the center of attention for the TV crew since he'd entered the room. Then Gil noticed that a funny light blue catlike animal with too many legs was perched on her shoulder. Well, it matched her dress.

He walked across the room, noticing that the TV news types seemed to have stopped questioning the redhead and were pointing their cameras at various places around the big wooden thing. Good timing, he thought, switching on his portable recorder again and inserting himself into the group.

"Excuse me, miss," he said, "you're Victoria Gordon, aren't you? I'm Gil Wegmann from *Newsweek*." He offered her his business card. "You were in the newspapers yesterday, the one who'd been kidnapped?" His eyes wandered to the little blue animal on her shoulder. Its big violet eyes seemed to be watching him with great interest.

"Yes, that was me," she said. A look of discomfort fleetingly crossed her face, to be replaced by calm. She had nice green eyes, he noticed.

"You seem to have bounced back," he said, looking her up and down.

"I was lucky," she said. "They were about to inject me with a terrible drug when I was able to get away. Professor Saxon wasn't so lucky."

Interesting sidebar, but surely not the main story, Gil thought. "Guess I can read all about that in yesterday's papers," he said. "I know almost nothing about what's going on here. Maybe you can explain it to me. Why are we here? What's going to happen?"

Miss Gordon paused and seemed to be studying him. The strange little cat did the same. "In about five minutes the big wooden ball over there will disappear," she said. She explained to him about David and the children. "They're coming home," she said.

Wegmann blinked and looked at the smooth wooden surface beside him, then reached out and rapped it with his knuckles. It seemed very solid. He struggled to formulate his next question. "Another universe?" he asked. "Look, uh . . . Miss Gordon, I've been a science reporter for a while, and I've never heard of anyone talk about other universes except sci-fi nuts and a few theoreticians. Is this some kind of a joke, or is it supposed to be real physics?"

Victoria Gordon smiled. "Brand-new physics," she said with enthusiasm, "the newest." She told him about the twistor effect, then paused and looked closely at him again. "In your work, Mr. Wegmann, have you heard anything about superstring theories? Or shadow matter?"

He paused. "Look, Ms. Gordon, I kinda wandered into science reporting, you know? My degree's in history and journalism. I was hired on as a foreign correspondent, but one of our science guys died and I was nailed with this job. When I first started a couple of years ago. I did a story about superstrings. But I mostly just interviewed some long-hairs at Princeton and Harvard and MIT and let 'em talk. Now that you mention it, one guy did go on about some kind of invisible matter, yeah, it was 'shadow matter,' that his theory predicted. Seemed kinda proud of that, though I would've thought he'd try to keep it quiet."

Miss Gordon smiled again. "Particle theorists don't have the least sense of shame," she said. "And that particular theory, as it turns out, is more or less correct. Shadow matter does exist, and we now have a way of changing it into normal matter and vice versa." She stroked the blue animal on her shoulder. "Until a couple of days ago, Shadow here was made of shadow matter."

"Are all the animals there that weird blue color?" Wegmann asked. "I mean," he added quickly, "it's a very pretty color for a dress, but kind of odd for an animal."

"Shadow's normal color is brown," she replied, "but he can change colors to adapt to surroundings rather like a chameleon. I think he matched his fur to my blue dress, though, as a kind of joke. He seems to have a well-developed sense of humor."

A wasp, perhaps attracted by the TV lights, buzzed nearby. The blue-furred animal reached out, lightning fast, and to Wegmann's amazement picked the insect out of the air, holding it firmly between a thumb and forefinger. It removed the wasp's striped abdomen and put it into its little mouth. It seemed pleased with itself for a moment, then suddenly made a wry face and spat the insect remains on Wegmann's white shirt front.

"Some sense of humor!" said Wegmann. "Does he do that often?" He attempted, with notable lack of success, to brush the mess from his shirt.

Victoria Gordon made no attempt to apologize. She shrugged and smiled.

Gil thought rapidly, grasping for a new angle. "So your colleague—Harrison, was it?—is presently on this shadow Earth and is about to come back?"

"Yes," she said. "David has some gasoline-powered electric generators over there, and he and the Ernst children are about to come back. We've been in contact with him for the past several days. The children's parents, Paul and Elizabeth Ernst, are over there." She indicated a couple sitting on folding chairs near the window. They looked to be in their mid-to-late thirties. They were talking quietly, and the man was holding the woman's hand in his lap. "Paul's a professor of theoretical physics in the department. He knows all about superstring theories. Maybe you'd like to talk to him." She looked at her watch.

Gil nodded, excused himself, and walked across the room. He introduced himself and was beginning the interview when he heard something like lawnmower engines behind him and a voice saying, "We're just about ready over here." He turned and noticed a round dark region near one of the long walls. The noise seemed to be coming from there.

Victoria Gordon called out, "We're all ready too, David. Come ahead."

A few seconds later the dark region winked out, and as it vanished the lawnmower sound ceased. Everyone in the room was turning toward the wooden ball. Gil turned also.

Quite abruptly, the big wooden ball was no longer there. There was a puff of wind, and before him sat a disheveled man with a scraggly beard. Two dirty children stood next to him watching a computer screen. They turned around and everyone clapped, the sound competing with the noise of several little gasoline engines. The TV cameras were running; cameras flashed.

The man, presumably Dr. David Harrison, rose and shut off the engines. The small blue animal that had been perched on Victoria Gordon's shoulder leaped to the floor, ran across the room with a peculiar gait, and jumped into the little girl's arms. The two children ran to their mother and father near where Gil was standing. The girl, who was introduced as Melissa Ernst, was very excited. She showed the little animal to her parents and then to Gil. Its color was now brown. Its little sixfingered hand gripped his finger like a handshake. It felt surprisingly strong.

The little boy hugged his mother for a long time, then proudly showed his parents the necklace he wore. A number of enormous, sharp, curving yellow teeth were strung on what looked like monofilament fish line. The child said they were "shadow-bear" teeth and that he and David Harrison had made it after they had killed the bear. The bear had wanted to eat him, he added. From the size of the teeth, Gil decided he would rather not meet the entire animal.

On the other side of the room the cameras were flashing again. Gil looked around. David Harrison was kissing Victoria Gordon. The cameras flashed for quite some time.

Gil decided that this might be one of the better moments in science reporting. Three separate stories were already taking form in his head, and he was sure that a cover story was among them.

Dr. Arthur G. Lockworth, Presidential Science Advisor and Director of the Office of Science and Technology Policy, pushed away from his desk and leaned back in his high-backed leather swivel chair. He looked out the window. The view from the high windows of the Old Executive Office Building always fascinated him. The city of Washington, D.C., part government nerve center and part Disneyland of the Potomac, had put on its evening finery. It was now after eleven. He was working late tonight because the president's speech announcing the success of the White Sands Laser

Launch Facility and the new Moonbase plans had to be ready for review at the seven A.M. breakfast meeting.

There was a single quiet two-tone chime, and a light on his telephone console began to flash. It was his direct private line, known only to his wife and a few close friends. And, of course, the president. He lifted the receiver.

"Art," said his wife's voice, "I think you'd better check the eleven o'clock news on Channel 6. Hurry or you'll miss it. Call me when it's over. 'Bye."

"OK, hon," he said, and replaced the receiver on its cradle. He took out the remote control from his desk drawer and zapped to life the flatscreen TV that masqueraded as a painting when it was turned off.

The announcer was doing a voice-over while the camera focused on a small blue catlike animal. It was perched on the shoulder of a pretty redhead, and it seemed to have six legs. They were saying something about a murder/kidnapping and something about physicists at a laboratory at the University of Washington in Seattle returning from "another universe." What the Hell did that mean? There were pictures of a grubby young man and two dirty children. Then there was a shot of the small boy standing by an enormous ugly animal that was apparently dead. The animal had six legs; its clawed feet projected into the air.

Finally they cut to a picture which seemed to have been taken in a forest of extremely large trees—trees such as Lockworth, a California native, had never seen. The same small boy was climbing down a crude ladder mounted on the side of one particularly large tree. He had a stick in his mouth. Lockworth examined the picture and noted its color values and block-pixel grain. He concluded that it must have been made with one of those new variable-resolution CCD-to-ROM digital electronic cameras. The U.S.A. had beaten out the Japanese on that development, he thought, satisfied.

The small boy turned and unrolled what was revealed to be a crudely drawn but accurate version of the U.S. flag attached to the pole. He turned to the camera, poked the butt of the flagpole into a dark patch of soil, and said in a high child-voice, "I, Jeffrey Ernst, claim this universe, this territory, in the name of the United States of America."

"God!" said Lockworth. He had the momentary illusion that he was looking at Pandora's box, standing with lid ajar while tiny winged creatures flew off in all directions. He reached for the gold-colored telephone, the one that connected him directly to the White House. This was going to be a long night.

David had only a few minutes with Vickie and Paul and the others before the interviews began. He had talked privately with the police and the FBI. They were particularly interested in the circumstances of his disappearance and of the death of Vickie's kidnapper. One of the policemen congratulated David for saving the taxpayers the expense of a trial.

Then he'd been interviewed at length by TV journalists and by reporters from several local newspapers, the wire services, and a national magazine. Finally he and Vickie had been able to leave Physics Hall together. His car was still parked in the underground garage where he had left it weeks earlier. It seemed strange to be driving through the streets of the University District once more. No giant trees, no six-legged animals.

They had gone to the Red Robin and David had reacquainted himself with "Earth food" in the form of three cheeseburgers and most of a pitcher of beer. Finally, completely exhausted but happy, they went to David's apartment.

It was just after ten as David, with Vickie holding his hand, entered the apartment for the first time in over two weeks. Unless, of course, one counted David's visits from the other universe. Flash had left the place in rather a mess, but they pushed the clutter aside for cleanup tomorrow. David felt totally, terminally, dead tired, a little drunk, and very much in love. But there was one item that couldn't wait. He switched on his little flat Mac III, retrieved a diskette from a lower desk drawer, and called Vickie to come and sit beside him.

They worked for about an hour making final changes, corrections, and updates. Then he used the internal 9600-baud modem to dial into the Physics HyperVAX. He uploaded the two files, briefly edited his standard address list, and summoned the MAIL utility. In a few more lines the job was done and he logged off.

As it turned out, they both had plenty of energy left.

At 7:55 A.M. Eastern Daylight Time, a key turned in the door of the offices at 1 Research Road, Brookhaven, New York. The assistant production editor of the American Institute of Physics Publications let herself in and went directly to her office. The computer terminal on her desk listed the papers that had been electronically submitted to the AIP journals overnight. She routed the first stack, the batch for *Physical Review Letters*, straight to the laser printer for conversion to hard copy. Then she made a full pot of coffee.

When she had returned with a steaming cup there were a pile of stapled manuscripts in the output stacker of the printer. As she carried them to the editor's office for first processing she glanced at the paper on the top of the stack. It read:

First Observation of an Extra-Dimensional Precession Effect Induced by the Rotation of a Spherical Electromagnetic Field

by
D. G. Harrison, V. A. Gordon, and A. D. Saxon[†]
Department of Physics FM-15
University of Washington
Seattle, WA 98195

And at the bottom of the page she noticed the line:
[†]Deceased.

"Is Allan Saxon deceased?" she wondered aloud. She made a note to relay the information to *Physics Today* so that an obituary could be run. He was no older than I am, she thought.

At precisely 8:00 A.M. Pacific Daylight Time, the doorbell of David Harrison's apartment rang. He swam to consciousness from a great depth and shook himself awake. He looked around, reassuring himself that he was in his proper universe. Careful not to disturb Vickie, still fast asleep beside him, he carefully closed the bedroom door, stumbled to the front door, and peered out through the chained opening. Two men with dark business suits and narrow ties stood on the threshold. David recognized one of them as Agent Bartley, the FBI man who had interviewed him yesterday evening.

"Good morning, Dr. Harrison," Bartley said.

"I suppose it is," said David, unchaining the door. "I wouldn't know. Haven't had the opportunity to observe much of it yet." He yawned.

Bartley introduced the other man as his associate, Agent Cooper. "Dr. Harrison," he said, "I'm afraid we'll have to impose on you again. We need for you and Miss Gordon to come down to headquarters with us. Immediately. On orders from Washington at the highest levels. I wonder if you'd wake her, sir."

David looked sharply at Bartley. "There isn't much you guys miss, is there?" he said.

"Part of the job, Dr. Harrison." Cooper leered. "If you don't mind, sir?"

"OK, dammit," said David. "Come on in. Have a seat. We'll be ready soon." He turned and stalked out of the room.

David looked at his watch. They'd been sitting in this bare office for almost two hours now. Bartley had provided coffee but no breakfast, and had not been particularly remorseful about the "hurry-up-and-wait" routine. It was probably part of the standard procedure.

Finally, at ten-thirty, Bartley came in again, accompanied by two other men. "Miss Gordon, Dr. Harrison, I'd like you to meet Hodgkins, the agent in charge of our Seattle office, and Mr. Pickering from Washington." They shook hands.

Pickering presented them with identification from a defense-related scientific agency of the U.S. government, one with which David was only vaguely familiar. "I apologize for keeping you waiting," Pickering said. "I was flown into McChord in a two-place military jet this morning, but then I got tied up in a traffic jam on the freeway between Tacoma and Seattle. Should've ordered a 'copter, I guess.''

"No problem," said David, "except that I would have liked to be able to eat breakfast while you were in transit. I haven't had an Earth breakfast in over two weeks, you know."

Pickering glanced at Hodgkins, who blinked. "Dr. Harrison, Miss Gordon," Pickering said, "I regret the inconvenience, but this is a matter of some urgency. I've come on direct orders from the highest levels of the White House. I'm here to discuss with you this new 'twistor' effect you've discovered. I specifically want to caution you to divulge no further information about it to anyone until its defense and espionage potentials have been evaluated and it can be assigned a security status."

David frowned. "Yes, Mr. Pickering, I thought it would be some BS like that," he said. "You're all ready to clamp a lid of secrecy on our work, whether we want it or not. Is that it?"

Pickering looked pained. "Dr. Harrison, this is a matter of protecting our national interest. The phenomenon you've discovered is dangerous. You've already used it as a weapon, to kill a man. Consider how, in the wrong hands, it might be used for political assassinations and terrorist acts. No political leader would be safe. Consider how it might be used in espionage to discover our national secrets. Think of the security problems. I assure you, of course, that we have no intention of keeping your work secret any longer than—''

"You're too late," Vickie broke in.

Pickering frowned. "What do you mean?" he asked, turning to her.

"We submitted the papers last night," she said. Then she smiled.

"But—" Pickering protested.

"I'm afraid," David added, "that you've wasted the taxpayers' money on a fruitless trip, Mr. Pickering. By now two scientific papers, one describing the twistor effect and the other the apparatus we used to make it, are in the hands of the editors of *Physical Review Letters* and *Review of Scientific Instruments.*''

Pickering stood. "I must make a phone call," he said.

"Just relax," said David. "If that was all, perhaps you could still intercept them. But preprints of the papers have also gone to physics groups all over this country and the world. The twistor effect is essentially already in the open literature. Sorry you had to come all this way for nothing, Mr. Pickering.''

Pickering scowled down at David. "I don't wish to question your veracity, Dr. Harrison," he said, "but what you say isn't possible. According to the TV coverage, you came back from this 'shadow universe' of yours only late yesterday afternoon. From our reports, you were interviewed at the physics building for several hours, ate a quick meal, and spent the remainder of the evening in the company of Miss Gordon. We know that all the lights in your apartment were out by eleven P.M.''

David frowned.

"How," Pickering continued, "could you possibly have had time to write and prepare two papers, have them typed and reproduced, and put them into the mail? There was simply not time to do all that, Dr. Harrison, and we would have observed you doing it.''

"You're mistaken," said David. " 'All that' took less than an hour last night. You see, the papers were already done. I'd written both of them more than two weeks ago. All Vickie and I had to do was make a few changes to bring them up to date. I transmitted them by phone to the physics department's HyperVAX. From there we mailed them electronically, using a computer network system called BitNet. We physicists use BitNet routinely for scientific communication. I just pointed the HyperVAX at the files with the papers and the file with the distribution list, and the rest was automatic. At this moment people in Osaka, Beijing, Tel Aviv, Zurich, Rome, Athens, Paris, and Berlin should be reading our papers. And at Los Alamos and Livermore too, Mr. Pickering. And they're probably using BitNet now to forward copies to their colleagues. I'm sure your NSA monitors foreign BitNet traffic and will be sending you copies soon. You're dealing with a *fait accompli*, Mr. Pickering. The twistor effect belongs to the world. You're too late."

Pickering looked crestfallen. David couldn't be sure, but he had the distinct impression that Agent Bartley was amused.

". . . and with the evil magician dead," said David, "Ton and Elle flew with the Surplice back to the house of Ton's father, where she met his family. Then they went on to the kingdom of Elle's father." It had been another long day for David and Vickie. The FBI had kept them in custody until early afternoon while Pickering conversed repeatedly with Washington. Finally, grudgingly, they were released.

Elizabeth had prepared an elegant homecoming dinner, and, even though it was not a Wednesday, David had consented to finish the story for the children after the dinner was finished.

"The old king was delighted to have his beautiful daughter returned to him. And he was very taken with young Prince Ton. He let it be known that he was willing to give half his kingdom to this powerful prince who had saved his daughter and who could now use his powerful magic to protect both halves of the kingdom from the powers of evil. And of course the king's daughter, Princess Elle, was included in the deal.

"Ton and Elle were married in a beautiful royal wedding that made all the papers. And they lived happily ever after." David glanced across at Vickie and smiled.

"The End," he concluded, and looked around.

Paul, Elizabeth, Vickie, and Melissa clapped enthusiastically. Jeff looked thoughtful, then clapped too.

"Halloween is in two days, David," said Melissa, acting quickly before her mother could mention bedtime.

"So it is," said David. "Do you have a costume yet?"

"I'm going to be a shadow kitten," said Melissa. "I'll wear my tan leotard and use some of Mom's pantyhose stuffed with cotton to make extra legs . . ."

Elizabeth looked surprised.

". . . and I'll have pointed ears and a tail like Shadow,"

she continued. "Shadow and I will go out trick-or-treating together. We'll be like twins. Only I'll be bigger."

"I'm gonna be Ton," Jeff spoke up. "I'll have a Surplice and a Pricklance and an Urorb, and I'll wear my shadow-bear necklace, too."

"Ton didn't have a shadow-bear necklace," said Melissa with a note of scorn.

"But I do!" said Jeff. He smiled, satisfied.

"It's bedtime now, Universe-Hoppers!" said Elizabeth.

Without complaint Jeff and Melissa, with Shadow on her shoulder, said good night to the guests and went to their bedrooms.

Elizabeth turned to Vickie. "How are things with your brother? How is he taking all the publicity and interviews?"

"William seems to be taking it all very well," said Vickie. "He went back to high school today after a week of hiding out. He seems delighted to get back to a more normal existence. And he has a new project. He's hard at work tonight cramming for the November SAT tests. He's decided that he wants to uphold the family tradition and go to CalTech, as Dad and I did. Some of his grades haven't been too hot, so he'll need some spectacular SAT scores to be able to squeak in."

"Does he still want to study computer science?" asked Elizabeth.

"That's the interesting thing," said Vickie. "He's decided that he wants to major in physics. He says that now that he's cracked the universe of computers, he's ready to take on real universes . . . all seven of them."

Paul smiled. "Talk him out of it, Vickie, before it's too late," he said. "We aging theorists don't need his kind of competition." From a tall, frosted-green bottle with a little gold centaur on the label he poured cognac into wide crystal snifters and passed these to his guests.

David swirled the amber liquid in his glass, inhaled deeply, and rolled his eyes heavenward in appreciation. "You know," he said, "this universe does have a lot to offer."

Paul raised his cognac snifter. "I'd like to propose a

toast,'' he said. ''To David and Vickie and their marvelous future, in this universe or any other.''

''And to the twistor effect and the better world it will bring,'' added David. Together they clinked glasses and drank the dark fragrant liquid.

The Physics of *Twistor*

Reading hard science fiction is a poor way to learn science. That can be better accomplished by the traditional methods of reading textbooks, attending classes, and receiving on-the-job training. However, there is a related function that hard SF can perform: to communicate the feel and the excitement of actually doing science and provide some insight into what the activity of scientific research is about and how it works. I have tried to do some of that in this book. The University of Washington Department of Physics is in fact the academic department where I teach and do research. The people in the book are my own creations, and bear no resemblance to my own colleagues on the physics faculty. In particular, our chairman is considerably more pleasant as a person and effective as a chairman than is Ralph Weinberger in the story. None of my colleagues, to my knowledge, operate private businesses or attempt to exploit their students or postdocs in the style of Allan Saxon. The characters and circumstances are changed, but the feel of scientific research is as real as I could make it.

Those who have an interest in picking up a bit of extra scientific information in reading hard-SF novels like this one should be warned of a trap lurking at the core of all hard science fiction. This trap is that by SF convention there are no indications or clues as to which science in the story is "straight stuff" and which is "rubber science": speculation, extrapolation, fabrication, or invention inserted by the author to add interest to the story and further the plot. In well-written hard SF the seam between true and rubber science is intentionally made visible to the reader. The reader must be carried smoothly from correct and accurate science into the speculative realm, without any suspicion that he's been had or when it happened.

In many ways this procedure resembles the technique of root grafting used by horticulturists: the lower portions of a sturdy tree that possesses a robust root structure, but is rather prosaic-looking, is joined to the upper part of another tree that is more delicate and fragile but produces rich and dramatic flowers. The good horticulturist makes the graft invisible, so that only the closest inspection will reveal its presence. The result is a tree that is both dramatic and well-grounded. Hard SF should be the same.

This literary device, however, may have an unfortunate side effect: that the reader is led to believe that the rubber science used in an SF novel is in fact correct. As Charles Sheffield has pointed out, many of us grew up believing that astronomers had discovered canals on Mars, that human and pig embryos were so similar as to be indistinguishable, that computers which reached the complexity of the human brain would exhibit intelligence, that spaceships could easily travel faster than the speed of light by slipping into hyperspace, that J. B. Rhine of Duke University had conclusively demonstrated the existence of telepathy, that the pineal gland of the brain was a rudimentary third eye and the seat of parapsychological powers, that the British physicist P. M. S. Blackett had produced a theory which connected magnetism, gravity, and rotation and would be the key to antigravity, and so on. Thus the reader of science fiction—and particularly hard SF—may "know" many things that are not so, if only through the process of osmosis.

Not all readers are necessarily interested in the underlying science of hard SF. Those who are more interested in the feel and texture of hard SF, or who would prefer *not* to view the backstage machinery that operates the sets and props, should feel no obligation to read what follows. But for those who would like to be shown where the boundaries are between the real and the rubber science in this novel, I've provided this Afterword.

* * *

1. *The Theory/Experiment Dichotomy*. In much of science fiction "the scientist" is a stock figure with glasses, a white coat, and a humorless and rather otherworldly attitude, rather like a medieval monk in habit and tonsure. This caricature is not particularly accurate, and it misses one of the most important distinctions in modern science: the distinction between experimentalists and theorists. The relationship between theoretical and experimental physicists as depicted in this novel is as accurate as I could manage. The necessary specialization of modern science is such that no one individual can remain in a forefront position in theoretical physics and at the same time actively participate in the design and execution of experiments. There are too many theoretical techniques to be mastered, too much new experimental technology of which to stay abreast. This is not to say that there are *not* some individuals who try to do both, but these are a rare breed and even in those cases one of their strengths usually dominates the other.

2. *Warm Superconductors and Holospin Waves*. Warm superconductors were discovered between the time the first and second drafts of this novel were written. The discovery happened at an ideal time to provide a backdrop for the condensed matter physics that plays an important role in the early part of this book. Layered fluoridated perovskite crystals are real and can be read about in the journal *Physical Review*. Holospin waves and memory devices, however, are my fabrications, based on my conjecture that holographic images might conceivably be stored in the bulk spin structure of a warm superconductor. As far as I know, there is no physical basis for this conjecture.

3. *Shadow Matter and Superstring Theories*. Superstring theories indeed exist and are presently *the* hot topic in particle physics. This may or may not persist until *Twistor*'s time period. The discussion of superstring theories here is as accurate as I could make it, but the reader should be cautioned that I am not an expert in this field. Shadow matter and shadow particles have indeed been predicted by certain variants of the superstring formalism. It is not clear, how-

ever, whether shadow atoms with identical chemical properties, etc., are a consequence of such theories. Further, the notion of a "shadow spin" vector which is three units long and leads to $(2*3 + 1)$ or seven distinct varieties of shadow matter is my own elaboration of conventional superstring theories and has no theoretical basis.

4. *The Dark Matter and Solar Neutrino Problems.* These are problems of contemporary physics that are at present unsolved. The dark matter problem comes from attempts to estimate the density of matter in the universe by various methods, in effect "weighing" the universe. One method uses Doppler shift techniques to estimate the orbital velocities of bright stars near the periphery of galactic clusters, in effect treating the whole cluster as a single mass producing the observed orbit. The result is that only a small fraction of the estimated mass can be accounted for as visible stars, even after corrections for subluminous Jupiter-like bodies and interstellar hydrogen are included. Estimates of the matter density in the early Big Bang that would have been required to produce the observed abundances of deuterium, helium, and lithium in the present universe also lead to a similar mass discrepancy. The conclusion is that at best we can account for only about one seventh of the mass in the universe, with the remaining six sevenths in some mysterious "dark matter" form.

The solar neutrino problem arises from a decades-long effort by Ray Davis and his coworkers from Brookhaven National Laboratory to use a very large counter system buried deep underground in a South Dakota gold mine to detect neutrinos from the sun. This massive effort detects a solar neutrino flux that is only one third of that predicted by standard solar models.

The structure of the shadow universes in *Twistor* is contrived to accommodate these two scientific mysteries: six extra shadow universes to account for the dark matter problem, and two extra suns so that or own sun need produce only one third of the net neutrino flux. This, at least at the superficial level, "explains" both results. Whether this "explanation" could withstand the rigors of closer scientific scrutiny is not known.

5. *The Geophysics and Astrophysics of Shadow Worlds*. An underlying assumption of *Twistor* is that our Earth and sun have shadow-matter counterparts in two of the other shadow universes, with Earthlike planets occupying the same orbits and even having the same rotational periods. Except for the matching rotational periods this is fairly plausible from the viewpoint of planet formation, since the gravity well produced by a planet in one universe would tend to attract matter in the others also. However, this scenario may have problems in the areas of both geophysics and astrophysics. On the question of whether two shadow Earths could be superimposed on ours in a plausible geophysical model, Paul's arguments in Chapter 17 of *Twistor* are essentially my own. Because conventional models hypothesize an enormous density for the Earth's interior, it would seem to be possible to accommodate two more Earths by simply reducing the density of the interior of each by one third. Whether such a model could be made compatible with the phase boundaries and structures in the Earth's interior known from seismology, however, I cannot judge.

Similarly, I do not know whether conventional astrophysical models of the sun could permit two thirds of the sun's hydrogen to be inert matter which contributes only to the gravitational field and still produce enough fusion and energy generation. I am doubtful if this could be fitted within the envelope of acceptable variants of solar models. As far as I know, it has never been considered as a solution to the solar neutrino problem, although it is no more bizarre than several other ideas that have been taken quite seriously in the literature of astrophysics.

The locking of the rotational periods of superimposed shadow Earths is needed in the novel so that all three planets (or at least two of them) rotate at the same rate. Otherwise the treehouse might have reappeared at any place on Earth that is located at 47° north latitude. There is a mechanism for locking the rotational periods, and I am grateful to Bob Forward for pointing it out. The tidal forces arising from irregularities in the mass distribution of the three planets (mountains, oceans, concentrations of heavy minerals, etc.) would provide a damping mechanism that would eventually bring the bodies to the same rotational period. I have not calculated the time constant associated with such damping, but it is plausible that the billion or so years since Earth's formation would be sufficient.

An object, i.e., the apparatus lost in Part 1, that is twisted into one of the empty universes and left to orbit there under the influence of the Earth's gravitational field will have very peculiar non-Keplerian orbital dynamics because the gravitational force would not be a simple inverse square law force. Rather, it would be fairly well approximated by a Hooke's law force that grows linearly with distance from the center of motion. The orbiting object would fall repeatedly through the Earth in a precessing orbit, passing within a few hundred miles of Earth-center on each trip and traversing from one side of the planet to the other in about thirty-eight minutes. The orbit would bring the object repeatedly back to or near ground level at widely scattered points on the Earth's surface.

I wrote an orbital dynamics program to investigate such orbits. For input I needed the best available data on the interior density profile of the Earth, and I had to use double-precision FORTRAN on my wife's Macintosh SE to get sufficient accuracy. The opportunity to "launch" a space vehicle by letting it fall through the Earth would lead to a completely new form of space technology and also to very rapid and energy-efficient surface transportation from one place to another on the Earth. But I will save that for a sequel to *Twistor*.

6. *Hacking and BitNet*. The computer-system penetration techniques used by Flash in the hacking scenes in *Twistor* are all known techniques which have been used to penetrate protected computer systems. However, as is said of the wrestling holds shown on TV, the reader is cautioned not to try these in his own home. One reason is that they are illegal and are growing more so as state legislatures gain better understanding of computer crime and write better

computer-protection laws. Another reason is that these techniques are presently well known, even to a nonhacker like the author. Software producers and system managers have already set up countermeasures to entrap and defeat any hackers who might attempt to use many of them. They are used in *Twistor* to create the "feel" of the penetration of a well-protected computer system and should not be taken as an instruction manual on how to do so.

BitNet is an actual worldwide computer network that is already in very active use by the physics community. However, at present it is used primarily for "mail" messages between users and for the transmission of data files and programs. It is not in general use for the transmission of scientific papers and preprints because these usually include a number of figures; for example, line drawings of equipment or data plots. Although CompuServe's GIF standard, Adobe's Post Script, and several others are looming on the horizon, there is presently no universal graphics standard that would permit the routine inclusion of figures in scientific papers, and so they are still distributed by conventional mail.

It is a good bet that this will soon change. The scientific journals published by the American Institute of Physics, e.g., *Physical Review*, already accept manuscripts submitted on computer media. It is very likely that within a decade physics papers for journal publication complete with drawings and figures will be submitted and preprints of such papers will be routinely circulated by BitNet or its successor. One can only hope that publishers of works of fiction (like the present novel) will also eventually emerge from the nineteenth century and adopt similar technology.

John Cramer
Seattle, Washington
December 22, 1987

THE CONTINUATION
OF THE FABULOUS
INCARNATIONS OF IMMORTALITY
SERIES

PIERS ANTHONY

FOR LOVE OF EVIL
75285-9/$4.95 US/$5.95 Can

AND ETERNITY
75286-7/$4.95 US/$5.95 Can